Praise for Stephen Leather

The Double Tap

'Masterful plotting . . . rapid-fire prose' *Sunday Express*

'One of the most breathlessly exciting thrillers around . . . puts [Leather] in the frame to take over Jack Higgins's mantle' *Peterborough Evening Telegraph*

'A fine tale, brilliantly told – excitement which is brilliantly orchestrated' *Oxford Times*

The Birthday Girl

'Action and scalpel-sharp suspense' *Daily Telegraph*

'Terrifying, fast-moving and exciting thriller' *Independent*, Ireland

'A whirlwind of action, suspense and vivid excitement' *Irish Times*

The Chinaman

'Will leave you breathless'   *Daily Mail*

'Plenty of visceral excitements'   *Guardian*

'A gripping story sped along by admirable, uncluttered
prose'   *Daily Telegraph*

Hungry Ghost

'The sort of book that could easily take up a complete
weekend – and be time really well spent . . . A story that's
as topical as today's headlines'   *Bolton Evening News*

'Very Complicated. Fun'   *Daily Telegraph*

The Eyewitness

'Atmospheric suspense'   *Daily Mirror*

'Raw and uncompromising, this is a compelling and disturbing thriller that will make you think'
Sunday Mercury, Birmingham

'Stephen Leather's novel manages to put a contemporary spin on a timeless tale of revenge and retribution ... Leather's experience as a journalist brings a sturdy, gritty element to a tale of horror ... which makes *The Eyewitness* a compelling read'   *Evening Herald*, Dublin

Tango One

'The novel has everything one has come to expect in a Stephen Leather thriller – a fast, page-turning pace, characters you hate to love, a satisfying resolution in which justice is seen to be done and a thought-provoking promise that makes the reader delve into his or her own moral centre.'
Deadly Pleasures

The Stretch

'The twists and turns in the plot continue up to and including the last page. Brilliant.'   *Middlesbrough Evening Gazette*

'[*The Stretch* is a] rollicking good read'
Peterborough Evening Telegraph

'*The Stretch* is well up to the outstanding thriller standard we have come to expect from Stephen Leather'
Bolton Evening News

About the author

Stephen Leather was a journalist for more than ten years on newspapers such as *The Times*, the *Daily Mail* and the *South China Morning Post* in Hong Kong. Before that, he was employed as a biochemist for ICI, shovelled limestone in a quarry, worked as a baker, a petrol pump attendant, a barman, and worked for the Inland Revenue. He began writing full-time in 1992 and he has written 15 novels. His bestsellers have been translated into more than ten languages, and *The Stretch* and *The Bombmaker* have been filmed for television. He has also written for television shows such as *London's Burning*, *The Knock* and the BBC's *Murder in Mind*.

Stephen Leather now lives in Dublin. Visit his website at www.stephenleather.com

Also by Stephen Leather

STEPHEN LEATHER

The Double Tap

CORONET BOOKS
Hodder & Stoughton

Copyright © 1992 by Stephen Leather

First published in Great Britain in 1992 by Hodder & Stoughton
This paperback edition reissued in 2004 by Hodder & Stoughton
A Division of Hodder Headline

A Coronet Paperback

The right of Stephen Leather to be identified as the Author
of the Work has been asserted by him in accordance with the
Copyright, Designs and Patents Act 1988.

16

A CIP catalogue record for this title is
available from the British Library

ISBN 0 340 62839 1

Typeset in Plantin Light by Palimpsest Book Production Limited,
Polmont, Stirlingshire
Printed and bound in Great Britain by Clays Ltd, St Ives plc

Hodder Headline's policy is to use papers that are natural, renewable
and recyclable products and made from wood grown in sustainable
forests. The logging and manufacturing processes are expected to
conform to the environmental regulations of the country of origin.

Hodder and Stoughton
A division of Hodder Headline
338 Euston Road
London NW1 3BH

For Wanda

She was the richest little girl in the world. Rich beyond the dreams of avarice, rich almost beyond comprehension. As she played in the surf, giggling and shrieking and running from the waves, the white-jacketed waiter slowly polished a crystal tumbler and tried to imagine what it must be like to have so much money. The interest on the interest was still more than he'd earn in a lifetime. In a thousand lifetimes, maybe. He polished the crystal diligently and when he held it up in the Mediterranean sunlight it sparkled like a diamond. He was wearing white cotton gloves so that his fingers wouldn't mark the pristine surface. He placed it on a solid silver tray and reached for another tumbler.

The little girl knelt down by the water's edge and picked up something, a sand crab perhaps, or a pretty shell, and she skipped across the beach to her guardians who sat together under a huge umbrella. The man was her grandfather, wealthy in his own right but nowhere near as rich as the little girl. The woman was her great aunt, a withered husk of a human being, wrapped in a black shawl despite the searing heat. The little girl showed them what she'd found and they smiled benevolently. That they loved and cherished her was beyond doubt. Even from his post a hundred feet from the umbrella, the waiter could see it in their eyes. The old man ruffled the girl's wet hair and her laughter tinkled like a glass windchime. The old woman smiled a toothless smile and said something in Greek.

'No, Auntie,' admonished the little girl. 'English today. Today we must speak English.' The waiter held up the second tumbler and inspected it. The little girl was learning English, Spanish and Russian in addition to her own language. She was only eight years old, but already she was being groomed for the life that lay ahead of her. A life of wealth and power, a life that few other people in the world would believe existed. What could it be like to have so much, the waiter mused? And yet, thought the waiter, she was also to be pitied because the immense wealth had come at a heavy price. She was an orphan: her mother and father had died in a power boat accident the previous year. Now, as she laughed and played, she had only the company of her aged guardians and the men in dark glasses.

There were three bodyguards, big men, wide shouldered and well-muscled, standing close to the umbrella, their heads constantly moving even though there wasn't a stranger within half a mile. It was a private beach, on a private island, one of the dozen or so homes around the world owned by her trust fund, but the bodyguards never let their concentration slip. They wore shorts and brightly coloured shirts and had white smears of sunscreen down their noses, but no one would ever mistake them for holidaymakers. Occasionally the sea breeze would lift their loose shirts to reveal a holstered handgun or a sub-machine pistol. In addition to the three bodyguards on the beach, there were another two in the house and ten more sleeping or relaxing in the barracks next to the swimming pool. The little girl was under guard for every minute of every day; even as she slept two men would stand outside her bedroom door and another two under her window. She was the richest little girl in the world and she was the most protected.

The waiter slid the tumbler onto the tray and covered it with a crisp white cloth so that the crystal wouldn't be desecrated by windblown sand. He was sweating and he had to resist the urge to wipe his forehead with the sleeve of his jacket. He kept a wary eye on the old man. It was almost noon and he would soon be wanting his first glass of ouzo of the day.

The little girl ran back to the sea, hopping across the hot sand until she reached the cooler fringes of the water's edge. She squatted down and splayed her hands, palms uppermost, releasing the crustacean she'd so proudly shown the old couple. It was a small crab and it scuttled sideways, seeking sanctuary in the wet sand. Within seconds it had burrowed to safety and the little girl waved goodbye.

Far out to sea, a powerful speedboat ploughed through the waves. One of the bodyguards put a pair of binoculars to his eyes and studied it for several minutes. He spoke to the other men in Yiddish. They were Israelis, as were all the child's protectors. It had nothing to do with religion, the waiter knew, it was simply that Israeli-trained bodyguards were the best in the world. If necessary they would die to protect their charge.

The old man looked towards the waiter and nodded. The waiter took the ice bucket and the bottle of ouzo out of the gas-powered refrigerator and placed them on the tray. He held it with both gloved hands as he walked gingerly across the burning sand, hot even through his leather-soled shoes. As soon as he stepped out of the shade of the massive umbrella above the bar he felt the sun beat down on his hair and a rivulet of sweat ran down his neck. The three bodyguards were now all standing fifty feet or so behind the little girl, looking over her head at the speedboat which was arcing through the waves, away from the beach. There was more Yiddish, and shrugs.

3

The ice cubes rattled wetly in the ice bucket and the waiter took extra care where he put his feet on the shifting sand. The old man had bent his head close to the old woman, listening intently. She was probably warning him about drinking too much, the waiter thought, and he smiled to himself. The bodyguards were to the waiter's side, still staring out to sea. He took his right hand off the tray and dropped the ice bucket lid onto the sand before grabbing for the silenced automatic. The metal had been chilled by the ice and he was aware of how pleasant it felt through the cotton gloves as he levelled the gun between the shoulder-blades of the nearest bodyguard and fired twice. The man dropped to the sand as the waiter fired two more shots into the back of the middle bodyguard. The gun made no more sound than a child's cough and the third bodyguard had only begun to turn when the waiter put two of the mercury-tipped slugs into his back. Out of the corner of his eye the waiter saw the old couple struggling to their feet but he knew there was nothing they could do. They were too old, too feeble, to do anything but watch.

The waiter stepped over the legs of one of the dead bodyguards, the gun now warm to the touch. The child was kneeling in the sand, trying to find the crab. She looked up at him as he approached, smiling because there were only friends on the island, friends and protectors. She frowned when she saw the gun in his hand. The waiter smiled down at her. 'Are you frightened?' he asked softly.

She looked up at him and smiled again, hopefully. 'No,' she said, 'I'm not.'

The waiter nodded and shot her in the head, then in the chest. Behind him he heard a mournful wail, more of a howl than a scream. He couldn't tell if it was the old man or the woman. In the distance, the speedboat headed in the direction of the shore, its twin engines roaring. The waiter ran towards it as the blood of the richest little girl in the world soaked into the sand.

Mike Cramer wiped the condensation from the window of the taxi and peered out. The rain had stopped, though the taxi's windscreen wipers continued to swish back and forth. 'You can drop me here,' he said to the driver, a sullen rock of a man who hadn't spoken a word all the way from the ferry terminal.

'Suit yerself,' said the driver, jamming on the brakes. Cramer couldn't remember having said anything that might have offended the man. Maybe he'd just heard some bad news. Cramer thrust a twenty pound note into the man's hands and told him to keep the change, taking some small pleasure from the fact that for the first time the driver's face cracked into a smile. 'You're sure now?' queried the driver, as if the large tip had provoked a change of heart. 'The place you're wanting is further up the hill, it's no trouble.'

'I want to walk,' said Cramer, opening the door and shouldering his duffel bag. He trudged up the hill, the wind at his back. He didn't quite understand himself why he was walking and not driving up to the door. It was symbolic somehow, but he wouldn't be able to explain the symbolism to anyone. It was something to do with arriving on his own two feet, walking like a man and not being driven like an invalid, but even that felt too simplistic. He slipped his hand into the pocket of the reefer jacket and

5

felt the two brass keys. One for the front door, the solicitor had said, and one for the kitchen door. The kitchen door was also bolted from the inside, so he'd have to go in the front way.

He rested the bag on the pavement and turned to look out over the harbour. To the left bobbed the fishing boats of Howth, sturdy working boats, huddled together as if sheltering from the bitter cold wind but more than capable of taking the worst that the Irish Sea could throw at them. To the right, the weekend boats of the yacht club, their steel lines singing in the wind, their pristine white hulls rocking gently in the swell, tethered neatly in rows along the wooden pontoons of the marina like soldiers on parade. The yacht club building was a creamy yellow colour, its modern lines at odds with the weathered fishing village. Behind the club was a car park, but only two vehicles were parked there and one was a delivery truck. Fair-weather sailors, thought Cramer, and today wasn't fair weather. He swung the duffel bag back up on his shoulder and grunted. High above his head, seagulls swooped and banked, screaming for attention. Cramer craned his neck back and stared up at them. They reminded him of vultures, gathering over a dying animal. Cramer smiled at the image despite himself.

The cottage was close to the brow of the hill, a hundred feet or more from its nearest neighbour. It was small and squat, a granite pillbox with tiny windows and a steeply sloping roof, built to withstand the raging sea and the storms that blew in from the north-east. It was a hardy home, a home that had outlasted the men who'd built it and that would be around for generations to come. The curtains were drawn and the windows were grimy. The cottage had been empty for more than six months, the solicitor had said.

The property market was in a slump and the house was too small for most people. That was why he'd been able to buy it so cheaply. There was another reason, Cramer knew. Few people wanted to move into a house where someone had died. Cramer didn't care either way.

He dropped the duffel bag onto the stone step and put the key in the rusting lock. The key grated, and for a moment he thought that it would refuse to turn, but then it clicked and he pushed the battered oak door open. He stepped across the threshold, dragging the canvas bag after him. The door opened into the living room, a large brick fireplace to his left, a cramped staircase to the right. An overstuffed armchair sat next to the fire. Cramer noticed that the leather was all scuffed on the arms and there was a dark, greasy patch on the back of the chair where the previous occupant had sat for hours, staring into the flames. He closed the door behind him. The air was stale and damp so he threw open the single window and allowed the cold salty sea breeze to blow in. Tattered curtains, long faded and thin in places, flapped in the draught like trapped birds. There were ashes in the grate, and on the floor by the chair was an earthenware ashtray containing a single cigarette, stubbed out and broken in half. Next to it stood a tea-stained mug, chipped and cracked. Cramer felt like a detective at a crime scene, though there had been no doubt what had killed the old man who used to live in the house: a massive heart attack in his sleep, brought on by too much whisky and fried food and not enough exercise, coupled with the fact that he'd passed his allotted three score years and ten by a decade or more.

A chipboard door led through into a compact kitchen containing an ancient refrigerator, a dirt-encrusted gas stove and a Welsh dresser. Cramer opened the refrigerator door and the light came on. The solicitor had promised to reconnect the electricity supply and he'd been as good as his word. A packet of long-forgotten cheese sat at the back of the refrigerator, black inside its plastic wrapper, next to a half-used bottle of Heinz tomato ketchup lying on its side as if it had been hurriedly thrown in. Cramer closed the door. The stairs led up to a single bedroom, and Cramer could smell what was within before he pushed open the door. The room was barely twelve feet by ten, little more than a cell with a single bed and a wardrobe. The sheets and blankets had been thrown aside as if the occupant had leapt out of bed, but Cramer knew that the old man had been taken away by ambulancemen, because he'd been dead for a week before anyone knocked at his front door. The sheets were stained with stale urine and faeces and there was long-dried blood on the yellowing pillow. Cramer opened the window and took a deep breath of fresh air.

A door in the corner of the room opened into a tiny bathroom containing a tub so small that he'd have difficulty sitting in it never mind lying down, a washbasin and a toilet. The white plastic lid was down and Cramer flushed without opening it. The cheese had been enough of an unpleasant surprise.

He pulled the soiled sheets and pillowcase off the bed and took them downstairs. There was a cardboard box by the fridge containing old tins and several empty whisky bottles. Cramer dropped the sheets onto the rubbish then unlocked the kitchen door and threw the box outside into a small walled yard. There was a rusting bicycle leaning against the wall, its saddle missing and its chain broken, a reminder of the days when the old man had been able to cycle around the village. Cramer closed the door. The air was fresher and he could breathe without fighting the urge to throw up, but now it was too cold to take off his jacket. There was coal in a brass scuttle and a newspaper on the windowsill, and he soon had a fire burning in the grate. He rubbed his hands and held them out, warming them in front of the flames as he sat in the old man's chair. 'There's no place like home,' he muttered to himself. Outside, the screams of the gulls grew louder and more insistent.

The Colonel put his elbows on his knees and leant forward over the chessboard, his forehead screwed into deep creases as he studied the pieces. He made a soft clucking noise as he considered his options. The rook seemed the best bet. He sat up and reached for the piece, then stopped midway, his hand suspended above the board. No, the bishop. The bishop first, then the rook. He moved the bishop, pressing the piece down hard on the board so that it registered with the computer.

A tiny red light flickered on the side of the plastic board, letting him know that the computer was thinking. The Colonel had developed an intense dislike of the flashing light. He'd only had the chess-playing computer for two weeks, but it was without doubt the most able player he'd ever faced. At its highest setting it could defeat him seventy-five per cent of the time, and he was determined to keep on playing until he could consistently better it. The telephone warbled and he picked up the receiver, his eyes still on the board. He was beginning to have second thoughts. Maybe it would have been better to have moved the rook first and then attacked with his bishop. 'Yes?' he said.

'Mike Cramer's surfaced,' said a voice that the Colonel instantly recognised.

'Where?' He sat back in his chair.

'Ireland. We spotted him at Holyhead boarding the ferry to Dun Laoghaire.'

'There's no doubt?'

The caller sniffed, once. 'None at all.'

'Where is he now?'

'Howth, north of Dublin. He's bought a cottage there.'

'He's what?' The Colonel closed his eyes as if in pain. 'What the hell is he up to?' he asked.

The question was rhetorical but the caller answered nonetheless. 'We were hoping you'd be able to tell us.'

Mike Cramer put on his reefer jacket and buttoned it up to the neck as he closed the front door behind him. He didn't bother locking it. He thrust his hands deep into his pockets and walked down the road. An elderly woman was standing on a stepladder cleaning the windows of the neighbouring cottage and as he walked by Cramer wished her a good morning. He found a general store facing the west pier and he bought coffee, milk, sugar, and a newspaper, not because there was anything in it he wanted to read but because he'd need it to get the fire going. He wasn't hungry but he nevertheless put eggs, bacon and a loaf of bread into the wire shopping basket before handing it to the young lad behind the counter. 'Are you here on holiday?' asked the boy as he totalled up Cramer's purchases and put them into a blue plastic carrier bag.

'Nah, I'm living here,' said Cramer, passing over a twenty pound note.

The boy frowned. 'In Howth? Jesus, I'm doing all I can to move out. There's nothing for anyone here.' He gave Cramer his change.

'It's got everything I want,' said Cramer. 'See you around.' He walked along the sea front to a pub built of the same stone as his cottage. Three fishermen in bright orange waterproof jackets were drinking at the bar and they turned as one towards him as he stepped inside. They looked like brothers, balding, broad shoulders, ruddy cheeks and hands gnarled from too much exposure to sea water and cold winds. Cramer nodded a greeting and went to the far end of the bar where he ordered a double Famous Grouse from the matronly barmaid. He downed the whisky in one go and smacked his lips appreciatively.

'Good?' asked the barmaid.

'Oh yes,' said Cramer.

'Another?'

'Definitely. And have one yourself. While you're at it, I'd like to buy the guys over there a drink.'

The barmaid beamed and refilled his glass. 'Are you celebrating or something?'

'Or something,' said Cramer. He raised the glass and toasted the fishermen.

*   *   *

The boy sat in front of the television set and watched the rocket soar through the sky. A flat emotionless voice was calling out numbers but the boy didn't know what they referred to. Nor did he care. He sat open-mouthed as the rocket and its three astronauts headed for the moon. The moon. They really were going to the moon. Just like in the comics. The boy leaned back and put his hands on the floor as he stared at the screen. He tried to imagine what it must be like to be in a space capsule, drinking through a tube and going to the toilet in a space suit. The boy wanted to go to the toilet but he didn't want to miss one second of the launch. He pressed his legs together and blocked out thoughts of his full bladder. He heard his name being called but he ignored it and shuffled closer to the screen until his feet were almost under the television set. Something fell away from the bottom of the rocket and for a moment he thought that something had gone wrong, but then he heard the clipped voice say that separation had been successful and he realised that everything was okay.

His mother shouted for him again and the boy leaned forward and turned up the volume. The rocket was a small dot in the sky with a thick white plume trailing behind it. The boy wondered at what point the rocket was actually in space and not in the sky, and if there was a line somewhere up there that separated the two.

There was a banging from his mother's bedroom, the sound of a walking stick being pounded against the threadbare carpet. The boy got slowly to his feet. The banging was repeated, more rapidly this time. The boy went into the hallway and looked up the stairs. His legs felt like lead. His mother called his name again and the boy put a hand on the banister. He put his foot on the first step. He wished with all his heart for his father, but he was at work and wouldn't be

*back for hours. From the sixth step he could see his parents'
bedroom door, painted in the same pale green colour as the
rest of the doors in the house. The boy had lived in the house
all his life and he couldn't remember them ever being any other
colour. He took the stairs one at a time, pausing between each
step, his eyes fixed on the door. 'Where are you?' his mother
shouted, then he heard her cough.*

*'I'm coming,' he called and ran up the last few stairs. He
gripped the doorknob and pushed open the door. His mother
was on the bed on her hands and knees, her body wracked
with hacking coughs. Her mousy brown hair was tangled and
matted, her eyes were red and puffy and there were stains
down the front of her blue flannel nightie. She looked up as
he walked into the room and stood at the foot of the bed.*

*Tears welled in the boy's eyes. 'What do you want, Mum?'
he asked.*

*His mother sat back on her heels and wrapped her arms
around her stomach. 'I just want to get better,' she cried.*

'Me too,' said the boy. 'That's what I want, too.'

*She held out her arms and he climbed up onto the bed and
clung to her. She smoothed the back of his head with her hands
and made small shushing noises. 'You've got to be strong,' she
whispered. 'I'm going to need your help.' The boy buried his
face in the flannel nightie and its smell of sick.*

The man in the wheelchair stopped to examine a rack of
brightly coloured ties, running the silk through his gloved
fingers. A salesman in an immaculate dark blue suit raised
an eyebrow but the man in the wheelchair shook his head.

Just looking. He put his hands on the wheels and pushed the chair forward. The people who passed him studiously avoided eye contact, as if they were embarrassed by his disability.

He rolled slowly towards the suit section. His legs were wrapped in a thick blue wool blanket and he felt sweat trickle down his thighs. An elderly man was being measured by a young assistant while his much younger fur-coated and clearly bored wife watched. Two Japanese tourists were pulling suits off the racks, holding them up and talking animatedly. The man in the wheelchair smiled to himself. Compared with Tokyo, the prices in Harrods were probably a bargain. He never paid Harrods prices for clothes, never wore anything with a label that could be recognised.

The Arab swept into the menswear department, flanked by two Harrods executives and a trio of bodyguards. The bodyguards were thickset men in black suits and tinted sunglasses and had matching thick moustaches. Saddam Hussein lookalikes. Their eyes swept back and forth like searchlights, but the man in the wheelchair noted with some small satisfaction that they looked right through him. Cripples were always invisible. The Arab was dressed in full desert robes and looked like something out of *Lawrence of Arabia*, totally out of place among the racks of tailored suits. Behind the Arab walked three black-robed women, their faces covered except for their eyes. One was clearly the Arab's mother, she was short and squat and moved like a buoy bobbing in a rough sea. The other two were his wives. The man in the wheelchair propelled himself forward.

One of the wives was a Saudi princess, and by all accounts she was built like a Russian weightlifter. The other, his second wife, was a former *Playboy* centrefold from Utah who'd been about to embark on a movie career when she'd settled for the sheikh and his millions instead. In the black robes, it was impossible to tell the two wives apart. The man slipped his hand under the blanket.

The manager of the menswear department was gushing about how honoured he was to see the valued customer again, rubbing his hands together and bowing obsequiously. One of the bodyguards walked close to the wheelchair, checking out a man standing by the changing rooms. The man in the wheelchair smiled up at the bodyguard, but he was ignored. The silenced automatic coughed twice under the blanket and the bodyguard fell backwards, blood spreading across his white shirt from two large black holes.

The man in the wheelchair stood up, slipping out from under the blanket like a snake shedding its skin. He took three paces forward and shot the second bodyguard twice in the chest. The man was dead before his knees crumpled. The third bodyguard was reaching for his gun when he took a bullet in the sternum. As he slumped forward, clutching at his chest like a heart attack victim, the man shot him in the head, blowing blood and brain matter across the display of ties.

Shoppers began screaming and running for the exits, but the man was an oasis of calm among the panic. He aimed his gun at the Arab. The Arab's eyes widened in terror, then almost at once he visibly relaxed. The old woman was backing away, her hands held up in front of her face, her mouth open and making loud snoring sounds.

The two wives stood stock still, frozen in terror. Close

up the man could see that one was dark, with brown eyes, pockmarked skin. Obviously not the centrefold.

He turned to the other woman, levelled the gun between her big blue eyes and fired, then stepped forward and shot her again in the chest as she fell.

The man spun on his heels and walked quickly to the stairs, the gun at his side. People ran from him, leaving his way clear. Shouts and screams came from behind him, but he kept on walking, his head down. He reached the stairs and went down to the ground floor, keeping the gun pressed to his side. He walked to the Egyptian Hall and took the escalator to the lower ground floor. The screams and shouts had faded away by now, and by the time he stepped off the escalator no one was paying him any attention. He turned left and walked briskly through to the stationery department, as if he had nothing more pressing on his mind than the purchase of an executive writing set.

The door to the stationery stock room was unlocked, as he knew it would be. The man slid the gun into his belt and buttoned his jacket over it as he walked across the store room and into the entrance of the tunnel. Heating pipes ran along the length of the roof of the tunnel and he jumped up and dragged down a brown warehouseman's coat he'd stuck there earlier. The tunnel curved to the right ahead and the man could see that he was alone. He dusted the coat off and slipped it on as he walked among boxes of merchandise waiting to be taken into the store. The tunnel was the main supply route into the store, and the reason why delivery trucks were rarely seen blocking the Knightsbridge streets above.

Glancing in a circular mirror positioned at the bend of the tunnel, he saw several workmen heading his way so he kept his head down and walked purposefully. He wasn't challenged, nor had he been when he'd tried a dry run two days earlier.

Several electric carts rattled past, piled high with more boxes, but the drivers paid him no attention. The tunnel was about five hundred feet long and led to two lifts which went up to the main Harrods warehouse facilities. The man ignored the lifts and raced up the stairs to the single exit door which opened onto Trevor Square. A fresh-faced security guard, a telephone pressed to his ear, was looking his way, his mouth open in surprise, and the man pulled out his gun and shot him in the throat without even breaking stride. The security guard was still dying as the man closed the exit door and walked out into the sunshine. Ten minutes later he was on the tube, heading for Victoria Station.

Mike Cramer held the half-empty bottle of Famous Grouse in his hand, swirling the whisky around as he stared into the fire. He'd made himself a bacon sandwich earlier but it sat untouched on a plate by the chair. He could feel the whisky burning away at the lining of his empty stomach and he knew that he should eat something, but he had no appetite. A shower of soot fell down the chimney, startling him. The flue probably hadn't been swept in years, though the fire burned well enough.

He looked at his wristwatch, more out of habit than because he wanted to know the time. It wasn't as if he had anywhere to go. It was almost midnight. He sat back in the old armchair. It was comfortable and seemed to mould itself to his shape like a living thing. He'd moved it so that he could see the front door and the window and keep his back to the wall – though he was still close enough to the fire to feel its warmth. Cramer rolled his head from side to side. He could feel the tension in his neck, the muscles taut and unyielding. He yawned and his jaw clicked, another sign of the strain he was under. He got to his feet and climbed the stairs.

He hadn't been able to buy fresh sheets or a pillowcase in the village so he'd made do with the rough blankets and the stained pillow. He'd spent the night in worse places, and he had no qualms about sleeping in a dead man's bed. Cramer was well past the stage of believing in ghosts. He smiled to himself. Famous Grouse was the only spirit he had any faith in these days. He put the bottle on the floor by the bed and then took the Browning Hi-Power 9mm automatic from his shoulder holster and placed it under the pillow. It was Cramer's fifth night in the cottage. He didn't think it would be much longer.

Thomas McCormack was putting the final touches to a bright red-feathered trout fly of his own design when the phone on his workbench rang. He sighed and stopped what he was doing. It was Aidan Twomey, an old friend and colleague, but after the bare minimum of pleasantries McCormack realised that it wasn't a social call.

'There's a Brit here, Thomas,' said Twomey, whispering as if he didn't want to be overheard. 'Looks like a Sass-man to me. Living in old man Rafferty's cottage.'

McCormack pulled a face as he studied the half-finished fly. 'Sure he's not a relative?'

Twomey snorted down the phone. 'Rafferty related to a Sass-man? You'll have him spinning in his grave, Thomas. Nah, Rafferty didn't have any relatives over the water. He was the last of his line. No kids and his wife died a few years back. A local solicitor sold the cottage, lock, stock and barrel. Then this Brit moves in.'

'And you think he's SAS?'

'I'd bet my life on it, Thomas. He's definitely army, that's for sure. I've seen enough of the bastards in my time, you know that. He was in the pub, on his own, drinking. And he's been taking long walks, like he was waiting for something.'

'Doesn't seem to be keeping a low profile, then?' said McCormack impatiently. He wondered why Twomey was bothering him with such a trivial matter. If the SAS were conducting an undercover operation in Howth, the man would hardly be drinking in the local pub.

'I was wondering if maybe the boys had anything going in Howth. Anything they'd rather keep to themselves.'

'Not a thing, Aidan. Take my word for it.'

'Aye, right enough, right enough. But it's the way he's carrying on. Like he was waiting for something to happen.'

McCormack clicked his tongue in annoyance. Initiative was all well and good, but he didn't appreciate having his time wasted. 'Well, thanks for the tip, Aidan. I'll make a note of it.'

'Cramer,' said Twomey. 'Mike Cramer. That's his name.'

McCormack's jaw dropped. 'What?' he said.

'Mike Cramer. That's his name. That's what he told Padraig in the pub. I checked with the solicitor, too, and that's the name on the deeds of the cottage.'

'This Cramer. Describe him.' McCormack sat hunched over the phone as he made notes on a sheet of paper, the fly forgotten.

'Just over six feet tall, thin but looks like he can take care of himself, you know. Deep-set eyes, his nose is sort of hooked and looks like it might've been broken. Brown hair, a bit long. His accent is all over the place, but he's definitely not Irish. He told Padraig he was from Scotland originally.'

'Did he tell Padraig what he was doing in Howth?'

'Enjoying the sea air is all he said. What do you think, Thomas? Did I do the right thing calling you?'

'Oh yes,' said McCormack. 'Jesus, Mary and Joseph, you did the right thing all right. Now listen to me, Aidan, and listen well. Stay where you are. I'll have someone down there as soon as possible. Make sure no one goes near him, I don't want anyone asking him questions. I don't want him frightened off, okay?'

'Sure. But I don't think your man's going anywhere. He's well settled in at the cottage.'

McCormack replaced the receiver and sat staring at his reflection in the mirror on the wall. Cramer the Sass-man back in Ireland, sitting in a pub as if he didn't have a care in the world. It didn't make sense. It didn't make any sense at all.

*　　*　　*

The young man slowed the blue Citroën to a walking pace as he scrutinised the numbers on the houses. 'There it is,' he said to his passenger. 'Number sixteen.'

'What's the guy's name?' asked the passenger, a redhead in his late teens, pale skinned with watery green eyes.

'Twomey. Aidan Twomey.'

'Never heard of him.'

The driver stopped the car and turned to look at his passenger. 'Yeah, well he's probably not heard of you either, Paulie. The difference is, Aidan Twomey did a tenner in the Kesh for the Cause and he's got McCormack's ear, so I'd be careful what you say, you hear?'

Paulie held his hands up in surrender. 'I hear you, Davie. Jesus, you're touchy today.'

Davie shrugged. He was a couple of years older than Paulie and since their father had died he'd become accustomed to being the man of the family. He ran his hand through his thick, sandy hair. 'This is important, Paulie. We can't afford to fuck up.'

'We won't,' said Paulie. He opened the glove compartment and took out a revolver, checking that all the chambers were loaded. It was an old gun and had once belonged to their father, though it had never been used in anger. For the last five years it had lain under the attic floorboards, wrapped in an oiled rag.

'What the hell are you doing with that?' hissed Davie.

'We might need it.'

'McCormack said we were to watch and report on this guy until the boys get here.'

'So?'

'So the word was watch, not shoot. We won't be needing a gun, Paulie.' He took it from his brother and shoved it

21

under the front seat. 'McCormack would have your balls if we got caught with that.'

'Who's gonna catch us? This isn't the North.'

Davie glared at him. 'Just do as you're told, will you? We watch, we wait, and that's it.'

'Then the boys from Belfast get the glory?'

'That's the way it goes. Don't you worry, our turn will come.' He climbed out of the car and walked down the path to the front door of the pretty bungalow with its views of the sea below. The garden was well-ordered, the grass neatly clipped and there was a stone bird bath in the centre of the lawn. Paulie followed him, glowering resentfully.

Davie rang the doorbell and the front door opened immediately. Twomey squinted at his two visitors as if he needed spectacles. 'Hello, boys, your dad's in the car, is he?'

'No, we're . . .' began Paulie, but Davie silenced him with a baleful stare.

'Thomas sent us,' said Davie.

'Oh, it's Thomas is it, not Mr McCormack?' said Twomey. He grinned impishly. 'I'm only messing with yer, lads, come on in.'

He ushered them into his sitting room and poured them large measures of whiskey without asking. He handed them brimming glasses and sat down on a flower-printed sofa. 'Is it just the two of you, then?' he asked.

'There are four coming from Belfast,' said Davie.

'Do you know their names?'

Davie shook his head. He felt his cheeks redden as he realised it was a sign of how low down he was in the organisation. 'Thomas wanted us to keep tabs on the Sass-man until they get here.'

Twomey drained his glass. 'I'd best be showing you where he is, then. We'll use my car. I'll get my coat, it looks like it's going to rain.'

Mike Cramer stood on the sea wall, his back to the harbour. His face was dripping wet and when he licked his lips he tasted the tang of salt. Through the misty rain he could see the huge hump of quartzite rock called Ireland's Eye, sitting in the boiling sea like a massive iceberg. The rain lashed against his face but it was a fine spray rather than a soaking downpour. If it hadn't been for the chill wind it would have been refreshing.

The wall curved around the marina, sheltering the yachts from the rough water, and at the far end was a lighthouse, its beam already flashing out to sea, guiding the fishing boats home. A black Labrador, its fur shining wet, walked over and sniffed at Cramer's boots, wagging its tail. Cramer patted it on the head absent-mindedly. He turned to walk back along the wall to the harbour. A solitary car was parked in the yacht club. There were three men sitting in it, an old man and two who couldn't have been much more than teenagers. 'It's started,' he said to the dog. The dog growled as if he understood, and Cramer smiled. An old man and two kids. There'd be more on the way, guaranteed.

*   *   *

The uniformed cop pushed back his wooden chair and stretched out his long legs. He yawned and turned to watch a pretty black nurse walk down the corridor. Her hips swayed sexily and as she turned a corner she looked over her shoulder and grinned. The cop grinned back. A cup of cold coffee sat untouched by the side of his chair, next to the afternoon edition of the *Baltimore Sun*.

The cop stood up and arched his back. He didn't enjoy sitting for long periods, especially in the corridor of a crowded hospital. He hated hospitals. When his turn came to die, he hoped it would be out in the street or between the sheets with a hot blonde, not in some antiseptic white-painted room with tubes running into his veins and a stinking bedpan on the floor. He shuddered involuntarily. This was no time to be thinking about death.

The elevator doors at the end of the corridor hissed open and a young doctor in a white coat stepped out. He was tall with a shock of black hair that kept falling over his eyes as he walked towards the uniformed cop. He was carrying a small stainless steel tray covered with a white cloth. The cop nodded a greeting, and the doctor made to go past. The cop held up a hand to stop him. 'Whoa there, partner,' he said.

The doctor frowned. He was wearing wire-framed spectacles and he squinted as if he wasn't used to them. 'I have to take a blood sample,' he said impatiently. The cop studied the plastic-covered identification badge pinned to the top pocket of the doctor's white coat. The small colour photograph matched the man's face. John Theobald, MD. Cardiovascular Department. 'I haven't seen you before,' said the cop.

'That's not really my problem, is it?' said the doctor. 'Now are you going to let me get to my patient, or not?'

'He's not your patient, though, is he?' asked the cop. He tapped the clipboard he was carrying. 'Your name isn't on the list of approved medical personnel.' He gingerly lifted the cloth and peered under it. On the tray lay a disposable syringe, a couple of cotton wool balls and a small bottle of antiseptic.

'I've been on vacation,' the doctor explained. 'This is my first day back.'

'Today's Tuesday,' said the cop, dropping the cloth back over the tray.

'What do you mean?' The doctor was irritated.

'I mean, wouldn't Monday normally be your first day back?'

'I missed my flight. Look, what is this? What's going on here?' His voice rose angrily.

The cop held up a hand as if he were stopping traffic. 'Doc, I'm just doing my job. That man in there is a very important witness in a federal case . . .'

'That man is a patient, a patient who has just undergone major heart surgery, and there are tests that I have to do on him to check that the operation went smoothly,' interrupted the doctor. 'Now, get the hell out of my way. If you're that worried, why don't you come in with me?'

The cop held the doctor's look for a few seconds, then he nodded slowly. He opened the door and followed the doctor inside. A heart monitor beeped quietly. The only other sound in the room was the patient's ragged breathing. The cop kept his hand on his holster as the doctor put the tray down on the bedside table. The doctor snapped on a pair of rubber gloves, pulled back the cloth and wiped antiseptic along the patient's left arm, then quickly withdrew a sample of blood and pressed a small plaster over the puncture.

'Satisfied?' said the doctor, putting the blood-filled syringe on the tray and carrying it to the door. The cop moved out of the doctor's way and held the door open for him.

'Doc, I'm just doing my job.'

'Yeah,' said the doctor. 'You and the Gestapo.' He looked as if he were going to say something else, but then just shook his head and walked out.

The cop bared his teeth at the back of the departing doctor and slowly closed the door. He walked over to the bed and looked down at the patient. The man's eyes flickered open as if he was aware that he was being watched. The electronic beep quickened. 'Am I going to be all right?' the patient rasped.

'Peachy keen,' said the cop, removing his gun from his glistening black holster. From the inside pocket of his leather jacket he took out a bulbous silencer and carefully screwed it into the barrel of the gun. 'Just peachy keen.' He pointed the weapon at the man's face and fired once, then as his body went into spasm he fired a second shot into the newly-repaired heart.

Aidan Twomey was brewing a pot of tea when the doorbell rang. He put the kettle back on the stove and walked through the hallway. He could make out four figures through the rippled glass of the front door. He opened it and took a step backwards. 'My God, talk about a face from the past,' he said.

The broad-shouldered man at the front of the group

was grinning widely. He was in his late forties, a decade younger than Twomey, with black, curly hair and a bushy beard. 'Aidan, you old rascal. How've you been?' said the visitor. The two men embraced. Aidan Twomey and Dermott Lynch had done time together in the cells of Long Kesh – Twomey for being in possession of an Armalite rifle, Lynch for assaulting a soldier at a checkpoint – and during their imprisonment it was Twomey who had shown Lynch how to brew the perfect cup of tea. In return, the younger man had taught Twomey how to manufacture explosives from fertiliser and engine oil. 'I thought you'd retired, and here you are bringing us a Sass-man,' chuckled Lynch. He introduced his three companions, hard-faced men with tough bodies. They were all carrying sports holdalls, like a football team geared up for an away match. There were two large nondescript cars parked on the roadside.

Twomey took them through to the sitting room and then brought out the teapot. Lynch shook his head in amazement. 'Your timing was always damn near perfect,' he said.

Twomey nodded at the cabinet by the window. 'Get the cups out, will you, Dermott? And there's a bottle of Jameson's there too.'

'Who's watching your man?' asked Lynch, pouring out generous measures of whiskey.

'Two wee boys. Davie and Paulie Quinn.'

'Aye, I knew their old man,' said Lynch. 'How are they shaping up?'

'They've been watching the cottage all day, one of them phones in every hour.'

Lynch pointed to one of the sports bags the men had carried in. 'We've walkie-talkies in there, there'll be no more need for phoning,' he said.

'Jesus, I hope you've brought more than walkie-talkies with yer,' said Twomey.

Lynch laughed heartily. 'You wouldn't be trying to teach your grandmother to suck eggs now, would you?' He leaned over and opened the bag by his feet. Inside was a Kalashnikov with a folding metal stock, disassembled into its component parts. He swiftly reassembled it and slotted in the curved magazine. He grinned. 'Now, show me the Sass-man.'

The telephone rang and Twomey went over to answer it. 'It's Davie,' he said, cupping his hand over the mouthpiece. 'Do you want a word?'

Lynch shook his head. 'Where's Cramer?' he asked.

Twomey relayed the question to Davie. 'He's on the harbour wall again,' Twomey said to Lynch, holding his hand over the mouthpiece.

'Doing what?'

'Just standing there. That's all he does. He walks and he stands looking out to sea.'

'You think he's waiting for something?'

Twomey shrugged. 'Maybe.'

Lynch nodded. 'Tell Davie we'll meet him in front of St Mary's Abbey.'

Twomey sat in the passenger seat next to Lynch as they drove to the ruins of the parish church which overlooked the harbour, reminiscing about the old days. It was still raining and the windscreen wipers flicked from side to side as they climbed the hill to the church. They found Davie standing with his arms folded across his chest, stamping his feet for warmth. He hadn't dressed for the outdoors. Lynch motioned for him to get into the back of the car, next to Pat O'Riordan, a stocky farmer from Ballymena who was responsible for the deaths of three British soldiers. Davie recognised O'Riordan and his eyes widened as he realised the calibre of the men who'd driven down from Belfast. He was in illustrious company.

'Where's your car?' asked Lynch, twisting around in his seat.

'My brother's got it,' shivered Davie. 'He's parked on the west pier, across from the Sass-man.' Water dripped off his hair and onto his pullover. He flicked his wet hair out of his eyes.

Twomey handed Lynch a pair of powerful binoculars. 'That's your man down there, on the sea wall,' he said.

Lynch focused the binoculars, using the steering wheel to steady his hands. 'That's him, right enough,' said Lynch.

'You know him?' Davie blurted out, then fell silent, embarrassed by his outburst.

'Aye, lad, I've met Sergeant Cramer before.'

'What do you want to do, Dermott?' asked Twomey.

'We wait,' he replied, the binoculars still pressed to his eyes. 'We wait and we watch.'

'You think it's a set-up?'

'Look at him, Aidan. Standing there as bold as brass. He's like a baited trap, and we're the rats. We're not going to do anything until we're sure he's alone.' He handed the binoculars to Twomey and turned back to Davie. 'What's he been doing?'

Davie rubbed his hands together. 'He walks along the beach, he walks up and down the harbour wall. According to the lad in the shop he buys some food: bread, milk, just the basics. Doesn't seem to eat much, he's more of a drinker. Famous Grouse. He buys a bottle a day from the pub.'

'Is there a telephone in the cottage?'

Davie shook his head.

'Has he spoken to anyone, any strangers?'

Another shake of the head.

'Visitors?'

'Not according to the neighbours. He keeps himself to himself, but he seems friendly enough to the locals. He's made no secret of who he is.'

'Good lad, you've done well.' Davie smiled with pride as Lynch turned the key in the ignition. 'Let's take a run by his cottage while he's down there,' he said. 'Show me the way.'

Thomas McCormack stared at the ripples on the surface of the river. 'What do you think, Joe? Think he'll take it?'

Joseph Connolly grinned. 'It's all in the wrist, Thomas. Give it a go.'

McCormack drew back his arm and sent his fly arcing through the air. It settled on the water but the trout below defiantly refused to bite. Connolly chuckled to himself. 'He's a cunning old bastard, right enough.'

McCormack wound in his line again. The two men had been standing thigh deep in the fast flowing water for the best part of thirty minutes, and neither had caught a thing, never mind the huge trout that was said to inhabit the shady spot beneath the riverside oak. 'Go on, let's see your best shot,' said McCormack. He pushed his horn-rimmed spectacles further up his nose. The glasses and his greying hair gave him a scholarly, almost schoolmasterly, appearance, belying his role as a member of the IRA Army Executive, a man who regularly made life or death decisions. It had been an impassioned speech by McCormack which had resulted in a massive car bomb, causing millions of pounds worth of damage to London's financial centre, and it had been McCormack's idea to bring in the American sniper with a high powered rifle who'd killed half a dozen members of the security forces with long distance shots across the border.

Connolly was one of the hardliners in the Army Council, and one of the harshest critics of the 1994 ceasefire and the peace process that had followed. Connolly's mistrust of the British Government bordered on the paranoid, and he had taken a lot of persuading before agreeing to back Gerry Adams's peace initiative.

McCormack watched as Connolly cast his fly, a smooth, fluid action that McCormack had to admire. Connolly had been fly-fishing for more than half a century and McCormack was a relative newcomer, but even if he fished for another hundred years he didn't think he'd ever be as good as the old man. 'Come on, you bugger, isn't that the loveliest, tastiest fly you've ever seen?' Connolly whispered to the unseen quarry. McCormack held his breath, certain that this time the fish would take the bait, but the glossy blue fly sat untouched on the surface. 'It's not my day, sure enough,' growled Connolly as he wound in his line.

McCormack pulled a pewter hip flask from the inside pocket of his waxed cotton jacket, unscrewed the top and offered it to his companion. Connolly's liver-spotted hand trembled slightly as he took the flask, but McCormack pretended not to notice. Connolly had just turned seventy, and while his mind was still razor sharp, he was rumoured to have developed Parkinson's disease. It wasn't as if the man was an invalid, and McCormack had noticed that there were no shakes when Connolly was concentrating on fishing. McCormack hoped that the rumours were wrong and that the trembling was nothing more than a symptom of old age, like the thinning white hair, the liver spots and the hearing aid tucked behind his right ear. The old man drank from the flask, handed it back and began to tie another fly onto his line. 'This Cramer,' he said without looking up. 'What do you think?'

McCormack smiled. The canny old bastard had read his mind. 'It's not a set-up,' he said, slowly. 'He's on his own. Whatever he's up to, he's not with the SAS any more.'

'Could be Five.'

'Nah. British Intelligence wouldn't touch him with a bargepole. Cramer was finished some time ago. He's too well known here, and he'd be bugger all use anywhere else. Besides, if Five were using him, why would they put him in Howth?'

Connolly shrugged as he concentrated on his knot. 'You tell me, Thomas. You're the one who won't let sleeping dogs lie.'

McCormack sensed admonition in the older man's voice and realised that he'd have to tread carefully. 'This is a murdering dog that deserves to be put down, Joe. Peace process or no peace process.'

'No argument here,' said Connolly, straightening up and looking him in the eye. 'I just don't want it to backfire on you, that's all.' He paused. 'There's no doubt that it's Cramer?'

'None. Dermott saw him five years ago, up close.'

'Close? How close?'

'We had Cramer in a farmhouse with another under-cover Sass-man. Cramer's partner died while he was being questioned, Cramer was lucky to get away with his life. Dermott was one of the team guarding him.'

'Does Cramer know Dermott?' asked Connolly.

'Dermott says no. Cramer was hooded or blindfolded most of the time.'

Connolly fixed McCormack with a beady stare. 'Dermott's got a personal interest, hasn't he?'

McCormack nodded. 'Aye. But that's not what this is about.'

'And Cramer's quite alone?'

'No question of it. Dermott's had him under twenty-four hour surveillance for the past three days. No one's gone near Cramer, he's made no telephone calls, and there are no other strangers in the village.'

'Do you think he's cracked? Had some sort of break-down?'

'It's possible. He's certainly not behaving rationally.'

'Why not bring him in?' asked Connolly.

'Because there's nothing we need from him. Other than to be an example of what we do to our enemies.'

A plopping sound at the far side of the river caught Connolly's attention. He shaded his eyes with his hand but couldn't see anything. 'Aye, the bastard deserves a bullet, right enough,' he said.

'So I have the Army Council's permission?'

Connolly smiled tightly. 'Let's just say there won't be

any tears shed. But we won't be claiming responsibility, not officially. Politically it's too sensitive; you know how things are at the moment. But Cramer's been the death of too many of our people for us to leave him be.' Connolly licked his lips and they glistened wetly. 'When?' he asked.

McCormack drained the flask and slipped it back into his pocket. 'Tomorrow morning. Early.'

Connolly put a hand on McCormack's shoulder. 'Just be careful, Thomas. If anything goes wrong . . .' He left the sentence hanging, and McCormack nodded. He understood. There must be no mistakes.

Dermott Lynch was tucking into sausage and chips in Aidan Twomey's spotless kitchen when the telephone rang. Twomey answered it in the hall and a few seconds later he appeared at the kitchen door. 'It's Thomas,' he said.

Lynch nodded and put down his knife and fork. 'This'll be it,' he said. He took a mouthful of tea and wiped his mouth with the back of his hand. He picked up the receiver. 'Aye, Thomas.'

'It's a runner,' said McCormack. 'Tomorrow morning.'

'Fine,' said Lynch.

'You're sure he's alone?'

'Dead sure.'

'And he suspects nothing?'

'He's not even looking over his shoulder.'

'Where are you going to do it?'

'The sea wall. Every morning first thing he takes a walk.

Stands near the lighthouse looking out over the sea like a fisherman's wife.'

'Be careful, Dermott.'

'He's a sitting duck.'

'Just mind what I say. I don't want anyone getting hurt.'

Lynch laughed softly. 'Except for Cramer, you mean?' He was still chuckling when he went back into the kitchen. Twomey was refilling their mugs with steaming tea. 'It's on,' said Lynch, sitting down at the table and picking up his knife and fork.

'What's your plan?' asked Twomey.

'We'll take him on the sea wall. There'll be nowhere for him to run.'

'You might be seen.'

Lynch snorted contemptuously. 'We might be seen, but I doubt there'll be any witnesses,' he said.

'Aye, right enough,' said Twomey, sipping his tea. He put his mug down. 'I'd like you to do me a favour, Dermott.' Lynch narrowed his eyes, his fork halfway to his mouth. 'Not for me, you understand, for the Quinn boys. They've been pestering me . . .'

Lynch grinned, understanding. 'And they want to be in on the kill?' Twomey nodded. 'Sure, no problem. It's about time the boys were blooded.'

Mike Cramer woke to the sound of seagulls screaming. He rolled out of bed and washed in the bathroom before dressing in the same clothes he'd been wearing all week.

Before going downstairs he took the Browning from under the stained pillow and slid it down the back of his trousers.

He made himself a coffee and sat in the old man's chair as he drank it. There were packets of bread and sausage in the kitchen but neither had been opened. The bottle of Famous Grouse sat half-finished in the hearth and he reached over and poured a slug into his mug. Not quite an Irish coffee, he thought wryly, but close enough. The gun was sticking into the small of his back so he took it out and placed it on his lap. The Belgian-made Browning with its thirteen cartridges in the clip was a good weapon to have in a fire-fight against multiple opponents. As a rule, Cramer would never get himself into a position where he'd have to fire at more than two targets, but he knew that the situation he was heading for was the exception that proved the rule. A one-off. He field-stripped the gun and checked the firing mechanism, then reassembled it with well-practised movements before draining his mug. Another reason for choosing the Browning was its rugged reliability and the fact that it rarely jammed. In all his years in the SAS he'd never had one fail on him. He stood up, wincing as he did.

The shoulder holster was hanging on the back of the front door, its supple leather glistening in the sun which filtered through the grimy windows. He eased it on, holstered the Browning, and slipped on his reefer jacket. He had a strong premonition that today was the day. The waiting was over.

* * *

From his vantage point amid the ruins of St Mary's Abbey, Paulie Quinn watched Cramer walk slowly down the road to the harbour, his hands in his pockets. Cramer kept his head bent down as if deep in thought. Paulie wondered what was going through the Sass-man's mind, whether he knew that today would be his last day on earth. Paulie put his walkie-talkie next to his mouth. 'He's on his way,' he said.

'I see him,' said Lynch who was sitting with Pat O'Riordan, parked in the yacht club car park.

Paulie put the walkie-talkie back in his pocket and pressed the binoculars to his eyes. He didn't want to miss a second. His only regret was that he wouldn't be closer to the action. He'd much rather have been down on the road with his brother, but Lynch had said someone had to be up on the high ground, and he was the youngest. One day, thought Paulie with a tinge of bitterness, one day he wouldn't be the youngest any more. He'd show them.

Cramer noticed the glint out of the corner of his eye, a flash of light from the old church. His heart began to race and he took several deep breaths. He fought the urge to turn his head and to look up the hill as he walked around the bend in the road and saw the harbour stretched out before him.

Two fishing boats were sailing away from the west pier leaving plumes of dirty grey smoke in their wake. Down on the beach two dark-haired men were throwing a stick for a black Labrador. They were walking slowly along the strip of sand, towards the marina. The dog raced back and forth, its bark whipped away in the wind before it could reach Cramer's ears. Cramer recognised the dog, but not the men. There were several cars parked next to the yacht club building. Two men sat in one of the cars, not moving. Cramer rolled his head around, trying to loosen the muscles in his neck. He was tensing up, and this wasn't the time to go stiff.

'Right, let's get the bastard,' said Lynch, shoving his walkie-talkie into the glove compartment. He opened the door and went around to the boot. Leaning over his navy blue holdall, he slipped out the Kalashnikov while O'Riordan stood behind him, shielding him from the road. Lynch was wearing a long raincoat, open at the front, and he held the assault rifle inside, pressing it close to his body. 'Okay,' he said, stepping away from the car while O'Riordan pulled a handgun from the holdall and slid it into the pocket of his leather bomber jacket.

They walked across the car park, the wind pulling at their hair and whipping up ripples in the puddles at their feet. Ahead of them, Cramer had stepped onto the sea wall and was walking out to the lighthouse.

Davie Quinn was sitting on a wooden bench in front of the public toilets, a newspaper on his lap. He stood up, holding the folded newspaper so tightly that his knuckles went white. He nodded at Lynch and began to walk along the road.

* * *

Cramer stood at the far end of the sea wall, staring out to sea. He moved his head slowly to his left and saw that the two men were closer now. Half a mile away. The dog was running in circles around them, but they'd stopped playing with it. The two big men had left their car and were walking purposefully across the car park. And the boy, the boy was walking down the road holding the badly concealed gun as if he feared it would break if he dropped it. Five, he thought. Five plus the one on the hill make six.

He wiped his face with his hands and yawned. It wasn't from tiredness, he knew. It was the tension. He pulled a packet of chewing gum from his pocket and unwrapped a stick. The wind blew the green wrapper from his fingers as he slipped the gum into his mouth, and he turned to watch it whirl through the air. He frowned as he saw the lone figure standing on the sea wall where it met the road. How had he missed one?

'Where the fuck did he come from?' hissed Lynch. He put a restraining hand on O'Riordan's shoulder. 'Hold a while, Pat. Let's see what that guy's up to.' Lynch looked across at the Quinn boy who was standing on the pavement, unsure of what to do. Lynch motioned with his head for Davie to go back to the bench.

'Maybe he's just out for a walk,' said O'Riordan hesitantly.

'Yeah. Maybe.'

The man was in his fifties, perhaps older, wearing a green Barbour, a cap and green Wellington boots. He walked with a stick, though it seemed to Lynch that it was for effect rather than because the man was unsteady on his feet. He strolled briskly along the sea wall, swinging the walking stick as if it were a military cane.

From where they were standing, Lynch couldn't see Fitzpatrick and McVeigh on the beach. He just hoped they'd have the sense to hold back.

Cramer didn't look around as the man in the Barbour jacket joined him at the edge of the sea wall. 'Nice day for it,' said the man amicably.

Cramer's upper lip curled back, but still he didn't turn to face the visitor. 'Nice day for what?'

'For whatever it is you're doing.' He tapped the ground with his stick. 'Just what the hell are you doing, Sergeant Cramer?'

'The only one with a rank these days is you, Colonel.'

The Colonel tapped his stick again. He turned around so that his back was to the sea. 'I count five,' he said. 'Do you think five will be enough?'

'Six,' said Cramer. 'There's one up on the hill.'

The Colonel acknowledged the correction with the merest hint of a smile. 'They must really hate you to do this, you know? The Unionists are bound to claim it's a breach of the ceasefire.'

'Maybe,' said Cramer.

'Unless they're planning to remove all the evidence. If there's no body, I suppose there'd be no proof that it ever happened. Not now you're no longer with the regiment. It's not as if you'd be missed, is it?'

'Thanks, Colonel,' said Cramer bitterly.

'Do you know who they are?'

Cramer shrugged. 'It doesn't matter.' He noticed for the first time that the Colonel was wearing a blue tie covered with small winged daggers. Cramer smiled. Only the Colonel would go up against a team of IRA hitmen wearing the regimental tie of the Special Air Service.

'Dermott Lynch's running the show. He's got Pat O'Riordan with him. Down on the beach you've got Gerry Fitzpatrick and Fergus McVeigh. We couldn't identify the youngster.'

'Lynch's good.'

'Oh yes, he's good. And he's got a personal interest in you, of course. We'd love to get hold of O'Riordan, too. But the rest are strictly second division.'

The Colonel looked at his watch, then turned back to face the sea again.

'What do you want, Colonel?'

'A chat. You've got time for a chat, haven't you?'

Cramer shrugged listlessly. 'I'd rather be on my own, if that's all right with you.'

'But you're not on your own, are you, Sergeant Cramer? There's an IRA active service unit armed to the teeth heading your way.'

'You'd best be going then, huh?'

The Colonel shook his head sadly. 'This isn't the way to do it, Joker.'

The nickname made Cramer smile. It had been a long time since anyone had used it. 'Do what?'

'You know what.'

Cramer sighed and hunched his shoulders. 'You don't know what you're talking about,' he said flatly.

'I know you're dying.'

For the first time, Cramer looked across at the Colonel. 'We're all dying,' he said venomously.

'How long?' asked the Colonel. 'How long did the doctor give you?'

'If you're here, you already know.'

'Two months. Three months at the most. The last few weeks will be in intolerable pain. You'll need to be on a drip, and even that won't be enough.'

'So you know why I'm here.'

'Because you're frightened of dying in a hospital bed, screaming in agony. Friendless. Alone.'

Cramer wrinkled his nose at the image. 'Thanks for sugar-coating it for me, Colonel.'

'Bowel cancer isn't a pleasant way to die.'

'You're telling me.'

'So you've decided to go down fighting. To die like a soldier, in battle.'

Cramer smiled and drew back his jacket so that the Colonel could see the Browning in the holster. He looked over his shoulder. The men on the beach were still heading in their direction. Lynch and O'Riordan were standing in the car park, talking. 'You should go, Colonel. This is going to get messy.'

'Hear me out, Joker. This isn't the way to do it.'

Cramer's eyes hardened. 'With all due respect, Colonel, you don't know what the fuck you're talking about.'

The Colonel thrust his square jaw forward. His jaw, and the wide nose which had been broken several times, gave the man a deceptively simple appearance, but Cramer knew that he had an IQ in the high 150s and was one of the top twelve chess-players in the United Kingdom. 'I can offer you a better way.'

'Yeah, right. What do you want me to do? Swallow my gun? I've tried, Colonel. I can't.'

The Colonel shook his head. 'That's not what I'm offering. I'm offering you a chance to do something worthwhile with your last few weeks.'

Cramer frowned, then looked away. 'I'm listening.'

'Over the last two years there've been a series of assassinations around the world. Businessmen, politicians, criminals, all killed by one man. A professional killer who'll hit anyone if the price is right. He's never been caught, and we have no idea who he is.'

'We? We as in the SAS?'

'The FBI, Interpol, MI6, the SVR, Mossad.'

'All the good guys, huh?'

The Colonel ignored the interruption. 'He likes to get in close, this killer. He always uses a handgun. We've dozens of witnesses, but we don't know what he looks like.'

Cramer frowned. 'That doesn't make sense.'

'Oh, we've dozens of descriptions all right. He's short. He's tall. He's thin, he's overweight, he's balding, he has a beard, blue eyes, brown eyes, pale skinned, tanned. The only thing we're sure of is that he's white and male.'

'A master of disguise,' said Cramer, smiling at the cliché.

The Colonel shrugged. 'He uses contact lenses, he grows facial hair as and when he needs it. He puts on weight, he takes it off. Maybe he even has plastic surgery. There isn't anything he won't do to succeed.'

Cramer turned around slowly. The men in the car park had started walking again. They'd soon be at the sea wall. He looked anxiously at the Colonel, who seemed unfazed by the approaching killers. 'What do you want from me?'

'Do you know what a Judas Goat is?'

Cramer shook his head.

'Say you're trying to trap a tiger. You can trample through the jungle all you want, you'll not see a hair of it. You're in his territory. You're wasting your time trying to hunt it. So what you do is you take a young goat, a kid, and you tether it in a clearing. Then you sit back and wait. The tiger seeks out the bleating goat, and BANG! One dead tiger.'

'A Judas Goat?' repeated Cramer. 'Sounds more like bait to me. That's what you're offering me? The chance to be bait?'

'I'm offering you the chance to go up against the most successful assassin in the world, Joker. To the best of our knowledge he's never failed. Never been caught, and never failed. Wouldn't that be more of a challenge for you? Those bastards down there might call themselves an IRA active service unit, but we know better, don't we? They're psychopathic thugs with guns, that's all. Sure, you'll die with a gun in your hand and the blood coursing through your veins, but there's no honour in being gunned down like a rabid dog. Sheer weight of numbers, that's the only advantage they'll have. They'll just keep firing until you're dead. You'll get a couple of them, maybe more, but look at the company you'll be dying in. Hell's fucking bells, Joker,

44

you wouldn't give those bastards the time of day and yet you want to die with them?'

Paulie Quinn swung the binoculars from side to side, scanning for Fitzpatrick and McVeigh. They flashed across his vision and he panned back slowly until he had them dead centre. They'd stopped on the beach and were watching Cramer and the new arrival. McVeigh scratched his head and Fitzpatrick shrugged. McVeigh said something and Fitzpatrick nodded, then they started to walk, pulling their guns from beneath their bomber jackets. Paulie turned the binoculars onto Lynch and O'Riordan, who were striding towards the sea wall. O'Riordan turned as he walked and motioned with his hand for Davie to follow them.

Paulie searched for his brother and found him walking quickly along the road, clutching a newspaper. Paulie smiled. His brother looked tense, but he was doing exactly as he'd been told, following behind Lynch and O'Riordan, ready to cut off Cramer's escape if he should try to get around them. Paulie wondered if Davie would get to shoot the Sass-man. God, he hoped so. He wondered who the man in the Barbour jacket was and why he was so earnestly talking to Cramer. Whoever he was, he was as good as dead. Lynch had obviously decided to take him out as well.

*   *   *

Cramer said nothing. He stared out to the horizon and took several deep breaths. The Colonel waited for him to speak. 'Why does he take risks?' Cramer asked eventually. 'Why does he always do it close up? There are easier ways to kill. Safer ways.'

The Colonel nodded. 'The FBI reckon it's because he enjoys it. He wants to see his victims as they die. He's a serial killer, but a serial killer who gets paid for his work. It's not a question of whether or not he'll kill again, it's when. He'll keep on killing until we stop him, because he's not doing it for the money. He's doing it for the thrill.'

'And you want this guy to try to kill me?'

The Colonel turned to look at Cramer. He shook his head slowly. 'No,' he said softly, his voice barely audible above the sound of the waves crashing against the sea wall. 'We're pretty sure that he'll succeed.'

Cramer didn't say anything.

'The man has never left any physical evidence behind,' the Colonel continued. 'No fingerprints, no blood or tissue samples, nothing. If we catch him close to you with a gun in his hand, it's not enough. It's not even attempted murder, it's just possession of a weapon and for all we know he might have a licence for it. Even if he points the gun at you, what have we got? Threatening behaviour? Maybe attempted murder. If we're lucky he'll go away for five years. No, he has to pull the trigger. Once he's done that, we've got him.'

Cramer nodded, finally understanding. 'And if he pulls the trigger, I'm dead?'

The Colonel nodded. 'But you'll have a chance. You'll be armed; if you see him coming for you you'll be able to shoot first. It's a better chance than the Judas Goat gets.'

'He'll kill me,' said Cramer flatly.

'But you'll die with honour. In battle. Against a real professional. Isn't that a better way to die? Better than being shot by these thugs?'

Cramer stared out to sea. 'Is that how you'd like to go, Colonel?'

'If I had the choice, yes.' The Colonel's voice was flat and level. 'It's your call, Joker.' If you want it to happen now, I'll just walk away.'

The Colonel looked towards the men on the beach. They were about a quarter of a mile away, still walking in their direction. The other two men had reached the end of the sea wall and the youngster was walking down the road behind them, the newspaper held in both hands. 'You don't have much time,' said the Colonel. He tapped his stick on the concrete and the cracks sounded like gunshots.

Cramer chuckled coldly. 'That's the truth,' he said. He paused. 'How do you know he'll come for me?'

'We know who one of his intended victims is going to be. I'll explain later, but we're looking for someone to take his place.' He paused. 'Well?'

Cramer rubbed his chin and then sighed. 'Okay.'

'You're sure?'

Cramer narrowed his eyes and studied the Colonel. 'What? Now you're trying to talk me out of it? I said I'll do it. I'll do it.'

The Colonel put his hand on Cramer's shoulder and squeezed. 'Thank you.'

Cramer shook his head. 'I'm not doing it for you, Colonel. I'm doing it for me. But first we've got to take care of them.' He nodded down the sea wall where the two IRA men were walking quickly towards them. The one in the raincoat was holding both hands to his sides, clutching something. A weapon, probably an assault rifle. The men on the beach had broken into a run, guns at the ready.

The Colonel took a small transceiver out of his coat pocket, pressed the transmit button and spoke rapidly into it. Cramer couldn't make out what the man had said, but seconds later he heard the roar of two massive turbines and a huge red, white and blue Westland Sea King helicopter appeared from behind Ireland's Eye. Its main rotor dipped forward and it sped through the air towards them. 'Damn you, Colonel,' Cramer shouted above the noise of the engines. 'You knew I'd accept, didn't you?'

The Colonel said nothing as the helicopter circled and then dropped so that it was hovering only feet above the harbour wall, the rotor wash flattening the water below. He motioned with his stick for Cramer to get in first. Cramer took one last look over his shoulder, deafened by the turbines. The bearded man had pulled a Kalashnikov out from under his raincoat and was holding it, seemingly unsure whether or not to fire. For one moment they made eye contact and Cramer could feel the hatred pouring out of the man, then a hand reached out of the belly of the Sea King and half pulled, half dragged him inside. .

Lynch upended the Kalashnikov and slipped it back under his raincoat as the huge helicopter lifted away and banked hard to the left.

'What the hell was that all about?' asked O'Riordan.

'Fucked if I know,' said Lynch. He stared after the Sea King as it flew off across the waves, his curly black hair blowing behind him. Fitzpatrick and McVeigh ran up, panting for breath.

'Put your guns away, boys,' said Lynch. 'We're not here to shoot helicopters.'

The two men thrust their handguns into the pockets of their jackets. 'What's going on, Dermott?' asked McVeigh.

Lynch ignored him. He whirled around and peered at the harbour road, half expecting to see a convoy of armed soldiers heading their way. The street was empty. It wasn't a trap. That was something to be grateful for, but it made the Sass-man's sudden departure all the more bemusing.

Fitzpatrick's walkie-talkie crackled and they heard Paulie Quinn's anxious voice. 'What's happening? Where's he gone?'

'Shut that thing off,' barked Lynch, heading towards the car.

Mike Cramer sat with his arms folded across his chest as the massive helicopter flew low and fast across the waves. One of the Sea King crewmen handed him a set of padded headphones and Cramer put them on, grateful for relief from the deafening roar of the engines. Cramer's head was full of questions, but he said nothing. The Colonel sat down on the seat in front of the emergency exit window and held out his hand. Cramer handed over his Browning Hi-Power.

Cramer looked around the cabin. This Sea King was like no other he'd ever been in. It was packed with electrical equipment, some of which he recognised. There was an extensive array of radar screens, far more than he'd expect to see in a search and rescue helicopter, and a Marconi LAPADS data processing station. The crewman who'd hauled him into the helicopter and given him the headset was seated in the sonar operator's seat in front of the sonar/radar instrumentation racks. In addition there was a lot of equipment Cramer had never seen before, equipment without brand names or labels of any kind.

The helicopter banked to the right, keeping low. Through the window behind the Colonel, Cramer saw a small yacht carving through the waves. They were heading east. Cramer smiled to himself at the thought of the IRA hit team standing on the sea wall. All foreplay and no orgasm, armed to the teeth and nothing to shoot at.

He wondered if he'd done the right thing, agreeing so readily to go with the Colonel. He owed the Colonel nothing. It was now more than seven years since Cramer had left the regiment. He'd only worked for him once since, and that had almost ended in tears. Cramer closed his eyes and leaned back against the metal bulkhead. The Colonel had used him as bait then, too, sent him to the States on the trail of Mary Hennessy, the IRA terrorist who'd tortured and killed Cramer's friend. At least this time Cramer knew what he was getting into. At least this time he knew the odds of surviving.

What had the Colonel said? A killer who loved to get up close. A killer who'd never been caught. A killer who was so successful that the only way to stop him was to use a Judas Goat. Maybe it really would be a better way to die. Cramer had seen a lot of men and women die and he knew that there were good ways and there were bad ways, and that most people didn't get the chance to choose. He opened his eyes again. The Colonel was unscrewing the cap off a stainless steel Thermos flask. He poured black coffee into a plastic mug and offered it to Cramer. Cramer shook his head.

The Colonel had always been able to read him like a book. He'd known that Cramer would accept the mission and had made all the arrangements accordingly. Cramer wondered if the man had had a fallback position, someone else who would have accepted the job if Cramer had turned it down. He also wondered if anyone else had already refused the mission.

Once well away from land, the helicopter began to gain height and they were soon several thousand feet above the sea. At first Cramer had assumed that they would be landing on a ship, but he soon realised that the helicopter was going to fly all the way to the British mainland. He settled back. There was nothing to do but wait.

Dermott Lynch and Pat O'Riordan drove into Dublin along the Howth Road. Lynch was fuming as he stared out of the window, his lips set in a tight line. The original plan had been to drop the weapons off and drive back up to the North, but Cramer's disappearance had changed all that.

They passed Trinity College, and Lynch scowled at the bright blue clock which topped the grey stone building. It was just after ten o'clock in the morning. 'Forget about it, Dermott,' said O'Riordan.

'Why was he there?' asked Lynch. 'It was as if he was waiting for us. Then suddenly he's whisked away. It doesn't make sense.'

'It doesn't have to make sense. He's gone and that's it.'

Lynch scratched his beard. 'The Brits are up to something, Pat. They're fucking with us and I want to know why. Maybe McCormack will know.'

'Do you want me to stay?'

Lynch shook his head. 'No need. You get back to your farm. I'll speak to McCormack then catch the train back tonight.'

O'Riordan braked sharply to avoid a bus. Lynch wasn't wearing his seatbelt and he lurched forward. 'Sorry,' said O'Riordan. 'I'm not used to driving in the city.'

'Just think of them as cows,' said Lynch.

'Aye, Dermott, I'll do that,' said O'Riordan with a grin. The traffic was crawling along Dame Street and O'Riordan was stamping on the brake as if he was at the wheel of a tractor. 'The Quinn brothers did all right,' he said.

'They were okay,' agreed Lynch. 'Davie has potential, Paulie's still a bit young.'

'They're both keen.'

'Yeah, but that's not always an advantage, Pat, you know that. I'm not sure that I'd ever want my life to depend on the likes of Paulie Quinn.' Lynch ran a hand through his beard and glared at the traffic, as if he could make it vanish through sheer effort of will. 'I'll get out here,' he said.

'Yeah, might be best.'

Lynch twisted around and picked the holdall off the back seat. It contained the Kalashnikov and the handguns they'd handled at Howth. Lynch had no qualms about carrying the weapons through the streets of Dublin. He said goodbye to O'Riordan, climbed out of the car and walked along the pavement. A crocodile of French students carrying red and green backpacks blocked his way and he moved through them with a smile. A pretty young girl with long blonde hair banged into his holdall and yelped. She rubbed her leg and looked reproachfully at Lynch. He smiled sympathetically. 'Sorry, love,' he said.

The helicopter started to descend and Mike Cramer swallowed to clear the pressure in his ears. Directly below were blue grey waves, to the left was a wide beach and beyond the stretch of sand were woodland and ploughed fields. He looked at his watch and did a quick calculation: assuming they'd been flying at the Sea King's normal cruising speed of 140 knots, they were probably somewhere over Wales. In the distance he saw three hills, wooded around the base but bare at the top, like balding men. There was a microwave radio station on the top of one, but Cramer didn't know the country well enough to be able to identify it. The helicopter banked to the right and down below he saw a large peninsula sticking out towards Ireland. As the helicopter continued to descend Cramer picked out lush green fields dotted with sheep, isolated copses and a scattering of small farms, then they flew over the ruins of a castle towards what looked like a large country house set in its own grounds. The helicopter circled over the house before dropping down to land.

Cramer's ears were aching from the constant roar of the Sea King's turbines and the padded headphones were damp with sweat. He disliked helicopters, even though one had saved his life seven years earlier, rushing him to hospital in Belfast with his guts ripped open. He'd have died in an ambulance, no question about it; only the Lynx could have made it to Belfast City Hospital in time. But that didn't mean he enjoyed travelling in the machines. He could never get over the feeling that the whole business depended on one nut keeping the whirling blades in place. If that went it was so long and good night. Still, there were worse ways of dying. Much worse.

Cramer's stomach heaved as the helicopter flared and came in to land and he tasted acid bile at the back of his throat. He swallowed and coughed and swallowed again and then the helicopter was down, its rotors slowing. The crewman climbed out of his seat and opened the door. Cramer climbed out after the Colonel. Cramer kept his head low, even though he knew that the rotors had plenty of clearance. They jogged to the front of the Sea King, away from the whirling tail rotor, then the Colonel gave the pilot a thumbs-up and the helicopter climbed back into the sky, the downdraft flattening the grass all around them and ripping at their clothes like a thousand tiny hands.

Cramer watched the helicopter fly off to the west. 'This way,' said the Colonel, leading him towards the building Cramer had seen from the sky. It was built of red brick, three storeys high and topped with a slate roof. There were two wings either side of a main entrance, where a circular driveway curved around a stone fountain which didn't appear to be working. There was an air of neglect about the place, as if it hadn't been occupied for some time.

The helicopter had dropped them inside a stone wall which surrounded the house and several acres of lawn. Cramer saw two men standing either side of a large wrought-iron gate, big men wearing leather jackets, jeans and training shoes.

'The building was a girls' preparatory school until a few

months ago,' the Colonel explained. 'It gets a little chilly at night but we won't be disturbed.'

Another guard stood at the entrance. He greeted the Colonel with a curt nod and acknowledged Cramer with a slight smile. They walked into a huge entrance hall which rose to the top of the building. A wide stone staircase wound upwards, past a long, thin chandelier, coated with dust. Corridors led left and right and Cramer glimpsed a succession of white-painted doors, all closed. 'Classrooms that way,' said the Colonel, indicating the left. 'We'll be eating in the dining hall, to the right. I'm using an office over there. I've allocated you a staff bedroom on the second floor.'

'How long will I be here?' Cramer asked.

'A week. Maybe longer. First I want you to read all the files, and there are some people I want you to meet.'

The Colonel headed up the stairs, his stick clicking on the stone steps. He took Cramer up to the second floor and along a corridor to a large room containing a bed, a sagging armchair, an old oak wardrobe and matching dressing table. Under a sash window stood a table piled high with files. The Colonel waved his stick at the paperwork. 'They're copies of the files held by the various law enforcement agencies who've been investigating the killings. For those in Europe I've only included the Interpol paperwork. Languages weren't your forte, I remember.'

'*Mais oui, mon colonel*,' Cramer replied dryly, his accent deliberately atrocious. He went over to the table and ran his hand over the files. His window overlooked the rear of the school and he could see a large car park with half a dozen vehicles bunched together in one section and, to the right, a line of single storey buildings with large metal chimneys. Through the windows he could just make out huge ovens, cooking equipment and rows of stainless steel cupboards and shelving so Cramer guessed they were the former school's kitchens.

'I'll have some food sent up to you. Read as much as you can today and we'll start in earnest tomorrow,' said the Colonel. He stopped at the door. 'Do you have any questions?'

Cramer shook his head. 'I probably will have after I've read all this. Just one thing.'

The Colonel smiled. 'Famous Grouse?'

Cramer was surprised. 'Am I that transparent?'

'I wouldn't have thought whisky was doing your stomach any good.'

Cramer shrugged. 'That might have been good advice a few years ago. Now it's a bit late.'

'The man whose place you're taking drinks red wine. He never touches whisky.'

'So when I take his place, I'll drink wine.'

'Just so you know.'

'I hear you, Colonel.' It was general practice in the SAS for troopers and noncommissioned officers to refer to their officers as 'Boss', but Cramer had never been able to bring himself to use the more informal term with the Colonel.

The Colonel tapped his stick on the bare floorboards. 'I'll have it for you this evening.' He closed the door behind him.

Half an hour later, while Cramer was still reading through the first file, there was a knock on the door. 'Come in,' he said, not looking up. A middle-aged woman, plump with a pleasant face, her hair tied back in a bun, elbowed the door open and carried in a tray containing a plate of sandwiches and a glass of milk. She introduced herself as Mrs Elliott, with the emphasis on the Mrs, and left the tray on the dressing table. He thought it best not to ask Mrs Elliott about the whisky. She didn't look much like a drinker.

The dogs leapt out of the starting gate at full stretch, their paws kicking up puffs of sand on the track. The crowd yelled and screamed as the greyhounds hurtled after the mechanical hare, but Thomas McCormack seemed more interested in the programme he was holding. 'Next race, number six,' he said out of the corner of his mouth.

'Yeah?' said Dermott Lynch. 'Is it one of yours?'

McCormack gave Lynch a crafty sideways look. 'No, but it's going to win.'

Lynch studied the dog's form as the greyhounds rounded the first bend. It had finished unplaced in its last three races, but he knew better than to question McCormack's advice. McCormack owned a string of greyhounds and on at least two nights a week he could be found at Dublin's Shelbourne Park dog track.

Lynch looked up as the favourite crossed the finishing line and was engulfed in the waiting arms of a girl. She was a pretty young thing, shoulder length hair the colour of copper, and a figure that even the blue overalls couldn't conceal. On any other day Lynch would have been tempted to strike up a conversation with her, but the visit to the dog track wasn't a social event. He'd been summoned there by McCormack.

Lynch looked up at the results board at the far end of

the stadium. The short odds on the favourite meant that no one would get rich on the race, but the dog McCormack had tipped would be running at twelve to one. The two men walked back inside to the betting hall and stood in a queue, waiting to place their bets.

McCormack gave the cashier a handful of notes and asked for it to be placed on number six, to win. Lynch took out his wallet. He dithered for a second or two and then took out all the banknotes it contained. He considered an each-way bet, but McCormack was standing at his shoulder, watching. Lynch handed over all the notes. 'Number six, to win,' he said. McCormack smiled and nodded.

They went outside to watch the dogs being walked. Number six looked good, its coat glossy, its hindquarters strong and well developed, holding its head up high as if it knew it was due for a win. 'Have you got a dog running in this race?' Lynch asked.

McCormack nodded at a brown dog at the far end of the line, sniffing listlessly at the shoes of its handler. 'He's coming on but it'll be a few months yet before he peaks.' They left the showing area and headed towards the track. 'So, Dermott, what happened?'

'A helicopter came from nowhere. Bloody nowhere. Lifted him off and flew away with him.'

'Army?'

'No. Not army. Red, white and blue it was. Not a soldier in sight. It's a mystery all right, and if there's one thing I can't stand it's a mystery.'

McCormack took off his horn-rimmed spectacles and polished them with his handkerchief. 'What do you think he was up to?'

'I don't know. Whatever it was, I think there was a change

of plan. I don't think he was expecting the helicopter. Or the man who appeared on the sea wall.'

'This man, any idea who he was?'

Lynch shook his head. 'Military, I think. He walked like a soldier. Carried a stick.'

'Armed?'

'Couldn't tell.'

'What about the helicopter? Did the crew have guns?' McCormack put his spectacles back on and peered over the top of them.

Lynch thought for a second and then shook his head. 'No. I only saw one of the crew, he pulled Cramer in, but he wasn't armed, I'm sure of that.'

McCormack tapped the programme against his leg as he walked, his head down in thought. He didn't speak for almost a minute. 'I think we're going to have to let this one go, Dermott.'

'I want the bastard,' said Lynch fiercely.

'Connolly wasn't over happy about us going after Cramer in the first place, you know. Let sleeping dogs lie, he said. He took some persuading.'

'Yeah?' Lynch scratched his beard as if it itched.

'Yes. I had to take sole responsibility for it. If it had gone wrong, I'd have been the one explaining to the Army Council. And it damn near did go wrong. We were lucky it wasn't a trap, right?'

'I wouldn't say that, Thomas. We had Howth pretty well sewn up. If the SAS had been there, we'd have known about it.'

'That's as may be. But whatever Cramer was doing, it's over now.'

'I want him,' said Lynch.

'I know you do. But you've got a personal interest, Dermott, let's not forget that.'

'Let me go after him. Please. I'm asking as a friend.'

McCormack snorted softly. 'You can't ask me that as a friend, and you know it. You can only make a request like that to me as a member of the Army Executive.'

The next race was about to start and the spectators began to pour out of the betting hall and cluster around the track. The on-course bookmakers were frantically chalking up new odds. Lynch could see that the odds on number six were already shortening. 'And if I do ask you as a member of the Army Executive?'

'Then I'd have to refuse your request. If you're adamant then I could put it before the Army Council, but I know what their answer would be. And so do you. They've too much to gain from the peace process, they're not going to jeopardise it over one man.'

'Not even a man like Cramer?'

'Not even for Cramer. Look, Dermott, if it was up to me, of course I'd say yes. Hell, I'd even help pull the trigger. But you know what we were told in 1994. No mavericks. No splinter groups. We speak and act with one voice.'

The handlers began walking the dogs towards the starting gate. 'We were so bloody close,' hissed Lynch. 'A minute earlier and we'd have got him.'

'But you didn't,' said McCormack softly. 'So now it's over.'

Lynch wanted to argue but he knew it would be futile. 'Whatever you say, Thomas.'

'Good man.' The race was about to start, but McCormack was already perusing the programme as if the outcome was a foregone conclusion. 'Number two in the race after this.

Guaranteed.' He looked up and smiled. 'You'll be able to use your winnings from this race.'

'Thanks. Thanks for the tip.'

'When are you going back to Belfast?'

'Tomorrow morning. I'll catch the first train.'

'Good. There's a wee job I want you to do for me when you get back.'

'Sure, Thomas. Whatever you say.'

McCormack studied the programme as the traps sprang open and the greyhounds burst out, like shells from a mortar.

Mike Cramer lay on his back and listened to the blackbirds, a pleasant contrast to the savage cries of seagulls he'd heard the last time he'd woken up. He opened his eyes and squinted at his wristwatch. It was just before five o'clock though it was already light outside. He rolled out of the single bed, padded across the bare floorboards to the window and pulled open the thin curtains. A thickset man in a grey sports jacket stood in the middle of the lawn, a walkie-talkie pressed to his mouth. He looked up and gave Cramer a half-wave. Cramer waved back.

To the right, beyond the lawns but still inside the wall that surrounded the property, were three tennis courts, lined up like playing cards in a game of Find The Lady, and beyond them a croquet lawn, the hoops still in place. Cramer ran his hands through his hair. He smelled his armpits and wrinkled his nose. He needed a shower, badly. By the bed stood a three-quarters empty bottle of Famous Grouse. The

Colonel had brought it up after darkness had fallen and had sat on the bed keeping Cramer company, drinking the whisky and toasting the old days, the days before Cramer had been shot and tortured and before the cancer had started to grow. Cramer unscrewed the cap off the bottle, swilling it around like a mouthwash before swallowing and grimacing as it went down his throat.

He tossed the bottle on the bed and went into the bathroom, which was tiled from floor to ceiling. The grouting was black and stained and a mouldy smell was coming from the bathtub. The showerhead was as large as a saucepan lid and Cramer turned it on. To his surprise the water came out steaming hot almost immediately.

On a shelf above the sink stood a can of menthol shaving foam, a pack of disposable razors, a toothbrush still in its plastic wrapping and a tube of Colgate tartar control toothpaste. Cramer picked up the toothpaste and smiled, wondering who had done the shopping and why they'd chosen the tartar control formula. He cleaned his teeth and shaved and then climbed into the bathtub and stood under the shower. There was no shower curtain and water cascaded off his body and onto the tiled floor. He noticed a fresh bar of soap in a shell-shaped soap dish and he used it to wash himself thoroughly. He hadn't realised how long it was since he'd felt truly clean.

He wrapped himself in clean towels and sat on the bed and read another of the files as he dried himself. It was an American killing; the victim had been a Chicago lawyer. The lawyer had several Mob figures as clients and the Chicago newspapers had suggested that the killing was one of a series of tit-for-tat murders, as two crime families fought for control of lucrative concrete-pouring contracts.

The police file was never closed, though, and the latest addition, a memo from the Marseilles field office of the Sûreté – in response to an official Chicago Police Department enquiry – pointed out that the lawyer's widow had remarried within the year and that she and her new husband were now living in the South of France. The new man in her life was twenty years younger and a good deal poorer than her husband had been. The file also contained a photograph of them together, she with the over-tight cheeks and slightly too-open eyes that indicated a face lift, he with a weightlifter's chest, slick-backed hair and movie star looks. She'd been questioned several times but there was no evidence linking her to the assassin. It looked like the perfect crime, but Cramer wasn't concerned about who'd financed the murder, it was the killer he was interested in.

The fact that it was the same man in both shootings wasn't in question. Two shots, one to the face, a second to the chest: that appeared to be the killer's trademark. When Cramer had attended the SAS's Killing House in Hereford, he too had been trained in the 'double tap' – two shots fired in quick succession. However, the SAS instructors had stressed the importance of aiming at the torso so that there was less chance of missing – head shots were deemed too risky.

The killer had walked into the lawyer's office and shot him dead in front of his secretary. The secretary's description of the killer was detailed, but unhelpful: brown hair, brown eyes, just under six feet tall, lightly tanned skin. Any or all of those characteristics could be altered, Cramer knew. Hair dye, coloured contact lenses, lifts in the shoes, sunbeds or tanning cream. There was an artist's impression based on the secretary's description, and a computer-generated photo-fit, and while they did resemble each other, they had little in common with the pictures in the other files Cramer had read.

All the files on killings which had taken place in America contained FBI Facial Identification Fact Sheets, which had been filled in by investigating agents prior to the photo-fits being generated. They contained a list of facial features, and witnesses were asked to tick the pertinent boxes. Cramer took the sheets from the various files and compared them. They were just as disparate as the photo-fit pictures. The shape of the head could be categorised as oval, round, triangular, long or rectangular. All of the boxes had been ticked by at least one of the witnesses. The mouth could be classed as average, both lips thick, both lips thin, lips unequal, large or small. Most of the witness reports ticked the lips as average, but there was at least one witness who ticked each of the other categories. The consensus seemed to be that the man's eyebrows were average, his ears were average, his chin was average and his nose was average, but there was no consistency. Two witnesses said the man had a double chin, one said his eyebrows met in the middle, another said he had protruding ears. Cramer was beginning to understand what the Colonel had meant when he'd said that they had plenty of descriptions but no real idea what the assassin looked like.

He finished drying himself and then looked around for clean clothes. There was none, the chests of drawers and the wardrobes were empty. Cramer shrugged and pulled on the clothes he'd arrived in. It seemed that the Colonel hadn't thought of everything.

As he went down the main staircase he smelled bacon

and when he walked into the dining hall the Colonel was already there, sitting at one of the long refectory tables and tucking into a fried breakfast. The Colonel picked up his coffee mug and nodded at the stainless steel serving trays which were lined up on a table by the door. 'Help yourself,' he said. 'If there's anything else you want, Mrs Elliott will get it for you. She's quite a cook.'

Cramer walked along the row of trays. There were fried eggs, scrambled eggs, crisp bacon, sausages, tomatoes, fried bread, even kippers, enough to feed a battalion. Cramer wasn't hungry but he knew that he'd have to eat. He spooned some scrambled eggs onto a plate and went over to sit opposite the Colonel. Mrs Elliott bustled out of the kitchen carrying two steaming jugs. 'Coffee or tea?' she asked. She sniffed and Cramer had the distinct impression that she could smell the whisky on his breath.

Cramer asked for tea. The Colonel waited until she'd gone back into the kitchen before asking Cramer how he'd slept. Cramer shrugged. 'Same as usual,' he said. The Colonel didn't have to point out the bags under his eyes, Cramer had seen them staring back at him as he'd shaved.

'Did you get a chance to read any of the files?'

'Half a dozen, in detail.'

The Colonel put down his mug of coffee. 'Any thoughts?'

Cramer shrugged and stirred his eggs with his fork. 'Half of the hits were in the States, right? That suggests that the killer is an American.'

'Maybe. Or it could imply that Americans are more willing to hire professionals to do their killings.'

Cramer nodded. 'I can't work out why he shoots them in the face first. You know the drill. Two shots to the chest, then one to the head to make sure, if you have the time. But only if you have the time. In the Killing House it's two chest shots, then on to the next target. We don't have the luxury of head-shots.'

'Which means what?'

'Which means, I suppose, that he's not SAS-trained,' answered Cramer. 'In fact, I can't think of any Special Forces group which trains its people to go for head-shots.'

'Perhaps he didn't agree with the way he was trained,' said the Colonel as Cramer put a forkful of eggs in his mouth and swallowed without chewing. 'Remember, he's always very close to the target. Within ten feet, often closer. At that range, head-shots are less chancy.'

Cramer shrugged and stirred his eggs again. They were good scrambled eggs, rich and buttery with a hint of cheese, but he had no appetite. 'It's a question of training, though,' he said. 'If it's drilled into you to kill one way, it's damn difficult to do it any other way.'

'We can talk that through with the profiler when he arrives,' said the Colonel, placing his knife and fork together on the plate. As if by magic, Mrs Elliott appeared and whisked it away.

'Profiler? What's the deal there?'

The Colonel wrapped his hands around his steaming mug. The dining hall was cavernous and the propane heater at the end of the table provided little in the way of warmth. 'The man we're looking for is a professional assassin, there's no doubt about that. That's how the police would look at it. A psychiatrist might take a different view. He could look at him as a killer who keeps killing. A serial killer. And serial killers develop patterns. By analysing those patterns we might be able to build up a picture of what makes him tick.

The FBI has a team of specialists based in Quantico who profile serial killers for police forces around the country.'

'And one of these profilers is working on our killer?'

'The FBI did the initial profiling, but now we've got a guy who used to work for the Bureau helping us,' said the Colonel. 'Name of Jackman. He used to be one of their best operatives, now he runs a private profiling agency in Boston.'

Cramer swallowed another mouthful of eggs without chewing. 'A private serial killer profiler?'

'He offers recruitment advice to companies, stops them hiring bad apples. He gets called in to help movie stars with problem fans, stalkers and the like. And he's helped resolve several kidnapping cases where the police haven't been called in. Some of the biggest insurance companies use him.'

Cramer frowned. He washed his eggs down with his tea. 'I don't get this, Colonel. Why isn't the Bureau helping us?'

'The FBI have less than a dozen profilers on staff and a single manager and they're on a tight budget. They do a total of about eight hundred profiles a year but they have to turn away at least two hundred. The Bureau's total budget for profiling is just over a million dollars a year, despite all the publicity the unit gets. They don't even have the time to do written profiles on a lot of the cases they handle – they offer advice on the phone to law enforcement agencies all across America. But Jackman can give us as much time as we need. He's had access to all the case files for the past three months. I want you to meet him before we put you in place.'

Cramer put down his fork. The bulk of his scrambled eggs remained untouched on the plate. 'What will he be able to tell me?'

'He might be able to give you an idea of what sort of man the killer is, give you a profile so that you recognise him when he moves against you.'

Cramer smiled thinly. 'Moves against me? You mean tries to kill me.'

'Whatever. It'll give you an edge.'

'I'll take whatever I can get,' said Cramer. He rubbed his stomach.

The Colonel leaned forward, concerned. 'Are you okay?'

'A bit sore, but nothing like as bad as it's going to be in a few weeks.'

'There's a doctor coming later. He'll give you a check-up.'

'I've been seen by experts, Colonel. I've had all the second opinions I need.'

'All the same, I want him to look at you. He might be able to prescribe something for the pain.'

Cramer shook his head. 'I don't think so,' he said. 'Painkillers will just slow me down. Besides, the pain lets me know I'm still alive.' He pushed the plate away and drained his mug.

They both looked over at the door as they heard footsteps in the hallway. A short, portly man carrying a large briefcase entered the dining hall, walking quickly as if he was behind schedule. He was wearing a dark blue blazer and black slacks and his shoes gleamed as if they'd just been polished. The Colonel stood up. 'The doctor?' asked Cramer.

'The tailor,' said the Colonel.

'A tailor? What the hell do I need a tailor for?'

'The man whose place you'll be taking wouldn't be seen dead in clothes like yours, Joker.'

The tailor put his briefcase on the table, opened it and

took out a tapemeasure and a small notebook. 'Up, up, up,' he said to Cramer, talking as quickly as he walked. Cramer got to his feet and held out his hands to the sides. The Colonel smiled as the tailor busied himself taking Cramer's measurements and scribbling them down in his notebook. 'Three suits, we said?'

'That's right,' said the Colonel. 'All dark pinstripe, double breasted, no turn-ups. A dozen shirts, all white, double cuffs. Socks, underwear, a selection of casual shirts and trousers. Conservative.'

'Of course, of course,' said the tailor, kneeling down in front of Cramer and deftly measuring his inside leg.

'And an overcoat,' said the Colonel. 'Cashmere.' Cramer raised an eyebrow. 'Quality shows,' the Colonel explained. 'Especially when you get up close.'

The tailor measured Cramer's arms, his waist and his chest. 'Which side will you be carrying?' the tailor asked Cramer.

'Carrying?' repeated Cramer, confused.

'Shoulder holster,' said the tailor.

'Left side,' said Cramer.

'Good, good.' The tailor turned to the Colonel. 'What about accessories?' he asked. 'Belts, ties, cufflinks?'

'I'll leave that up to you,' said the Colonel. 'Bring a selection.'

'Certainly,' said the tailor. 'Certainly.'

'And you can supply shoes?'

'Of course, of course.' The tailor looked up at Cramer expectantly.

'Ten and a half,' said Cramer.

The tailor made a note, stood up, picked up his briefcase and left.

'Regular whirlwind,' said Cramer, his hands still out at his sides.

'He puts the guys in Hong Kong to shame,' said the Colonel. 'He'll have it all ready within forty-eight hours.'

'And I get to keep them after it's all over?'

The Colonel began to reply, then he realised that Cramer was being sarcastic. He shook his head, almost sadly. 'I'd forgotten why they called you Joker,' he said.

Cramer shrugged and sat down again. 'So when does it happen?'

'A few days. There's still some preparation to be done.'

'Just don't leave it too long,' warned Cramer.

The top shelf of the larder was just out of the boy's reach so he had to stand on a chair to reach the tin of beef stew. He opened the can, emptied it into a pan and stirred it carefully on the gas stove. When the stew began to bubble and spit he poured it onto a plate and carried it upstairs with a glass of milk. His mother was sitting up, her back propped up with pillows. The walking stick lay on the covers next to a stack of old magazines. 'I made you lunch,' said the boy.

His mother smiled. 'You're a good boy,' she said.

The boy carried the plate and glass over to the bedside table and put them down next to a box of tissues. He handed his mother a fork. 'It's beef stew,' he said.

'My favourite.'

'It's not your favourite. Your favourite is roast chicken, you always say. But I couldn't make roast chicken.'

'This is my favourite today.' She took the fork and the boy

held the plate for her as she speared a small piece of meat. She chewed slowly, then nodded. 'Delicious.'

'Yeah? Are you sure?'

'Sure I'm sure.' She reached over and ruffled his hair. 'How was school today?'

'Okay, I guess.' He stood watching her, waiting for her to take a second bite, but she put the fork back on the plate and lay down, wincing as she moved. 'Try some more,' he urged. 'It's good.'

'Maybe later.' She sounded tired. She always sounded tired, the boy thought. As if she'd given up hope.

'Didn't I cook it right?' he asked, frowning.

She smiled. 'You cooked it just fine. I'm tired, that's all.'

The boy put the plate on the bedside table and gave her the glass of milk. 'Milk's good for you,' he said. She took a sip. It left a white frothy line across her upper lip. He reached over and wiped away the milk on her lip with his hand. 'When are you getting better, Mum?' he asked.

'I don't know,' she said.

'Soon?'

'Maybe soon.' She patted the edge of the bed and he climbed up and sat next to her. 'Do you know where Daddy keeps my medicine?' she asked. The boy nodded. 'I think I need some more,' she said. 'Can you bring it up to me?' The boy chewed the inside of his lip. 'You can do that for me, can't you?' she said. The boy shrugged. 'Go and get it for me. Please.'

'Daddy says . . .' He tailed off, unable to finish the sentence.

His mother reached over and patted his leg. 'Your daddy says what?'

The boy sighed deeply. 'Daddy says only he can give you the medicine. He said you're not to have it.'

71

His mother nodded as if she understood. 'I'm sure that if Daddy knew how much I needed my medicine he'd give it to me.'

The boy turned his head away and stared at the door. 'Daddy said not to.'

His mother began to cough. The boy picked up the box of tissues and pulled one out for her. She took it and pressed it to her mouth as her chest heaved. He watched anxiously until the coughing spasm was over. When she took the tissue away from her mouth it was spotted with blood. His mother screwed the tissue up as if hiding the evidence of her illness. 'You're going to have to help me,' she said.

Dermott Lynch drove the Ford Granada slowly down the rutted track, the steering wheel threatening to tear itself from his gloved hands. It was only after he'd picked up the car that he realised it was an automatic and he was having trouble remembering not to use his left foot. It wasn't as if he had a choice – the vehicle had been appropriated for him by two teenagers acting under IRA orders, and left in a car park close to Belfast railway station with its ignition key in the exhaust pipe. The Granada belonged to an old couple who lived in the outskirts of Belfast and they wouldn't report it stolen until the following day, not if they knew what was good for them.

Davie Quinn sat in the front passenger seat, sniffing as if he had the beginnings of a cold. His brother Paulie was in the back. From occasional glances in the driving mirror, Lynch could see that the younger Quinn brother was nervous. His cheeks were flushed and there was a thin sheen of sweat on his forehead. 'You okay, Paulie?' Lynch asked.

Paulie jerked as if he'd been stung. 'What? Oh yeah. I'm fine.'

'Good lad,' said Lynch, smiling to himself. Thomas McCormack had insisted that the Quinn boys be taken on the job. They'd both conducted themselves well in Howth, but no shots had been fired and no one had been hurt. It was important to discover how the boys would react under pressure. He looked across at Davie. Davie was by far the more confident of the two brothers and had all the makings of an ideal volunteer. He had a sharp intelligence but he kept quiet when necessary. Lynch was all too well aware of how many operations had been blown by a youngster who was the worse for drink showing off to his mates or a girlfriend. The ceasefire meant that it was more important than ever before for the organisation's volunteers to conduct themselves well. The IRA wasn't being dismantled, it was simply going even further underground, waiting for the call to return to violence if the political process failed to come up with the goods. Discipline had to be maintained, volunteers had to be trained, and active service units continued to gather data on prospective targets in Ireland and on the mainland.

If Davie handled himself well, Lynch would recommend that he be put forward for specialised training, with a view to sending him to the mainland as part of a deep cover active service unit. There was no doubt that he was committed to the Cause. His father had been gunned down in a Falls Road pub by three UFF men in ski masks, for no other reason than he'd been a Catholic. There had been no military honours at Paddy Quinn's funeral, no pistol shots or tricolour draped over the coffin, because he had refused to have anything to do with the IRA. But his sons, they were a different matter. They'd joined the organisation a week after their father's funeral, despite their mother's protests.

The track curved to the left and O'Riordan's farm came into view, a ramshackle collection of weathered stone buildings, a grey metal barn and a gleaming white silo. Lynch parked in front of the silo and told the Quinn brothers to stay in the car.

O'Riordan had the door of the farmhouse open before Lynch reached it, his arm outstretched. They shook hands and Lynch could feel the hard callouses on O'Riordan's palms. It was a small farm and even with European Community subsidies it didn't generate enough income for O'Riordan to employ more than two labourers, so he had to do much of the heavy work himself.

The acrid smell of pig manure wafted over from one of the outbuildings and Lynch pulled a face. He preferred his pork sliced into rashers and sizzling in a frying pan. O'Riordan laughed at his discomfort and slapped him on the back. 'You never could stand the countryside, could you?'

Lynch cleared his throat and spat on the grass. 'I suppose you need something to keep the cities apart,' he growled. 'Are you ready?'

'Yeah. The stuff's in the stable.' O'Riordan stuck his hands into his brown corduroy trousers and walked with Lynch to a single storey stable building. He pushed open a door to an empty stall and held it open while Lynch walked inside.

'Jesus, Pat. How can you live with this stink?' asked Lynch, holding his nose.

O'Riordan stepped in the stall and closed the door. He

breathed in and grinned. 'Nothing wrong with a little horseshit,' he said. 'It brings the roses up a treat.' He picked up a shovel that was leaning against a whitewashed wall and used it to clear away the straw from a corner. He pushed the edge of the shovel into the gap between two of the flagstones and levered one up. Underneath were three stainless steel milk churns. 'Give me a hand, will you?' said O'Riordan as he placed the shovel on the floor. Together they pulled out the churns. O'Riordan unscrewed the caps and one by one emptied out more than a dozen polythene-wrapped parcels. 'Choose your weapons,' he said.

Lynch peered at the parcels. 'What have you got?' he asked.

'A sawn-off, an East German Kalashnikov, a Czech Model 58V assault rifle, a couple of Uzis, a . . .'

'We're not going to war, you know,' interrupted Lynch.

O'Riordan ignored him and continued to rattle off his list. '. . . half a dozen Czech M1970s, they're just like the Walther PPK, a Romanian TT33, a Chinese Tokarev, a couple of Brownings, a 9mm Beretta . . .' He prodded the parcels with his foot. 'Oh yeah, an old Colt .45, but it hasn't been fired for ten years or so and it'll probably take your hand off.' He stood up and put his hands on his hips. 'What do you feel like?'

Lynch pursed his lips and scratched his beard. 'Italian,' he said eventually. 'I feel like Italian.'

O'Riordan bent down and picked up one of the packages. Lynch unwrapped the polythene. Inside was the Beretta wrapped in an oiled cloth with two clips of ammunition. He checked the action and nodded his approval. 'Have you used it?' Lynch asked.

'Yeah, but it's clean. What about the boys?'

'Brownings. But make sure the safeties are on.'

O'Riordan grinned. 'And I'll have the shotgun. Just in case.'

'Just in case?'

'Aye. Just in case we have to get heavy.'

'We won't,' said Lynch.

'We'll see.' O'Riordan replaced the remaining weapons in the metal churns and Lynch helped him put them back into the ground.

'Regular arsenal you have here,' said Lynch as he lowered the flagstone back into place and kicked straw over it.

'It's always good to have a little put by for a rainy day.' O'Riordan was wearing a specially-made nylon sling under his coat and he slipped the sawn-off shotgun into it, then went outside. While Lynch carried the pistols over to the Granada, O'Riordan led a brown and white mare from a neighbouring stall into the one containing the hidden weapons. Lynch handed the still-wrapped Brownings through the window to Davie. 'Check them, then hide them under the seats,' he said.

He tucked the Beretta into the back of his trousers and slid the spare clip into the inside pocket of his leather jacket before going back to join O'Riordan as he bolted the door to the stall. The horse snorted inside as if objecting to being locked up. Lynch knew just how the mare felt. He'd spent three years listening to the sound of cell doors clanging shut and it wasn't an experience he'd care to repeat.

O'Riordan winked at Lynch. 'You ready?'

'Sure.' He looked at his watch. It was two o'clock. He wanted the job done before five, before the man of the house came home. 'Where's the drill?'

'Charging.'

'Charging?' Lynch frowned.

'Charged,' said O'Riordan, correcting himself. 'I had it plugged in overnight. The wife thought I was planning some DIY. She's going to be disappointed, isn't she? I'll go get it.'

O'Riordan disappeared inside the farmhouse and a minute or so later he reappeared with a Black and Decker cordless drill. He pointed it at Lynch and pulled the trigger and the bit whirred. 'Okay, let's go,' he said, putting the drill into a white plastic carrier bag.

Davie Quinn climbed into the back of the Granada without being asked. O'Riordan got in the front seat and nodded a greeting to the two brothers, but didn't say anything.

The four men drove to West Belfast in silence. As they entered the city they passed a convoy of grey RUC Landrovers driving in the opposite direction, their windows protected by steel mesh. 'Bastards,' hissed O'Riordan under his breath.

Lynch smiled tightly. 'Just be grateful they're not heading our way,' he said. He turned the Granada down a side road and parked in front of a pub. Like the Landrovers', the pub's windows were shielded with wire mesh. Two young men in anoraks and jeans stood in the entrance smoking cigarettes. The taller of the two nodded at Lynch.

Lynch didn't bother locking the car doors and the four men walked purposefully down the road, Lynch and O'Riordan in front, the Quinn brothers following closely behind. A woman in a cheap cloth coat walked by pushing two crying babies in a buggy. Two boys with dirty faces and scabby knees sat on the kerb with their feet in the gutter and turned to watch the men go past.

Lynch wasn't worried about witnesses, he was on Catholic territory.

The house they were looking for was in the middle of a brick terrace, one of hundreds of near-identical homes, distinguished only by the colour of the peeling paint on the woodwork. Lynch pressed the doorbell and O'Riordan motioned for the Quinn brothers to stand to the side, out of sight. They heard footsteps, then the door was opened by an overweight grey-haired woman in a flowered print dress and a baggy green cardigan. Before she could speak, Lynch pushed her back into the hallway and pulled out his Beretta. The woman began to shiver and opened her mouth to scream. Lynch glared at her. 'Be quiet,' he hissed and clamped his hand over her mouth. O'Riordan slipped by and stood at the foot of the stairs. 'Where's the boy?' whispered Lynch. The woman's eyes gave her away, flicking towards the stairs. Davie Quinn closed the front door and locked it. From the kitchen Lynch could hear the tinny sound of a transistor radio. 'Anyone else in the house?'

The woman tried to speak and Lynch moved his hand away from her mouth. 'My daughter,' she said. 'She's only twelve.'

'Where is she?'

'Please don't hurt us, son. We're good Catholics. The boy wouldn't hurt a fly.'

'Where is she?' Lynch repeated, holding the gun in front of her face.

'The kitchen. There's been a mistake, son, you can't . . .'

Lynch motioned to Paulie and the teenager used his hand to silence the woman. Paulie and Davie both had their guns out. Paulie was sweating but Davie seemed

78

calm. They were both looking at Lynch, waiting for instructions.

'Take her through into the front room,' Lynch whispered to Paulie. As Paulie bundled the woman into the room, Lynch went along the hall to the kitchen with Davie. A young girl with mousy hair tied back in a ponytail was sitting at a small table reading a magazine. She looked over her shoulder as Lynch walked up behind her and her eyes widened in horror.

'You're here for Ger, aren't you?' she asked, her voice trembling like a frightened rabbit. 'I told him. I told him you'd come for him one day. I fecking told him, so I did.'

Lynch ignored the question. He picked up a tea towel and tossed it at Davie, then grabbed the girl by the shirt collar and pulled her to her feet. He half-dragged, half-carried her down the hallway to the front room.

The woman was sitting hunched on a threadbare sofa, playing with a rosary. Lynch dropped the girl down next to her mother. 'Please, son, don't hurt my boy,' whined the woman. She put an arm around the girl and pulled her close.

'Your boy's been selling drugs to kids,' said Lynch flatly.

'Oh no, son, you're wrong. My Ger's a good boy. A bit wild, maybe, but he's a good heart . . .' She began to cry softly.

On the wall above the woman's head hung a portrait of the Pope, and next to it a black-framed photograph of John F. Kennedy. The woman looked up and stared at the pictures, as if pleading for their support. Lynch felt no sympathy for her. He knew that she'd already been warned about her son's drug-dealing. If she wasn't prepared to keep her family in order, the organisation was. By whatever means it took.

'Keep them here,' he said to Paulie. He knelt down in front of the woman and put a hand on the rosary. 'We're not going to kill your boy, but if you tell anyone, anyone at all, we'll come back. Do you understand?'

'Don't hurt him,' she sniffed. 'Please don't hurt him.'

'Do you understand?' Lynch repeated. 'Say anything and we'll be back. And it won't just be for the boy.'

The woman nodded. She averted her eyes and began to mumble the Lord's Prayer as she fingered the polished amber beads of the rosary. Lynch straightened up and motioned with his head for Davie to follow him. They joined O'Riordan at the foot of the stairs. O'Riordan had taken his sawn-off shotgun from under his coat. He nodded at Lynch and they moved silently up the stairs, Davie bringing up the rear.

There were four doors leading off the top landing. Only two were closed. Lynch put his ear to one of the doors but heard nothing. He eased it open. It was the bathroom, a cheap yellow bathroom suite and a green knitted cover on the toilet seat, with a matching cover on a spare toilet roll. He closed the door.

Davie was breathing like a train, his nostrils flaring. He had the tea towel in his left hand, the Browning in the other, and Lynch was pleased to see he had the safety off and the barrel pointing straight up. His finger was outside the trigger guard, just as he'd been told. Davie swallowed nervously as Lynch brushed by him and stood by the second door. Lynch seized the handle, nodded at O'Riordan, and thrust open the door.

The boy was standing in the middle of the bedroom,

his back to them. He was listening to a Sony Walkman through headphones and playing air guitar, whipping his long red hair backwards and forwards in time to the music. The three men filed into the room and Davie closed the door behind them. It was a typical teenager's room: rock 'n' roll posters on the wall, a pile of dirty laundry in one corner, a cheap veneered bookcase filled with paperbacks, and a single bed with the bedclothes in disarray. It smelt of old socks and sweat and was almost as unsavoury as the stable where O'Riordan kept his arms cache.

The boy whirled around then froze as he saw his visitors. His mouth fell open, then he was suddenly galvanised into action, throwing himself across the bed and clutching for the window. O'Riordan dropped the carrier bag on the floor, stepped forward and grabbed one of the boy's legs, pulling him hard and throwing him onto his stomach. The boy began to scream as O'Riordan sat across the base of his spine, pinning him to the bed. The boy lashed out with his arms but O'Riordan wriggled up his back and used his knees to hold him down. 'Fuck off, yez bastards!' the boy screamed, bucking and twisting even under O'Riordan's weight.

'Davie, come on lad,' urged O'Riordan. 'Get on with it.'

Davie rushed forward and used the tea towel to gag the struggling boy, then moved around to the foot of the bed and grabbed the boy's ankles. O'Riordan put his head down close to the boy's face. The towel muffled his screams. His cheeks were pockmarked with old acne scars and his red hair was unkempt and dirty, flecked with dandruff. O'Riordan grabbed a handful of hair and yanked his head back. 'Listen to me, Ger. This is going to happen whether you struggle or not, do you hear me?' The boy said nothing but continued to try to get up. O'Riordan thrust the barrel of the shotgun against the boy's temple and tapped it, hard enough to hurt. 'If you cooperate, they'll be able to patch you up and you'll be on your feet in a few months. Carry on fucking with us and you'll never walk again. It's up to you. Am I getting through to you, Ger?' The boy suddenly went still. 'That's better,' said O'Riordan. 'Now take your punishment like a man and we can all get on our way.' He sat up, keeping his weight pressed down on the boy's shoulderblades.

Lynch reached around to the front of the boy's waist, unclipped his leather belt and pulled his jeans down to his ankles. 'Sit on his calves, it'll stop him kicking out,' Lynch told Davie and the young man obeyed. The boy began to cry, his tears staining the pillow.

Lynch was a veteran of more than a dozen kneecappings and he knew how important it was to seize control from the outset and to give the victim no opportunity to resist. Kneecapping was a particularly brutal form of punishment, but it worked, serving as a permanent reminder both to the victim and to others. No matter how good the surgeons – and the surgeons in Belfast were the best in the world at repairing and replacing shattered joints – the knee would never be as good as new. Even after the ceasefire, the IRA used kneecapping to punish drug dealers, rapists and joyriders, and men like Lynch had become experts at the technique. O'Riordan hadn't lied when he'd told the boy it could be done easily or painfully. Depending on how the gun or drill was used, the kneecap could be merely damaged or the leg destroyed. Drilling from the side was painful enough, but drilling from the back of the knee would shatter the kneecap into dozens of splinters.

Lynch took the drill out of the carrier bag and switched it on. He pressed the trigger and the bit whirred and buzzed. The boy's body went into spasm and Lynch pressed down with both his hands. The pillow and the gag stifled most of the noise.

'Okay?' asked O'Riordan.

'Yeah,' said Lynch. He looked over his shoulder and saw that Davie Quinn had his eyes closed. Lynch smiled. The first was always the hardest. Lynch placed the whirling bit against the side of the boy's left knee with all the precision and care of a surgeon. There was very little blood as the bit tore through the flesh, then the noise of the drill changed from a high pitched whine to a dull grinding sound as it ripped through the cartilage. The drill shuddered in Lynch's hand as the bit grated against bone and he fought to keep it steady.

Davie opened his eyes but shut them quickly when he saw the bit emerging at the far side of the knee, covered in blood and flesh and bits of white cartilage. The boy went still on the bed, his face deathly pale. They usually passed out, Lynch knew, more from fear than from the pain. If they really wanted to make the victim suffer they'd wake him up before working on the second knee, but the boy was being capped more as a warning to others than to hurt him. Lynch kept the bit turning as he pulled it out of the injured knee so that it wouldn't jam, then wiped his forehead with the back of his arm and went back to work, drilling through the second knee as easily as the first. When he'd finished, he pulled out the bit, switched off the drill and put it back into the carrier bag. O'Riordan climbed off the unconscious boy and untied the gag. Saliva dribbled onto the pillow.

Lynch checked the boy's wounds. There was some bleeding, but it was far from life-threatening. He took a sheet and wrapped it around the boy's legs. 'He'll be okay,' he said. 'You can get off now, Davie.'

The three men went downstairs to the sitting room, where Paulie was standing over the woman and her daughter, his Browning in both hands. 'Wait five minutes, then call an ambulance,' O'Riordan told the woman. 'Make sure they take him to the Royal Victoria and if you get the chance, ask for Mr Palmer. He's the best for kneecaps, okay?'

The woman nodded and kissed her rosary. 'Thanks, son,' she whispered. The girl burst into tears and buried her head in her mother's lap.

Lynch drove the Quinn brothers to the Falls Road and dropped them off a short walk from their home, then headed for the M2 and Ballymena. 'Did I ever tell you about the first capping I was on?' asked Lynch. O'Riordan shook his head. 'It was a guy who'd been taking pictures of little boys, naked. Didn't touch them, but he was heading that way, so he had to be taught a lesson. Do you know Paddy McKenna? He's in the Kesh now.'

'Heard of him, yeah.'

'Yeah, well we picked the guy up, four of us, and took him out to Kilbride to do the dirty deed. Paddy brought the drill. It was his first capping as well. So, we have the guy pinned down in the field, and we tell Paddy to get on with it. He starts looking around. What the fuck are you waiting for, we say. "Where's the socket?" he asks. "Where's the fucking socket?"'

O'Riordan laughed uproariously. 'Easy mistake to make,' he said, wiping his eyes.

It wasn't until they were driving down the track that led

to O'Riordan's farm that he raised the subject of Mike Cramer. 'What did McCormack say?' he asked.

'Let sleeping dogs lie. That's what he said.'

O'Riordan snorted softly. 'Fuck that for a game of soldiers.'

'Yeah. But what can we do? How am I going to track down a helicopter? They could have gone anywhere.'

O'Riordan shook his head. 'Not anywhere, Dermott. What goes up must come down. And Air Traffic Control must have been tracking it. You might try asking them.'

'Oh sure, I'll just phone them up and ask them if they saw a helicopter pick up a Sass-man in Howth. I can just imagine their answer.'

'It was a Sea King, wasn't it? That's what it looked like to me.'

'I suppose so. It was a big bugger, that's for sure, not a normal army chopper. I've never seen a red, white and blue chopper before. They're usually grey or green.'

'What about the Queen's Flight?' said O'Riordan.

'Aye, it could have been the Duke of Edinburgh himself, coming to lift our man off. How far can they go, any idea?'

O'Riordan shrugged. 'A few hundred miles maybe. They were heading east, but that doesn't mean anything. They could have circled around and headed up north.'

'Belfast? Yeah, that's possible. Do we know anyone in Air Traffic Control?'

'I'll ask around. But you'd best be careful. McCormack won't like it if he thinks you're going behind his back.'

'Yeah, yeah, yeah.'

'I mean it, Dermott. McCormack is a dangerous man to cross.'

'I know. I'll just be making a few enquiries, that's all.'

*　　*　　*

Mike Cramer was walking around the croquet lawn,
deep in thought, when he heard the Colonel calling
him from the French windows at the rear of the main
building. He looked up. The Colonel was waving his
walking stick as if he was trying to call back an errant
retriever. Cramer smiled at the thought. A Rottweiler
would be a better comparison. During his last few years
in the SAS, the Colonel had tended to use Cramer on
operations where the qualities of a highly-trained attack
dog were more in demand than the ability to bring back
a dead bird.

Cramer walked across the grass. Away to his left, by the
line of tall conifers which separated the tennis courts from
the lawn, stood a broad-shouldered man in a dark blue
duffel coat, one of several SAS troopers on guard duty.
The wind caught the coat and Cramer got a glimpse of a
sub-machine pistol in an underarm holster.

The Colonel had gone back inside by the time Cramer
reached the window. It led into a large, airy room which
appeared to have been the headmistress's office. The
Colonel sat behind a huge oak desk. The walls were bare
but there were oblong marks among the faded wallpaper
where framed photographs of netball and lacrosse teams
had hung for generations. As Cramer stepped into the room
he noticed another man, standing by an empty bookcase.
'Cramer, this is Dr Greene,' said the Colonel.

The doctor stepped forward and shook hands with
Cramer. He was just under six feet tall, in his early fifties

with swept-back grey hair and gold-framed spectacles with
bifocal lenses. He was wearing a brown cardigan with
leather patches on the elbows and was carrying a small
leather medical bag. 'Strip to the waist,' said the doctor.

'Top or bottom?'

The doctor looked at Cramer over the top of his
spectacles, an amused smile on his face. 'Whichever you'd
prefer, Sergeant Cramer.'

Cramer took off his reefer jacket and unbuttoned his
shirt. The Colonel made no move to leave. He read the
look on Cramer's face. 'You don't mind if I stay, do you?'
he asked and Cramer shook his head.

The doctor whistled softly between his teeth as Cramer
dropped his shirt onto the desk. He walked over and
gently touched the thick raised scar that ran jaggedly
across Cramer's stomach. 'Across and up. As if someone
had tried to disembowel you.'

'That's pretty much what happened. I lost a few feet of
tubing and I had to wear a colostomy bag for the best part
of a year, but I guess I was lucky.'

'And this?' The doctor touched Cramer's right breast.
There was a mass of scar tissue where the nipple had
once been.

Cramer shrugged. 'Pruning shears.'

The doctor walked around Cramer, noting the rest of
the scars on his body. He touched him lightly on the left
shoulder. 'A .45?' he asked.

'A .357, I think. It went right through so they never
found the bullet.'

'And this?' The doctor pressed a small wound on the
other shoulder.

'A fruit knife.'

'And this thin one that runs around your stomach?'

'A Stanley knife.'

The doctor shook his head in wonder. 'You seem to have a lot of enemies, Sergeant Cramer.'

'Just one.'

'One man did all this to you?'

'It was a woman. She did most of the damage.'

'A woman?' The doctor whistled through his teeth. 'I wouldn't like to meet her on a dark night.'

'Mary Hennessy, her name was. She was an IRA terrorist. She's dead now.'

The doctor stood in front of him again and studied the thick scar across his stomach. 'That must have done a lot of damage inside.'

'Tell me about it. If I hadn't been helicoptered to hospital I'd have died.'

'She was torturing you, this woman?'

'She was torturing a friend of mine. He died moments before I was rescued. She did that to my stomach just before she fled. I guess she wanted me to die slowly, in a lot of pain. She almost had her wish. The rest of the stuff she did to me two years later.'

The doctor had Cramer open his mouth and took a small torch from the pocket of his cardigan. He peered at Cramer's throat, then pushed his fingers against the side of his neck as if checking for lumps. 'That seems fine,' he murmured, then he pressed Cramer's stomach with the flat of his hand. Cramer winced. The doctor pressed again, lower this time, and Cramer grunted. 'That hurts?' asked the doctor.

'A bit.'

'Did the doctors in Madrid think that the cancer could be a result of the trauma?'

Cramer nodded. 'That, coupled with the stress. And my drinking.'

The doctor nodded. 'How much pain are you in, generally?'

'Generally, it's okay. Twinges now and then. It hurts most when I eat.'

'What about your appetite?'

'That's pretty much gone. Partly because it hurts, but mainly I'm just not hungry most of the time.'

'Bleeding?'

'Yeah. That's why I went to the hospital in the first place. My shit went black.'

'And you were losing weight?'

'I went down from 184 pounds to 170. I thought it was because I'd stopped eating.'

'And you're still losing weight?' Cramer nodded. 'The doctors in Spain, how long did they give you?'

'Three months. Max.'

The doctor sniffed. 'I've seen the X-rays, and the scans. I'd say they were being optimistic.' He straightened up and went over to his bag. 'I'll give you a vitamin shot now, and some tablets to take.'

'Not painkillers. I don't want painkillers.'

'Just vitamins. But you'll be needing painkillers before long.'

'Yeah, well I'll face that when I have to.'

'I'll leave you something, take it if and when you have to. And you'll need something much stronger towards the end. I'll arrange for you to have morphine and you can dose yourself.'

'It won't come to that.'

'You think that now, but nearer the . . .'

'It won't come to that,' Cramer insisted.

The doctor held his look for a few seconds and then nodded acceptance. He opened his bag and took out a plastic-wrapped syringe and a vial of colourless liquid. He injected the vitamins and gave Cramer a bottle of tablets. 'These are just multivitamins,' he explained. 'They'll make up for what you're not getting from your food. I'd drink milk if I were you, eggs maybe, if you can keep them down. Fruit would be good for you, but in small amounts. Better to eat a little often than to try to force down big portions.' He looked over his shoulder at the Colonel. 'Normally I'd tell him to take it easy, but I suppose that's not an option in this case, is it?'

'Sergeant Cramer's going to be working, that's true.'

'Well God help him, that's all I can say.'

'I doubt that he will, but thanks for the sentiment,' said Cramer acidly.

The doctor handed Cramer another bottle, this one containing green capsules. 'For the pain,' he said. 'Not on an empty stomach. Not more than one at a time. And not more than six in any one twenty-four-hour period.'

'Thanks, Doc,' said Cramer.

'I meant what I said about arranging morphine for you.'

'And I meant what I said about it not coming to that,' said Cramer, putting his shirt back on.

Dermott Lynch was sitting with his feet on the coffee table watching the BBC *Nine O'Clock News* when the phone rang. He let his answering machine take the call as he watched the BBC's industrial correspondent explain the latest gloomy trade figures. He popped the tab on a chilled can of draught Guinness and poured it deftly into a tall glass as the recording announced he couldn't get to the phone. He put down the glass as he heard Pat O'Riordan's voice and picked up the receiver. 'Yeah, Pat, I'm here.'

'Screening calls, are we?' said O'Riordan.

'Just taking the weight off my feet. Figured I deserved a rest. How's things?'

'Don't suppose you fancy giving me a hand cleaning out the pigs, do you?'

'You're dead right.'

'Fancy a drink?'

Lynch looked at the Guinness as it settled in the glass, a thick, creamy head on the top. 'You read my mind,' he said.

Mrs Elliott served up a chicken stew with herb dumplings along with freshly-made garlic bread and buttery mashed potatoes. The Colonel and Cramer ate alone in the huge dining hall next to the propane heater. The Colonel had opened a bottle of claret but Cramer had refused. He had a glass of milk, instead. With a large measure of Famous Grouse mixed in.

Cramer toyed with his food, eating small mouthfuls and chewing thoroughly before swallowing. The Colonel watched him eat. 'Bad?' he asked.

'The food's fine.' Cramer put down his fork. 'I never had

much of an appetite even when I was fit.' He picked up the file that he'd been reading before dinner. 'Have you read this one?' he asked. 'The Harrods killing?'

'The Saudi Foreign Minister's second wife. Ann-Marie Wilkinson. The Met think it was the first wife who paid for the hit.'

'Cheaper than divorce, I suppose.'

'I don't think the Saudis bother with divorce, do they?' said the Colonel. 'I think they just take as many wives as they want.' Cramer shrugged and took a long drink of milk, then added another slug of whisky. 'Anyway, the first wife had the money,' the Colonel continued. 'She was related to the Saudi royal family and it seems that she resented all the attention Ann-Marie was getting.'

Cramer held up a photocopy of a typewritten report. 'She was pregnant.'

The Colonel nodded. 'I know. That's another reason why they think she was killed. He had three children by the first wife, it could be that she didn't want any competition. What's on your mind?'

'He murdered a pregnant woman. It takes a particular sort of killer to shoot a pregnant woman, don't you think?'

The Colonel put down his knife and fork. 'I've known plenty who would, without a second thought.'

'Professionals? You think so?'

The Colonel leaned forward over his plate. 'You've killed women, Sergeant Cramer. For Queen and country. And a soldier's salary.'

'I've killed terrorists who were female, Colonel. There's a difference. And the Kypriano killing. The girl. Eight years old. He killed an eight-year-old girl.'

The Colonel gently swirled the red wine around his glass

and stared at it. 'He's well paid for what he does. Half a million dollars a hit, we hear. Perhaps the money makes it easier.'

'I don't think so.'

'Are you saying that if you were offered half a million dollars you wouldn't do it?'

Cramer looked up sharply. 'A child? No, I wouldn't. Would you?'

'Of course not. Not for any amount. But we're not talking about me, we're talking about someone who's prepared to kill for money. You've been trained to kill. And you've killed for no other reason than that you've been ordered to. Okay, so there are some things you wouldn't do, but not everyone has the same degree of moral judgement.'

Cramer nodded noncommittally, but his eyes narrowed as he studied the Colonel's face. 'What if it was in the interests of national security, Colonel? Would you do it then?'

The Colonel looked at Cramer for several seconds, though to Cramer it felt as if the silence was stretching into infinity. The Colonel stopped swirling his wine and drained his glass. He was about to answer when Mrs Elliott appeared. The Colonel put down his glass while she collected their plates, frowning at the amount Cramer had left. As she went back into the kitchen, the Colonel stood up and excused himself, saying that he needed an early night. The unanswered question hung in the air like black rain cloud.

*   *   *

The pub was just off the Falls Road, a red brick building with metal shutters over the window and an orange, white and green tricolour flag hanging over the front door. A thickset man in a brown raincoat stood by the door, his hands deep in his pockets, his eyes ever watchful.

'Evening, Danny,' said Lynch.

'How's yerself, Dermott?' asked the man.

'Getting by. Busy tonight?'

'Aye, there's a fair crowd in.' He pushed open the metal door and Lynch heard the sound of a fiddle being played with more enthusiasm than ability.

Lynch grimaced. 'That should soon clear them out,' he said, and the doorman laughed.

Several heads turned as Lynch made his way to the bar. In the far corner the fiddler, a bearded man in his sixties, wearing a plaid shirt and baggy cotton trousers, was sawing away on his fiddle with gusto. Behind him was an anorexically-thin blonde girl with an accordion and a middle-aged man with a tin whistle, though they sat with their instruments in their laps as they watched the old man perform.

Two men in donkey jackets moved apart to allow Lynch to the bar. The barman came over immediately and greeted him by name. There were few bars in the Falls area where Dermott Lynch wasn't known and respected. He ordered a Guinness and scanned the bar for familiar faces as he waited for it to be poured. A grey-haired old man in a sheepskin jacket with a tired-looking shaggy-haired mongrel sitting at his feet nodded a silent greeting and Lynch nodded back. A group of teenagers fell quiet as Lynch's gaze passed over them. Lynch spotted one of the lads who'd kept an eye on the Granada while he'd done the kneecapping, but he made no sign of recognising him.

The fiddler sat down to scattered applause, then the blonde girl began to play her accordion, nodding her head backwards and forwards as she concentrated, her lips pursed. The barman placed the pint of Guinness in front of Lynch and took his money. Lynch drank deeply and wiped his mouth with the back of his hand. Pat O'Riordan appeared at his elbow. 'You looked like you enjoyed that, all right, Dermott.'

Lynch grinned and winked at O'Riordan. 'You'll be taking a pint yourself?'

O'Riordan watched the blonde girl play her accordion. 'She's a fine looking girl, sure enough.'

'Bit stringy for me,' said Lynch as he caught the barman's eye and pointed to his glass, indicating that he wanted another Guinness for O'Riordan. O'Riordan was married with four young children and Lynch knew he was devoted to his family, but he liked to pretend that he had a roving eye. O'Riordan's Guinness arrived and he sipped it appreciatively. The fiddler and the pipe-player joined the accordion player in a rebel song that had several of the drinkers tapping their feet and singing along. The two men listened to the music for a while, enjoying the atmosphere of the pub, the well-being that came from knowing that they were among friends. Lynch drained his glass and ordered two more drinks. While they waited for the Guinness to settle, O'Riordan slipped Lynch a piece of paper. 'That's your man,' said O'Riordan. 'He's based at Dublin Airport. His brother is in the Kesh doing a five-stretch, he's been told to expect a visit from you.'

There were two telephone numbers on the piece of paper, a home number and one at the man's place of work. 'I'll drive down tomorrow morning,' said Lynch.

The rebel song came to an end amid rapturous applause and stamping of feet. 'Not tomorrow you won't,' said O'Riordan. 'There's a wee job McCormack wants you to do for him.'

Lynch sighed. 'Not another capping?'

O'Riordan shook his head. 'Bigger, Dermott. Much bigger.'

Mike Cramer sat on the bed, his back against the wall. On his lap lay the file on the first killing which had been attributed to the assassin. It had taken place in Miami, almost exactly two years earlier. A Colombian drugs baron had been sitting in a nightclub with his two seventeen-year-old girlfriends, sniffing cocaine and drinking champagne. Three bodyguards had been sitting at an adjacent table. The file contained photographs of the aftermath: the three bodyguards sprawled on the purple carpet, their guns still in their holsters, the drugs baron still sitting upright, a third eye in the middle of his forehead, blood all over his shirt.

More than two hundred people had been in the nightclub and there were almost as many versions of what had happened. Even the drug dealer's blondes differed on the colours of the Hawaiian shirt the assassin was wearing and the type of gun he was carrying. One of the girls thought it was an automatic, the other said it was a .357 Magnum. Cramer figured that their descriptions were useless. He doubted if either of the girls knew anything about guns, and in a dark nightclub with everyone screaming and panicking there was little chance of them being able to describe the weapon accurately.

The killer had been on the dancefloor, dancing alone, and he'd walked towards the bar, waiting until he was right next to the table where the bodyguards were sitting before pulling his gun out. Leaving aside what the girls had said, Cramer reckoned that it would have been a small pistol, something that could easily be concealed. According to the Medical Examiner's report it had been a 9mm calibre, but that only narrowed down the number of possibilities, it didn't even come close to identifying the weapon.

Using a 9mm for the hit made sense, it was standard issue to anti-terrorist groups around the world. Its main drawback was its tendency to go right through the target. Unlike a .22, which would spin and tumble, ripping through internal organs and blood vessels, a 9mm would pass through a human body unless it struck bone, leading to potential problems in hostage situations. The SAS used Splat frangible rounds, bullets made of a mixture of polymer and non-lead metal which were guaranteed to break up on impact, but which were also capable of passing through cover first. The killer had used a form of accelerated energy transfer rounds with plastic cores, which would spin on contact, mimicking the action and massive tissue damage of a .22. Cramer wasn't sure why the killer had bothered – the nature of the bullet made little difference in a point-blank shot to the face.

In all, the assassin had fired nine shots. One each for the three bodyguards, two for the drugs dealer, then two more into the chest of one of the bodyguards who'd been trying to pull his own gun out despite being shot in the throat. On the way out of the nightclub the assassin had been challenged by one of the tuxedoed doormen and he'd shot him twice. Nine bullets. Definitely not a revolver.

Many 9mm handguns held eight or nine in the clip, but Cramer doubted if the killer would have gone into a place as crowded as the nightclub and fired off all his shots. He'd have wanted the security of something in reserve. A second clip wasn't out of the question, but changing clips would take time and he'd be vulnerable during the changeover. Cramer's weapon of choice would have been the Browning Hi-Power, effective up to forty feet and with thirteen rounds in the magazine, but he figured the killer had used something like a SIG-Sauer P226, which held fifteen cartridges. It was only a guess because he knew there were literally dozens of other possibilities: Heckler & Koch of Germany made a thirteen-shot 9mm handgun, the P7A13; the French had the MAB P15 with a fifteen-shot magazine; the Italians had the Beretta Model 92 series with magazines ranging from eight to fifteen; the Czechs had the fifteen-shot CZ 9mm Model 75; the Austrians had the Glock, made from lightweight polymer and available with fifteen, seventeen and nineteen round magazines. Most European countries had factories churning out large capacity 9mm handguns, and tens of thousands found their way to the States, legally or otherwise.

Cramer massaged the bridge of his nose and blinked his eyes. Even if the killer had a favourite weapon, and even if he could identify it, the knowledge wouldn't do him any good. By the time Cramer was staring down the barrel of whatever gun it was the killer was using, it would be too late. Bang. One bullet in the face. Bang. The second in the heart. Then nothing but darkness.

There was a knock on the bedroom door. 'Come in, Mrs

Elliott,' he said, closing the file and dropping it onto the bed. He recognised her knock, two taps in quick succession, like the double tap in the Killing House.

Mrs Elliott carried a tray into the room and put it down on a chair by the bed. 'A snack for you, Mr Cramer,' she said. 'Hot milk and ham sandwiches.'

'Thank you, Mrs Elliott. You shouldn't have bothered.' Most of the food she brought up to his room ended up being flushed down the toilet, though he usually drank the milk. Her glance barely passed over the bottle of Famous Grouse but Cramer could sense her disapproval.

'It's no bother, Mr Cramer,' she said, and disappeared out of the door, her dress cracking like a sail in the wind.

Cramer poured a double measure of whisky into the milk and sipped it as he picked up the file again. Cramer wondered what significance there was in the fact that the Miami assassination had been the first. The only links between all the killings in the files that Cramer had read were the handgun and the placing of the two shots. The Miami assassination had been quick and efficient, as if the killer knew exactly what he was doing. Cramer wondered if he'd actually killed before, but using a different method so that the deaths hadn't been included in the investigation. The killing seemed too professional to have been a first. Perhaps he'd killed in many different ways before focusing on his preferred method?

There was also the question of how the killer had been hired in the first place. Becoming a contract killer wasn't like setting out to be a doctor or an accountant – you couldn't simply move into an office and put a sign on your door. Contract killers had to have a track record, they had to prove that they could kill and get away with it, and they had to prove that they could be trusted. Cramer had heard of former soldiers and mercenaries who'd become contract killers, but generally such assassins were Mob-trained, career criminals who had served their apprenticeships before becoming fully-fledged killers. Killers didn't just appear from nowhere. There were skills to be acquired, techniques to be mastered. Cramer knew, because he was a killer, and he'd been trained by the best.

He dropped the file on the floor and picked up the next one. It was several times thicker than the Miami file, and as Cramer flicked through it, he soon realised why. The victim had been a British Member of Parliament, a Scot earmarked for a ministerial post who had been a close friend of the Prime Minister. Cramer vaguely remembered reading about the assassination, but at the time he'd been more concerned about the pain in his guts and the grim faces of the Spanish doctors. He scanned the police reports. The killer had been dressed as a motorcycle cop and had flagged down the MP's official Rover as it drove away from a newly-opened semiconductor plant. The killer had calmly waited for the driver to wind down his window, then he'd shot the MP's minder in the shoulder and killed the MP with two shots, one to the face, one to the heart. The descriptions provided by the injured bodyguard and the driver were worse than useless – the killer had kept his full-face helmet on, the tinted visor down, and he'd been wearing black leather gloves. Medium height, medium build.

Strathclyde Police had started a preliminary investigation but a team of Special Branch officers were sent up from the Metropolitan Police to take over. Despite the heavyweights,

the investigation stalled. A burnt-out motorcycle was discovered in a field outside Carlisle a few days later, but it
provided no forensic evidence.

Cramer read a memo from Special Branch to the Security
Service requesting possible motives for the assassination
and the reply, sent two days later, was noncommittal.
The MP was married with two teenage children, had no
known sexual liaisons outside the marriage, was a lawyer
by profession and had no controversial business interests.

The Security Service did however point out that the MP
had helped organise a campaign to stop an American oil
company developing two huge offshore oilfields for Iran.
The company had been about to sign the billion-dollar
contract when the MP raised the matter in the House of
Commons. The British had been pressing the Russian Government not to supply the Iranians with nuclear reactors,
and the MP made a stirring speech complaining that it was
unfair to ask the Russians to stop trading with Iran at a
time when the Americans were about to help the country
develop its oil resources. The State Department stepped in
and the deal was blocked. 'It is possible,' the Security Service
memo concluded, 'that the assassination was revenge for the
blocked contract.' Cramer smiled thinly. The memo didn't
say whether the Iranians or the oil company might have
paid for the hit. The way big business operated these days,
it could have been either.

There was a sheaf of correspondence between Special
Branch and the FBI, exchanging information on hired
assassins who might be prepared to kill such a high-profile
target, but it was clear that the investigation was going
nowhere. A memo from Special Branch to the Prime Minister's office some three months after the killing suggested

as much. The Prime Minister hadn't replied to the Special Branch memo; instead he had written a seven word memo to the Colonel. 'Immediate action required. Report directly to me.' The unsigned memo explained something that had been troubling Cramer ever since he had started working his way through the stack of files. Cramer had wondered why the Colonel and the SAS should be leading the hunt for a paid assassin, especially one who appeared to be most active in the United States. Now the answer was clear; it wasn't just to prevent further killings. The Prime Minister had taken it personally. He wanted revenge for a dead friend.

The mist came rolling off the hills around Crossmaglen, a cold, damp fog that chilled Lynch to the bone. He shivered and looked over at O'Riordan. 'Nice day for it,' he said.

'I don't suppose a city boy like you gets up before dawn much,' said O'Riordan. He was wearing a green waterproof jacket, a floppy tweed hat and green Wellington boots. Had it not been for the Kalashnikov he was cradling in his arms, he would have looked every inch the gentleman farmer.

'Forecast was for sun,' said Lynch, rubbing his hands together for warmth.

O'Riordan pulled a face. 'You can't forecast the weather here,' he said. 'It changes from one minute to the next. You should have worn a waterproof jacket, right enough.'

'Yeah, now you tell me.' Lynch had put on a black leather jacket with a sheepskin collar which was already wet through, and blue denim jeans which were soaking up the damp like a sponge. Beads of dew speckled his beard and moustache, and water trickled down the back of his neck in rivulets.

The two men stood by O'Riordan's Landrover which they'd parked under a chestnut tree, but it provided little in the way of shelter, as the moisture was all around them like a shroud. Lynch looked at his wristwatch. It was just before five. O'Riordan was right, he rarely got out of bed before ten and he disliked mornings, with a vengeance.

Davie and Paulie Quinn jumped down from the back of a mud-splattered truck a short distance away, then reached inside and pulled out large spades.

'Think we should help them?' asked O'Riordan.

Lynch grinned. 'The exercise will do them good,' he said.

'Didn't you tell them to bring gloves? They'll have blisters the size of golfballs by the time they've finished.'

'Slipped my mind,' said Lynch. He sat down on the bumper of O'Riordan's Landrover and groaned. 'God, I hate mornings,' he said.

Davie walked over, his spade over his shoulder. 'Okay?' he asked cheerfully.

O'Riordan stood with his back to the tree and counted off twenty paces. He raked his heel through the damp earth. 'Here there be treasure, me hearties,' he growled.

'How deep is it?' asked Paulie as he joined his brother.

'Six feet. Maybe a bit more. Put your backs into it, boys. We haven't got all day.'

As the brothers began to dig, O'Riordan went back to Lynch. Lynch looked at his wristwatch again.

'We'll be okay,' said O'Riordan. 'Half an hour, then fifteen minutes to load up, fifteen minutes to refill the hole. We'll be away in an hour.'

'I just don't like being exposed, that's all.' He squinted up at the reddening sky. Birds were already starting to greet the approaching dawn.

O'Riordan leant his assault rifle against the vehicle and ducked his head through the driver's side window. He took out a Thermos flask. 'Coffee?'

Lynch nodded and O'Riordan poured steaming black coffee into two plastic mugs. Paulie Quinn looked over at them but O'Riordan nodded at the hole. 'Keep digging, son.'

Mike Cramer lay on his back, staring up at the ceiling. He was thinking about death. His own death. Cramer wasn't scared of dying. The act was usually less painful and stressful than what led up to it. Death could often be a welcome release, an escape from pain, a way out. His right hand stroked the raised scar across his stomach as he remembered how he'd been so sure that he was dying as he lay on the floor of the Lynx helicopter, his trousers soaked with blood, his entrails in his hands.

It had taken maybe twenty minutes for the chopper to reach the hospital in Belfast and he'd been conscious for every second. Two troopers had tried to stem the bleeding but they hadn't known what to do about his guts, other than to cover the wound with a field dressing. There had been surprisingly little pain, and that had been why Cramer was so sure that he was dying.

He closed his eyes and shuddered as he remembered how Mick Newmarch had died. Death for Mick hadn't been easy, but then Mary Hennessy hadn't intended it to be. She'd used bolt-cutters on his fingers and a red-hot poker to cauterise the wounds so that he wouldn't bleed to death. She'd tortured him for hours like a cat toying with a mouse, then she'd castrated him and watched him bleed to death. It had been Cramer's turn then, his turn to be tied to the kitchen table in the isolated farmhouse, to be interrogated while armed IRA men stood outside. He remembered how she'd scowled as she'd heard the men shout that they had to go, that the SAS were on their way, and he remembered the way she'd smiled as she'd shown him the knife, letting it glint under the fluorescent lights before stabbing him in the stomach and cutting him wide open. 'Die, you bastard,' she'd whispered as the blood had flowed, then she'd left without a backward look. But Cramer hadn't died. The troopers had bundled him into the chopper and sat with him, urging him to stay conscious as they flew to the city, then the doctors had put him back together again, patched him up as best they could. Six months later he'd left the regiment. A booze-up in the Paludrine Club – the SAS bar at the Stirling Lines barracks in Hereford – a couple of paragraphs in *Mars and Minerva*, the regimental magazine, and back to Civvy Street. Yesterday's man.

No, death held no fear for Mike Cramer. Not any more. He'd stared death in the face and he had been prepared to embrace it with open arms. Now it was only the manner of his death that concerned him. And the Colonel had given him a way, a way to die with honour. In battle.

*　　*　　*

Seth Reed popped the last piece of black pudding in his mouth and chewed with relish. Reed's nine-year-old son, Mark, screwed up his face. 'Dad, how can you? That's pig's blood you're eating!'

Reed sat back in his chair and patted his ample stomach. 'Yup. And it was dee-licious.'

'Yuck.' The boy was still halfway through eating his breakfast, and Reed pointed at the rasher of bacon and half a sausage that remained on his plate.

'What do you think that is?' he asked.

'Bacon.'

'Pig. That's what it is.'

'Yeah, but it's not pig's blood.'

Kimberlee Reed's spoonful of cereal came to a sudden halt on its way to her mouth as she glared at her husband and son. 'Guys, can we please give it a rest?'

'He started it,' said Reed, pointing at Mark.

'Did not.'

'Did too.'

Kimberlee sighed and shook her head. 'You two are impossible. I don't know which of you is worse.'

Reed and his son pointed at each other. 'He is,' they said in unison.

The landlady, a tall, stick-thin woman with her greying hair tied back in a tight bun, appeared in the doorway, a pot of coffee in her hands. 'Is everything all right?' she asked.

'Perfect, Mrs McGregor,' said Kimberlee.

'More coffee?'

Kimberlee flashed her little girl smile. 'Do you have any decaff?' she asked.

Mrs McGregor shook her head. 'I'm afraid not, dear. What about a nice cup of tea?'

'Decaffeinated tea?'

Mrs McGregor shook her head again as she refilled Reed's cup. 'We don't get much call for it, I'm afraid.'

'That's okay. Orange juice will be fine.'

Mrs McGregor refilled the coffee cups of the family sitting at the next table and bustled out of the dining room.

'Are we ready to go?' asked Kimberlee.

Reed drained his cup and smacked his lips. His son finished his orange juice and mimicked his father's actions. 'Sure,' said Reed. 'Why don't you get the check while I get the bags?'

There was a bellpush in the entrance hall and Kimberlee pressed it while her husband went upstairs. Mrs McGregor came out of the kitchen, drying her hands. Kimberlee gave her the money for the night's bed and breakfast and the notes disappeared underneath Mrs McGregor's apron like a rabbit bolting into its burrow. 'So where are you going to next, dear?' she asked.

'Waterford, in the south,' said Kimberlee. 'We're going to look around the crystal factory. I want to buy some champagne glasses.'

'That'll be nice, you make sure you drive carefully now.'

'Oh, Seth'll be driving, Mrs McGregor. We couldn't get an automatic and I can't handle a stick shift. Not with my left hand.'

Reed struggled back down the stairs, a suitcase in either hand and a travel bag hanging on one shoulder. Kimberlee looked at him anxiously. He'd had a minor heart attack the previous year, and while the hospital had given him the all-clear she still worried whenever he exerted himself. The high-cholesterol fried breakfast wouldn't have helped his arteries, either, and he was drinking too much coffee. She reached out to take one of the suitcases, but he shook his head. 'Honey, I can manage.'

The family said goodbye to the landlady and then Kimberlee and Mark followed Reed down the path to their parked car. He loaded the cases into the boot and five minutes later they were on the A29, heading south. It was an almost 160 mile drive to Waterford but they were in no rush and Reed decided to drive on the back roads so that they could enjoy the lush countryside, a far cry from their home in Phoenix, Arizona.

They'd been driving for less than half an hour when Mark announced that he wanted to use the bathroom.

'A bathroom?' said Kimberlee, looking over her shoulder. 'This is Ireland, honey, not the Interstate. There are no pitstops here.'

'Mom . . .' Mark whined.

'If he's gotta go, he's gotta go,' said Reed.

'Can't you wait a while, honey?' asked Kimberlee. Mark jogged up and down in his seat and pressed his legs together. 'I guess not,' muttered Kimberlee. She picked up a folded map from the dashboard. 'Dundalk is the nearest town, Seth. Can we make a detour?'

'Mom . . .' pleaded Mark from the back.

'Honey, please,' said Kimberlee. 'Just wait a while, can't you?'

Mark shook his head and Kimberlee sighed. She put the map back on the dashboard and patted her husband on the thigh. 'We'll have to stop.'

'Here?'

'Anywhere.'

*   *   *

'How's it going, lads?' Lynch called. He could only see the tops of the heads of Paulie and Davie Quinn as they shovelled wet soil out of the hole. When he didn't get an answer he walked across the field and stood looking down at the two boys. They were sweating and breathing heavily but to their credit they were digging as quickly as when they'd first started. 'How's it going?' he repeated.

Davie Quinn looked up and wiped his forehead with his sleeve. 'It's okay,' he panted.

Paulie Quinn attacked the soil with his spade and used his foot to drive it deeper. 'Best start taking it easy, Paulie,' said Lynch.

'I'm all right,' said Paulie, heaving the soil out of the hole with a grunt.

'Aye, you might be, it's the Semtex I'm worried about.'

Paulie stopped digging. He stared at the soil underfoot, then up at Lynch. 'Semtex?' he said.

'Yeah,' said Lynch laconically. 'You know, the stuff that goes bang.'

Paulie looked at Davie. 'Yez didn't say anything about no Semtex,' he said.

'I didn't know,' said his brother. 'But it doesn't make any difference, does it?'

Paulie frowned. 'I guess not.' He tapped the ground gingerly with the end of his spade.

'You'll be okay, lads,' said Lynch, who didn't want to take the joke too far. He wanted to be out of the field as quickly as possible. 'I wouldn't be standing here if it was dangerous, now would I?'

Davie grinned and started digging again. Paulie followed his example, but he was still a lot less vigorous than before. Lynch watched. O'Riordan came up behind him, still cradling his Kalashnikov.

Davie's spade hit something plastic. Paulie flinched as if he'd been struck and Lynch smiled at the boy's discomfort. 'Pass me up the spades, lads,' he said. 'Then scrape away the soil with your hands.'

The boys did as they were told. They dug away with their hands like dogs in search of a bone. After several minutes of digging they came across a large rubbish bin, sealed in plastic. Lynch looked at O'Riordan. 'That's ammunition,' he said. 'Armour-piercing cartridges for the M60s.'

Lynch nodded. 'Okay, lads. Pass that here.'

The Quinn brothers heaved the bin up and Lynch and O'Riordan dragged it out of the hole.

The boys went back to digging. They unearthed two more large packages, long and thin and wrapped in thick polythene. 'The M60s,' said O'Riordan.

'Them too,' said Lynch.

Lynch and O'Riordan carried the three bulky parcels over to the truck and loaded them into the back while Davie and Paulie carried on digging. 'Any idea what McCormack is planning to do with this?' asked Lynch.

'Bury it somewhere else, I suppose,' said O'Riordan. 'He wants to keep the good stuff and hand the old stuff over to the army.'

Lynch wiped his hands on his jeans. 'So it looks as if we're demilitarising when all we're doing is throwing out our junk.'

'It's just public relations, Dermott, you know that. It makes Dublin and London look good, it's a photo opportunity for the army, and we get rid of gear that would probably blow up in our faces anyway. Seems like a hell of a good deal for everyone. The Prods are doing it, too.'

They went back to the hole. Davie and Paulie had uncovered two more plastic bins and a polythene-covered chest. O'Riordan pointed at the chest. 'That's the Semtex,' he said.

'How long's it been here?' asked Lynch.

'Three years,' replied O'Riordan. 'But it was moved around a lot before that and it's well past its sell-by date. It got here in 1985 but it was sitting in a warehouse in Tripoli for God knows how long before that. McCormack wants it leaving here.' He pointed at one of the plastic bins. 'Those are handguns and ammunition and a few hand grenades. They stay.' He pointed at the other bin. 'Those are Belgian disposable mortars. They're state-of-the-art, but McCormack wants them left here, too. They'll be a trophy for the army, and it makes it look as if we're serious about the ceasefire.'

O'Riordan peered into the hole. 'There should be one more package,' he said.

Davie got down on all fours and dug with his hands. After a few minutes he sat back on his heels. 'Got it,' he said triumphantly.

'Now that,' said O'Riordan, pointing at a polythene-wrapped parcel, 'is something really special. It's a 66mm M72 A2.'

Lynch sighed wearily. 'I love it when you talk dirty,' he said. 'What the hell is it, Pat?'

'A bazooka,' grinned O'Riordan. 'From the States. It's a one-man, single-shot throwaway, it's got a one kilo rocket that can blow a tank wide open.'

'Jesus,' said Lynch. 'How many of those have we got?'

'Just the one that I know about,' said O'Riordan. 'It was sent over as a sample shortly before the 1994 ceasefire. We were going to buy more but then the FBI got hold of our supplier.' O'Riordan leaned over the hole. 'Pass it up, Davie. And be careful.'

Davie handed the polythene-wrapped parcel up to O'Riordan, who cradled it tenderly in his arms.

Lynch held out his hand to Davie and pulled him out of the hole. They both helped Paulie out. 'Right, lads. Now fill it in.'

The brothers were exhausted but they set to with a will, shovelling the wet earth back into the hole. Lynch went back to the truck where O'Riordan was placing the bazooka with the rest of the arms cache. 'Can you handle it from here on?' Lynch asked.

O'Riordan raised an eyebrow. 'What's on your mind?' he asked.

'I want to go to Dublin to see your man. He gets off work at noon.'

'Yeah? Then what?' asked O'Riordan. He threw a tarpaulin over the weapons.

'Depends on what he tells me. If I can get a lead on that chopper, I want to go after Cramer.'

O'Riordan's eyes narrowed and he clicked his tongue. 'Remember what I said before. You'll need to clear it first.'

'I know.'

'How are you going to get to Dublin?'

Lynch grinned. 'I was hoping I could borrow the Landrover. You'll be in the truck, right?'

O'Riordan chuckled. 'You'll do anything to avoid work, won't you?'

'Come on, Pat, it's all downhill from now on. The hard work's over. It's not like it was in the old days – the border's no barrier at all any more. You can do it with your eyes closed. And the Quinn boys can do all the carrying for you.'

O'Riordan climbed down out of the back of the truck. 'Aye, go on then, you soft bastard.'

As Lynch was driving off in the Landrover, he saw Davie and Paulie shovel the last of the earth into the hole. Paulie threw down his spade and showed his palms to his elder brother, obviously complaining about his blisters.

The tailor arrived just as Cramer and the Colonel were finishing their breakfast, bustling into the room as if he was behind schedule. 'Good morning, good morning,' he said. He was carrying two large Samsonite suitcases and he grunted as he swung them onto the far end of the table which the two men were using.

'*Voilà!*' he said, opening the cases with a flourish.

'*Voilà?*' repeated Cramer, amused by the portly man's enthusiasm.

The tailor paid him no attention and began dropping brown paper parcels onto the table. 'Shirts, white, double cuffs. Shirts, polo. Underwear, boxers, a variety of colours. Socks, black. Ties, a selection, all silk of course.'

'Of course,' repeated Cramer.

'Slacks, brown. Slacks, khaki. Slacks grey.' He held up a paper bag like a conjurer producing a rabbit from his top hat. 'Accessories. Belts, cufflinks, I took the liberty of including a selection of tie pins.' The tailor looked at the Colonel. 'I would prefer to make some adjustments to the suits and the overcoat if we have time,' he said. 'I could have them back here tomorrow morning. It's not essential but . . .' He gave a small shrug.

The Colonel nodded. 'Tomorrow will be fine.'

'Excellent, excellent,' said the tailor. He produced a suit and held it out to Cramer.

Cramer nodded. 'Looks great,' he said.

The tailor tut-tutted impatiently. 'Try it on, please,' he said.

Cramer did as he was told, then stood stock still as the tailor fussed around him, making deft marks on the material with a piece of chalk and scribbling into his notebook. Cramer tried on the three suits, then the cashmere overcoat, and the tailor spirited them back into the cases.

'So, I'll see you at the same time tomorrow,' the tailor said to the Colonel. He disappeared out of the dining hall as quickly as he'd appeared.

'Does he do your suits?' Cramer asked the Colonel.

'I couldn't afford his prices,' said the Colonel with a tight smile.

Cramer refilled his tea from a large earthenware pot. Mrs Elliott brewed her tea in the army style, piping hot and strong, and for all he knew, with a dollop of bromide thrown in for good measure. 'This guy I'm standing in for,' he said. 'When do I find out about him? I don't even know who he is.'

'One step at a time, Joker. First I want you to know what you're up against.'

'I think I've got a good idea.'

'That's as maybe, but I'd like you to read through all the files before we move on to the next stage. And there are a few more tests.'

'Medical?'

'No. I'm bringing in an instructor from Training Wing.'

'Anyone I know?'

The Colonel smiled thinly. 'I doubt it,' he said. 'You've been away a long time.'

Seth Reed brought the car to a halt by a gap in the hedgerow. He turned around and nodded at his son. 'There you are,' he said.

'A field?' said Mark, his face screwed up in disgust.

'Beggars can't be choosers,' said Reed. 'Would you rather wait until we get to Dundalk?'

'I can't wait,' said Mark, reaching for the door handle.

'Watch out for the rats,' warned Reed.

Mark's hand froze in mid-air. 'Rats?'

'As big as cats. Mrs Mcgregor told us about them.'

Mark looked at his mother.

'Your father's joking,' said Kimberlee. 'It's his sick sense of humour.'

Mark opened the car door and looked at the thick grass running along the hedgerow.

'Go on, kiddo. I was joking.'

'You're sure?' asked Mark, still not convinced.

'Cross my heart.'

Mark slid out of the car and walked gingerly over the damp grass, through the gap in the hedge and into the field. 'Shouldn't you go with him?' asked Kimberlee.

'What? With rats as big as cats out there?'

'I just thought . . .'

'Honey, this is Ireland. We're in the middle of nowhere. He's hardly likely to get mugged in a field, is he?'

Kimberlee pouted. Reed gave it a five full seconds before opening the door and following his son. He knew from experience that the pout was only the first weapon in his wife's impressive armoury. It was always less painful to concede early on. 'Thanks, honey,' she called after him.

Davie Quinn crashed the truck into gear and bumped along the rutted track. Pat O'Riordan put a hand onto the dashboard to steady himself. 'Easy, Davie,' he said. 'Take it slowly. We're in no rush. Remember what we've got in the back.'

'Okay. Sorry.' Davie's face reddened.

'Just be grateful we don't have the Semtex on board,' said O'Riordan. He chuckled. 'You okay back there, Paulie?' he called.

Paulie Quinn was in the back, making sure that the weapons didn't shift around too much. 'Yeah. No problem.'

Davie guided the truck off the track and onto the narrow road that ran between the fields. O'Riordan looked at his watch. 'Are we late?' asked Davie, clearly anxious.

O'Riordan smiled at the boy's enthusiasm. He was so eager to please that it was almost painful. 'A bit, but nothing to worry about.' O'Riordan wasn't worried in the least about crossing the border into the South. Since the ceasefire all the roads linking the Republic with Northern Ireland had been reopened and the border posts dismantled. There were no longer any soldiers checking vehicles and it was now as easy to drive across the border as it was to drive from London to Manchester.

'What happens to the stuff we left behind?' asked Davie.

'It'll be called in after a few days. Give the weather a chance to obliterate the evidence. The organisation is preparing to hand over more than a dozen arms stockpiles to the authorities as a sign of good faith.'

'But we hold on to the good stuff, right?'

O'Riordan winked. 'You got it.'

Seth Reed stood by the hedgerow as he waited for his son to finish going to the toilet. The South Armagh scenery was breathtaking: rolling hills, the forty-shades of green his travel agent had promised, even the cloying mist had an ethereal quality that softened the colours and gave the view the feel of a hastily-painted watercolour. It was hard to believe that until recently the area had been one of the most dangerous in the world, where British troops had to be ferried about in helicopters because they faced death and injury if they dared to venture on foot.

When his wife had first suggested they spend their vacation touring Ireland he'd been reluctant. Her family originally came from the Republic and she was keen to go back to her roots and to get a feel for the country her ancestors had left almost a century earlier, but Reed believed that it was still too early, that the peace had yet to prove that it was a lasting one. She'd pouted, and had talked the travel agent into calling him direct. The travel agent had been persuasive, he'd even joked that the Reeds would be safer in Ireland than virtually anywhere in the States, and that the biggest danger they'd face would be hangovers from the Guinness. Between them, Kimberlee and the travel agent had talked Reed into it, and after a week in the country Reed was glad that they'd come: there were relatively few tourists around, the roads were a joy to drive on, and the people were unfailingly friendly and welcoming. When he got back to the States, he was definitely going to recommend the Emerald Isle to his friends. A few spots of rain splattered on his jacket and when he looked up more fell on his face. 'Come on, Mark,' he called. 'It's raining.'

Mark appeared from behind a bush, wiping his hands on his knees.

'Okay?' said Reed.

'Sure,' said Mark. They went back to the car together. 'Can I sit in the front, Dad?'

'Ask your Mom.'

Kimberlee agreed. She climbed out of the car and got into the back while Reed started the engine. The only thing he'd disliked about the trip so far was the choice of rental car which the travel agent had booked. It was a four door but it wasn't an automatic and it had none of the extras that Americans take for granted, such as airbags and air-conditioning.

Mark climbed into the seat vacated by his mother. Reed tried to get the windscreen wipers going but he pushed the wrong control lever and his turn indicator went on instead. He switched the turn indicator off and fumbled with the windscreen wiper lever as he accelerated. 'Seatbelt, honey,' chided Kimberlee behind him. 'That goes for you too, Mark.'

Reed gripped the steering wheel with his right hand as he groped for the seatbelt buckle. The rain got suddenly heavier, obscuring his vision. He'd only put the windscreen wipers on intermittent, he realised.

'Honey, you're on the wrong side of the road,' said Kimberlee.

Reed cursed himself under his breath. He was always forgetting that the Irish, like the Brits, insisted on driving on the left. He let go of the seatbelt buckle and reached for the windscreen wiper controls as he twisted the steering wheel to the right. The wipers came on, sweeping the water off the windscreen. It was only then that he saw the truck heading right for them. In the back, Kimberlee screamed.

O'Riordan didn't see the white car until they were almost upon it, careering across the road as if the driver had lost control. Davie Quinn banged on the horn and slammed on his brakes, but O'Riordan felt the big truck start to slide on the wet tarmac. He grabbed for the steering wheel.

'It's okay, I've got it, I've got it!' Davie shouted.

Despite Davie's protests, O'Riordan could see that the truck was heading for the car. He pulled harder on the wheel, trying to get the truck over to the left, out of the car's way. The road was narrow; there was barely enough space for the two vehicles even if they'd been driving perfectly straight. With the car in the middle of the road, a collision was inevitable.

O'Riordan saw the driver, a middle-aged man with greying hair, wrestling with his steering wheel. He glimpsed a child in the front passenger seat, his mouth open in terror. Then there was a dull crump and the car spun away to the right, the windscreen shattered.

Davie was shouting but O'Riordan couldn't make out what he was saying as the offside wheels of the truck left the tarmac. Wet branches slapped across the windscreen and the truck tilted sharply to the left. The truck was half off the road and the tyres on the grass verge gripped harder than those on the wet tarmac, so the more Davie braked, the more the truck veered to the left. The steering wheel twisted out of Davie's hands. O'Riordan felt his seatbelt dig into his chest and the truck bucked and reared and slammed through the hedge. O'Riordan pitched forward, his knees thumping into the dashboard, his arms flailing with the impact. Suddenly everything went still.

O'Riordan shook his head. The seatbelt was tight up against his neck making it hard to breathe, and he felt around for the buckle. He found it and unclipped the belt, gasping for air as the nylon strap went slack. He rubbed his throat and looked across at Davie, who was hunched forward over the steering wheel. O'Riordan shook him by the shoulder. 'Davie?' he said.

Davie turned slowly. His eyes were glassy and O'Riordan realised he was in shock, but other than that he appeared to be unharmed. O'Riordan twisted around in his seat. 'Paulie?' he shouted. 'You okay?'

'Yeah, I think so,' said Paulie from the back of the truck. 'What happened?'

O'Riordan couldn't help but grin at the banality of the question. He tried to open the door but it was jammed. 'Davie, we're going to have to get out your side,' he said.

There was a hiss of escaping steam and a series of clicks from the engine as if it hadn't quite died. Davie fumbled with the handle and pushed the door open. The truck was leaning at a forty-five degree angle and they had to drop down from the open door onto the ground. Paulie was on his hands and knees, dragging himself out of the back of the truck. Davie went to help his brother as O'Riordan surveyed the damage. The offside wheels of the truck were in a ditch and it was resting on a hedge. The front axle was broken, a shattered tree branch had speared one of the tyres and the front of the vehicle was a twisted mess. The truck wasn't going anywhere, even if they could find some way of getting it back onto the road.

Davie helped Paulie to his feet. The truck made a groaning noise like a dying elephant and lurched further to the left, its offside wheels sinking deeper into the ditch. O'Riordan rubbed his chin, wondering what the hell they were going to do.

The car they'd hit had slewed across the road and was resting nose down in the ditch on the far side of the road. Its boot had sprung open and O'Riordan could see it was filled with suitcases. On the ground next to the car lay a small bundle of clothes, but as O'Riordan looked at it closely he realised it was a child. A boy. He went over to see if there was anything that could be done but before he even got close he could see from the blood and the angle of the boy's neck that he was dead. He'd obviously been thrown through the windscreen on impact.

Davie came up behind O'Riordan. 'Pat, what are we going . . . ?' His voice tailed off as he saw the body. 'Oh Jesus,' he said. 'Is he . . . ?'

'Yeah,' said O'Riordan. 'Go back to the truck. Keep an eye out for other vehicles.' O'Riordan stepped around the body of the boy and peered into the car. The driver was sprawled halfway through the shattered windscreen, his throat ripped open and his lower jaw a bloody pulp. The rain washed his blood across the bonnet, a red streak on the white metal. There was a woman in the back seat, unconscious but still held in place by her seatbelt. O'Riordan wiped his forehead with his sleeve. He shaded his eyes with the flat of his hand and peered into the car. She didn't seem to be bleeding. She was probably the wife of the dead man, mother of the dead child. Tourists, by the look of the suitcases. 'Christ, what a mess,' O'Riordan muttered to himself.

He went back to the Quinn brothers. O'Riordan knew he had to make a decision, and quickly. The area they were in wasn't highly populated, but it was only a matter of time before another vehicle came along. They could wait and hope that a van or a truck appeared which they could then commandeer and use to take away the consignment, but if the police turned up they'd be in deep trouble. If only

Lynch hadn't taken the Landrover. The Quinn brothers watched him nervously, waiting for him to make up his mind. Paulie was staring wide-eyed at the body of the boy on the ground. Davie had a hand on Paulie's shoulder as if restraining him. The rain was coming down heavier now, the drops pitter-pattering on the roof of the truck. At least the bad weather meant they were unlikely to be spotted by a passing helicopter. O'Riordan stood with his hands on his hips and stared at the disabled truck. They could carry the arms, but not far. If they buried them in a nearby field, the police would be sure to find them.

O'Riordan turned to look at the Quinn brothers. 'On your way, lads,' he said. 'Cut across the fields, keep out of sight. Get as far away from here as you can. Give it a couple of hours, then hitch. Okay?'

Davie nodded but Paulie continued to stare at the small body. 'Paulie, there's nothing we can do,' said O'Riordan. 'It was an accident.'

'He's okay,' said Davie. 'I'll look after him.' He pulled his brother to a five-bar gate and helped him over. They disappeared into the rain.

O'Riordan climbed into the back of the truck and ripped the polythene from the disposable bazooka. He was one of half a dozen volunteers who'd attended a training course on the operation of the M72. A former Green Beret had flown over from the States to demonstrate the firing of the weapon, using a replica.

O'Riordan walked down the road until he was some fifty metres from the truck, then dropped down into the ditch. He pulled open the telescopic launcher-tube and flipped up the front and rear sights. The M72 was surprisingly light, weighing just about three pounds. He armed it and put it to his shoulder, gripping the weapon tightly in anticipation of the recoil.

'Jesus, what a waste,' he whispered. He fired, and immediately there was a deafening whooshing sound as the tube jerked in his hands. The missile shot towards the truck, leaving a white smoky trail behind it. It hit the truck just behind the driver's cab and exploded in a ball of yellow flame. O'Riordan ducked his head as bits of debris flew by him. There were hundreds of smaller bangs as the ammunition exploded. O'Riordan kept down low into the ditch until the explosions subsided. A piece of metal smacked into his shoulder but not hard enough to do any damage. It lay in the sodden grass close to his foot. It wasn't a bullet, it looked like a piece of the truck chassis.

When he looked up again the truck was burning with thick plumes of smoke spiralling up into the leaden sky. O'Riordan went as close as he could and threw the mortar tube onto the fire. The truck was burning fiercely despite the rain and O'Riordan doubted that there'd be much of it left by the time it burned out. He ran to the gate, vaulted over it, and jogged across the recently ploughed field.

Dermott Lynch was halfway through a pint of Guinness in a pub in the Temple Bar district of Dublin when he saw the news flash. The barman turned up the volume on the television set fixed to the wall by the entrance to the Gents toilet and stood watching it, his arms folded across his chest. The RTE1 announcer was reading from a sheet of paper. A man and a child killed. A woman in hospital. At first Lynch thought it was a road traffic accident, but then the picture cut away to footage of the burnt-out wreckage of the truck half-lying in a ditch.

Lynch put down his Guinness. A cold prickling feeling ran down to the base of his spine. What the hell had gone wrong? The newsreader said that the truck was believed to have contained arms and ammunition. The police were looking for the driver of the truck, but there were as yet no witnesses to the accident. Lynch frowned. If the truck had been destroyed in the accident, what had happened to Pat and the Quinn boys?

Lynch considered the consequences of the deaths. The IRA Army Council would mount an investigation and demand to know what had gone wrong. He'd have to explain why he'd left O'Riordan and the Quinn brothers, and while he didn't think that he'd made a mistake by doing so, he doubted that McCormack would see it that way. The police would pull out all the stops to find out what had happened, and there'd be political ramifications, too. The Protestant paramilitaries wouldn't hesitate to claim that the incident was a breach of the ceasefire. Lynch knew that he'd have to call McCormack, but he wanted to talk to the air traffic controller first. McCormack would demand an immediate meeting, Lynch was sure of that. And he'd insist that Lynch lie low, maybe even stay in Dublin until it had all blown over.

The newsreader was replaced by an American soap opera and the barman turned down the volume. Lynch stared at the screen with unseeing eyes. He wondered where Pat was, and if he was okay. He must have got away with the Quinn boys, but that didn't explain the state of the truck.

Maybe he'd set fire to the truck to destroy the evidence. That at least made sense. Lynch shook his head to clear his thoughts. There was no use crying over spilt milk. He sipped his Guinness and wiped the creamy froth from his beard with the back of his hand.

Lynch had a copy of the *Daily Telegraph* on the table in front of him, not because he was a regular reader of the British newspaper but because it would act as a clear signal to the man he was there to see. A stooped figure entered the smoky gloom of the pub and looked left and right. Lynch knew even before they made eye contact that it was the man he was there to meet. His name was Luke McDonough. He'd never been a member of the IRA but he was sympathetic to the Cause, and while he would never take an active role in any terrorist operation he was happy enough to supply information.

McDonough came over to Lynch's table and looked down at the newspaper. Lynch stood up and shook the man's hand. McDonough's skin was pale and pasty as if he didn't get out in the sun much, and his fingernails were bitten to the quick. Lynch wondered if it was as a result of the man's high-pressure job or if he was just the nervous type. He asked what McDonough wanted to drink. 'Orange juice,' he said, almost apologetically and sat down while Lynch went to buy it. When Lynch came back to the table, McDonough was flicking through the paper. He put it down and took his drink, toasting Lynch before drinking. 'I'm working the early shift tomorrow,' he said, by way of explanation.

'Yeah, I bet you need a clear head in your job, right enough,' agreed Lynch sympathetically.

'Tell me about it,' said McDonough. He put down his

drink, steepled his fingers under his chin and looked at Lynch as if he was studying a radar screen. There were deep crow's feet either side of his pale grey eyes, as if he spent a lot of time squinting. 'Your man asked me about a helicopter flying in and out of Howth a few days back. A Sea King, he said.'

Lynch nodded. 'Yeah. It came around Ireland's Eye, picked up two men, and flew off to the east. Did you see it on your screens?'

'Not personally, no. I was working ground control. But I've checked our records and we were in contact with it. Hardly surprising, Dublin radar goes down to about thirty feet above sea level all around there. He couldn't have got within twenty miles of Howth without being spotted.'

'Where did it come from?'

McDonough began to bite at the flesh at the corner of a fingernail, gnawing away like a gerbil. His teeth were yellow and ratlike, and he glanced furtively around as if he feared being chastised for the habit. 'No way of telling,' he said. 'They hadn't filed a flight plan. They came in on a heading of 280 degrees but that doesn't mean anything.' McDonough stopped biting his nails. 'Your man said the Sea King was red, white and blue. Red tail, white body, blue on the bottom?'

'That's right,' said Lynch.

McDonough's eyes sparkled. He folded his hands together and put them under the table as if hiding them. 'I reckon it could have been one of the Westlands operated by the Ministry of Defence Procurement Executive.'

'Not the army?'

McDonough shook his head. 'Nah, they use them for radar trials and experimental work. It's a mystery what it was doing in Howth, it shouldn't even be in Irish airspace.'

'Okay, so let's assume it was an MoD chopper,' said Lynch. 'Where could it have gone?'

'They certainly didn't land at Dublin, and whichever way they went they must have given the airport a wide berth. I checked with Belfast and they've no record of a Sea King landing there at the time you're talking about. They're were plenty of army Lynxes and Pumas around and a couple of Chinooks, but no Sea Kings.'

'But they could have landed anywhere else, away from the airports?'

'Oh sure. A field, even on a ship at sea. From the sound of it, I'd say they went to the mainland.'

'Yeah? Why?' Lynch sat forward, suddenly interested.

'Why else would they use a Sea King? It's got a huge range, more than 750 miles with a standard fuel load. And if it was a Procurement Executive chopper, it could have easily been fitted with extra tanks. It could have gone all the way to London. A Lynx's range would be less than 400 miles, and they're a hell of a lot more common in Ireland than Sea Kings. Even the Westland Wessex that 72 Squadron uses in the north can only fly about 350 miles on standard tanks, maybe 500 with auxiliary fuel. No, if they went to the trouble of using a Sea King, there must have been a reason, and the range is the only thing I can think of. If they were staying in Ireland or landing at sea, they'd have used a Lynx or a Wessex for sure.'

Lynch nodded excitedly. 'Okay, so if we assume it crossed the Irish Sea, how do I find out where it landed?'

'You'd need to speak to someone like me over in the UK. Wales first. That's where the pilot would have checked in.

But I don't know anyone over there, not anyone Irish, anyway. But I could have a go myself.'

'How long will it take?' Lynch asked.

'Depends,' said McDonough. He ran his finger around the rim of his glass, then licked it. 'There are plenty of reasons why Dublin ATC might request information on a flight to the mainland. If I meet any sort of resistance I'll back off immediately, but I don't think there'll be a problem. I didn't want to try without checking with you first.'

'Good man,' said Lynch. 'I'll call you tomorrow to see how you got on.' He drained his glass and stood up. He shook McDonough's hand firmly. 'Keep the paper, it's a bit right-wing for my taste.' Lynch left the pub and walked through Temple Bar looking for a call box. A teenager in blue denim dungarees was playing a saxophone, bent almost double at the waist as he put his heart and soul into it, the mournful notes echoing off the narrow alley where he was standing with his case open at his feet. Lynch dropped a couple of coins into the case as he went by but the guy had his eyes closed and showed no reaction. It seemed that every second building in Temple Bar was being renovated by entrepreneurs attracted by the city council's tax breaks. Until recently the area, to the south of the River Liffey, had been the rundown haunt of drug addicts, muggers and prostitutes, but it was gradually being turned into an entertainment centre along the lines of London's Covent Garden with restaurants, bars and speciality shops. He found a call box and McCormack answered on the third ring. 'Thomas? It's me.' Lynch was as reluctant to use names on an open line south of the border as he was in Belfast.

'Where the fuck have you been?'

Lynch frowned. It wasn't like McCormack to use profanity, even under stress. 'I'm here. In Dublin.'

'You've heard what happened?'

'Yeah.'

'We need to meet. Now.'

'Yeah. I know.'

'Where are you?'

'Temple Bar.'

'I'll pick you up in thirty minutes. College Green, in front of the Bank of Ireland.'

'I'll be there.' The line clicked in his ear. Lynch tapped the receiver against the side of his head. McCormack was unhappy. Very unhappy.

The Colonel settled back in his chair and put his stick on the desk. Cramer stood at the French windows, looking out over the lawn towards the main gate where two men in jeans and sports jackets were standing, their backs to the building. Cramer had seen at least twelve different guards over the past few days, all of them members of 22 SAS. It was ironic, when he'd most need protection, when he was out in the real world taking the target's place, he'd be more or less on his own. A Judas Goat. Bait. Waiting for the assassin to strike.

The Colonel's voice jarred him out of his reverie. 'You've read all the files in detail?'

Cramer turned to face him. 'Yes. All of them.'

'So you know what you'll be up against? He's never failed. Never been caught. Never pulls his gun until he's up close. What do you think your chances are, Joker?'

Cramer tilted his head to the side. 'Long term, nil.'

The Colonel cleared his throat as if something there was irritating him. 'I meant your chances of taking him out.'

Cramer shrugged. He was wearing a denim shirt and black Levi jeans. The suits, even though they were made-to-measure, always felt confining and he took every opportunity to change out of them. 'If I can get him in my sights I think I've a good chance.' He folded his arms across his chest. 'The problem is, I can't pull the gun out until I'm sure it's him. And I won't be sure until he's pointing his gun at me.'

The Colonel studied Cramer with unblinking brown eyes. 'And how do you feel about that?'

'Come on, Colonel, we both know why I'm doing this. Who shoots who first doesn't really matter, does it?'

'I'm not sending you on a suicide mission, Joker.'

Cramer returned the Colonel's stare. 'Aren't you?'

The two men looked at each other in silence. It was the Colonel who spoke first. 'And you're still prepared to go ahead?'

'That's why I'm here.'

The Colonel tapped his fingers on the desk. 'The next stage is to take photographs of you, and those will be sent to the FBI in Miami along with details of the target's movements. From there they'll be forwarded to Zurich. Once the contract is placed with Zurich, there's no going back. You understand that, Joker? The way this killer works, there's no further contact once the contract has been placed.'

'Just do what you have to, Colonel.'

The Colonel nodded slowly. 'I will.'

'So when do I leave here?' Cramer sat down and crossed his legs at the ankles.

'We've still got some work to do,' said the Colonel.

'You haven't yet explained what it is that I'll be doing. And what's happening to the guy I'm replacing?'

'I wanted to be sure that you were committed to the operation, first.' The Colonel picked up a thin blue file and passed it across the desk. 'This is the target. Andrew Vander Mayer. A multi-millionaire, self-made.'

Cramer opened the file. There were only two sheets of paper inside. 'This is it?'

'That's it. There's very little about Vander Mayer in the public domain. And there are no photographs. That's in our favour. No matter how much research the assassin does, he won't get more than you have there.'

'And who is it who wants him dead?'

'A former business partner, a lawyer by the name of Frank Discenza.'

Cramer frowned. 'Italian? Why didn't he get the Mafia to do the hit?'

The Colonel smiled. 'Not all Italians are connected to the Mafia, Joker. And the Mafia can be a double-edged sword. If they do something for you, eventually they'll come looking for the favour to be repaid. Our man works only for cash.'

'And how did you know this Discenza was planning to have Vander Mayer hit?'

'The IRS and the FBI mounted a joint surveillance operation on Discenza earlier this year and they picked up the Zurich connection on one of their phone taps. Discenza was being circumspect, but one of the FBI agents heard enough to realise what was going on.'

'Who was Discenza calling?'

'A banker in Zurich. A very small bank, private clients only, just a brass plate on a wall and a couple of telephones. The banker's just a middle man, a conduit. The client contacts the banker, the banker lodges the fee and passes on the details. It's a damn near perfect system.'

'And Discenza is cooperating?'

'He's got no choice. The FBI have him for conspiracy to commit murder, the IRS have him for major tax evasion. He was facing a long jail sentence on both counts, so yes, he's cooperating.'

Cramer frowned. 'But what exactly am I supposed to do?'

'You live Vander Mayer's life. You visit his homes, you travel in his personal jet.'

Cramer shook his head. 'Live his life? How will I know what to do? Where to go?'

'You'll have help. He has a personal assistant who travels everywhere with him and she'll be with you every step of the way. Vander Mayer will be on his yacht, he'll effectively run his business from there, but he'll act as if he's where you are. If you're in his London flat, he'll say he's calling from London, and so on.'

Cramer studied the sheets. 'An arms dealer? He's an arms dealer?'

'More of a middle man than an actual dealer. You don't go to Andrew Vander Mayer if you want to buy a couple of dozen Kalashnikovs. But if you want to equip your air force with the latest air-to-air missiles and your country is on the UN blacklist, then he's your man.'

'I don't know anything about arms dealing.'

'You don't have to,' said the Colonel. 'You won't be in

on any business meetings, Vander Mayer will handle it all from his yacht. His assistant will deal with any small things that crop up.'

The second sheet in the file contained a list of dates and places. 'This is my itinerary?' asked Cramer. The Colonel nodded. 'I'm getting around. London. New York. Hong Kong. Paris. St Petersburg.'

'That's the sort of life that Vander Mayer lives.'

Cramer looked up from the itinerary. 'This is for the next two weeks.'

'We don't know how long it'll be before the killer makes his move. Hopefully it'll be sooner rather than later.'

'Hopefully,' Cramer repeated quietly. His right hand moved towards his stomach as if it had a mind of its own and Cramer stopped it. He scratched his ear instead. The fact that the cancer was gradually eating him away was never far from his thoughts, even when the pain had retreated to little more than a dull ache. Four weeks. It was a long time when you were waiting to die.

'You're all right with that?' asked the Colonel.

'Fine.'

The Colonel opened a drawer and took out a blue American passport. He held it out. 'You'll be needing this when you leave the country.'

Cramer took the passport. It was his photograph, but the name inside was Andrew Vander Mayer.

'It's genuine, you won't have any problems with it,' said the Colonel. 'We've got the full cooperation of the US State Department.' He tossed over three more passports of various colours: one was a European-style British passport, another was Uruguayan, a third was Israeli. Cramer frowned. 'He's Jewish?'

The Colonel shook his head. 'No, but he's done a lot of business with Israel. Done a lot of favours for them, too.'

Cramer flicked through the passports. They all contained his photograph but Vander Mayer's details.

'He travels with whatever passport is most convenient. His assistant will take care of all your travel arrangements, just as she does for him. She'll tell you which one to use.'

Cramer nodded and put the passports back on the desk. 'This girl. The assistant. How much does she know?'

'She's knows that Vander Mayer has been threatened, and she knows that you'll be taking his place for a while.'

'Does she know that she's at risk, too?'

'There's no indication that she's in danger. The killer goes for the bodyguards and the target.'

'He hit the security guard in Harrods.'

'But no innocent bystanders. He's very selective.'

'I hope for her sake you're right. When do I meet her?'

'Tomorrow. She's flying in from the States.'

'And Vander Mayer?'

'It's best you don't know where he is.'

Cramer looked at the two printed sheets in the file, nodding slowly. 'So the killer comes looking for Vander Mayer and he finds me. And how will you catch him? Assuming he gets by whatever bodyguards you give me, and assuming he manages to take me out, what then?'

'I'll have other men shadowing you at all times. He won't get away, I promise you that.'

Cramer closed the file. 'He's got away before.'

'We weren't on the case then.'

'But if your men are too close, they'll scare him off.'

'They won't be too close,' the Colonel said emphatically.

Cramer slid the file onto the desk. 'You're going to use snipers, aren't you? You've no intention of trying to bring him in. You're just going to blow him away.'

The Colonel raised an eyebrow. 'There will be occasions when there will be snipers in the vicinity, yes. But you're not going to be out in the open that often and a sniper isn't going to offer you any protection when you're indoors. When you're inside, I'll have men close by, but they are not going to be able to defend you from an attack. If they're close enough for that, they'll be close enough to be seen. They're there to apprehend the killer, not to stop the attempt. Am I clear on that?'

'As crystal, Colonel. I'm right, aren't I? You don't intend to apprehend him, do you? This isn't about bringing him in, it's about taking him out, right?'

The Colonel exhaled through his nose, his lips set in a tight line as he studied Cramer. 'Is that a problem for you?'

Cramer shook his head. 'Whatever it takes, Colonel. Whatever it takes.'

'Good man.' The Colonel opened a drawer and took out another file, this one consisting of more than a hundred A4 sheets in a clear plastic binder. 'I've been wondering whether or not to show you this. It's the report we received from the profiler, Bernard Jackman.'

'The FBI expert you were talking about?'

'Former FBI expert,' the Colonel corrected.

'I thought you said that I was going to meet him.'

'You are. He's expected tomorrow or the day after. But he gave me this report. It's his profile of the man we're looking for.' The Colonel tapped the file with his thick, stubby fingers. 'The problem is, if we focus on his profile and it turns out Jackman's wrong, you might be blinded to the real killer.'

Cramer nodded. 'Okay, but at least it might give me some clues as to who we're looking for.'

The Colonel tossed the clear plastic file across the desk and it landed on top of the Vander Mayer file. 'Just bear in mind that it's not an exact science. There have been several cases where profilers have got it wrong. Sometimes with disastrous consequences. Read it with care.'

Cramer picked up the two files. A sudden pain lanced through his stomach and he grunted. A wave of nausea rippled through his guts and he took a deep breath as he tried to quell it.

'Are you okay?' asked the Colonel, clearly concerned.

Cramer forced a smile. 'I will be,' he said.

A gentle drizzle was floating down from the leaden sky when McCormack arrived in front of the Bank of Ireland in a black convertible BMW. It was the first time Lynch had seen McCormack's car and it caught him by surprise. McCormack had to sound his horn twice before Lynch realised it was him. Lynch had expected him to be at the wheel of an estate car or a comfortable saloon, not a high-powered sports car.

Lynch climbed into the front seat. McCormack made no move to shake hands, but Lynch couldn't tell if it was because the man was angry or because he was simply keen to get moving. The traffic was heavy and McCormack put the car in gear and moved away from the kerb, edging cautiously in front of a bus. Lynch looked at the soft top of the car and wondered what on earth had persuaded McCormack to buy a convertible. Irish summers were notoriously brief and it rained more often than not.

'My car's in the garage,' said McCormack as if reading his mind. 'This is the wife's.' The windscreen wipers swished back and forth, whispering like assassins.

'Nice car, right enough,' said Lynch. He ran a finger along the roof and wondered what Mrs McCormack was like. McCormack drove with great care, constantly looking in his mirror and twisting around to check his blind spots. He indicated religiously, rarely got the car out of second gear, and left such a big space between the BMW and the car in front that he was constantly being overtaken. Lynch didn't know if McCormack always drove so cautiously or if it was simply because he was at the wheel of his wife's car.

McCormack waited until they were driving through Phoenix Park before speaking. 'So what went wrong?' he asked.

Lynch shrugged and looked out of the side window. In the distance was the stark towering cross which marked the spot where Pope John Paul II had addressed hundreds of thousands of Catholics on his visit to the country in 1979. 'Fucked if I know, Thomas. Have you spoken to Pat?'

McCormack shook his head. 'No. And there's no sign of the Quinn boys either. It's a mess, Dermott.'

'I only know what I saw on the TV. It must have been an accident.'

'An accident?' said McCormack sharply. 'It's a bloody disaster.' They drove by the imposing residence of the American Ambassador. 'This is going to cause all sorts of problems in the States,' he said.

'Yeah,' agreed Lynch. 'Tourists, the TV said.'

'A nine-year-old boy,' said McCormack. 'We killed a nine-year-old boy.' Lynch had to admire the way McCormack said 'we', as if he was including himself in the fiasco rather than distancing himself from it. 'Why did you come to Dublin, Dermott?' McCormack asked.

'I had to see somebody.'

'Do you mind telling me who?' The question was put smoothly, but Lynch knew that he was being interrogated by an expert and that there was no point in lying.

'A guy who works at Dublin Airport. Luke McDonough. Pat gave me his name.'

'And why would you be wanting to talk to this McDonough?' McCormack peered through the windscreen, then indicated and turned left and drove by a small lake, holding the steering wheel as if it was made of porcelain.

'He works for air traffic control,' said Lynch. 'I was trying to find out what happened to the helicopter that picked up Cramer.'

McCormack's lips pressed together so tightly that they almost disappeared. Lynch shivered as if the temperature in the car had dropped ten degrees. 'I thought I'd made my view plain on that matter,' McCormack said eventually.

'I just wanted to find out where the helicopter went.'

'And then?'

'Then I was going to tell you I knew where Cramer was, and ask your permission to go after him.' McCormack looked sideways at Lynch, peering over the top of his horn-rimmed spectacles like a concerned uncle. The appearance was deceptive, Lynch knew. There was nothing avuncular about Thomas McCormack.

'And because you wanted to drive down to Dublin, O'Riordan only had the one vehicle? The truck?'

'I suppose so. Yes.'

McCormack put the car into third gear for only the second time since Lynch had climbed into the BMW. Lynch licked his lips. He said nothing. There was nothing he could say. 'So, because you decided to ignore what I said about chasing Cramer, we lost a stock of high grade munitions, two innocent bystanders have died, we're set to lose God alone knows how much money from the States, and the media north and south of the border is going to be baying for our blood. Is that a fair summary of the situation, would you say?'

McCormack's words were cold and emotionless as if he was detailing a shopping list. Lynch wasn't sure whether or not he should apologise. He knew that an apology wouldn't count for anything. 'The fault was mine,' Lynch said quietly. 'I'll take the responsibility. I asked Pat to finish off while I drove to Dublin. He wasn't happy about it.'

'At least one of you was being professional,' said McCormack, shifting down to second gear again and braking gently. The BMW was doing just under 25mph. 'The Army Council is meeting tonight, Dermott. I'll do what I can.'

'What do you think will happen?'

'If you're lucky, a verbal warning. A smack across the knuckles. You're a good volunteer, you've done more than your share. Everyone's allowed one mistake.' McCormack increased the speed of the windscreen wipers, even though the rain seemed to be slacking off. 'I'm going to have to play down your reason for coming to Dublin, though. We wouldn't want everyone to know that you were disobeying orders, would we?'

'Thanks, Thomas. I appreciate it.' Lynch quietly tapped his fingers on the dashboard as McCormack put on his indicator and pulled into the side of the road. They were back in front of the Corinthian pillars and Ionic porticos of the Bank of Ireland.

'Take care back in Belfast, Dermott,' said McCormack. 'And forget Cramer, okay?'

Lynch opened the door and climbed out into the drizzle. 'Sure, Thomas. And thanks again.' He closed the door and watched the BMW pull slowly out into the traffic, its indicator light winking. Lynch put the collar of his jacket up, hunched his shoulders, and headed towards his car. There was no way he'd be able to forget Cramer. Not until he was dead and buried and Lynch had danced on his grave.

The boy tossed and turned in his single bed, unable to sleep. He pushed back the covers and sat up. He pressed his ear against the wall, screwing up his face as he listened. His mother was crying, crying like she used to when she'd watched a sad film. Suddenly she started to scream. Screams of pain. Screams of anguish. The boy bit down on his lower lip, hard enough to draw blood. He could hear his father trying to comfort her but she was shouting at him; telling him that she'd had enough, that she wanted to die. The boy dropped down onto his bed and buried his head under the pillow, trying to shut out the screams. Despite the pillow, he could still hear her.

He began to hum to himself, using his own voice to drown out the sounds of her suffering.

Cramer walked along the corridor to the gymnasium, his footsteps echoing off the green-tiled walls. Every dozen steps he passed a green-painted steel radiator, cold and unused now that the school was empty. The Colonel had explained that the institution had fallen victim to the recession and a growing reluctance among parents to send their children away to boarding schools. Planning permission had been granted to turn the building into a conference centre but in the meantime it had been requisitioned by the Ministry of Defence.

At the end of the corridor was a set of double doors. Cramer pushed them open and stepped onto the wooden floor of the gymnasium. It was large enough to contain two netball courts and its walls were lined with climbing bars. At one end of the room thick ropes hung down from the ceiling some thirty feet overhead, and various items of dust-covered gymnastic equipment were stacked against the wall: a vaulting horse, a trampoline, wooden benches, a box of netballs. At the other end stood a man in a grey sweatshirt and blue jeans. He was broad shouldered with short, dark blond hair, and was busily slotting bullets into a magazine. He looked up and nodded at Cramer. 'Sergeant Cramer?' he asked. He was taller than Cramer, about six feet four, with a boxer's frame and a large chin he jutted forward as he waited for Cramer to reply.

'The name's Mike,' said Cramer. 'My soldiering days are behind me. A long, long way behind me.'

The man grinned and stuck out a large hand with perfectly manicured nails. 'Allan,' he said. 'Training Wing, 22 SAS. Good to meet you, Mike. I've heard a lot about you.' As Cramer shook it he felt the strength in Allan's thick fingers. It was a killer's hand, and even though the man was smiling Cramer knew that he was looking into a killer's eyes. Allan had the slightly distant look that came from seeing too many men die and the knowledge that he was responsible for their deaths. It was a look Cramer recognised. He saw it every time he looked into a mirror.

Allan was standing by a long table which held a box of cartridges and several pairs of ear protectors. A wall of sandbags twice the height of a man had been built against one of the walls and in front of it were five cardboard figures with bullseye targets over the hearts. The targets were about twenty feet away from the table. 'You favour the Browning Hi-Power, right, Mike?' asked Allan. For the first time Cramer realised that he had a faint Irish accent. Dublin, maybe, certainly not from the North.

Cramer nodded and Allan slotted a clip into a Hi-Power and handed it to him. It was Cramer's own gun, the one the Colonel had taken from him in the helicopter: a Belgian-made FN Hi-Power Mark 3, eight inches long and weighing just under two pounds. The double-row staggered magazine gave the gun a thick grip, just one of the reasons that Cramer favoured the weapon.

'Most of our guys use Glocks now,' said Allan. 'They're lighter and they've got bigger clips.'

'Yeah, so I heard,' said Cramer. 'I didn't like the recoil myself. I prefer a heavier gun.'

'Different strokes,' admitted Allan with a shrug, and he handed one of the sets of ear protectors to Cramer. 'Let's see what you can do,' he said, putting on his own headset. 'Take the target on the left.'

Cramer pulled back the slide and chambered a round, keeping the gun pointed down as he turned to face the targets. 'Fast or slow?' he asked.

'Up to you.'

Cramer nodded. He raised the Browning in a two-handed grip, sighted along the barrel with his arms fully extended and fired once. The bullet struck just below the heart and slightly to the left. He compensated and fired again, then emptied the entire clip in groups of two.

The bitter tang of cordite filled the air and the palm of his right hand ached. He removed his ear protectors and walked over to the target. 'Nice grouping,' admitted Allan. 'Very nice.' Six of the shots were dead centre of the bullseye, all but two of the rest could have been covered by a tea cup. 'You cheated with the sighting shot, though. You don't get those in the Killing House.'

'Yeah, I know. You want me to go again?'

Allan grinned, showing a small gap between his top two front teeth. 'Mike, we've only just started,' he said, patting him on the back. His huge hand felt like a shovel between Cramer's shoulders. 'Train Hard, Fight Easy, that's the Training Wing's motto.'

Allan asked Cramer to fire another clip into a second target and this time he managed to get all thirteen shots within the bullseye. Allan nodded his approval. 'Better,' he said. 'You always use the double tap?'

'Pretty much.'

Allan took the Browning from Cramer and removed the

clip. 'We've started teaching our recruits sustained firepower as part of our close quarter battle training. Let's see you empty the clip as quickly as possible.'

'Into one target?'

'Sure. You never know whether the terrorist has a remote control on him or a hidden weapon. Two shots might not be enough to take him out instantly.'

Cramer raised an eyebrow. 'You reckon? I've never had a problem.'

'I've seen a guy try to crawl away with two slugs in his chest. More than enough time to detonate a bomb.' He loaded another clip into the Browning and handed it back. 'This time, grip tighter with your left hand and relax your right. That'll help control the recoil and allow your trigger finger to be more flexible.'

Cramer took the gun, frowning. 'You know what I'm going up against, right?'

Allan nodded. 'Sure. Bear with me, Mike, we'll get there eventually.' Cramer stood in front of the middle target as Allan took a stopwatch out of his back pocket. 'When you're ready,' he said.

Cramer steadied his breathing, steadied his arm, and fired thirteen times, pulling the trigger as fast as he could. When he finished, his trigger finger was aching and his wrist felt as if it had been broken. He ejected the clip and looked at Allan.

'Five point two seconds,' said Allan.

Cramer waved his right hand, trying to restore the circulation to his trigger finger. 'Is that good?'

Allan shrugged. 'With practice, you should get down to below three seconds.'

'I don't see the point.'

'The point? You're going to have a guy coming at you, eight, maybe nine feet away from you with a loaded gun in his hand. His adrenalin's going to be up, he's going to be moving towards you, you're going to have to pull out your weapon, aim and fire in one, maybe two, seconds. With the best will in the world your aim is going to be all over the place. One shot might not cut it. Even two. You're going to have to keep firing until the guy's dead to have any hope of beating the clock.'

Cramer smiled thinly. In the old days SAS troopers who died in action were listed on plaques on the Regimental Clock Tower. When the SAS barracks and headquarters were rebuilt in 1984, the plaques were moved to outside the Regimental Chapel, but beating the clock still meant staying alive. Cramer realised that Allan wasn't aware of the irony of his statement – that Cramer stood absolutely no chance of beating the clock.

Allan walked up to the target. 'Your accuracy went to pot. Look at this.'

Cramer joined him by the cardboard target. He was right. One of the shots had hit the target in the head, and while most were still in the heart area, there was a much bigger spread than before. 'Yeah, I see what you mean,' Cramer said. At least three of the shots weren't stoppers. 'So we're going to keep practising, right?'

Allan shook his head. 'You'll be practising, I'll be watching.'

Cramer went back to the table and picked up a fresh clip. On the floor there stood a stack of boxes containing fresh rounds. Hundreds and hundreds of rounds.

THE DOUBLE TAP

* * *

Davie Quinn carried the tray of drinks over to the table and put it down in front of his brother. He handed one of the pints of Harp lager to Paulie and placed the glasses in front of the two bleached blondes. They'd been drinking with the girls for the best part of a couple of hours and Davie was having trouble remembering their names. 'And Malibu and pineapple juice for the ladies,' he said, sliding the tray behind his chair with a flourish.

'Thanks,' said the taller of the two blondes, a typist who Davie seemed to remember was called Noreen. Her friend, he was reasonably sure, was Laura, and she was unemployed, like most of the girls Davie knew. Davie and Paulie had met the girls three pubs ago, and they'd been happy to tag along with the brothers, so long as they didn't have to buy their own drinks. The girls were pretty enough and good fun, and it looked as if they'd be happy to go the whole way. Laura certainly was, she'd allowed Davie to put his hand halfway up her skirt and once, when Noreen had gone to the Ladies and Paulie was at the bar buying another round of drinks, she'd stuck her tongue in his mouth and damn near suffocated him. She gave him a beaming smile and raised her glass to her lips. Davie winked at Paulie, encouraging him to try to enjoy himself.

Davie had taken his brother out in an attempt to cheer him up. They'd walked for the best part of four hours before hitching a ride with a delivery van which was heading for Belfast. They were cold, wet and miserable and the driver had taken pity on them, offering to share his flask of chicken soup. The man had been curious as to why they were hitching without any bags and Davie had spun him a story about having a row with their girlfriends, adding that the girls had dumped them outside a country pub and taken the car. The man had laughed uproariously at that, showing a mouthful of nicotine-stained teeth.

They'd waited in until early evening, but Pat O'Riordan hadn't got in contact. Davie decided there was nothing to be gained by staying at home so he'd persuaded his younger brother to go out for a drink. Just a quick one, that had been the original plan, but then they'd met the girls.

Paulie was nursing his lager, his head down as if in prayer. Davie decided that Paulie had had enough to drink and that it would soon be time to call it a night. Laura put down her glass. There was a greasy smear of lipstick around the rim that matched the colour of her fingernails. Davie couldn't take his eyes off the nails, they were the longest he'd ever seen and he kept imagining how they'd feel scraping along his back. 'You ready to go soon?' asked Laura, brushing her long, blonde hair behind her ears.

'Go where?' asked Davie.

'My parents are down South. Visiting my uncle in Cork.'

'Really?' Davie couldn't believe his luck.

'Yeah, they won't be back until tomorrow night.' Her leg pressed against his under the table.

Davie sent up a silent prayer of thanks to whichever saint was watching over him that night. 'Come on, Paulie, drink up,' he said.

Paulie didn't look up. 'He's pissed, bless him,' said Noreen.

A can rattled by Davie's ear and he looked around.

148

A teenager with red hair and a straggly moustache was holding the can and he pushed it forward, almost under Davie's nose. 'For the Cause,' he said. Davie shoved his hand into the pocket of his jeans and pulled out a fifty pence piece. He dropped it into the can and the teenager waved it in front of Paulie. Paulie struggled to focus on it. 'For the Cause,' the teenager repeated.

'Fuck off, we've done our bit for the Cause today,' said Paulie.

The teenager rattled the can again. There was a paper tricolour on it, orange, white and green, and the letters IRA stencilled on it with black ink.

'I said fuck off. We already gave.' Paulie sat up, his eyes bloodshot and watery. 'We almost died for the Cause today, we almost fucking died.'

Realising he wasn't going to get a donation from Paulie, the teenager moved to another table. A thin man in his early twenties, wearing faded jeans and a black leather motorcycle jacket, dropped several coins into the can without looking up. 'What do you mean, you almost died?' asked Noreen, her curiosity piqued.

'Nothing,' said Davie quickly. 'He doesn't mean nothing.' He leant forward and pushed a warning finger in front of his brother's face. 'Just shut the fuck up.'

Paulie grabbed the finger and shook it solemnly. 'Okay, Davie. Mum's the word.'

Davie glared at his younger brother and picked up his pint of lager. He drained it and put the empty glass down. 'I'm taking him home,' he said.

'What about . . . ?' said Laura, but Davie ignored her and pulled his brother to his feet.

'Maybe some other time,' he said.

Laura looked at him pleadingly. 'Look, why don't we help you take Paulie home, then you can come back with me.' She flicked her hair to the side, knowing that it was her best feature. She flashed her blue eyes. Her second best feature.

Davie succumbed to her charms. 'Okay,' he agreed.

'Great,' said Laura. She picked up her handbag, then helped Davie half carry his brother to the door. Noreen followed, walking unsteadily on white stiletto heels.

As the Quinn brothers left the pub, the man in the motorcycle jacket finished his pint of Guinness, picked up his newspaper and waved goodnight to the barman.

Stepping into the cold air, the man looked left and right, then walked slowly down the street, slapping the newspaper against his leg and whistling softly. He stopped to look into the window of a shoe shop and bent to stare at a pair of brown leather cowboy boots, using the reflections in the glass to confirm that he wasn't being followed. The street was clear. Somewhere off in the distance a bottle smashed, and from high overhead came the clatter of an unseen helicopter, but other than that he could have been alone in the city.

Robbie Kirkbride, 'Sandy' to his colleagues in the army's 14th Intelligence Company, had been working undercover in Belfast for seven months, doing little more than sign on the dole and hang around the city's pubs, picking up tidbits here and there, a name, a face, scraps of information that the experts in the Intelligence and Security Group would hopefully be able to use to put together the bigger picture, biding his time until he felt confident enough to infiltrate the lower echelons of the IRA. Ceasefire or no ceasefire, the army was continuing to gather intelligence on the organisation, in the same way that the IRA was continuing to collate information on possible targets. Both sides were determined to be ready should violence restart.

On the way to the telephone box he dropped his paper and as he bent down to pick it up he checked behind him one last time. Still clear. He went into the call box and dialled the number of his controller.

Cramer, Allan and the Colonel sat in the dining room with cups of coffee in front of them. Cramer was dog-tired, both his hands ached from the constant firing practice and his ears were ringing. During his six-week close quarter battle training course in the Killing House in Hereford he'd fired more than a thousand rounds a day, but there was a world of difference between close quarter battle training and standing in front of a target, firing a handgun at arm's length.

'So how did he do?' the Colonel asked Allan.

'Just fine,' said Allan. He'd changed into khaki Chinos and a white T-shirt which emphasised his weightlifter's forearms. 'Tomorrow we'll see how he gets on with the smaller guns.'

'Am I missing something here?' asked Cramer. It was the first he'd heard of using a different gun. He'd assumed that he'd be using his Browning.

'The man you'll be standing in for doesn't carry a gun,' explained the Colonel. 'There's no way you'll be able to keep a gun the size of a Browning on you without it being seen.'

'And it's not the sort of gun you'll be able to draw quickly,' added Allan.

Cramer sighed in exasperation. 'So what was today all about? You're saying I've been wasting my time?'

Allan shook his head. 'Absolutely not. I wanted you to get used to rapid fire with the Browning, then when you use a smaller weapon you'll find it that much easier. It'll be like switching from a standard army issue parachute to a ramair canopy.'

The Colonel looked at Cramer, his head tilted slightly to one side as if he expected an argument. Cramer felt like complaining about the way information was being fed to him on a piecemeal basis, but he knew that that would appear unprofessional so he said nothing.

'You're only going to get one chance to take on this guy,' said the Colonel. 'I want you to be as prepared as possible.'

'And that means using a smaller gun?'

The Colonel nodded. 'The way this killer operates, he won't pull out his weapon until he's a few paces away from you. You can't afford to react until he's blown his cover.'

'So when you see his gun, you're going to have to move immediately,' said Allan. 'The type of gun isn't going to matter, not at such close range. You're just going to have to point and keep firing. What's more important is that you get the gun out as quickly as possible. And the Hi-Power is just too big a weapon.'

Cramer drained his cup. Allan picked up the coffee pot to pour him a refill but Cramer shook his head. 'What about bodyguards?' he asked. 'Does the target normally have protection?'

'Yes, two, one of them doubling as a driver,' said the Colonel. 'We're going to stick to that.'

'And how do they feel about that?' asked Cramer.

Allan smiled. 'It should be fun,' he said, raising his cup to Cramer.

Cramer's eyes widened in surprise. 'You?'

'Sure. The target's usual bodyguards are good but they're not SAS-trained. Plus, this operation requires special skills, it's not a straightforward bodyguarding job.'

'What do you mean?'

The Colonel cleared his throat. 'What Allan means is that a bodyguard's normal function is to protect the client at all cost, to throw himself in front of the bullet if necessary. But in this case the prime function is going to be to apprehend the assassin.'

'Apprehend? Or kill?'

The Colonel smiled thinly. 'Whatever.'

Cramer looked at Allan with renewed respect. In most of the files he'd read, the killer had taken out the target's bodyguards first. Allan must have known what he was letting himself in for, but he appeared to be totally calm at the prospect. Allan smiled at the look on Cramer's face. 'It's not as crazy as it sounds,' he said. 'We'll be wearing Kevlar body armour, and we'll be expecting the hit.'

Cramer nodded. Allan was right, most of the bodyguards had been shot in the chest. It was only the primary targets who'd taken bullets in the face. 'Who's the other bodyguard?' he asked.

'A guy called Martin,' said Allan. 'Former Irish Army. Ranger Wing. He's been running his own security firm for the last few years, bodyguarding mostly. You'll meet him tomorrow.'

Cramer stood up and stepped away from the bench seat that ran the full length of the table. The propane gas heater hissed, its bluish flames wavering in the draught that ran the full length of the massive dining room. 'I'm away to bed,' he said. 'I'll see you tomorrow.' He left the Colonel and Allan sitting in silence as he made his way to his bedroom.

Paulie Quinn was lying on top of his bed, reading a comic and eating his way through a packet of digestive biscuits. His window was open a few inches to allow fresh air into the room and he could hear the sound of children kicking a football around in the streets below. He brushed crumbs off his chest and took another biscuit from the packet on his bedside table.

Downstairs the telephone rang. His mother called for Davie and a couple of minutes later there was a knock on Paulie's door. He looked over the top of his comic. It was Davie. Davie closed the door and sat down on the end of the bed. 'That was Pat O'Riordan,' he said.

'Yeah? What's he want?'

'We're to lie low. He heard we were out last night and he's not happy. We're to stay at home until we hear from him.'

'He's mad at me, isn't he? He heard I was pissed. Shit. I'm sorry about last night. I was out of order.'

'Yeah. You've got to be careful what you say, Paulie. We're not kids any more. Big boys' rules, you know?'

'Yeah, I know. It won't happen again, that's for sure. At least it wasn't a complete loss, though. You got your hole, right?'

Davie grinned lecherously. 'That's for me to know and you to dream about,' he teased. 'Did you get Noreen's number?' he asked.

Paulie shook his head. 'I wasn't really interested,' he said. 'She wasn't my type, you know?'

Davie smiled at his younger brother. Eighteen years old and still nervous with girls. 'I've got her number,' he said. 'She wants you to give her a call.'

Paulie beamed. 'Are you serious?'

'Sure. She liked you. God knows why.'

Paulie put the comic down on his chest and stared up at the ceiling. Davie could see that he had something on his mind. 'What's up?' he asked.

Paulie wrinkled his nose. 'What happened yesterday. With the American kid. And his dad.'

'It wasn't our fault, Paulie.'

'Yeah, but we killed them. They're dead and we did it.'

Davie rubbed his chin. He hadn't shaved but his skin was still smooth, with only a hint of stubble. 'We didn't kill them, Paulie. They were driving on the wrong side of the road, for fuck's sake. And if anyone's to blame it was Pat for grabbing the steering wheel.'

'I guess,' said Paulie. He didn't sound convinced.

Davie stood up and went over to the window. 'Look, Pat did everything he could. He called an ambulance for the woman and she's okay. The guy and the kid were dead, there was nothing anyone could have done for them. It was an accident, Paulie. If it hadn't been us on the road it could have been anyone else. They were just in the wrong place at the wrong time.' Davie put his hands on either side of the window and craned his neck to look down.

'What is it?' Paulie asked.

'Cops,' said Davie.

Paulie went to stand by his brother. Down below he saw three grey armoured Landrovers. A couple of housewives in thick wool coats and headscarves watched them drive by. In the days before the ceasefire, the RUC Landrovers would have been accompanied by rifle-carrying troops and the air would have been filled with the sound of crashing metal as the women in the area banged dustbin lids on the pavement, sounding a warning to the Catholic community that the army were coming. Now the police passed through the area without incident.

'The bastards are out in force,' said Davie. 'Wonder who they're after today?'

'It's us, isn't it?' Paulie said anxiously. 'It's us they want.'

Davie leant on the windowsill and peered down. 'Relax, there's no reason they'd be looking for us. They could be after anyone.' The first two Landrovers sped by the building, and Davie breathed a sigh of relief. But he caught his breath when all three screeched to a halt and RUC officers wearing bullet-proof vests fanned out, guns at the ready. They rushed across the strip of grass in front of the block of flats and towards the entrance. Paulie backed away from the window. The comic fell from his hands, forgotten. 'It is us, Davie. I know it is.'

Davie smiled reassuringly. 'Nah, there's lots of flats. There's no reason for them to be after us.'

'Yeah, but . . .'

Davie interrupted him. 'There's no reason for them to be after us,' he repeated. 'Remember that.' He was about to say more when he heard footsteps pounding up the concrete stairs, followed by the crash of a boot against the front door.

'Oh Jesus, it is us,' said Paulie. 'They've come for us.' His face had gone white and his hands were shaking.

'It's okay, we're clean,' said Davie. 'Just don't panic.' Downstairs, their mother was screaming. The front door was kicked again, harder this time.

Paulie knelt down and pulled out an old tartan suitcase from under his bed, his hands trembling. Davie frowned as Paulie flicked the latches and opened it. Inside was his comic collection. Davie was on his way to the bedroom door when Paulie threw a stack of comics onto the floor and took out their father's revolver. Davie stopped in his tracks. 'Oh fuck, no,' he said.

'I was going to throw it away, Davie, honest I was.'

There was the sound of splintering wood, more screams from their mother, then urgent male voices telling her to get out of the way. She screamed again, but the scream was cut short. Heavy boots tramped up the stairs. Something smashed to the floor.

Paulie was sitting on the floor with the gun in his hands, staring at it as if he didn't know what it was. Davie looked at the revolver, then at the window. He had to get rid of it, somehow. Maybe he could throw it up onto the roof, hide it in the guttering, do something, anything, before the police burst into the bedroom. He grabbed the weapon from Paulie and dashed to the window. His heart was racing, the blood pounding in his head. He pushed the sash window up but before he had it fully open he heard the door crash behind him. He whirled around, holding the gun up to show that he wasn't going to use it, his mouth open to shout that they weren't to shoot, but before he could get the words out he realised it was too late. Time seemed to freeze. The policeman standing in the doorway couldn't have been much older than Davie, he had acne on his forehead and a mole with hairs growing out of it on the

157

side of his nose. His handgun was centred on Davie's chest and Davie could see his finger tightening on the trigger. Behind the young policeman stood another man with a gun. He shouted that Davie was to drop the weapon. Davie wanted to explain that the revolver wasn't even loaded, but the words wouldn't come. He felt his bladder empty and he was suddenly ashamed that he'd wet his pants like a frightened child. Paulie's hands were up in the air as if he was surrendering on his brother's behalf, his eyes wide and unbelieving.

Davie knew what was going to happen but he was powerless to do anything to stop it. The young policeman's gun jerked up and Davie felt the bullets thud into his chest as he staggered backwards, his head slamming into the window. He heard the glass shatter but didn't feel the shards tear into his scalp. He slid down to the floor, his hands clutched to his chest, his mouth opening and closing soundlessly.

Cramer was towelling himself dry when there was a knock on the bedroom door. 'Yeah?' he called, wrapping the towel around his waist. It was Allan, holding a large pair of scissors. He clicked them, a mischievous grin on his face. 'What are they for?' asked Cramer suspiciously.

'Got to make you look decent,' said Allan. 'Colonel's instructions.'

'Yeah? What part of my anatomy are you planning to remove?'

'Short back and sides,' explained Allan, motioning for Cramer to sit on the bed.

Cramer sat down. 'Do you know what you're doing?'

'Not really, but I'm willing to give it a go.' He clicked the scissors menacingly.

'You've got to be joking.'

'Come on, Mike. How difficult can it be? Just keep still, that's all.' He move towards Cramer, the scissors held high.

Cramer put his hands over his ears and lay back on the bed. 'Keep those things away from me, you mad bastard,' he shouted.

Allan roared with laughter and pulled open the door to reveal Mrs Elliott standing there. 'Afraid of a little snip.' He handed her the scissors. 'Mrs Elliott here'll be doing the business.'

'I've got three children, Mr Cramer, so I know what I'm doing,' said the woman.

Cramer squinted up at Allan. 'Why?'

'Have you looked at yourself in a mirror lately. You look like shit.'

'Thanks, Allan.'

'Nah, seriously, we've got to get you ready for the photographs. The way you look, no one's going to believe you're a man worth bodyguarding. You look like you've been in a ditch for the past three weeks, your hair's . . .'

'Okay, okay,' said Cramer, sitting up. 'I get the message.' He saw Mrs Elliott looking at the scars on his stomach and chest with a look of horror on her face. 'The last barber did that to me,' he said. 'That's why I'm nervous of scissors.'

Mrs Elliott frowned, then realised that he was joking. She tutted, went into the bathroom and came out

159

with another towel which she draped over Cramer's shoulders.

'Do you have a parting there somewhere, Mr Cramer?'

'The left side, I think,' said Cramer. It was almost a year since he'd been inside a barber's shop. He usually did the job himself with a pair of nail scissors when it got too long. Allan stood watching, his hands on his hips. 'Haven't you got anything better to do?' Cramer asked him.

'No,' said Allan, grinning at Cramer's discomfort.

Mrs Elliott began to comb Cramer's hair, the wet strands sticking to the side of his face. Cramer knew that Allan was right, he did look like shit. They might be able to change his appearance but he doubted if a new haircut was going to change the way he felt.

Paulie Quinn lay face down on the mattress, but even with his eyes closed there was no escape from the light. He'd banged on the cell door and yelled until his throat was raw, but they wouldn't turn off the fluorescent lights which glared down from behind a sheet of protective glass. They'd taken away his clothes and given him a pair of green overalls to wear. They were way too big for him and rough against his skin, like fine-grade sandpaper.

This wasn't how it was supposed to be, he knew. He should have been asked if he wanted a solicitor, he should have been allowed to make a phone call, they should have at least given him a drink of water. His throat was so painful he could barely swallow. He had no idea how long they'd keep him in the cell, or how long he'd already been there.

With the constant light he had no way of knowing if it was day or night.

He rolled over onto his back and rubbed his eyes, still wet from crying. The RUC officers who'd dragged him into the armoured Landrover had refused to answer his questions, they'd just sat next to him in sullen silence, nothing but contempt and hatred in their eyes. There had been no windows in the vehicle and he had no idea where they'd taken him. He was eventually dragged out and handed over to three men in casual clothes, tough-looking men with short haircuts and wide shoulders who looked like they might be army but weren't wearing uniforms.

Paulie sat up and rested his back against the whitewashed wall. Apart from the mattress on the floor, the cell was empty. There wasn't even a toilet. As far as Paulie knew, there were always toilets in police cells. And observation hatches in the door so that they could look inside. The door to the cell was white-painted metal and there was no hatch, not even a keyhole. Wherever they'd taken him, it wasn't to a police station. He buried his head in his hands and began to sob. He wanted his mother, and he wanted Davie. Thoughts of his brother made him cry all the more. Davie had been shot three times, maybe four, and Paulie had seen the life ebb from his eyes, leaving them cold and staring. The police hadn't allowed Paulie to touch his brother, he'd begged and pleaded but they'd dragged him away.

It was his own fault that his brother had been killed. He should never have kept the gun, never given it to Davie. He began to bang the back of his head against the wall, softly at first, then harder, not caring about the pain, wanting to turn back time, wanting to die in his brother's place.

*   *   *

Mike Cramer heard the gunshots as he walked along the corridor to the gymnasium. He counted the rapid-fire shots. There were eighteen in all, fired in less time than it took Cramer to take two strides. He opened the door to see Allan inspecting one of the man-size cardboard targets. 'Morning, Mike,' he said over his shoulder.

'How did you do?' asked Cramer.

'You don't want to know, it'd just depress you,' grinned Allan, popping the empty magazine out of the pistol. 'First-class haircut. Maybe I'll ask Mrs Elliott to give me a going over.' The floor was littered with empty brass casings. 'Have you seen one of these?' He handed the gun over, butt first.

Cramer shook his head. Across the barrel were the words Heckler & Koch and VP70 was stamped into the butt. 'It's a Heckler & Koch VP70 machine pistol. Fires double action only, so there's no safety, muzzle velocity of 1,180 feet per second, eighteen in the clip, weighs two and a half pounds fully loaded.'

'Feels good,' said Cramer, weighing it in the palm of his hand. 'Are you going to be carrying this?' He gave it back to Allan.

'Nah, this is Martin's, I'm just playing with it. I'll stick with a Glock 18.' Allan picked up a shoulder stock from the table and slotted it into the back of the pistol. 'This is the kicker, There's a selector switch here on the top front of the stock that lets you set it to fire three-round bursts, fully automatic.' He gave Cramer a pair of ear protectors. 'Watch this.'

Allan flicked the selector switch to '3' and aimed at the target, pushing the stock into his shoulder as he sighted down the barrel. He pulled the trigger and three shots rang out, so close together as to be almost indistinguishable. Allan fired all eighteen shots at the target, and Cramer was impressed to see that they all hit the centre of the bullseye. Allan was one of the best shots Cramer had ever seen.

Cramer nodded his approval. 'Nice shooting.'

'Yeah, well I'm not used to it. Like I said, it's Martin's baby really.'

He walked over to the table and waved his hand over a selection of handguns. 'Have a look at these, Mike.'

Cramer bent over the table and studied the three handguns. All three were considerably smaller than his Browning Hi-Power.

'The one on the right is a . . .'

'Walther PPK,' interrupted Cramer. '7.65mm calibre, blowback, semi-automatic. Seven in the clip.' He pulled back the slide and chambered a round. 'It's what James Bond used, right?'

'That I don't know, but it was designed for the German services. PPK stands for Polizei Pistole Kurz. And that's a 9mm version you've got there. We've given it a very light trigger, just over two pounds pull will do it. That goes for all the guns here.'

Cramer clicked the safety on and put it back down on the table. The second gun was a Beretta Model 1934. Cramer picked it up. It was shorter than the length of his hand by at least an inch.

'It weighs the same as the PPK, about one and a quarter pounds, and it's also got a seven-round magazine. It's another 9mm. Not much to choose between it and the Walther, to be honest.'

Cramer put it back down on the table and picked up the third handgun. It looked like a child's toy and the word 'Baby' was spelled out at the bottom of the butt. Above it he noticed the FN logo that denoted the Fabrique National Herstal Liège Company of Belgium, the manufacturers of Cramer's Browning.

'That's the baby brother of your Hi-Power,' said Allan. 'It was actually marketed under the name Baby Browning. FN have manufactured them since 1906 but you don't see too many of them about these days. They're banned in the States.'

Cramer raised an eyebrow. 'Because they're so small?'

'That's right. Too easy to conceal. For you, that's a real plus.'

Cramer felt the weight. 'Half a pound?' he asked.

'Seven ounces,' said Allan. 'It's really something, isn't it? Barrel length of two and one-eighth inches, total length, four inches.'

'It's a lady's gun,' said Cramer.

'Don't you believe it,' said Allan. 'Mechanically it's the same as the .25 ACP vest pocket automatic that Colt used to make. You wouldn't use it in a fire-fight and beyond ten feet it's a peashooter, but close up it'll bring a man down.'

Cramer stared down at the gun. It was hard to believe that the tiny weapon could kill a man. The barrel was shorter than his index finger. 'I don't know, Allan,' he said. 'Doesn't look like it'll pack enough of a punch to me.'

Allan shrugged vaguely. 'It's up to you. We don't have to decide yet, but I'd like you to get familiar with all three.' He handed Cramer a leather underarm holster with webbing straps. 'Put this on. It's time we started to practise the draw.'

Cramer put down the Baby Browning and Allan helped him fasten the straps and adjust the holster so that it lay flat against his shirt. Cramer picked up the Walther PPK. The leather was smooth and supple and the gun slid in and out with the minimum of friction.

'Take it easy at first,' said Allan. 'Withdraw the weapon with your right hand, then as you push the gun forward, bring your left hand over your right, same as you were doing with static firing. Remember, a strong grip with your left hand and relax the right.'

'Got it,' said Cramer, sliding the gun in and out of the holster.

'Fire off a few clips to get the feel of the draw, take your time and fire with your arms fully extended. Once you're familiar with the action, I want you to forget about the sight picture. I want you firing before your arms are extended, just empty the clip as quickly as possible. You're going to be so close to the target, aiming will be a waste of time.'

Cramer donned his ear protectors. 'Okay, let's get to it.' Allan took down the target he'd been using and fitted a fresh one. 'Seven shots, rapid fire,' said Allan, standing to the side.

Dermott Lynch yawned and opened his eyes. He rolled over and stared at the long auburn hair of the girl lying next to him, wondering how quickly he could get rid of her without causing offence. She was a nice enough girl, and an amazing lay, but Lynch liked to be alone in the morning. Maggie, her name was. Maggie O'Brien. She was voluptuous, plump even, with a pretty face and the greenest eyes he'd ever seen outside of a cat. She worked as a barmaid in a pub off Grosvenor Road and was an occasional visitor to Lynch's bed. She had only just turned twenty and knew that the relationship had no future, but the sex was great and Lynch was perfectly happy to turn to her for physical comfort from time to time. He just wished she'd get into the habit of leaving before morning.

Lynch had several girlfriends in Belfast. He'd made the decision many years earlier not to get married, not even to enter in a long-term relationship. His position as an active member of the IRA meant that relationships made him vulnerable, both to the security forces and to Protestant terrorist organisations. Better to be single. He came from a big family and had more than enough nephews and nieces to make up for the lack of children of his own.

Whenever possible Lynch preferred to make love to his girlfriends on their turf, so that he could slip away afterwards, a quick kiss on the cheek and then a cab home. Maggie lived with her parents, however, so he had no alternative but to take her home with him to his small terraced house. She murmured in her sleep and pushed back against him. Her naked flesh was warm against his thighs but Lynch moved away, putting distance between them. Sex was for the night, something to be done in darkness. Maggie's hand slid behind her and reached between his legs and he realised that she wasn't asleep. She took him in her hand and squeezed softly, encouraging him, wanting him, but Lynch wasn't aroused in the least. He slid out of bed and padded to the bathroom.

'Dermott. Come here,' moaned Maggie.

Lynch pretended that he hadn't heard and closed the bathroom door. He leant over the washbasin and stared at his reflection in the mirror. His eyes were bloodshot, the result of a heavy night's drinking, and there were crumbs in his beard. He'd eaten a bag of salt and vinegar crisps before going to bed. He grinned wolfishly. God alone knew why Maggie wanted to touch him first thing in the morning. He looked like shit. He cupped his hand around his mouth, breathed out, and then sniffed. Yeah, he smelled rough, too.

He ran a bath as he cleaned his teeth. As he spat foam into the sink, his front doorbell rang. He wrapped a towel around his waist and went back into the bedroom. Maggie was sprawled across the bed, covered only by a sheet. It did little to conceal her ample body, but Dermott wasn't tempted. He went over to the window and peered out. It was Pat O'Riordan, dressed as if he'd come straight from his farm.

Lynch went downstairs and let him in. O'Riordan looked at his wristwatch pointedly. 'I know, I know,' said Lynch. 'I had a rough night. What's wrong?'

'The cops were at the Quinns' house yesterday. Davie's dead and Paulie's disappeared.'

'Fuck,' said Lynch.

'Yeah. Fuck.'

'Do you want a coffee?'

'Got anything stronger?'

'Never touch the stuff,' said Lynch with a smile. He took O'Riordan through to the sitting room and poured large measures of Jameson's whiskey. They clinked glasses and drank. Lynch waved O'Riordan to the sofa.

'It gets worse,' said O'Riordan.

'Worse? How can it get worse?'

'You haven't seen the papers, have you?' Lynch shook his head. O'Riordan let out a sigh. 'The guy who was driving the car, he's related to an American politician. A member of the House of Representatives.'

'Oh fuck,' said Lynch. He rested his head on the back of his chair and stared up at the ceiling. 'Fuck, fuck, fuck.'

'Yeah, tell me about it. He's been one of the guys pushing for more Green Cards for the Irish.'

'Oh Jesus.'

'There's more. His wife's related to the Kennedys. The Kennedys, Dermott.'

Lynch closed his eyes. 'Pat, if you tell me that she's the Pope's sister, I think I might just top myself.'

'This is going to get very messy,' said O'Riordan. 'They're going to move heaven and earth to get us. The Americans are going to put pressure on the Irish Government, and the Brits. We're up shit creek.'

Lynch sat up and ran his hand through his beard. 'Only if they know it was us,' he said. 'Davie's dead, you say?'

'Shot by the cops. He had a gun.'

'Not one of ours?'

O'Riordan shook his head. 'His father's. From what I've heard, it wasn't even loaded.'

'Poor bastard.'

'Yeah, well, if you ask me it serves them right for having the bloody thing.' He paused. 'You haven't asked the big question,' he said.

Lynch sat down on an overstuffed easy chair and put his bare feet up on the coffee table. 'You mean why were the police at their house?'

O'Riordan raised one eyebrow. 'Careless talk costs lives.'

'It wouldn't have been Davie. I'm sure of that.' He took a mouthful of whiskey and rinsed it around his mouth before swallowing. 'Paulie's gone, you said?'

'We've sent a solicitor to the family, and he's trying to find out where he is. But we don't think the RUC have got him any more.'

'What, you think Five are holding him? If they are, he'll talk.'

'Yeah. I know.'

'Can we reach him?'

'We don't even know where he is.'

The two men sat in silence for a while. Upstairs, Maggie had commandeered Lynch's bathwater. O'Riordan grinned at the sound of splashing. 'Anyone I know?' he asked.

'Aye. Your missus.'

O'Riordan pulled a face and finished his whiskey. He held out the empty glass but Lynch motioned with his head for O'Riordan to help himself.

'You've already spoken to McCormack?' asked Lynch.

'Yeah. That's why I'm here. He wants us to lie low. Until they've taken care of Paulie. He's furious.'

'Terrific,' said Lynch. He banged his glass down on the table. 'Shit, shit, shit. It was McCormack's fucking idea to take the Quinns with us.'

'He knows that, Dermott, but I wouldn't go throwing it in his face, if I were you.'

'What are you going to do?' Upstairs, Maggie began to sing an Irish folk song.

'I'm going south. I've got friends in Killarney, but I'll keep moving.'

'What about the farm?'

'McCormack's going to send someone to help out.' O'Riordan leaned over and refilled Lynch's glass. 'He wants you out of the country.'

Lynch nodded. 'No problem. I'll cross the water.'

'Where will you stay?'

'Best you don't know, Pat. I'll keep in touch with McCormack.' He took another drink. 'This has got really messy, hasn't it?'

'Tell me about it.' He looked up at the sound of splashing. 'Are you going to introduce me to your friend?'

'All I'm going to introduce is my foot to your arse,' said Lynch.

O'Riordan put down his empty glass and got to his feet, grinning. He stuck out his hand and Lynch stood up and shook it, firmly. O'Riordan stepped forward and held Lynch in a bear hug, squeezing him so tightly that the air exploded from his lungs. 'You take care of yourself, yer soft bastard,' O'Riordan said.

'Aye, you too,' replied Lynch, gasping for breath.

After he'd shown O'Riordan out, Lynch went back upstairs. Maggie was in the bedroom, towelling herself dry. 'Who was that?' she asked.

'No one,' said Lynch.

Maggie smiled slyly and let the towel fall to the floor. She put her hands on her ample hips, glanced across at the bed and then back at Lynch. She raised one eyebrow invitingly, but he turned his back on her and headed for the bathroom. 'Show yourself out, will you, love?' he said.

He heard her slam the front door a few minutes later as he was shaving off his beard with short, careful strokes of a cut-throat razor.

THE DOUBLE TAP

When Cramer and Allan walked into the dining room, the Colonel was already tucking into bacon and eggs. Sitting opposite them was a new face, a big man with close-cropped dark hair, slightly shorter than Allan but with equally wide shoulders. He introduced himself as Martin, the second bodyguard and driver.

Cramer helped himself to scrambled eggs and then poured himself a mug of Mrs Elliott's treacly tea. Martin's plate was piled high – eggs, bacon, sausage, baked beans, black pudding, tomatoes, and on a side plate he had half a dozen slices of buttered toast. He smiled as he saw Cramer's tiny portion of eggs. 'No appetite, Mike?' he asked through a mouthful of food.

The Colonel looked up at Cramer and Cramer saw his eyes narrow a fraction. He realised that Allan and Martin hadn't been told about his illness. Cramer nodded almost imperceptibly and then grinned at Martin. 'Never was one for early-morning scran,' he said, using the SAS slang for food.

'The haircut's a big improvement,' said the Colonel.

'Yeah, she knows what she's doing,' agreed Cramer.

Allan sat down opposite Martin with a plate of fried food. 'When did you get here?' he asked.

'Late last night. I was in London bodyguarding a Hollywood star and his boyfriend.'

'Yeah? Going to name names?'

Martin shook his head. 'The sort of money they pay me guarantees confidentiality.'

Allan laughed and told Cramer the names anyway. 'I didn't know he was queer,' said Cramer.

'Yeah, neither does his wife,' said Martin, biting a chunk out of a slice of toast.

They were interrupted by the arrival of the tailor, bustling in with a suitcase in either hand. 'Good morning, good morning,' said the tailor, hefting the cases onto one of the tables.

Martin looked at Allan. 'The tailor,' said Allan. Martin nodded as if that explained everything.

Cramer put down his fork and tried on one of the suits as the tailor walked around him, nodding and biting his lip. 'Good, good,' he said, brushing Cramer's shoulders and kneeling down to check the trousers.

'A perfect fit,' said Cramer, his arms out to the sides.

'Of course,' said the tailor primly. He helped Cramer on with the overcoat and then stood back to get a better view.

'First class,' said the Colonel. The tailor nodded enthusiastically, picked up his empty cases, and half ran out of the dining room.

'Is that guy on something?' asked Martin, shaking his head in amazement.

'Fastest tailor in the west,' said Cramer, walking up and down in the overcoat. 'He knows his stuff, though.'

'We'll be taking photographs this afternoon,' said the Colonel. He nodded at Cramer's scuffed Reeboks. 'Don't forget the shoes.'

'Photographs?' repeated Cramer, mystified. 'What photographs?'

'For the killer,' said the Colonel. 'He's going to want to know what the target looks like.'

The overcoat suddenly felt heavy, like a suit of armour. Cramer took it off and folded it over his arm. Allan and Martin both bent their heads over their plates and concentrated on their food. Cramer shivered as if he'd just noticed a draught. It was the first time he'd been referred to as the target.

Dermott Lynch took a taxi to the airport and bought a ticket on the next Aer Lingus flight to London Heathrow. He picked up a copy of the *Irish Times* and sat down to read it. A large photograph dominated the front page, a middle-aged man, a pretty blonde and a young boy. Seth Reed and his family. The father and son killed in the collision with a truck full of IRA weaponry. The woman was sedated and was waiting for her relations to fly over from the States. Lynch scanned the story.

There were the usual vitriolic quotes from Protestant politicians condemning the incident, and a brief statement from the Provisionals saying they regretted the deaths of the two tourists but that they had not been involved in the incident. An IRA spokesman claimed that they had no knowledge of the arms cache being moved and that they had launched an internal investigation, while an unnamed spokesman for the security services said that it was clear that the weapons were being taken away with a view to being hidden.

The newspaper's journalists had also contacted several top American politicians who were unanimous in their anger and sorrow. A spokesman for the Northern Ireland Tourist

Board warned that the deaths could result in the loss of millions of pounds to the province. There had already been dozens of holiday cancellations from Americans who feared a return to the violence of the past.

Nowhere in the paper was there any mention of the arrest of Paulie Quinn, or the shooting of his brother. Lynch wondered how long it would be before the boy talked. Harder men than Paulie Quinn had cracked under interrogation. He dropped the newspaper into a rubbish bin and walked to the boarding gate.

Cramer stood facing the full-length mirror. Even in the tailored suit and the bulky cashmere overcoat, he could see that he'd lost weight. The clothing helped to conceal how ill he was, and at least he didn't look too gaunt. His eyes had always been deep-set and ever since he was a teenager he'd looked as if he needed a good night's sleep, no matter how rested he was. Allan had brought the mirror down from one of the bedrooms and placed it in the gymnasium so that Cramer could practise drawing his weapon. It was hard going. Cramer had no problem in firing the PPK. Under Allan's guidance he'd become as adept with the pistol as he was with his preferred Browning, and his grouping at ten metres was as good as ever he'd achieved when he was in the SAS. But he wasn't getting any better at drawing the weapon. The action seemed totally unnatural, his arm had to move up and then in, his fingers had to reach the butt, his trigger finger had to slip into the trigger guard and he had to pull the weapon out so that it didn't snag on his clothing.

Cramer squared his shoulders and felt the underarm holster tighten against his chest. There was one advantage to rehearsing in the coat: when he finally took it off he'd find it that much easier to pull out the gun. He stared into his eyes and bared his teeth. 'You talking to me?' he asked his reflection. The reflection grinned back. 'Are you talking to me?' said Cramer, his voice louder this time.

His hand darted inside his jacket and pulled out the PPK, his eyes never leaving those of his reflection. He pointed the gun at the mirror, his finger on the trigger. 'I said, are you talking to me?'

Allan chuckled from somewhere behind him. 'You're getting better,' he said. 'I'd leave out the De Niro impersonations, though.'

Cramer straightened up and put the PPK back in its holster. 'I'm still too slow, aren't I?' he asked.

'Maybe,' admitted Allan. 'It depends.'

'Depends? On whether or not he forgets to tie his shoelaces and then trips over them?' He turned to face Allan as he smoothed down the collar of his coat.

'On whether he can get past Martin and me.'

Cramer sighed and nodded slowly. 'Yeah, I keep forgetting that he's probably going to try to slot you first.'

'He's always taken the bodyguards out before going for the target,' agreed Allan.

Cramer patted Allan on the shoulder. 'Thanks,' he said.

Allan looked surprised. 'For what?'

'For the training. For pushing me.'

'Fuck it, Mike, that's what I do. I train people. You're just another job.' He grinned. 'But fuck up on the day and I'll swear I had nothing to do with you.'

Cramer chuckled and turned back to the mirror. 'Let's try it again,' he said. He squared his shoulders again, then stiffened as he realised someone had just come into the gymnasium. It was a girl, Oriental with short black hair, and she was staring at Cramer, a quizzical look in her dark brown eyes. Cramer frowned as he looked at her reflection. He hadn't heard the gymnasium door open, nor had he noticed her walk across the wooden floor. As he turned to face her, he saw that Allan too was momentarily confused.

'Are you looking for something, miss?' Allan asked.

The girl continued to scrutinise Cramer. She was a little over five feet tall though black high-heeled boots added a couple of inches to her height. She was wearing black jeans and a black jacket over a white T-shirt and had a single gold chain around her neck. He found it difficult to judge her age; she had the soft, unlined skin of a teenager but the poise and authority of a woman in her thirties. 'He doesn't look anything like him,' she said.

The Colonel stepped through the door and tapped his stick on the floor. 'He doesn't have to,' said the Colonel. 'Very few people know what he looks like.' The Colonel turned to Cramer. 'This is Su-ming, Vander Mayer's assistant.'

Cramer wasn't sure how to greet the girl. He stepped forward and offered his hand, but instead of shaking it she turned it palm upwards. She had the hands of a child, soft and smooth, but the nails were long and painted a deep red. The contrast between the child-like fingers and the adult adornment was disturbing and Cramer's throat tightened. She looked down at his palm and slowly traced the lines with her forefinger, the nail scratching across his skin. Cramer shivered.

The Colonel walked across the floor and stood behind the girl as she studied Cramer's palm. His footsteps echoed around the huge gymnasium and it was only then that Cramer realised that Su-ming had made no noise when she walked, despite her boots.

'See anything you like?' joked Cramer, but she didn't react. She ran her fingernail along the base of his thumb. The gesture was sensual, and under any other circumstances he'd have thought that the girl was flirting with him, but her concentration was total.

The Colonel sniffed impatiently, but Su-ming ignored him and continued to stare at Cramer's hand. Cramer looked down at the top of the girl's head. Her hair was jet black and glossy and it glistened under the fluorescent lights. Suddenly she looked up and he found himself looking directly into her eyes. 'Do you read palms, is that it?' Cramer asked.

'I read people,' she said, her voice loaded with disdain. She let go of his hand and turned to the Colonel. 'It won't work,' she said.

The Colonel raised his eyebrows. 'What do you mean?'

The girl put her head on one side and wrinkled her nose. 'You're wasting your time. This man is unsuitable.'

'Unsuitable?' repeated Cramer in disbelief. 'What do you mean, unsuitable?'

'Sergeant Cramer is a highly trained soldier,' said the Colonel. 'I have every confidence in him.'

The girl didn't reply but gave a barely perceptible shrug that could have meant anything. To Cramer it signified contempt; for some reason the girl had taken an instant dislike to him.

'Can you tell me why you feel this way?' asked the Colonel quietly.

'Mr Vander Mayer never asks me to explain myself,' said Su-ming. 'I merely offer observations. It's up to you whether or not you act upon them.'

Cramer looked at his palm, as if the network of lines and creases would reveal to him whatever had upset her. 'What did you see?' he asked.

The girl turned back to him. She took hold of his hand again and ran her fingers across his palm. Cramer felt his spine go cold and he shivered. He was suddenly certain that Su-ming knew what was wrong with him, that she had somehow detected the cancer that was growing inside him. Cramer swallowed. His mouth had gone dry. She looked up at him and he knew that the word on her lips was death and that she was going to say it out loud. He cleared his throat. 'What do you see?' he repeated.

The girl's face was devoid of emotion. She looked up at him with no more compassion than she would show a piece of machinery, as cold and impassive as a catwalk model. She tilted her head back a fraction and her lips parted to reveal perfect white teeth. The gymnasium was totally silent. Cramer was unable to take his eyes off the girl, but he could sense the Colonel and Allan straining to hear what she would say. Su-ming nodded as if she'd decided to tell him, but it was still a second or two before she spoke. 'Sadness,' she said softly. 'I see great sadness.'

Cramer took back his hand and slipped it deep into his overcoat pocket as if trying to hide it from her. She carried on looking deep into his eyes and this time Cramer realised he could see something there; something that looked disconcertingly like pity.

The girl suddenly turned around and walked away, her boots making no sound on the wooden floorboards. The three men watched her go. Only when the door had closed behind her did Allan turn to look at Cramer. 'I don't know about you, Mike, but I'd give her one.' Cramer didn't laugh.

Paulie Quinn paced around his cell like a caged animal. He hadn't slept, partly because of the light but also because someone kept banging on his cell door at irregular intervals. He hadn't been given anything to eat or drink and he had a pounding headache. He was also scared, more scared than he'd ever been in his life. He realised that the police hadn't stormed the house because of the old revolver. They must have known that he'd been involved in the deaths of the tourists. He was facing a murder charge. Life imprisonment. He paced faster and faster. Life behind bars. He was only eighteen years old. Did life mean life? Would they really keep him in prison until he died? It wasn't fair. All he'd done was to dig out the stuff and sit in the back of the truck.

Paulie wondered if Lynch and O'Riordan had also been arrested. He stopped pacing as he was struck by the thought that one of them had given his name to the police. Tears welled up in his eyes again. He heard footsteps outside, then the sound of bolts being drawn back. The door was thrown open. Two men in leather bomber jackets and jeans walked in purposefully. 'I want a solicitor,' Paulie said, but the men ignored him. They grabbed an arm each and frogmarched him out. Waiting in the corridor was a third man, older with greying hair and reddish cheeks. He had a black hood in his hands and he thrust it over Paulie's head.

'I want to make a phone call,' protested Paulie. He was dragged along the corridor and into a room. He was pushed backwards and he fought to keep his balance, but instead of falling to the floor he collapsed into a chair. He heard a door slam and then the hood was ripped off his head.

A man in a dark brown suit was sitting at a table, a notepad in front of him and a fountain pen in his hand. The tie he was wearing had little ducks on it. Paulie blinked and shook his head. He felt sick and he retched and tasted bile in his mouth. 'Who was with you, Paulie?' the man asked. He was in his mid-thirties, with dark brown hair that kept falling across his eyes and an upturned, almost feminine nose.

'Who are you?' asked Paulie.

'Who was with you?'

Paulie realised there was another man standing with his back to the door and looked over his shoulder. He was slightly older than the man with the pen, wearing a green tweed jacket and black trousers. In his hand was the hood.

'I want a solicitor,' said Paulie.

'No, you don't,' said the man at the door.

'I want to phone my mum.'

'Mummy's boy, are we?' said the man with the pen.

Paulie's face flushed. 'She'll be worried about me.'

'She's going to be even more worried when she finds out what you did.'

'I didn't do nothing. Are you the cops?'

The man with the pen smiled and wrote something down on the pad. 'We know your brother was with you. Who else?'

'I don't know what you're talking about.'

'The truck. The arms. Heavy stuff, Paulie. Very heavy stuff.'

Paulie swallowed. He could still taste the bile and he snorted, trying to clear his throat. 'I don't know anything about no arms.'

'You know a kid died, Paulie?' Paulie shrugged. 'We know you were just a hired hand, Paulie. It's not you we want. It's the big boys. We want their names.'

'You know what they do to touts.'

The man with the pen smiled thinly. 'They're going to do it to you anyway, Paulie. Unless you help, you're as good as dead.'

Paulie's jaw dropped. 'You can't keep me here,' he said.

'Oh yes we can,' said the man at the door. 'Besides, you're here for your own protection.'

'What the fuck are you talking about?'

'They know we've got you, Paulie,' said the man with the pen. 'And they know you'll talk. You think they trust you to keep quiet? A boy like you?' He shook his head. 'No, Paulie. They think you're spilling your guts right now. And the longer we keep you, the more they're going to be convinced that you're talking.'

'You're not the police?' Paulie knew they weren't RUC because the RUC took the IRA volunteers they arrested to their interrogation centre at Castlereagh. And wherever he was being held, it wasn't Castlereagh. There were no cameras recording the interview and Paulie had been told that the police had to record all their questions.

'No, we're not. But we do have the right to screen you prior to RUC interrogation. You'll know when that

181

happens, Paulie, because you'll be arrested and they'll be over you like a rash. You're better off talking to us, believe me. But if you really want us to hand you over to the RUC, we will.'

Paulie frowned in disbelief. 'You will?'

The man sat back in his chair and tapped the pen on his notepad. 'Sure. We could arrange that right now.'

Paulie stood up. 'Okay. That's what I want.' The overalls were flapping around his legs and the sleeves hung down over his hands.

'I can assure you that within twelve hours of putting you into police custody, you'll be dead.'

'Dead?'

'The IRA won't risk letting you live, Paulie. I can guarantee it. They'll protect the big boys.'

'Bullshit. You don't know what you're talking about,' said Paulie, his voice rising in pitch. 'Who are you anyway?'

The man with the pen smiled. 'Five,' he said quietly. 'MI5.'

Paulie felt his legs go weak. He sat down and ran his hands through his greasy, unwashed hair.

'How's that?' shouted Cramer, standing with his hand on the door handle of the gleaming grey Mercedes 560 SEL.

'Too posed,' answered the photographer from the second-floor window. 'Look to your right, then slowly move your head back.' Cramer did as he was told amid a series of clicks and whirrs from the camera's motordrive. 'Better,' shouted the photographer. 'Okay, Su-ming, you can get out of the car now.' Su-ming opened the car door and climbed out, a bored look on her face. The camera clicked again.

The Colonel stood at the entrance to the building, leaning on his stick and watching. Allan moved to stand in front of Cramer as if shielding him. The camera clicked again, like an automatic weapon firing rapidly. The Colonel stepped onto the gravelled drive and looked up at the photographer. 'Get the driver as well, will you?' he shouted. 'And make sure Su-ming is in all the shots.'

'Yes, boss,' the photographer answered.

Martin was sitting in the driver's seat, his hands on the wheel. He climbed out of the Mercedes and went to stand next to Cramer and Allan. Su-ming brought up the rear. Above the Colonel's head, the camera continued to click. It was vital for the photographs to look as if they'd been taken at long range and without the knowledge of the subjects.

The two bodyguards were wearing lightweight bullet-proof vests under their shirts. The vests were barely noticeable, but the Colonel knew that the assassin was a professional. He'd realise that they were wearing body armour and shoot accordingly. The Colonel hadn't mentioned the fact to Allan and Martin but they were professionals too, and were well aware of the risks they were running. The tailored suits looked well on Cramer, as if he belonged in a boardroom and not in a hospital bed. Cramer wasn't wearing a bullet-proof vest. There was no point. The assassin's first shot at his intended target was always to the face.

*　　*　　*

It was a two-bedroomed flat on the second floor of a Maida Vale apartment block. The flat was long and thin and Dermott Lynch had to walk through the kitchen to get to his bedroom. The room was about the size of a prison cell, three paces by two paces, with a wooden bed, a built-in wardrobe and a single chair.

'It's not the Savoy,' said the man who was showing Lynch around. He was a building contractor originally from Castlebar in County Mayo, a squat man with wide shoulders, a ready smile and a tendency to crack bad jokes. His name was Eamonn Foley and ten years previously he'd lived in Belfast and had been active in the IRA, mainly fundraising and helping to launder the organisation's illicit revenues. He'd continued to offer whatever support he could after he'd moved to London.

'It's fine,' said Lynch, dropping his suitcase onto the bed.

'Any idea how long you'll be staying?' Foley asked.

'I'll be moving on in a week or so. Is that a problem?'

'Stay as long as you want, Dermott. *Mi casa es tu casa.*'

Lynch looked out through the window at the gardens below. A small boy was playing on a swing, kicking his legs up in the air as he swung to and fro. He wondered how old the boy was. Probably the same age as the Reed kid.

'Tea?' asked Foley behind him.

'Sounds good. Why don't I make it?' Lynch had drunk Foley's tea before and it wasn't an experience he cared to repeat.

*   *   *

The pony kept pulling to the right and it took all the little girl's strength to keep it heading straight for the fence. She kicked it hard in the flanks with her heels and the pony snorted and jumped, clearing the red and white striped bar with inches to spare. The girl reined the pony to a halt, her face flushed with excitement. The spectators burst into applause at the announcement that it had been a clear round, the first of the afternoon.

'She's a natural, right enough,' said Thomas McCormack, nodding his approval.

'Natural, my arse,' said Joseph Connolly, 'she's been trained by the best. My daughter reckons young Theodora is going to be Olympic standard by the time she's sixteen. I tell you, Thomas, it's costing a fortune.'

'Worth it, though.'

'Huh? What did you say?'

'I said it's probably worth it.'

Connolly tapped the hearing aid behind his right ear with his finger. 'This damn thing's been playing up all week,' he complained. 'Say something else.'

'What do you want me to say?'

'Anything.'

McCormack looked over the top of his horn-rimmed spectacles. 'Testing, testing, testing. One two three.'

'Ha bloody ha,' scowled Connolly. 'Come on, let's walk.'

As they headed away from the outdoor arena, the little girl came running up. 'Grandpa, Grandpa, did you see me?'

'Indeed I did,' said Connolly, bending down to beam at her. 'A clear round.'

'The only clear round,' she said proudly. 'Did you see how I nearly hit the third fence?'

'No, you jumped it just right.'

Theodora wrinkled her nose. 'I'll do better in the next round, I'm sure.'

'I just bet you will.'

'I'm going to be needing a bigger pony soon.'

'Yes, your mummy was telling me. We'll see what we can do when Christmas comes around.'

'You mean it, Grandpa?' she said, jumping up and down. 'Do you really mean it?'

'We'll see, Theodora. Now go and find your mummy.'

The little girl ran off, and Connolly smiled ruefully at McCormack. 'It never stops, does it? You just finish paying for your children, and then a whole new generation comes along.' Behind them a buzzer sounded as another rider started around the course. Connolly tapped his hearing aid again. 'This Crossmaglen business. It's a bloody nightmare.'

'Aye, bad enough that a tourist was killed, but to kill a man related to a heavyweight American politician. Jesus, Mary and Joseph, luck doesn't get any badder than that.'

'And the kid. Don't forget the kid.'

'Aye, Joe. I hadn't forgotten the kid.'

'We're going to have to do something,' said Connolly. 'Something drastic.'

McCormack nodded and took his pewter hip flask out of his pocket and offered it to Connolly. The old man shook his head. 'Not right now, thanks,' he said.

'The Army Council is baying for blood and Sinn Fein's nose is out of joint, too. They want to know what they were doing with the weapons in the truck. You can see their point, can't you?'

McCormack nodded. He put the flask away, unopened.

'I did make it clear, didn't I? I did tell you that the arms cache was to be handed over intact, didn't I?'

'You did.'

Connolly narrowed his eyes. 'You're sure about that, Thomas?'

McCormack met his gaze steadily. 'Dead sure, Joe.'

Connolly nodded, satisfied. 'All we've got to do, then, is to tidy up the loose ends.'

'What have you got in mind?' Connolly didn't answer and McCormack wondered whether or not he'd heard the question. The two men walked along a line of empty stalls. A teenage stablegirl threw a bucket of water into the end stall and began to scrub the floor with a stiff brush. The men gave her a wide berth so they wouldn't get splashed.

'The Quinn boy's going to talk,' said Connolly. 'He'll be crying like a baby before Five have finished with him. He'll give up Pat and Dermott. He'll give up his own mother.'

McCormack's stomach went cold. He had a good idea what was coming next. 'Do we know where he's being held?'

'I do. But we can't get to him. It's totally out of the question. Where are they?'

McCormack removed his horn-rimmed spectacles and polished them on a red handkerchief. 'Pat's staying with a cousin in the South. Dermott's in the UK.'

'It's only a matter of time before they're pulled in.'

'Or taken out.'

Connolly shook his head. 'No, the SAS won't kill them, I'm sure of that. The Brits will want a trial, they'll want to show the Yanks that they've got the situation under control.'

'We'll get to the Quinn boy eventually. If there's a trial,

he'll need a solicitor. We'll get to him that way. His solicitor will explain to him what'll happen to his family if he gives evidence.'

'It'll be too late by then. The damage will have been done.' A cheer went up behind them and they heard the announcer say that another rider had gone around without any faults. 'Theodora won't be pleased about that,' muttered Connolly, almost to himself.

'The worst possible scenario is that Pat and Dermott stand trial,' said McCormack. 'But they won't talk. I guarantee that.'

'I know,' said Connolly. 'I know they won't talk.'

McCormack finished polishing his spectacles and put them back on. 'They're good men, Joe. They've given their lives to the Cause.' Connolly turned his head to look at McCormack and McCormack knew exactly what was going through his mind. 'Oh Jesus, Joe. No. There has to be another way,' he said.

'We can't have them in court,' said Connolly softly. 'It'll destroy us.'

'So we help them disappear.'

'Where? Where can they go where they'll never be found? The world's a smaller place than it used to be, Thomas. There's nowhere to hide any more. Not for terrorists.'

The two men walked in silence for a while. McCormack thrust his hands deep into his overcoat. He shivered. 'I'll take care of it,' he said.

'Good man. I knew you would. Are you still on for Saturday?'

'Absolutely,' McCormack replied. He smiled half-heartedly. 'I've got this new fly I'm dying to try. I've used part of a peacock feather, glossy bluish-green. It's going to be a winner, I'm sure of it.'

Rob Taylor drummed his fingers on the steering wheel as he watched the sun go down, smearing the sky a raspberry red. Normally there was nothing he'd rather do than watch an African sunset, but the man sitting behind him was becoming increasingly impatient and even the ready supply of ice cold gin and tonics from the cooler hadn't placated him. Taylor had to have a kill before the night was over or he'd be in big trouble.

Taylor had written dozens of letters of applications and phoned countless times before he'd eventually landed the job of ranger on the MalaMala game reserve, and when he'd first put on the khaki uniform he'd never been so happy. Just then, however, he'd have given anything to be back on his father's sugar cane plantation.

There were only two guests in the Landrover, a huge bull of a man, a minister of the government of Zimbabwe who took up a bench seat normally big enough for three, and his French mistress, a strikingly pretty brunette who was sitting in the passenger seat next to Taylor and whose silky-smooth right arm kept bumping against his own far too often to be accidental. Right at the back of the vehicle, on a seat set higher than the rest, sat John, the Zulu tracker, who was scanning the area with narrowed eyes. He was as anxious as Taylor to find a kill.

The minister had flown into the game reserve that morning en route to a meeting in Pretoria and had insisted that he be shown the big five – elephant, rhino, lion, leopard and buffalo. And he'd also insisted on watching one of the predators devouring its kill. Taylor had drawn the short straw and had spent most of the afternoon racing up and down the reserve in search of the animals. It was a good time to be in the park, the river was close to running dry so the game was sticking close to the water supply, and within hours he'd shown the minister a huge elephant with tusks more than seven feet long, a herd of water buffalo that was moving slowly westwards out of the neighbouring Kruger National Park, two rhinos and a leopard that had been patiently staking out a warthog hole. At one point Taylor had thought that he'd have it all sewn up before dusk, but try as he might he couldn't find a lion, much less one with a kill.

He'd suggested that they watch the sunset with a few drinks, but it seemed that the more the minister drank, the more objectionable he became, warning Taylor that he had friends in high places and that if a lion wasn't forthcoming then Taylor's job was on the line. Taylor doubted whether he'd get the sack just because lions were scarce, but a large part of a ranger's job was public relations, and he didn't want the boss to think that he wasn't up to it. Over his headset he could hear another ranger talking about a large male king cheetah that was walking up to the Marthly waterhole, but its belly was swollen and it clearly wouldn't be hunting for a couple of days. A king cheetah was an unusual sighting, but Taylor knew that the minister wouldn't be satisfied with anything less than a lion.

Taylor unclipped the microphone from the dashboard and pressed it against his lips. 'Rob here, any sign of a lion?'

'Negative,' replied a voice. It was Karl, a recently-recruited ranger who was driving a group of Japanese tourists to see the leopard.

'Nothing here,' said Rassi, a former armoured personnel carrier driver who was clearly taking delight in Taylor's discomfort. Taylor could tell that Rassi would have liked to have said more, but it was an open channel monitored back at camp, and fooling around on the job wasn't tolerated by the boss.

'Well?' boomed the minister, leaning forward to massage his mistress's neck. There was something predatory about the gesture, and Taylor could picture the man breaking her pretty little neck with one squeeze and then feeding on her soft parts. He shuddered involuntarily.

'They've found tracks,' he lied, knowing that the minister wouldn't have been able to hear what had come over the headset. 'Shouldn't be long now.'

'Good,' said the minister, nodding like an elephant preparing to charge. 'About time.'

He sat back in his seat and the Landrover's suspension squeaked as if in pain.

'See anything, John?' Taylor asked his tracker in Zulu. He'd carefully tested to see if the minister understood Zulu but had drawn a blank, so he'd carried on using the tracker's native language when speaking with him, just in case there was bad news.

'Nothing,' John replied. He shrugged to show that he sympathised with the ranger. 'Maybe we could try Mamba Waterhole?'

'Yeah, we'll give it a go.' Taylor rubbed his chin and sniffed. He felt as if he was coming down with a cold. That was all he needed. The minister was telling his mistress about the time Margaret Thatcher visited MalaMala with F. W. de Klerk when he was President of South Africa. The South African President hadn't seen the Big Five, but Thatcher had claimed to have had a glimpse of a leopard and so managed to get one up on him. The minister thought that was hilarious and he threw back his head and laughed, his gold front tooth glinting in the dying light of the sun. The girl smiled across at Taylor as if soliciting his sympathy.

'So, I too am going to beat de Klerk,' boomed the minister. 'Isn't that right? Tonight we'll see a lion, and a kill, huh?'

'Yes, sir,' said Taylor. He looked back at John. 'Put the searchlight on,' he told the tracker, 'let's drive around and see if we can't get lucky.' He collected the minister's empty glass, stashed it away in the coolbox at the rear of the Landrover, and climbed back into his driving seat. The sun dipped below the horizon and stars twinkled overhead. Over his headset Taylor heard Rassi calling in a herd of impala. The deer were as common as rabbits at that time of the year, and Taylor knew that Rassi was only doing it to annoy him.

The minister pounded the back of Taylor's seat impatiently. Taylor reached for the ignition key, but before he could start the engine he heard the roar of an approaching Landrover. Taylor frowned. Rassi had given his position as more than twenty kilometres away at Buffalo Bush Dam and Karl was still sitting next to the leopard. As far as he knew there was only one other ranger out and he was parked next to the Marthly waterhole.

A Landrover came crashing through the undergrowth to Taylor's left. Its halogen searchlight cut through the night, blinding Taylor so that he had to shield his eyes with one hand. He picked up the microphone with the other and pressed the transmit button. 'Hey, careful with the light,' he said.

There was silence in his headset as the approaching Landrover revved its engine and ran over a clump of elephant grass.

'Who are you talking to, Rob?' asked Rassi's voice.

The Landrover stopped less than fifty feet away from Taylor's vehicle, but the searchlight still blinded him so he couldn't see the driver. 'John, can you see who it is?' Taylor asked in Zulu.

'No, but it's one of our Landrovers,' said the tracker.

'What the hell's going on?' asked the minister. 'Get him to turn that light off.'

Taylor felt a soft hand stroke his knee and his leg jerked involuntarily. The girl was insistent, and she slowly walked her fingers up his thigh. Taylor was too busy concentrating on the Landrover to even think about what the girl was doing. He heard a thud as the driver jumped down onto the sand. Taylor began to get a bad feeling about the situation. He put his right hand on the Sako .375 Magnum rifle that was strapped across the bonnet. It was already loaded.

'What's wrong?' asked the minister, slapping the back of Taylor's seat.

Taylor squinted into the bright white light. Suddenly a black silhouette stepped into the beam and walked slowly towards Taylor's Landrover. 'Who is it?' called Taylor. When the figure didn't reply, the ranger yanked the rifle out of its mount. Before he could shoulder the weapon he felt a sudden blow to his chest. He looked down and was surprised to see a red stain spreading across the khaki material. He could hear his blood pounding in his ears as he

began to fight for breath and the rifle fell from his nerveless
fingers. The last thing he saw was the black silhouette take
another step towards the Landrover, then Taylor slumped
forward, his forehead smacking into the steering wheel. The
girl began to scream hysterically and the minister cursed
as he struggled to stand up. Before Taylor died he heard
two more shots, but he didn't see the two bullets strike the
minister, one in the head, one in the heart.

Dermott Lynch put a pound coin in the slot and dialled
Thomas McCormack's number. He didn't identify himself
when McCormack answered but McCormack recognised
his voice immediately. 'Where are you?' McCormack
asked.

'London,' replied Lynch.

'Where exactly? I'll need an address.'

'Is this line safe?'

'For God's sake, Dermott, my phones are swept every
day. You're going to need cash and I have to know where
to send it.'

'I'm staying with Eamonn Foley.'

'In Maida Vale?'

'Yeah. What's happening there? Has the Quinn boy
turned up yet?'

'No news. But they don't seem to be looking for you.
No one's been to your house and O'Riordan seems to be
in the clear, too.'

'Maybe Quinn's tougher than we thought.'

'Yeah, maybe, but you're better off out of it, Dermott.

Stay where you are and keep your head down. We'll get this sorted out.'

Pat O'Riordan drove the tractor into the barn and killed the engine. It continued to run for a few seconds and he made a mental note to check the timing when he had the chance. He climbed down and arched his back. He'd been sitting on the machine for the best part of four hours and he was suffering. The farm was a bit larger than his own holding in Ballymena but the owner, Seamus Tierney, had given over two of his fields to mobile homes and caravans, a cash crop that pulled in several thousand pounds a month during the summer. Tierney was renovating several of the mobile homes and so O'Riordan had volunteered to do some work about the place. It was the least he could do, considering Tierney and his wife were giving him free room and board.

One of the farm's many cats walked stiff-legged into the barn, its ears pricked up and its tail flicking to and fro like a metronome. O'Riordan bent down to rub its head but it ran off. When O'Riordan straightened up he saw the two men standing in the doorway, big men wearing green anoraks and black ski-masks. One of the men was holding a sawn-off shotgun, levelled at O'Riordan's chest. The other man was holding a cardboard box about the size of a television set. O'Riordan slowly raised his hands. He heard a noise behind him. There was another man there holding an assault rifle. He must have been hiding at the back of the barn. The cat was rubbing itself along the man's legs.

Another man, this one carrying a length of rope, entered the barn. The man with the shotgun gestured with the weapon. 'Don't go making this difficult for us, Pat.' The accent was Belfast, hard and nasal.

'What's going on, lads?' asked O'Riordan. The man with the box put it on the ground and opened it. He took out a large white quilt. O'Riordan frowned. 'What's the game?' O'Riordan took a step back but the barrel of the assault rifle brought him up short.

The man with the shotgun had pale blue eyes and they stared back at O'Riordan, unblinking. O'Riordan knew he was in trouble. Serious trouble. The man with the shotgun gestured again. 'You can put your hands down now. And don't try anything stupid.' O'Riordan did as he was told. The man with the quilt walked towards him, holding it up.

'What is it you're after?' asked O'Riordan. He was genuinely confused. If they were SAS they wouldn't be using a shotgun, if they were UFF or UDV or any of the Protestant paramilitaries they'd have just blown him away and left him dead on the ground. The quilt and the rope just didn't make any sense at all. Unless they were planning to kidnap him. Maybe that was it. But why would anyone want to kidnap him? He stood stock still as they wrapped the quilt around him, leaving his head clear. He expected them to tie him up with the rope, but to his surprise two of the men grabbed him, one around the chest, the other around his legs. It was almost comical, and if it wasn't for the sawn-off shotgun and the weapons he'd have thought it was some sort of April Fool's joke.

The man with the rope threw one end up in the air and it looped over a girder up in the roof. It was only then that O'Riordan saw the noose. He began to struggle, but the noose was deftly placed over his head and pulled tight, stifling his cries. The man holding the end of the rope jumped in the air and pulled down on his end with all his strength. O'Riordan was jerked off his feet but the two men holding him kept the soft quilt pressed around him so that he couldn't struggle. He died with only one mark on him, the rope burn around his neck.

Cramer walked through the dining hall and pushed open the double doors which led to the kitchen, expecting to find Mrs Elliott fussing around the stove. He was surprised to see Su-ming, chopping vegetables with a large knife. She used the knife quickly and confidently, the steel flashing only millimetres from her fingers as she sliced green peppers, scallions, mushrooms and other vegetables which Cramer didn't recognise. She had taken off her jacket and hung it over the back of a chair. In the T-shirt and jeans she looked about eighteen years old.

She didn't look up as Cramer went over to the fridge and took out a carton of milk. Cramer drank from the carton and watched her as she poured a splash of oil into a large steel wok.

'Mrs Elliott will cook for you if you ask her,' said Cramer, wiping his mouth with his sleeve.

'I sent her away. I didn't want her near my food.' She put the wok on the stove and turned on the gas. 'You realise she's poisoning you with all that animal fat?'

Cramer looked at the milk carton and shrugged. He

peered at the vegetables on the wooden chopping board. 'What are they?' he asked.

'Ginger root, bamboo shoots, water chestnuts,' she replied. She threw the vegetables into the smoking oil and stirred them vigorously with a wooden spatula.

Steam billowed around the wok and Cramer sniffed appreciatively. 'Do you cook for your boss?'

'I do many things for Mr Vander Mayer,' she said, dropping a handful of snow peas and bean sprouts into the mixture. 'And yes, I advise him on his nutrition.'

'And you read people for him, too?'

She looked at him over her shoulder. 'I advise him on many subjects.' Cramer drank from the carton again. 'You're not eating, are you?' she asked.

Cramer shrugged. 'Milk does me just fine.'

'You're not well.' It was a statement, not a question.

'You read that in my palm?'

Su-ming took the wok off the burner and poured the stir-fry mixture into a bowl. She used the spatula to spoon boiled rice from a pan into another bowl and put them both on the kitchen table. She stood looking at Cramer for a few seconds then nodded as if she'd reached a decision. 'There's a bowl and chopsticks on the draining board,' she said and sat down.

Cramer joined her at the table and she spooned rice and vegetables into his bowl. He had trouble using the chopsticks and she smiled at his clumsy attempts. 'Would you prefer a fork?' she asked.

Cramer shook his head and persevered. Su-ming used neat, economic movements to carry the food from her bowl to her mouth.

'It's good,' said Cramer. The vegetables were crisp and

tasty, and while he still had little appetite, at least he didn't find the food hard to swallow.

'I know,' she said. 'And it's better for you than the animal fats and starch which that woman is feeding you.'

Cramer adjusted the chopsticks. His fingers felt large and clumsy. 'How long have you worked for Mr Vander Mayer?' he asked.

Su-ming's chopsticks stopped in mid-air, suspended over her bowl. 'Fifteen years,' she said.

'Fifteen?' repeated Cramer. Su-ming nodded and continued to eat. Cramer frowned. He couldn't believe that Su-ming was more than twenty-five, which meant she'd joined the arms dealer when she was just ten years old. 'What happened to your parents?' he asked.

Su-ming put her chopsticks down on the table. Her eyes were cold, her face impassive. 'I am here because Mr Vander Mayer said that I should cooperate with your Colonel,' she said in measured tones, as if she were a parent talking to an uncooperative child. 'That is the only reason. I have already made my feelings clear on the matter, but Mr Vander Mayer insists. I am not here to make small talk with you. I do not wish to become your friend or to have you become mine. I certainly do not wish to divulge personal details to you. Do I make myself clear?'

Cramer sat stunned. She hadn't raised her voice or shown any sign of emotion, but her words had cut right through him. 'Hey, I'm sorry,' he said. 'I was just . . .'

'. . . making small talk,' she said, finishing his sentence.

'That's right. Small talk.'

Su-ming picked up her chopsticks again. 'Life is too short for small talk,' she said and popped a snow pea into her mouth.

*   *   *

The Colonel poured himself a large whisky and held up the bottle to show Allan. 'Are you sure you don't want one?' he asked.

'No thanks, boss,' Allan replied.

The Colonel put the half empty bottle back on the side table and went over to his desk. 'How's Cramer's drinking?'

'Under control. You were right, once we started training, he cut back.'

The Colonel sipped his whisky. 'He needs a goal, does Mike Cramer. He needs something to aim for, to focus on. Without it he tends to fall apart. Don't underestimate him, Allan.'

'I won't, boss.'

'How's he doing otherwise?'

'His marksmanship is getting better. I'll be starting him on the set pieces tomorrow, we'll see how he does under pressure.'

'Do you think he'll be ready in time?'

'I don't know. He's out of condition, he looks like he's been living rough for months, but he's all we've got, right?'

'That's right.' The Colonel raised his tumbler in a toast. 'And if anyone can turn a pig's ear into a silk purse, you can.' He drank again as Allan chuckled.

A cellular phone warbled on the windowsill. 'I'll see you tomorrow,' said the Colonel. He waited for Allan to leave before taking the call. It was the last person he expected to hear from: Andrew Vander Mayer.

'Colonel, I need a favour,' said Vander Mayer.

'Where are you, Mr Vander Mayer?' the Colonel asked.

'It's okay, I'm on the yacht,' said Vander Mayer.

'I don't think it's a good idea to be calling,' said the Colonel. 'I thought I made it clear that there was to be no contact until the matter has been resolved.'

'This is important.'

'And a contract on your life isn't?'

Vander Mayer ignored the rhetorical question. 'You will be in London in two days, am I right?'

'That's right. For forty-eight hours. Then we move to New York.'

'I have a business deal that requires my presence in London.'

The Colonel leaned forward, his body tense. 'Out of the question,' he said. 'Absolutely, totally, one hundred per cent out of the question.'

'Colonel, I agreed to cooperate with you on condition that my business was not affected. This meeting is vital. The man who wishes to see me is doing so at great personal risk to himself and if I do not meet him in London, I will not get the chance again. And there are plenty of other buyers for what he has to sell.'

The Colonel frowned. 'This man, you've met him before?'

'No. But I know of him.'

'You realise that this could be the assassin?' There was no reply from Vander Mayer. 'This could be the hit,' said the Colonel.

'I see,' said Vander Mayer.

'So you understand why you must not come to London?'

There was another long silence. 'Very well. But I want Su-ming to meet with him. Alone.'

'I wouldn't recommend that either,' said the Colonel. 'That would be an indication that you were not available, and if this man is our killer, it would tip him off that something was wrong. Can't you postpone the meeting?'

'I've already told you, that's not possible.'

'What does this man have that's so important?' asked the Colonel.

'Something I've been trying to get hold of for a long time,' said Vander Mayer. 'Okay, your man will have to meet him. There's no other way. What's his name?'

'Cramer. Mike Cramer. What's the point of the meeting, Mr Vander Mayer?'

'I'm to take delivery of a sample and some documentation.'

'So it won't be necessary for Cramer to have an in-depth knowledge of your business?'

'Not really. In any case, he's Russian and speaks little or no English so Su-ming will have to translate everything.'

The Colonel considered Vander Mayer's suggestion. If this was the assassin making his move, the worst thing the Colonel could do would be to pull Cramer out of the firing line. 'Very well,' said the Colonel. 'When and where?'

'It'll have to be in my Kensington office. According to the itinerary you gave me, your man Cramer is going to be there in the afternoon on Thursday, so I'll have the meeting arranged for half past four. I'll need to brief him first.'

'You'll have to do that before we leave for London,' said the Colonel. 'Under no circumstances are you to contact me or him once the operation is under way. We've no idea what scanners or listening equipment he has.'

'No problem. I'll just sit on deck and soak up the sun.'
'One thing, Mr Vander Mayer. This sample, what is it?'
'It's an industrial compound. Nothing dangerous. But valuable.'

Dermott Lynch left the Warwick Castle public house in Little Venice and walked back to the flat along Blomfield Road. To his left, the other side of a row of black-painted railings, was a canal, its banks lined with pretty narrow boats, many of them bedecked with flowers, homes rather than working vessels. As Lynch walked along the pavement, a rusting blue Ford Transit van came up behind him and slowed to match his pace. The window on the passenger's side wound down. Lynch looked over at the vehicle. The passenger in the front seat was in his early twenties, a long, thin face and unkempt greasy hair. 'Is this the right way to Elgin Avenue?' the man asked. Lynch recognised the accent. West Belfast. The man had probably been born within a mile of Lynch's own home. It was too much of a coincidence.

Lynch kept on walking. 'Straight on, then take the second right. You'll find it.'

The passenger nodded. 'Are you Dermott?'

Lynch shook his head. 'Not me, mate,' he said. He quickened his pace. With his beard shaved off, his hair cut short and the wire-framed glasses he was wearing, there was no way he could have been recognised. Unless they were specifically looking for him.

'Dermott Lynch,' said the man.

'Don't know him,' said Lynch. The only way they could have known that he was the man they were looking for was if they'd staked out the flat. But there was only one person who knew where he was and that was Thomas McCormack. So if Thomas had sent them, why hadn't they simply knocked on the door? There was no need for late night assignations on a deserted street. Lynch knew he was in trouble. There were no windows in the side of the Transit so he had no way of knowing how many people were in the back.

'You sure? We've got something for you. From McCormack.' Lynch stopped. So did the Transit.

Lynch stood with his hands free, his legs apart. He wasn't armed, not so much as a knife. 'Yeah? Now what would that be?'

'This.' The man's hand appeared at the open window, holding an envelope.

Lynch smiled. It looked like an envelope full of cash, but he knew without a shadow of a doubt that he was being set up. The money could just as easily have been handed to him in the pub, or at the flat, or the man could have telephoned and arranged the handover. There was no reason to do it out in the open. Lynch walked towards the van, his hand outstretched, an easy smile on his face. 'Why didn't you say so in the first place?' he asked.

The passenger grinned. He was holding the envelope in his left hand, his right was hidden. As he got closer, Lynch saw that the man's jaw was clamped tight, a sure sign of tension, and his eyes had a fixed stare. They weren't planning to kill him there and then, he decided. They had other plans for him.

'What's your name, son?' asked Lynch. The question caught the man by surprise. Lynch saw him frown, but before he could reply Lynch reached out, grabbed the man's hair and smashed his face into the window frame. The cartilage of the man's nose cracked with a satisfying splintering sound. Lynch banged the man's head down a second time and this time his face made more of a soft crunching noise. There was blood everywhere. The driver began yelling and Lynch heard the clatter of feet in the back of the van.

Lynch grabbed the passenger's hair with both hands and yanked him through the window. He was struggling wildly so Lynch kicked him in the ribs, hard. The man was still holding the envelope and in his other hand was a pistol. Lynch grabbed at the weapon and wrestled it out of the man's grasp. He pointed it at the back of the man's neck and fired. The explosion echoed from the row of houses bordering the road. Lynch knew the police would arrive within minutes, maybe sooner.

Lynch swung around to face the van. The driver had a pistol in his hands and he pulled the trigger, gritting his teeth as he fired. To Lynch's amazement, nothing happened. 'Shit!' screamed the driver and Lynch realised with a feeling of satisfaction that the man had left the safety on. Lynch fired his own weapon and the driver slumped back, a gaping red hole where his nose had been.

The back doors of the van crashed open. Lynch leaned inside the passenger window. One of the men was standing silhouetted by a street lamp, about to jump down. Lynch shot him in the back then threw himself to the ground, rolling to the side as the fourth man appeared at the side of the van, bent double with a Kalashnikov in his arms. The Kalashnikov exploded, the bullets spraying across the side of the van, thudding through the metal as if it were cardboard. Before the man could lower his aim, Lynch put a bullet in his throat. The man whirled around and dropped the assault rifle, his hands clutching at his neck. His mouth opened and closed but no words came out. Blood trickled from between his teeth. Lynch got to his feet. The man's eyes glazed over and he fell to his knees, gurgling. Lynch walked past him and checked the back of the van. The man there was dead, lying face down on the metal floor. Lynch went through his pockets and pulled out his wallet.

In the distance he heard a siren. He ran around to the driver's side of the van. The driver was covered in blood and there was a smear of brain matter and bone fragments across the windscreen and a strong smell of urine. Lynch prised the gun from the dead man's fingers and patted down his bloodstained jacket until he found his wallet in an inside pocket. The siren was getting louder and Lynch heard shouts from the houses which overlooked the road. He ran down the pavement, vaulted over the railings and onto the towpath, escaping into the darkness.

Cramer's chest heaved and he threw up, the yellow vomit splashing over the wooden toilet seat and dribbling down into the bowl. He groaned. His head was throbbing, his stomach felt on fire. He massaged his temples and spat, trying to get the bitter taste out of his mouth. As the waves of nausea subsided he struggled to his feet and drank from the cold tap, swilling the water around his mouth and then spitting it out.

There was a timid knock on the bedroom door. 'Yeah,

wait a minute,' he called. He cleaned his teeth, using lots of toothpaste to get rid of the lingering bitterness. He splashed cold water over his face and then wiped the toilet seat with a piece of tissue and flushed it.

When he opened the door, Su-ming was waiting there. 'Is there something wrong?' she asked.

Oh yes, thought Cramer, there's something very wrong. There's a cancer growing in my guts and there's an assassin out there with a bullet with my name on it, and if one of them doesn't kill me soon I'm feeling so much pain that I'll be putting a gun in my mouth and pulling the trigger myself. 'I'm fine,' he said.

'Mr Vander Mayer wants to speak to us,' she said.

'He's here?'

'No. We have to telephone him.'

'The Colonel knows about this?'

'Mr Vander Mayer has already spoken to him.'

Cramer leant against the door frame. He felt weak but he didn't want Su-ming to know how ill he was. 'What's going on?' he asked.

'I think Mr Vander Mayer wants to tell you himself, but it's about a meeting he wants you to have the day after tomorrow.'

'In London?'

Su-ming nodded. 'Are you sure nothing's wrong?'

Cramer straightened up. 'Which phone?' he asked.

'The Colonel's study.' She turned and walked down the corridor. Cramer stood and watched her go, then followed her downstairs.

The only light on in the study was a green-shaded desk lamp which illuminated the desk and little else. The Colonel

207

was sitting behind the desk, a cellular telephone in front of him.

'I thought he was supposed to keep his head down until this was over,' said Cramer.

'Something came up.'

'Something so important that he thinks it's worth risking his life?'

The Colonel nodded in agreement. 'I told him, but he insists. And we do need his goodwill for this to work.'

'His goodwill? There's a contract out on his life.'

'He says that unless you and Su-ming meet this man, he'll come over himself. And if he appears on the scene, the whole thing's dead in the water.'

Cramer sat down in one of the armchairs. 'This man I'm supposed to meet, who is he?'

'All Vander Mayer would say is that he's a Russian with something to sell.'

'And I'm supposed to negotiate with this guy? But I don't know anything about Vander Mayer's business.'

'Which is why he wants to brief you first.' He handed the phone to Su-ming.

She tapped in a succession of numbers and held it to her ear. Vander Mayer answered within seconds. 'It's me,' said Su-ming. She listened intently. 'Yes,' she said, looking at the Colonel. 'Yes,' she repeated. She lowered the phone. 'Mr Vander Mayer asks if we could have this conversation in private.'

The Colonel got to his feet. He picked up his walking stick and tapped it on the wooden floor. He looked as if he was going to argue, but he walked stiffly to the door and let himself out. 'Okay,' Su-ming said into the phone. She listened again for what seemed to be several minutes, nodding as she held the phone to her ear. 'Okay, I'll put him on,' she said eventually. She walked over to Cramer and gave him the phone.

'Yeah,' said Cramer, laconically.

'Mike? Is it okay if I call you Mike?'

'Sure,' said Cramer. There was a distinct delay on the transmission and he could hear a faint echo of his own voice as he spoke. It was distracting and he concentrated hard.

'Okay, Mike, has your boss told you what's happening?' His voice was over-friendly, the sort of cheerful bonhomie used by double-glazing salesmen and television evangelists. The accent was American, from one of the southern States, Cramer figured. The vowels were long and drawn out and there was a laziness about the voice, as if it was too much of an effort to talk quickly. It was the sort of voice that Cramer could tire of very quickly, he decided.

'You want me to meet a Russian, that's all I know.'

'Okay, great. His name is Tarlanov. He speaks hardly any English but Su-ming is fluent in Russian.' Cramer raised his eyebrows in surprise. He would have expected her to be able to speak Oriental languages, but fluency in Russian was an unexpected talent. 'Tarlanov will have something for you, a sample of a chemical I'm interested in buying. Less than a kilo in weight, it'll be sealed in a metal flask. I want you to look after it for me until I can get to London.'

'What's in the flask?'

There was a pause and all Cramer could hear was a series of clicks and faint whistles. 'How much are you being paid for this job, Mike?' Vander Mayer asked eventually.

'What?' asked Cramer, taken off guard by the direct question.

'You're being paid for this, right?'

Cramer realised that he'd never discussed money with the Colonel. When the job had been offered, it had been the last thing on his mind. Even when he'd been serving with the regiment, he'd never been concerned about how much he was being paid and under his present circumstances he hadn't given it a second thought. 'I'm not doing this for money,' he said.

'You're doing it out of the goodness of your own heart, is that it?'

'I was asked to help.'

'You're putting your life on the line, that's what you're doing. It seems only fair that you should be well paid for that.'

'What's your point, Mr Vander Mayer?'

'Andrew. Call me Andrew. Seeing that you're taking my place, it only seems fair that we're on first name terms.'

'What's your point, Andrew?'

'The point is that I'm willing to offer you a substantial fee for your help. Shall we say a quarter of a million dollars?'

Cramer caught his breath. 'For what?'

'I want you to work for me. I want you to see this man Tarlanov and to take what it is he gives you. But I also want your discretion.'

'You want to buy my silence, is that it?' Su-ming looked at him, a worried frown on her face.

Vander Mayer chuckled softly. 'You're not a man to beat around the bush, are you, Mike? All right, yes; I don't want you telling anyone else about my business. You're in a very privileged position, you're going to be seeing and hearing things of a very confidential nature, things that a lot of my competitors would dearly love to know.'

'Look, Mr Vander Mayer, I'm here to do one thing, and one thing only, and that's to trap the man who's been paid to kill you. As soon as he's taken care of, it's over. Paying me a quarter of a million dollars isn't going to affect the way I do my job one way or the other. And I'm going to have to know what's in this container you want me to take from Tarlanov.'

'I'd rather keep that confidential,' said Vander Mayer. 'And please, Mike, call me Andrew.'

'I don't see how you expect me to meet this man if I don't know what it is I'm supposed to be taking from him.'

'Su-ming will handle the conversation. All Tarlanov wants is to see a man called Vander Mayer in person. There's a lot of con men in this business, Mike, and he insists on a face to face meeting. But he's not going to have much to say at this stage, he's just giving me a sample to test and some documentation to back it up. If the sample is what he says it is, I'll follow it up directly.'

'So there's nothing you want me to ask him?'

'Su-ming will ask the questions.'

'Won't that seem a little strange, like the tail wagging the dog?'

'Not if Tarlanov's English is as bad as I think it is.'

'And what if it isn't? What if he understands more than you think?'

'Su-ming will be able to handle it, Mike, don't worry. Just play your part. Be polite, offer him a drink, shake his hand, then get him the hell out of my office.'

'Is it dangerous?'

'Is what dangerous?'

'The material he's giving me. Are there any special precautions I should take?'

Vander Mayer chuckled again. 'You're fishing, Mike. Just accept the sample and take it back to the apartment. There's a safe in the study, Su-ming has the combination. Put the material in the safe along with any documentation he gives you. Do that for me, don't ask any questions, respect my privacy, and you'll receive a quarter of a million dollars when this is over. Now, would you put Su-ming back on, please?'

Cramer took the portable phone from his ear and stared at it for a few seconds, shaking his head in astonishment, almost unable to believe that a man he'd never met was offering to give him a small fortune for no apparent reason. He could only imagine how rich Vander Mayer must be to be able to offer such a sum without a second thought.

'Cramer?' said Su-ming, holding out her hand for the phone.

Cramer shook his head to clear it. 'What? Oh, yeah, he wants a word with you.'

He gave her the phone. She walked to the far side of the study as if afraid that he might overhear. She stood by the curtained window, nodding into the phone as she spoke. Cramer could only hear her last few words before she cut the connection. 'Yes,' she said, her voice barely a whisper, 'I love you, too.'

The phrase stuck in Cramer's mind long after he'd got back to his bedroom. She'd said it without feeling, flat and devoid of emotion, as if Vander Mayer was forcing her to say the words.

*   *   *

Paulie Quinn sat on his mattress with his back to his wall, his arms wrapped around his knees, hugging them to his chest. He was praying, saying the Lord's Prayer over and over again, but there was no solace in the words. Tears streamed down his face. He would never see his mother again, he knew that. He'd never leave the cell. He hadn't told them anything, but he knew that he wouldn't be able to hold out much longer. It wasn't that they were violent, they hadn't beaten him or even threatened to hurt him. They just kept repeating the same questions again and again, returning him to his cell when they wanted to rest but denying him the sanctuary of sleep. He knew that they wouldn't let him go until he'd told them everything. He stared up at the lights, then at the locked door. There was only one way to escape. One way out.

He crossed himself, the way he'd done whenever he entered church, the way he'd done at his father's funeral. 'Dad,' he said through the tears. 'I'm sorry. I'm so sorry.' He put his fingers into his mouth and took out the metal paper clip he'd managed to take from the interrogation room. It had been on the floor and he'd pretended to faint and managed to slip it under his tongue without the MI5 men seeing. He straightened the clip out, then wiped his tears away with the sleeves of his overalls. It was a mortal sin, but there was nothing else he could do. He'd tell them everything eventually, and then his life would be over anyway. At least this way his mother would be taken care of, and he'd have a hero's funeral. At least he'd be remembered with pride and not branded forever as a tout. He held out his left wrist and looked at the blue-green veins under his skin. He believed in Heaven, and he believed in Hell. Paulie sobbed. Even after death he'd never see his father or brother. Suicides never went to Heaven. 'I'm sorry, Dad,' he muttered through the sobs as he ripped away at his wrist with the end of the metal clip. The first few cuts were little more than scratches, but he closed his eyes and thrust the metal deep into his flesh as he recited the Lord's Prayer like a mantra.

Cramer found the Colonel outside, standing in front of a flowerbed which had become overgrown with weeds. 'It's a pity there's no one to look after the grounds,' said the Colonel. He sounded distracted, as if his thoughts were a million miles away from the untidy flowerbed.

An owl hooted off to Cramer's left. He shivered. 'I'm not happy about this meeting Vander Mayer's arranged,' he said. The owl flew out of an oak tree on the other side of the wall which surrounded the school's grounds.

'Why not?'

'You know he wants me to take something off this Russian guy?'

'A sample, he said. And documents.'

'Yeah, but he won't tell me what it is.'

'Does that matter?'

'Colonel, he's an arms dealer. It could be anything. Germ warfare, nerve gas; hell, it could be a bomb, for all I know.'

'I think that's most unlikely,' said the Colonel. He used the end of his walking stick to rearrange the foliage around a small flowering shrub.

'You know he offered me a quarter of a million dollars to work for him?'

'Did he?' said the Colonel. 'Now why would he do that?'

'To stop me asking questions, and to make sure that no one else sees what the Russian is giving me.'

The Colonel walked by the side of the school along a gravel path and Cramer followed him. 'This could be a set-up, it could be the killer making his move. You have to go through with it.'

'I know. But what about the stuff the Russian gives me?'

'I gave Vander Mayer an undertaking that we wouldn't be looking into his business. He has a similar undertaking from the Americans.'

'So even if what he's doing is illegal, there's nothing we can do?'

The Colonel nodded. 'We're not here to investigate him, we're here to catch a killer.'

'So I just take this sample, whatever it is, and I don't ask any questions?'

'What does he want you to do with it?'

'He said to put it in the safe in his apartment.'

'So that's what you do.'

Cramer exhaled deeply. He could see that there was nothing he could say that would change the Colonel's mind.

'And, of course, you get to keep the money,' the Colonel added without a trace of irony.

'Terrific,' said Cramer. They walked together around the back of the school. Two men in bomber jackets and faded blue jeans were patrolling the perimeter. One of them waved at the Colonel, who raised his stick in salute. 'The Americans know what we're doing, right?' Cramer asked.

'Absolutely. I'm liaising with the FBI in Washington, and

they'll be providing extra manpower once you get to New York on the same basis that the SAS will be covering you in London.'

'So why are you involved? Why has this become a British operation?

'Because we have the expertise. Because the Prime Minister has taken a personal interest.'

'But the target's an American and from the files I've read I'd say there's a good chance that the killer's a Yank, too.'

'You might be right.'

'So why are you running the operation? The Americans have got Delta Force and all sorts of covert people buried in the CIA. It'd be a great opportunity to earn a few Brownie points from the PM.'

The Colonel stopped. He held the walking stick as if it were a shotgun and sighted along it. 'There are security considerations that I'd rather not go into,' he said. He mimed pulling a trigger. 'But it was felt that it would be more appropriate for the operation to be run from here.'

Cramer had a sudden flash of inspiration. 'They've used him, haven't they? The Yanks have bloody well used him.'

'There's no proof of that,' said the Colonel, starting to walk again. 'But we can't rule it out. Like you say, there are lots of dark corners in the CIA that haven't seen light for a long time. There are people with hidden budgets answerable to no one who wouldn't be averse to paying a freelance to take care of a little business. And at least two of the victims wouldn't exactly be missed by the US Government, if you get my drift.'

'So the FBI doesn't even trust its own people?'

'No, the Bureau's safe, at least the people I'm dealing with are. But the fewer Americans involved, the better.'

Cramer nodded. 'Understood.'

'Are you okay?' the Colonel asked.

Cramer realised that he'd been holding his stomach. 'Yeah,' he said.

'Are you sure?' The Colonel's concern was genuine.

'It's not just indigestion, Colonel. This pain isn't going to go away.'

'I could get painkillers from the Doc. Something strong.'

'Not yet,' insisted Cramer. 'I want to go into this with a clear head, I don't want anything that'll slow me down.'

'It's your call,' said the Colonel.

'I know.' Cramer wiped his face with his hands. He was sweating, despite the cold night air. He desperately wanted to change the subject; it wouldn't take much for the Colonel's concern to change to pity. He started walking again and the Colonel followed. 'This banker, the guy who takes the contracts for the assassin. How do his clients know how to get in contact with him?'

The Colonel frowned. 'What do you mean?'

'Well, he can't advertise, can he? So how does he drum up business?'

The Colonel pulled a face. 'Word gets around,' he said. 'The sort of people and organisations who can afford his fee talk to each other. Phone numbers are exchanged. He's a neutral, he doesn't take sides, he's a tool to be used by anyone with enough money.' The Colonel narrowed his eyes. 'Let's face it, Joker, if you wanted someone killed, you know people who'd do it for a couple of thousand pounds. Maybe less. Hell, you probably know people who'd do it for you as a favour, right?'

217

'Right,' Cramer agreed.

'This guy's the same, he just operates for much bigger sums. The people who need him know how to get in touch. Word gets around.'

'Okay, but if you and the Yanks know who the banker is, why can't you just haul him in and put pressure on him?'

Cramer smiled without warmth. 'We both know people who'd love the opportunity for a spot of show and tell.'

'Wouldn't do any good,' said the Colonel patiently. 'They never meet, I doubt that they even talk to each other. The banker is like a circuit breaker – if we trigger him the killer will know we're on to him. He'll just disappear, then start up again somewhere else. It's a perfect system.'

'What about the money? Can't that be traced?'

The Colonel shook his head. 'It's not even worth trying,' he said. 'All he's got to do is press a few buttons and it can be routed through the Cayman Islands, Paraguay, anywhere. Forget it, Joker. This is the only way we're going to catch him.'

Cramer rubbed the back of his neck. The skin was damp there, too. 'The way he does it. The way he shoots them in the face, then the heart.'

'What about it?'

'It doesn't feel right. I'm sure the guy has a reason for doing it that way.'

'You can ask the profiler when he gets here.'

'There's nothing about it in his report.'

The Colonel scraped his walking stick along the gravel path. 'What are you getting at?'

'You shoot a guy in the head if he's tied up. If he can't fight back. That's how the IRA do it. They tie the guy up and they shoot him in the head. Bang! That's how the

Mafia do it, too, if they can. Tie the guy up and blow him away. Maybe that's how the guy used to operate, and the head-shot became a habit.'

'Possible,' said the Colonel.

'Or maybe he did it that way by accident the first time. Maybe he killed a guy before he became a pro. Maybe he got into a fight and shot a guy, got him in the head with the first shot. It worked so he figured that's how he'd do it in future. It could be as easy as that.'

'You're just guessing,' said the Colonel.

'Maybe. But did the FBI check if there had been any other killings using the same method, killings that weren't high profile assassinations? Killings that might have taken place while our guy was learning his trade?'

The Colonel nodded thoughtfully. 'Okay. I'll find out. And don't worry about Vander Mayer's consignment. It's his business, not ours. You just concentrate on what you've got to do.'

Cramer grinned. 'Concentrate on being bait, you mean? Sure, I can do that.'

The Colonel returned the grin. 'Yeah, I knew you were the right man for the job.'

Dermott Lynch dropped a coin in the slot and dialled Eamonn Foley's number. The two handguns were tucked into the back of his trousers, hidden by his jacket. They pressed into the small of his back as he leaned against the side of the call box and waited for Foley to answer the phone. Everything depended on how he reacted to the sound of Lynch's voice. If he was in on it, Foley would be surprised and Lynch doubted if he was good enough an actor to hide that.

Foley picked up the receiver. 'Yeah?'

'Eamonn. It's Dermott.'

'Hiya, Dermott. You on the piss?'

'Yeah. I had a few pints down the Warwick.'

'Feeling no pain?'

'Aye, you could say that.' Lynch couldn't sense any tension in Foley's voice. 'Has anyone been asking for me?'

'No, mate. You expecting someone?'

'No phone calls?'

'What's wrong?' Foley's voice was suddenly serious. Lynch decided that he could trust the man. Besides, he had no other choice.

'I'm in deep shit, Eamonn. Can you get my stuff and bring it to me?'

'Now?'

'Now.'

'What's happened?'

'I don't have time to explain. Just put everything in the suitcase and bring it to Edgware Road tube station.'

'The tube's not running this time of night.'

'I know, I know. I'll be waiting outside. And Eamonn, make sure you're not followed.'

'Jesus, Dermott. Who'd be following me?'

'Just be careful. Ten minutes, okay?'

'Fifteen.'

'Ten, Eamonn. You can make it if you leave right now. What sort of car have you got?'

'Ford Sierra. Blue.'

'Leave straightaway, okay?' Lynch replaced the receiver.

He waited exactly one minute and then dialled Foley's number again. It rang out and Lynch cut the connection immediately. Foley wasn't calling anyone. That at least was a good sign.

Lynch jumped as a siren went off and the call box was lit up by a flashing blue light. Instinctively he reached behind him, going for one of the guns, but then he smiled as he saw the ambulance rush by. 'Easy, boy,' he whispered to himself. He kept the phone pressed against his ear as he waited for Foley. He could see the front of the Underground station from his vantage point, its entrances now closed behind metal gates, and he was safer in the call box than he would be out in the open.

Foley arrived exactly eight minutes after Lynch's phone call, which Lynch took as another good sign. He slipped into the passenger seat and told Foley to drive. 'Where to?' asked Foley.

'Just drive.' Lynch twisted around and quickly checked through the contents of the suitcase on the back seat. His passport was tucked into a side pocket, along with an envelope containing five hundred pounds. He took out a green pullover and closed the case.

'Something strange happened just after you phoned,' said Foley as he drove down the Edgware Road. 'The phone rang, then went dead.'

'Don't worry about it,' said Lynch. He bent his head to look in the wing mirror.

'There's no one following us,' said Foley. 'Are you going to tell me what happened? Maida Vale was swarming with cops.'

'Four guys in a Transit attacked me.' Lynch pulled out the wallet he'd taken from the driver. There was a

221

driving licence and a Barclaycard inside. 'They were from Belfast.'

'UFF?'

'The driver was from the Falls Road. Name of Sean O'Ryan. Does that sound like a Prod to you, Eamonn?'

Foley shook his head. 'Doesn't make sense, does it?'

Lynch pointed to a car park. 'Drive in there and let me out,' he said.

'Don't be daft. You're safe in my flat.'

'I don't think so. I'm going to have to lie low.'

'Okay, you know best.' Foley drove into the car park and turned to face Lynch.

'I'm sorry about this, Eamonn.'

'Hey, don't worry about . . .' His face fell when he saw the pistol pointed at his chest. 'Don't,' said Foley. Lynch quickly wrapped the pullover around the gun to muffle the noise. 'Dermott, please. You can't.'

'I don't want to, Eamonn, but I don't have any choice.' The muffled bang would be loud in the confines of the car, but Lynch doubted if the sound would travel too far.

'Let's talk about this, Dermott. You can't just shoot me.'

Lynch wasn't happy at having to kill Foley, but McCormack had given him no choice. The IRA had passed a death sentence on him, and Lynch would do whatever it took to survive. 'I've just killed four of the boys,' said Lynch. 'I don't know what the fuck's going on, but I'm a marked man. And they'll use you to get to me.'

'Shit, I don't know where you're going, Dermott. Just run. I'll not say anything. I swear on my mother's life.' Foley's voice was wavering, his eyes wide and fearful. 'Please.'

Lynch looked at Foley. He gnawed his lower lip. Foley was right. He didn't know anything. If he'd been in on it, they'd probably have waited for Lynch inside Foley's flat.

'Take the car, Dermott. Take my wallet. Take everything. Just don't kill me.'

Lynch's finger tightened on the trigger, but something held him back. The only information Foley had was that Lynch had cut his hair and shaved off his beard, but McCormack wasn't stupid, he'd have considered that possibility anyway. His new appearance hadn't fooled the hit team, and it wouldn't fool anyone else they sent after him.

'Please,' begged Foley as if sensing Lynch's change of heart. 'You can keep the car. I won't even report it stolen.'

Lynch licked his lips. He was about to agree when Foley lunged to the side, grabbing for the gun. Lynch fired instinctively. The bullet caught Foley in the throat, ripping through the soft flesh and cartilage and lodging in his lower jaw. Foley tried to speak but his voice box was shattered and all he managed was a grunting sound. Blood frothed from the wound and his chest heaved, then his eyes glassed over and he slumped forward. Lynch grabbed him by the collar and hauled him away from the steering wheel, keeping his body off the horn.

'You stupid bastard,' said Lynch sorrowfully. 'You stupid, stupid bastard.' He climbed out of the car, and when he was satisfied that the car park was deserted, he pulled Foley's body out of the driver's seat and dragged it around to the boot. After he'd covered the corpse with a tartan blanket he locked the boot and wiped Foley's blood off the front seat with a rag.

Lynch sat behind the wheel as he considered his options.

Going back to Ireland was out of the question, he wouldn't last ten minutes on IRA territory. He wanted to confront McCormack, but that too would be a death sentence. He had no choice but to hide, but Lynch didn't like the idea of running to ground like a hunted fox. He smiled as another possibility sprang to mind.

He left the car park and found a call box. He dropped a pound coin in the slot and dialled the number in Dublin. Luke McDonough answered on the third ring. 'How did you get on?' asked Lynch.

'No sweat,' answered McDonough. 'They were in contact with Swansea ATC most of the way. Since that Chinook went down on the Mull of Kintyre and killed all those intelligence and security chiefs, MoD chopper pilots tend to play by the rules more often than not. Trouble is, they didn't land at an airfield, civilian or military. They flew close to Swansea airspace but landed somewhere to the north. All I've got is a map reference.'

'That's fine, Luke. Just let me get a pen.' Lynch took a black ballpoint pen from his inside jacket pocket. He didn't have any paper but there were several postcards advertising massage services stuck to the call box wall. He took one down and turned it over. 'Shoot,' he told McDonough. McDonough read out the numbers and Lynch wrote them down and then repeated them to make sure he'd got it right. A mistake in just one digit and he could be out by hundreds of miles. 'Thanks, Luke,' said Lynch. The line went dead.

Lynch stared at the phone, his thoughts elsewhere. A plan was beginning to half-form at the back of his mind. All bets were now off, he didn't have to obey McCormack's instructions any more. Lynch could track down the Sass-man and exact his revenge, but for that he needed money. He had credit cards in his wallet, but his bank account was in Belfast and he'd be limited in how much he'd be able to withdraw in London. Besides, if he used his credit cards he'd leave an electronic trail that the organisation would have no problem tracking. Lynch needed cash, a lot of it.

There were several listings for M. Hennessy in London, the operator told him, but only one lived in Notting Hill Gate.

Jim Smolev walked to his Dodge which he'd parked behind the two-storey building that housed the FBI's Miami field office. Smolev had fifteen years with the Bureau under his belt, but he'd only been attached to the Miami office for three months. Prior to that he'd been based in New York, which is where he'd first come across the assassin. It had been sheer luck that he'd been involved in the investigation into Frank Discenza, and had realised the significance of the lawyer's phone call to Zurich.

Smolev climbed into his car, dropped the padded envelope onto the passenger seat and drove the few blocks to Interstate Route 95. The envelope contained the photographs that had just arrived from the UK, the photographs of the man who would be taking the place of Andrew Vander Mayer. As he drove, Smolev wondered how the Brits had managed to persuade the man to step into Vander Mayer's shoes. The assassin had been responsible for at least six killings in the States and as far as Smolev knew, he'd never failed. A contract placed with the assassin was as good as a death sentence.

Smolev ran his tongue along one of his back teeth. It had been troubling him for several days but he hadn't had time to get to the dentist. Frank Discenza was taking up all his time, and would be for the foreseeable future. Until the assassin was apprehended. Or killed.

It took Smolev half an hour to drive to the hotel where Discenza was being held. As part of the deal negotiated with the Bureau and the IRS, the lawyer was holed up in a luxury hotel with round-the-clock protection. The Bureau was quite happy with the arrangement, despite the massive cost, because it meant they were able to control the situation. Discenza spoke to no one, and no one could get in touch with him.

Two agents stood guard outside Discenza's suite and nodded as Smolev went in. Discenza was sprawled across a sofa, a napkin tucked into his shirt collar as he ripped apart a boiled lobster. 'Hiya, Jimmy, want some?' he asked, dunking a chunk of white flesh into a dish of butter.

Smolev shook his head. 'The pictures have arrived,' he said. 'It's time to contact Zurich.'

'Jeez, let me finish my dinner first, will ya? Besides, it's past midnight in Switzerland.'

Smolev flicked the edge of the padded envelope with his thumbnail. 'We'll need to arrange the money trans-fer, too.'

'I'm working on it,' said Discenza. He wiped his mouth with the back of his hand and then took a drink from a bottle of Budweiser. 'Wanna Bud?' Smolev shook his head. 'I'm gonna get this money back, right?' said Discenza. 'That's what we agreed. Half a million dollars is a lot of money, you know?'

'Yeah, Frank, I know. It's about three per cent of what you owe the government, right?' Smolev probed his aching tooth with his tongue. The pain was getting worse.

Discenza's grin widened. 'Yeah, I never thought of it like that. America, it's a great country, isn't it?' He ripped a claw off the lobster, waved it in the air. 'Where else in the world, huh?' Smolev looked at the man, barely able to conceal his contempt. He hated doing deals with men like Discenza, but he was enough of a realist to know that there was no other way of catching the assassin. 'And Andrew doesn't know what's going on, right? I mean, he doesn't know it was me that was planning the hit, right?'

Smolev smiled. 'No, Frank. He doesn't know.' A sudden thought hit Smolev, and it made him smile all the more. Andrew Vander Mayer didn't know that Discenza had been planning to have him killed, but when all this was over, when the assassin had been captured, then maybe the arms dealer would receive an anonymous tip. An unsigned letter. Or a late night phone call. Smolev would have to be careful, of course. These days, you never knew who was listening in.

Mike Cramer sat on his bed reading the file provided by the American profiler. The first section listed the killings in the order that they happened, starting with the assassination in Miami and ending with the murder of a trial witness in a Baltimore hospital two weeks earlier. A second section detailed the common features of the killings, with the profiler focusing on the physical appearance of the assassin. The profiler had concentrated on the descriptions provided by witnesses who could be expected to be reliable – such as law enforcement officials and bodyguards – which is what Cramer himself had done when reading the individual case reports.

There were several facts which were constant. The killer was white, male, able-bodied, had no visible scars, and he was right-handed. There were other factors which were variable but fell within certain parameters, he was between five feet seven and six feet two inches tall, his weight was somewhere between one hundred and seventy pounds and two hundred and ten pounds, and estimates of his chest measurement varied between forty inches and forty six. Of less use were the characteristics which the killer changed on a regular basis – hair length, hair colour, eye colour, facial hair. Cramer scanned the lists. There was nothing that he hadn't read for himself in the individual reports on the killings.

Jackman had compiled his own reports on each of the killings. They each came with a heading sheet which read VICAP Crime Analysis Report and a logo which spelled out what VICAP stood for: Violent Criminal Apprehension Program. Stripped across the bottom of the sheet were the address and telephone number of the FBI Academy in Quantico, Virginia. Each case had its own VICAP number as well as an FBI case number, and went on to classify the crime, the victim, the MO, the cause of death and any forensic evidence. Like the FBI Facial Identification Fact Sheets, most of the questions were answered by ticking appropriate boxes which resulted in a scientific analysis of the facts rather than subjective comments. The VICAP reports emphasised the similarities between the actual killings, but they also threw up the differences in the victims and the descriptions provided by the witnesses.

The next section was more interesting; Jackman's profile of the assassin. The profiler said the assassin had a military background, possibly Special Forces, and was likely to have risen to the rank of non-commissioned officer. He had probably left the services, perhaps for health reasons, and had had trouble maintaining steady employment afterwards. He was gregarious and liked crowds but had a tendency to pick fights. He would be above average intelligence, with a feeling of superiority to most people he came into contact with. He was possibly divorced, or had a string of sexual contacts, and was probably good looking. He was certainly attractive to women. He would have committed a number of motoring offences, and his licence had possibly been suspended.

The killer probably came from a family where emotional abuse was the norm, but the home was stable, at least during his early childhood. He may have been a bully at school, and despite his intelligence probably didn't go on to university.

There was plenty of detail, though the report was peppered with 'probably' and 'possibly' as if Jackman was afraid of being proved wrong and was therefore constantly hedging his bets. There was little in the way of explanation for the various conclusions, though Cramer guessed that the killer's familiarity with different weapons would suggest the military background. He had no idea why Jackman thought that the assassin would have had his driving licence taken away.

Most of Jackman's observations concerned the killer's psychological make-up and his childhood, and while they made fascinating reading, Cramer knew that they wouldn't be any use to him. The fact that the assassin didn't have a university degree wouldn't make him stand out in a crowd. Cramer needed a description, physical characteristics that he could watch out for. Cramer slid his feet off the bed. He padded over to the bathroom in his bare feet and drank from the tap. He wanted to use the toilet but he fought the urge. The last time, he'd seen blood in the bowl and it had frightened him.

Dermott Lynch parked the Sierra in Kensington Park Road and walked to Ladbroke Gardens. Marie Hennessy's flat was in a terrace of white-painted stucco houses, once homes to the rich but now subdivided into flats for the almost-wealthy. Her name wasn't on the entry-system bell but she'd told him that she was in flat C and when he pressed the button she answered immediately, as if she'd been waiting for him. 'I'm on the third floor, come on up, I'll buzz you in,' she said, her voice crackling over the speaker.

The lock buzzed and Lynch pushed the door open. He could feel the Czech 9mm pistol pressing into the small of his back. The gun had a fifteen round magazine and there were ten bullets still in it. The gun he'd taken from the driver was a slightly smaller Russian-made Tokarev with eight rounds in the magazine. He'd left it in the boot along with the body of Eamonn Foley. The hallway was in darkness but as he stepped inside the lights came on. The stair carpet was dark blue and plush and there were framed watercolours on the walls. The staircase spiralled up and mahogany doors led off to the flats, two on each floor. The door to Marie's apartment was already open when he reached the third floor, though she'd kept the security chain on. She waited until he got close before taking off the chain and opening the door wide. 'I wouldn't have recognised you if you hadn't told me you were coming,' she said.

'I shaved off the beard,' said Lynch, stepping inside. He had recognised her immediately. The chestnut hair, the slightly upturned nose, the blue eyes that had been brimming with tears the last time they'd met.

'And you've cut your hair,' said Marie, closing the door behind him. 'And you weren't wearing glasses. Go on through.'

'You've got a good memory, right enough,' said Lynch as he walked into the sitting room. It was expensively furnished with comfortable antiques, very much a girl's room. A small circular table held a collection of painted miniatures behind which he saw several framed photographs. Lynch recognised Marie's mother, Mary, and her father, Liam. The last time Lynch had seen Marie was at her mother's funeral three years earlier. Lynch bent down to look at a photograph of Mary and Liam, she in a wedding dress, he in tails, a stone church in the background. Mary was in her early twenties back then, Liam maybe a decade older. 'You look just like your mum,' said Lynch.

'I know,' said Marie, closing the sitting room door.

Lynch straightened up. There was a large gilt-framed mirror hanging over the marble fireplace and in it he saw Marie studying him, a look of concern on her face. 'Are you alone?' he said to her reflection.

She nodded. 'Why do you ask?'

Lynch turned to face her, smiling to put her at ease. 'Because I wouldn't want anyone to overhear us, that's all.'

'I'm alone,' she said. 'There's only one bedroom. You can check for yourself if you don't believe me.'

'I believe you,' he said.

'I'm honoured.'

Lynch grinned.

'What are you smiling at?' she asked archly.

'It's the sort of thing your mother would have said.'

She narrowed her eyes and looked at him as if deciding whether or not he was trying to flatter her. Then she smiled, showing white, even teeth that would have done credit to a toothpaste advert. 'Would you like a drink?'

'Coffee, please. Black.' If he was going to get through the next few hours, he was going to need a clear head.

Marie went into the kitchen. While she made his coffee he studied the photographs again. Liam Hennessy, the Sinn Fein adviser who'd been murdered by the SAS. Mary Hennessy, shot by a police sniper in Baltimore. Both had given their lives to the Cause, literally. Lynch wondered how their deaths had affected Marie, and if he could trust her.

One of the photographs was of Marie and a young man. Lynch recognised the man as her brother, Philip, one of the pall bearers at Mary Hennessy's funeral. Philip, at twenty-five, was a couple of years older than Marie and Lynch seemed to recall that he was now working in the Far East, something to do with banking or insurance. Marie returned with his coffee. 'How's Philip?' he asked.

'Fine,' she said. 'I haven't seen much of him, not since . . .'

She didn't finish and Lynch realised she had been about

to say 'the funeral'. Marie placed the tray and two coffee mugs onto a low table, then sat down in a Queen Anne chair and crossed her legs. She was wearing a short black skirt and a large beige pullover that tried but failed to conceal her figure. She had good legs, long and shapely, another thing she had in common with her late mother. 'So, what brings you to London?' she asked.

'I need your help.'

Marie narrowed her eyes. 'You? Or the organisation?'

To the best of Lynch's knowledge, Marie had never been an active member of the IRA. Neither had her brother. 'Me,' he said.

Marie stirred her coffee slowly. 'I'm not sure that there's anything I can do for you, Mr Lynch.'

'Dermott,' said Lynch. 'Mr Lynch is my dad.'

Marie gave a small shrug as if she didn't care either way what she called him. 'What is it you want?'

Lynch sat down on a hard, uncomfortable couch and leaned forward, his hands clasped together. 'You know Mike Cramer. The SAS sergeant who . . .'

Marie's hand froze above her coffee mug and she spoke quickly, interrupting him before he could finish. 'Yes. I know who Cramer is.'

'I think I might be able to get to him.'

'Where is he?' Her voice was monotone, almost mechanical. The silver spoon remained suspended in her hand.

'Best I don't tell you too much.' He ran his hand across his face. The beard had gone but it still itched. 'I'll need money.'

Marie frowned. 'Surely the organisation would . . .'

Lynch shook his head. 'I've been told not to take it any further. The Army Council doesn't want the boat rocked. They don't want anything to derail the peace process.'

'They what? Cramer is one of the men who killed my father. And he was directly responsible for my mother's death.'

'I know. I know. But they say I'm not to go after him. Let sleeping dogs lie, they said.'

'Who said?'

'Thomas McCormack. But he was speaking for the Army Council. Even if I find out where Cramer is, they won't allow me to do anything.'

Marie leaned forward and put her coffee back on the tray. 'And you're prepared to defy the Army Council?'

Lynch put two heaped spoonfuls of sugar into his own coffee. 'Cramer also killed my girlfriend. She was part of an ASU in London during the late eighties.'

'ASU?'

'Active Service Unit. Cramer was among a group of SAS soldiers who stormed the flat where she was living.'

'And you want revenge, is that it?'

Lynch studied her, trying to read what was going on in her mind. 'Don't you?' he asked quietly.

She held his look. 'Yes,' she said eventually. 'Yes, I do.'

'So you'll help?'

'There's a limit to what I can do. I have a job. I have a life, I have . . .'

'It's okay, Marie. I need money, that's all.'

Marie relaxed. She uncrossed her legs, keeping her knees pressed primly together as if she thought Lynch might peer up her skirt. 'That's one thing I can provide. How much will you need?'

'As much as you can give me. I've got to tell you, Marie, it won't be a loan. I doubt that I'll be able to pay you back.'

'Like I said, I've got a job.' She stood up and walked over to a Victorian side table. Lynch admired her legs as she bent to open a drawer. Under other circumstances maybe he would have tried to look up her skirt, but Marie Hennessy was the daughter of Mary Hennessy and as such was untouchable. Sacrosanct. She straightened up, a bank statement in her hands. 'I can let you have two thousand tomorrow morning as soon as the bank opens. Will that be enough?'

Lynch smiled. 'That'll be just great.'

'Do you have somewhere to stay?' Lynch shook his head. 'You can use my room,' she said. 'You're too big for the sofa. I'll sleep in here.'

'Marie, I can't thank you enough.'

'You don't have to. Just get that fucker Cramer. That'll be thanks enough.' She smiled sweetly, the girlish grin at odds with the obscenity.

Mike Cramer could feel the sweat trickle down his back and soak into the handmade shirt. It wasn't a cold night but he was wearing the cashmere overcoat over his suit. Allan's orders. Allan was standing slightly ahead of him and to his right, Martin was two paces to Cramer's left. Both bodyguards were wearing dark suits that glistened under the floodlights. They were walking together across the tennis courts. The nets had been taken down, giving them plenty of space to work in. Cramer had been about to go to bed when Allan had knocked on his door and told him to report outside in his Vander Mayer clothing.

One of the lights was buzzing like a trapped insect but Cramer blocked it out of his mind. There were three men standing at the far end of the tennis courts, whispering. Martin moved to cover Cramer, getting between him and the three men. Cramer's throat was dry and he was dog tired, but he forced himself to concentrate. The three men started to walk, fanning out as they headed in his direction. Cramer kept walking. The overcoat felt like a straitjacket and the shoes were rubbing his heels.

Allan's head was swivelling left and right, keeping track of the three men. The man in the middle of the group, stocky and well-muscled with a receding hairline, moved his hand inside his jacket. Cramer tensed, but the hand reappeared holding a wallet. The man on the left of the group bent down as if about to tie his shoelace but Cramer could see that he was wearing cowboy boots under his jeans. Martin moved to block the kneeling man, but as he did the third walker pulled a large handgun from under his baseball jacket. Without breaking stride he fired at Martin, one shot to the chest. Cramer stopped dead, his right hand groping for the gun in its leather underarm holster. Allan began to scream 'Down! Down! Down!' and reached for his own gun. Before he could bring it out the man fired again at close range and Allan slumped to the ground.

Cramer grabbed the butt of his Walther PPK. The man walked away from Allan, holding his own gun at arm's length. He was the tallest of the three, with a swimmer's build, a baseball cap pulled low over his eyes as if to shield them from the glare of the floodlights. He was only six feet away from Cramer, his mouth set in a straight line, his eyes narrowed. Cramer yanked out the PPK, swinging it in front of him, trying to slip his index finger into the trigger guard but he was too late, the gun was in his face. The explosion jerked him back and he flinched, his eyes shutting instinctively so that he didn't even see the second shot being fired.

'Shit!' he screamed.

Allan rolled over and looked at Cramer. 'Bang, bang, you're dead,' he said.

'It's this fucking coat,' said Cramer.

Martin got to his feet and dusted down his trousers before walking over to Allan. He held out his hand and pulled him to his feet.

'You're getting better,' said Allan.

'I missed the trigger,' said Cramer. 'I had the gun in my hand but I couldn't get my finger on the trigger.'

'You just need practice,' said Allan. 'You're not trained in quick-draw. In the Killing House you go in with guns blazing, not stuck in underarm holsters.' He slapped Cramer on the back. 'You'll be fine, Mike. Trust me. Come on, back to the starting position.' Allan, Martin and Cramer went back to their end of the tennis courts while the three other SAS men regrouped.

Cramer slipped his PPK back into the holster, then tried drawing it quickly. It snagged on the pocket of his jacket and he cursed. As he tried again he saw the Colonel open the gate in the tall wire-mesh fence which surrounded the three tennis courts.

The Colonel walked across the red clay playing surface. 'How's it going?' he called.

Cramer pulled a face. 'Twenty-three runs and I've taken a bullet every time.'

'You don't have much longer to practice. The photographs have arrived in Miami. They'll be sent by courier tomorrow. The money is being transferred through the banking system.'

'I'll be ready.'

'Good. The profiler will be here tomorrow. Then you leave for London.'

Cramer shrugged his shoulders inside the coat. 'I'm going to need a few more rehearsals. I've got to get my reaction time down.'

The Colonel nodded and tapped his stick on the playing surface, hard enough to dent the clay. 'There's been another killing. In South Africa.'

'He gets around, doesn't he? Have gun, will travel.'

'There's no turning back now, Joker.' There was a flat finality about his words, a coldness Cramer hadn't heard before, as if he was already distancing himself.

The boy heard his mother's screams as he opened the front door. He fought the impulse to pull the door shut and run away as he stood on the threshold listening to the animal-like cries of pain. He closed his eyes and rested his forehead against the door-jamb. The screams stopped and the boy sighed deeply. He closed the door as quietly as he could but the lock clicked and his mother called out his name. The boy dropped his book-filled carrier bag on the floor and climbed the stairs with a heavy heart.

His mother was curled up on the bed, her arms wrapped around her legs, tears streaming down her cheeks. The boy stood by the bedroom door, watching her. 'I can't take any more of this,' she said.

'You'll get better, Mum,' he said.

'No, I won't,' she said.

'You will. I know you will.'

'It hurts,' she said, curling up into a tighter ball.

She was so thin, the boy realised. Her arms were like sticks and the skin seemed to be stretched tight across her face. But she was still his mum. 'Shall I call the doctor?' he asked, his voice trembling.

'The doctor can't help,' she said. 'He can't make the hurt go away.' Her breath started coming in short gasps as if she was having trouble breathing.

'Do you want me to get you some milk?' His mother shook her head. 'What about something to eat?'

'You have to help me,' she pleaded.

'I will,' he said. 'I will, Mum. I'll do anything to make you better.'

She shook her head again. 'You can't make me better,' she said. She fixed him with her tear-filled eyes. 'But you can stop the hurting. You have to get me my medicine.'

Dermott Lynch woke instantly at the sound of the shower being turned on. At first he couldn't remember where he was, the wallpaper with its yellow flowers and the ruffles on the curtains gave the bedroom a feminine feel and there was a fluffy white bear on the dressing table which stared at him with blue glass eyes. Sun streamed in through the thin curtains and then he heard someone step into the shower. Marie Hennessy. Lynch looked at his watch. It was just before nine o'clock but he'd only slept for a few hours. Marie had kept him up late, talking over old times, begging him to tell her stories about her mother and father.

Lynch had taken care to sanitise what he told her. While her parents had both died for the IRA, Marie had never shown any interest in joining the organisation and Lynch didn't think she knew the full extent of their involvement. Liam Hennessy had been an adviser to Sinn Fein, the political wing of the IRA, during several bombing campaigns on the mainland during the late Eighties. He had also been the driving force behind the bomb attack on the Brighton hotel which had come close to taking the life of the then Prime Minister, Margaret Thatcher. Following the death of Liam Hennessy, his wife Mary had assumed an even more active role, going underground and taking part in several high profile bombings, or spectaculars as the IRA Army Council liked to call them. A lot of people had died.

He sat up in bed and rubbed his face with his hands. It still felt strange without the beard, as if the skin belonged to someone else, but he was pleased with the shorter hair as he no longer had to keep pushing it out of his eyes. He leant over the side of the bed and put his hand on the pistol to reassure himself that it was still there. He got out of bed and was about to pull the curtains aside when he had second thoughts. The flat was overlooked by the houses on the other side of the road and it would be smarter not to let the neighbours know that Marie had had a visitor. It was warm in the bedroom and Lynch suddenly remembered the body in the boot of the Ford Sierra, parked down below. It would soon start to smell and it would only take one curious passer-by to have the whole area flooded with police.

The bedroom door opened and he turned to see Marie standing there, swathed in a purple towel, her hair dripping wet. She showed no embarrassment at his nakedness, and in fact it was Lynch who blushed. 'Shower's free,' she said brightly.

Lynch stood with his hands across his groin like a footballer in a defensive wall. 'Great, thanks,' he said.

Marie's grin widened and she raised one eyebrow. For a moment it looked as if she was going to say something else, but then she turned and left him alone.

Lynch went into the bathroom and locked the door before running the shower. Above the washbasin was a mirrored cabinet and he stared carefully at his own reflection. He ran a hand through his hair, wondering what else he could do to change his appearance. Marie hadn't recognised him but the man in the van clearly had, despite the absence of a beard and the wire-framed glasses. He opened the cabinet door and looked inside: aspirins, contact lens cleaning solution, bottles containing different coloured contact lenses, cotton-wool balls, tweezers, a bottle of witchhazel, and several packets of contraceptive pills. 'Tut, tut, Marie, a good Catholic girl like you,' Lynch muttered to himself. She was a fine looking girl, and Lynch couldn't help but wonder who she was sleeping with and what she was like between the sheets.

The coloured contact lenses were a good idea but he had perfect eyesight and whatever Marie's prescription, they'd be an irritant if he tried to wear them. What he'd really hoped to find was hair dye.

He closed the cabinet door and stared at his reflection again. He looked younger without the facial hair, and the glasses made him resemble a vicar welcoming the faithful to a church garden party. There was a sudden knock on the door. 'Tea or coffee, Dermott?' called Marie.

'Coffee. You don't dye your hair, do you?'

There was a short pause as if Marie was trying to work out why he'd asked the question. Then realisation must have dawned. 'No,' she said through the door. 'But I can get you some stuff from the local chemist, if you want. After breakfast.'

Lynch smiled to himself. Smart and beautiful. Just like her late mother.

Martin was tucking into a cooked breakfast when Cramer walked into the dining hall. His plate was piled high with sausages, bacon and scrambled eggs and there was a stack of buttered toast on a side plate. Martin winked, and raised his coffee mug in salute.

Cramer shook his head in amazement. Martin swallowed. 'Hollow legs, Mike. Family trait.' He picked up two pieces of toast, slapped a sausage and two rashers of crispy bacon between them, and slotted them into his mouth, as if posting a letter.

Cramer poured himself a mug of coffee and sat down opposite. A neighbouring table held a large television set and a video recorder, and a white power cord trailed across the oak floorboards to a socket in the wall. Cramer nodded at the television. 'What's going on?' he asked.

Martin shrugged and washed his food down with a mouthful of coffee. 'Dunno. The Colonel set it up first thing.'

'Where's Allan?'

'On the tennis courts with the boys. Running through a few set pieces.'

'How do you think it's going?'

'Could go either way, Mike. I wish I could say I was confident that we'd get him, but we've got so little time to react, you know?'

'Yeah. I know.' Under Allan's guidance, Cramer's reaction times were getting shorter and shorter, but he was still failing to draw his weapon more often than not. And even when he did manage to get his gun out, he'd yet to get in a killing shot before being shot himself.

'Allan and I'll do everything we can to give you extra time, but at the end of the day it's like two gunfighters, except that you don't know who you're drawing against.' Cramer sipped his coffee. 'Not eating?' Martin asked.

'Is there anything left?'

Martin grinned and made himself another bacon and sausage sandwich. Cramer heard the Colonel walk into the dining room behind him. 'Good morning,' said the Colonel, lifting the lids off the stainless steel serving dishes and sniffing like a golden retriever tracking game. 'How are the sausages this morning?'

'First class,' said Martin. 'I don't know why Mike here isn't tucking in.'

'Maybe later,' said Cramer.

The Colonel spooned scrambled eggs onto a plate and

used tongs to pick up two grilled tomato halves. 'I spoke to our friends in the States,' the Colonel said to Cramer. 'They're going to run a check on previous murders using shots to the head. They'll get back to us if they turn up anything.'

Cramer nodded in acknowledgement. The dining room was cold despite the portable gas heater and the Colonel was wearing his Barbour jacket. He went over to the video recorder and put in a cassette before sitting down next to Cramer. Martin slid to the side so that they could all get a good view of the screen. From his pocket, the Colonel took a remote control device. Before pressing the 'play' button, he pushed the plate of eggs and tomatoes in front of Cramer. Cramer started to protest but the Colonel silenced him with a wave of his hand. 'Eat,' he ordered and Cramer reluctantly picked up a fork. The television flickered into life. 'These were taken by the security cameras in Harrods,' said the Colonel. 'The quality isn't as good as it might be, but as you'll see, it doesn't really matter.'

On screen an Arab in desert robes moved through the store, preceded by three bodyguards. There were two other men in suits either side of the Arab, but they looked more like store executives than protection, and behind the Arab walked three women in black robes, their faces covered. Cramer didn't hear the shots but he saw the first bodyguard slump to the floor and then the killer appeared on the screen, his arm outstretched as he aimed his weapon at the second bodyguard. The silenced gun fired twice again, two shots to the man's chest. The third bodyguard died before he could draw his own weapon. Cramer's mouth was dry. The killer was fast. Fast and accurate, faster even than the SAS men he'd been practising with on the tennis courts. The killer's face was turned away from the security camera as he walked past the Arab and shot one of the women, a bullet in the face, one in the chest, then he walked quickly out of range of the security camera.

Cramer put a forkful of scrambled eggs into his mouth and chewed slowly as the screen flickered. This time the view was of the stairs. Two elegant blondes in designer coats were smiling and nodding and a young man in a denim jacket turned to admire their legs. The killer came into view, walking quickly, his head down and his face turned away from the camera, a handgun pressed to his side. One of the blondes put a hand to her mouth, her eyes wide and fearful, and then the killer was gone. Cramer frowned. 'Was he limping?' he asked.

'Left leg,' agreed Martin. Allan arrived, wearing a dark blue blazer and grey flannels, looking for all the world like an Olympic referee. Allan stood behind the Colonel, his arms folded across his chest. He nodded a silent greeting to Cramer, then studied the screen.

'This is the Egyptian Hall,' said the Colonel as the screen flickered again. The killer walked by a life-size copy of the Rosetta stone and past a display of small statues. Cramer put down his fork. There was no doubt about it, the man was limping. Again it was impossible to identify the man, his head was turned away from the security camera. As he passed out of the camera's field the screen flickered and was replaced by a shot of the stationery department.

'He's really camera-shy, isn't he?' mused Martin as he assembled another bacon and sausage sandwich. No one seemed to be paying attention to the killer as he walked purposefully to a stock room door, even though he was still holding the silenced gun. He opened the door and disappeared behind it and the screen flickered once more.

The next shot was of the underground tunnel. This time the killer was wearing a warehouseman's coat and there was no sign of his gun. He walked past two workmen but they ignored him. The limp seemed to be less pronounced, Cramer noticed.

The final section of the video showed a young security guard on the telephone. The guard looked to his left, opened his mouth to speak and then fell back, blood pouring from his throat. The killer appeared briefly at the bottom left of the screen, revealing nothing more than the back of his head and his shoulders. The Colonel used the remote control to switch off the television set. 'That's the only time our man has been captured on film,' he said. 'I want you all to play it as many times as it takes until you get a feel for the way he moves.'

'The limp,' said Allan. 'He was faking it?'

The Colonel nodded. 'We had an orthopaedic surgeon take a look at it and he says it's not genuine. It's redirection. You spend so much time looking at the limp that you're not aware of his other characteristics.'

'He knew where all the security cameras were,' Cramer pointed out. 'He must have staked the store out first.'

'Agreed,' said the Colonel, 'but the security tapes are wiped regularly. We have tapes for the forty-eight hours prior to the assassination and we've gone through them, but there's no sign of him.'

'Well, we know he's white and we know he's right-handed,' said Martin. 'And he's cool.'

'Cool? He's ice,' said Allan. 'There's no nervousness about him, no tension. It's like he's on a Sunday afternoon stroll in the park. I've never seen anything like it. He takes out three bodyguards and his target and then he walks away without even looking back.'

'It's like he doesn't care,' said Cramer.

Martin shook his head. 'No, he's a real pro. He knows that hurrying or looking around will just draw attention to him.'

Allan put a large hand on Cramer's shoulder. 'Ready, Mike?'

Cramer drained his mug and stood up. The Colonel raised an eyebrow at Cramer's unfinished breakfast but said nothing.

'We'll run through some moves in the gymnasium,' said Allan. Cramer walked out of the dining hall with Allan and Martin either side. The suit felt like a straitjacket, even though it was a perfect fit. He would have much preferred to have been wearing a bomber jacket and jeans, but he realised how important it was to dress the part. It was camouflage, as vital to the role he was playing as the green and brown fatigues he'd worn in the Falklands and in the border country of Northern Ireland. He reached inside his jacket and touched the butt of his PPK as if to reassure himself it was still there.

Their footsteps echoed off the tiled walls of the corridor as they headed towards the gymnasium. Martin pushed open the door and stood to the side to allow Cramer in first. 'Cheers,' said Cramer. He felt rather than heard the man behind the door, and as he turned his right hand reached for the PPK. His fingers were still inches from the butt when the first shot rang out, and he felt the heat from the explosion on his cheek. He carried on turning and he saw his assailant, a blond-haired man in his late twenties holding a Smith & Wesson. The second shot rang out, aimed at Cramer's chest.

Cramer whirled around and pointed his finger at Allan. 'What the hell are you playing at?' he shouted.

'We're not playing at anything, Mike,' said Allan calmly. 'This isn't a game. There's no bell between rounds. The moment you accepted this job, your life was at risk. You can't afford to let your guard down. Ever.'

Cramer calmed himself. He took a deep breath and nodded. He could hear his pulse pounding in his veins and his fists were clenched tight. He forced himself to relax. He knew that Allan was right, he was just annoyed at his own stupidity. Martin should have gone into the room first, to check that it was clear, but from the way he was grinning it looked as if he'd deliberately set him up. Cramer nodded. 'Okay, Allan. You made your point.'

Allan slapped Cramer on the back. The man who'd shot Cramer with blanks was already walking back into the gymnasium. Three others were standing by the wall bars, dressed casually and wearing shoulder holsters. 'You'll be okay, Mike,' said Allan. 'I just want to make sure you get through this in one piece.'

Cramer's ears were still ringing from the shots and he massaged his temples. 'I know, Allan. I know. Let's get on with it.'

'I've got something I'd like to show you,' said Allan. 'You and the guys come at me and Martin, you decide who's going to be the trigger man.'

Cramer grinned. It would be nice to be on the winning side for once. He went over to the four men at the far side of the gymnasium and explained what they were to do.

'Ready?' called Allan.

Cramer gave him a thumbs-up. Martin stood by Allan's side and together they began to walk slowly across the wooden floor. Cramer and the four men fanned out, all keeping their hands swinging freely by their sides. One of them pretended to sneeze and Martin tensed as the man's hands went up to cup his nose. Allan straightened his tie with his right hand, his eyes hard and watchful. Cramer waited until he was six feet away from Allan before pulling out his PPK. Allan reacted immediately, his right hand slipping inside his left sleeve and reappearing with a stiletto. He stepped forward, thrusting the knife upward towards Cramer's chin. Cramer's finger tightened on the trigger but he was too late, Allan's left hand had whipped up, knocking Cramer's arm to the side in a blur of blue blazer. The stiletto pricked Cramer's neck. Allan froze, holding Cramer's stare. He smiled. 'What do you think?' He removed the stiletto and handed the weapon to Cramer.

Cramer examined it, frowning. The spike wasn't made of metal but of black plastic-like material. 'You knew I'd be the one firing, didn't you?' he said.

Allan shrugged. 'I guessed you'd want a crack at me, but it wouldn't have made any difference. As long as I see you going for your gun, I should be able to get the knife out first.' He held out his left arm and pulled back the sleeve. There was a leather sheath strapped to his forearm over his shirt. 'With your hands down by your sides, it's always going to be quicker to draw the knife than to pull a gun. But you're going to have to move forward, towards the killer. Towards the gun.'

'What's it made of?' Cramer asked.

'It's the latest thing from the States,' said Allan. 'I got a sample from a friend in Delta Force. It's a composite carbon fibre mixture, a spin-off from the space programme, very lightweight, practically unbreakable and never loses its edge.' He grinned. 'You can even shave with it. The advantage from your point of view is that it's virtually impossible to detect.'

Cramer nodded thoughtfully, his eyes on the stiletto. 'Let me try it.'

Marie Hennessy put a jug of milk and a box of muesli on the kitchen table next to a plate of wholewheat toast, Flora margarine and honey. 'I'm a vegetarian,' she said as Lynch looked up.

'Aye, well you look good on it,' said Lynch, grinning. He wondered if he should say anything about the Charles Jordan shoes he'd seen lying in the hall but decided against it. They were clearly expensive and definitely not plastic. There were also several leather-bound books scattered through the two bookcases in the sitting room. Whatever else she might be, Marie Hennessy was obviously selective about her moral stances.

'I'll go and get your money,' she said, taking a quick look at her watch. She slipped into a blue blazer and checked her hair in the gilt-framed mirror over the mantelpiece before leaving the flat.

As she closed the front door behind her, Lynch picked up the box of muesli and sniffed it. 'Rabbit food,' he muttered to himself and put it back down. Spreading honey thickly onto the toast, he ran through a mental list of what he still had to do. The only location he had for Mike Cramer was a map reference, lines of longitude and latitude, and for that to mean anything he'd need an Ordnance Survey map of the area. There was no doubt in his mind that he would kill the Sass-man. He had two guns, the Czech Model 75 in the bedroom and the Tokarev in the car, and he'd been well trained in the use of small arms. When in Ireland he generally preferred to use a Kalashnikov, but the handguns would be easier to conceal. He leaned over to go through the pockets of his jacket which was hanging on the back of a chair. He pulled out the two wallets which he'd taken from the hit team in Maida Vale. There was more than three hundred pounds in cash, along with the Barclaycard and driving licence. Lynch had been surprised to find the driving licence, as IRA volunteers on active service were instructed to remove all means of identification. He picked up the licence and looked at it. It appeared real enough, as did the Barclaycard, but Lynch doubted if they were genuine. He just hoped they would stand up to scrutiny when he went to pick up a rental car. But first he'd have to get rid of the Ford Sierra parked in the street outside.

Cramer was practising pulling the stiletto from its leather sheath when a helicopter roared overhead and rattled the gymnasium windows. He saw a flash of green through the dirt-streaked windows and then it was gone. 'Ready, Mike?' asked Allan.

Cramer nodded. He adjusted his sleeve and dropped his hands to his sides. Allan walked away, then stood facing Cramer with his hands on his hips. Martin joined him.

Allan and Martin moved together as if some unspoken signal had passed between them, but whatever it was, Cramer missed it. They walked at a medium pace across the wooden floor. Cramer stayed where he was. Waiting. It was Allan who made the first move, reaching inside his jacket and pulling out his Glock automatic. Cramer's right hand slid into his left sleeve and grabbed for the stiletto. As Allan swung up his arm to take aim with the gun, Cramer thrust out with the stiletto, but Allan swayed out of the way. The big man was deceptively light on his feet and moved as fluidly as a flyweight in an opening round, keeping the Glock pointed at Cramer's face as Cramer lashed out with the knife again. Allan pulled the trigger twice in quick succession and Cramer was almost deafened by the explosions. 'Shit,' said Cramer dejectedly.

Allan ejected the clip and slotted in two more blanks. 'You got it out all right, but you weren't moving forward,' he said, replacing the gun in its holster. 'It's only going to work if you get in close. In close and under the chin, straight up into the brain.'

'Yeah, I know,' said Cramer.

'We're getting there,' said Martin, opening a pack of Wrigley's gum and offering Cramer a piece. Cramer shook his head.

They were interrupted by the gymnasium doors opening. Blackie, one of the Colonel's troopers, shouted that Cramer's presence was required in the headmistress's study. Allan and Martin grinned. 'Sounds like six of the best to me,' said Martin.

Cramer walked along the corridor to the study. He took off his overcoat, draped it over his right arm, and knocked on the door. The Colonel ushered Cramer in. A man stood looking out of the window and didn't turn around as the Colonel closed the door. The man was just under six feet tall and had his hands clasped behind him like an undertaker overseeing a funeral. There was something funereal about the man's attire, too; a black suit and black shoes polished to a shine and an inch of starched white cuff protruding from each sleeve. He had dark brown hair which he'd pulled back into a small ponytail which curved on his collar like a carelessly-drawn comma. Cramer didn't generally make snap judgements about people, but he took an instinctive dislike to the man. It was partly the way the man dressed, partly the ponytail, but mainly it was the man's crass rudeness – unless he was stone deaf, his posing by the window was solely for effect.

The man turned slowly as if he had only just become aware of Cramer's presence. His hair was swept back from an unlined boyish face and for a second or two he studied Cramer through a pair of red-framed spectacles, then he grinned and reached out his hand. 'You must be Mike Cramer,' he said. He shook hands with Cramer. He had a strong grip and Cramer noticed that his nails were perfectly clipped. They reminded Cramer of Allan's neatly manicured hands. 'I'm Bernard Jackman.' He pronounced his first name with the emphasis on the second syllable in a slow Texan drawl.

'The profiler?' said Cramer.

Jackman tilted his head on one side. 'At your service.'

The Colonel walked over to his desk and sat down, nodding to Cramer and Jackman to take leather armchairs by the unlit fireplace. Jackman straightened the creases of his trousers before crossing his legs. There was something very precise and measured about all the man's movements, as if he was giving a performance.

'Bernard is passing through on his way to South Africa,' said the Colonel, placing his walking stick on the desk. 'We thought it would be a good opportunity for a briefing.'

'Do we have a report on the South African killing yet?' asked Cramer.

'It's on its way,' said the Colonel.

'I've already spoken to one of the investigating officers,' said Jackman. 'All the signs are that it was as professional as the rest. He was dressed as a ranger and driving a Landrover, obviously well planned. I'll be visiting the crime scene to see what else I can get. I'll compile my reactions while I'm there and either fax or phone you.'

'Any idea who paid for the hit?' asked Cramer.

'He had plenty of enemies, both in Zimbabwe and South Africa,' said the Colonel. 'The sort of enemies who'd have no problem coming up with our man's fee.'

Jackman turned to Cramer. 'You've read my profile of the killer?'

Cramer nodded. He eased a finger into his shirt collar. 'It was interesting,' he said noncommittally.

'Interesting?' repeated Jackman. 'I hoped you'd find it more than interesting.'

Cramer flexed his shoulders inside the suit. 'No offence, but a lot of it seemed to be guesswork.'

'Guesswork?' Jackman repeated slowly, stressing the two syllables.

Cramer looked across at the Colonel. The Colonel nodded that he should continue. 'You say that the guy we're after is intelligent, but that's a given because he couldn't do what he does if he was stupid,' Cramer said.

'Sure,' said Jackman.

'Yet you go on to suggest that he was a bully at school, and that he didn't go to university.'

Jackman steepled his fingers under his chin and studied Cramer. 'And I stand by that.'

'That has to be guesswork, right?'

'What else aren't you happy with?' asked Jackman, ignoring Cramer's question.

'You say he has a military background, and again I'd say that would be a given. But you say he left and had trouble keeping a job afterwards. I'd have thought that someone with army training, someone with above-average intelligence, wouldn't have a problem finding and keeping a job.'

'Like yourself?' said Jackman quietly. Cramer held the profiler's look for a few seconds. Jackman smiled tightly. 'Anything else?'

'Yeah. What makes you think he lost his driving licence?'

The Colonel made a soft snorting sound as if he was suppressing a laugh, but Jackman kept his eyes on Cramer. Jackman pushed his spectacles higher up his nose with his forefinger. 'I feel like Sherlock Holmes about to explain himself to Dr Watson. But it won't be the first time.' He uncrossed and recrossed his legs, taking care to adjust his creases again. 'How much do you know about profiling?'

'I saw *Silence of the Lambs*.'

Jackman gave Cramer another tight smile. 'Okay, I can see how an outsider would think that what I do is guesswork, but you've got to remember that I've got thousands of case histories to draw on, data on murderers and their victims from all around the world. Those cases allow me and profilers like me to draw certain conclusions, to assign certain characteristics to killers. In about five per cent of the cases dealt with by FBI profilers, the profiles lead directly to the arrest of the perpetrator. In another ten per cent of cases, the perpetrator is arrested as a result of the investigation being refocused following the profile. And in almost all cases, when a successful conviction is made, the criminal closely matches the profile. Profiling works, Mike, there's no doubt about that.'

Jackman rubbed his hands together, making a soft whispering sound. His eyes were fixed on Cramer's with almost missionary zeal. 'Leaving aside the specifics of the man we're looking for in this case, it's a general rule that serial killers are white and male. That holds true almost without exception, so even if we didn't have witnesses I'd be assuming that our killer fits those two characteristics.'

'So you're assuming that a paid assassin fits the same criteria as a serial killer?' asked Cramer. 'I thought serial killers were all crazy.'

Jackman shook his head. 'It's a common misconception,' he said. 'In fact, only two per cent of serial killers are ever classified as insane. My research leads me to believe that there is a valid comparison to be made between a serial killer and the man we're looking for. He kills on a regular basis, the killings appear to be happening at decreasing intervals, and he has a consistent method of killing. These are all characteristics of an organised serial killer.'

Cramer frowned. 'Organised? What do you mean, organised?'

'We divide killers into two types: organised and disorganised. Basically, an organised killer plans his crime in advance, a disorganised killer is an opportunist. An organised killer will take his weapon with him, a disorganised killer might pick up a knife at the scene of the crime and use that. An organised killer will often travel to carry out his murder and will cover his traces afterwards, a disorganised killer will kill close to home and won't care about how quickly the body is found or whether he's left fingerprints.'

'We know our man is organised,' said Cramer. 'He'd have to be to be a contract killer.'

'Exactly,' said Jackman. 'The man we're looking for is the ultimate organised killer. Which means there's every reason to assume that he fits the profile of an organised serial killer.' The profiler stood up and went over to the window. He stood there looking out, his hands clasped behind him as he continued his lecture.

'Organised killers and disorganised killers tend to come from different backgrounds,' Jackman added. 'We know this not because of some great psychological insight, but because at the FBI's Behavioral Science Unit they've constructed profiles of every serial killer that's ever been caught. I used to be with the BSU and part of my job was to interview these guys, to get inside their heads and to find out what makes them tick. By comparing their backgrounds, we can start to draw conclusions about their common characteristics.'

Jackman turned around and faced Cramer. He held up his left hand and began counting off on his fingers. 'One, organised serial killers tend to be of above average intelligence. It isn't unusual for them to have an IQ above 120.

'Two, partly because of their generally high IQs, organised killers tend to have feelings of superiority, and that leads them to pick fights, to drive too fast, to argue with their bosses at work. You asked why I thought our man has lost his driving licence. That's because most of the organised killers profiled by the BSU had a string of driving offences, and more than half had had their licences taken away. Telling them they're driving too fast doesn't have any effect, because they think they know best.

'Three, organised killers tend to come from families where the father had a job but where there was little discipline at home. Disorganised killers often have a family background of mental illness or drugs and more often than not there's also a history of abuse. Not necessarily sexual, but almost certainly beatings and the like.

'Four, organised killers are usually very sociable, on the surface at least. Disorganised killers are loners, organised killers are happier in groups.

'Five, organised killers generally have numerous sexual partners and are good in bed.' He saw the look of disbelief on Cramer's face and grinned. 'It's true. They're often very good-looking and great talkers, but because of their nature they usually can't sustain long-term relationships.'

'They bore easily,' said the Colonel.

Jackman nodded his agreement. 'That, and they have a tendency to pick faults in their partners. Also, despite their success with women, a lot of organised killers have a deep-seated hatred of the opposite sex. You've got to remember that most serial killers choose women as their victims, but that might not apply in this case. I think it's reasonable to assume that our killer comes from some form of dysfunctional family. I doubt he suffered sexual abuse. Divorce, maybe, or an early parental death.'

'You're saying that the loss of a parent makes a child

more likely to grow up to be a serial killer? That seems like a hell of a generalisation.'

Jackman folded his arms. 'The way you put it, it is. And it's obviously not true. Plenty of children from single parent families grow up to be perfectly respectable, hard-working citizens. I lost my mother when I was ten, but I didn't grow up to be a killer. It's what happens afterwards that's important, it's how the remaining parent treats the child that counts. Children have to be taught the difference between right and wrong, they have to be taught to be sociable, they have to realise that they're not the centre of the universe, that other people matter, too. It's the lack of that training that produces the sort of personality which is capable of becoming a serial killer. Are you with me so far?'

Cramer nodded. He didn't like being lectured, and he didn't like Jackman's overbearing confidence, but if Jackman held any clue to the killer's identity, Cramer wanted it.

'The Bureau began compiling profiles of convicted killers in the late Seventies,' Jackman continued. 'They started with assassins and would-be assassins, guys like Sirhan Sirhan and James Earl Ray, running them through a sixty-page questionnaire, looking for common features, something that sets assassins apart from other people.'

'Other than the fact that they kill people,' said Cramer. The Colonel flashed Cramer a warning look but Jackman ignored the interruption.

'Most assassins kill to attract attention to themselves,' Jackman continued. 'They might claim to be acting in the name of some political cause or another, but generally they're seeking attention. Often they keep diaries, for instance. When you get your man, I think you'll find that somewhere he kept a diary or a record of what he's been doing. Almost certainly with photographs, newspaper clippings, maybe even video recordings of news broadcasts.'

Cramer shifted in his chair. 'Okay, I see what you're saying,' he said. 'But I don't see how it's going to help me identify the killer.'

'In terms of being able to pick him out of a crowd, you're right,' Jackman admitted. 'Profiles don't work like that. What the FBI and other law enforcement agencies do is to use the profile to select the most likely suspects, so that they concentrate their resources in the most productive way.'

Cramer exhaled deeply and rubbed the back of his neck. It seemed that the more he tried to get specifics from the profiler, the more nebulous he became. It was like grabbing mist. 'What about his nationality?' Cramer asked.

Jackman shrugged. 'American or British would be the most likely, possibly Australian or South African.'

'Why?'

'The man's calmness under pressure and his marksmanship suggest Special Forces training.'

'So why not German?'

Jackman removed his glasses and twirled them around in his right hand. 'German is a possibility, yes. But whatever his nationality it's clear he has an affinity for languages. Witnesses who heard him talk disagree completely as to his voice and accent. He was working as a waiter for three days before the killing of the Kypriano girl and spoke fluent Greek. We have witnesses in Miami who were sure that he had a New York accent and a bodyguard whose client was shot in Bangkok says the assassin is Scottish.'

'Scottish?'

'The bodyguard was from Glasgow and he swears that

the accent was genuine. I'm not convinced that a German would be able to speak perfect Greek and English without a trace of a German accent.'

There was a knock on the door and Mrs Elliott appeared pushing a tea trolley. The Colonel smiled his thanks as she placed the trolley by the side of his desk and left the room.

'There was something I didn't read in your report that I thought would have been worth mentioning,' said Cramer.

Jackman raised his eyebrows and stopped twirling his glasses.

'The way he kills. Close up, one shot to the face, one to the chest.'

Jackman nodded. 'It's his signature. It's a way of telling the world that he did it. Like Zorro carving a Z with his sword.'

'There are easier ways of killing. The head-shot is risky. It's not the way we're trained to shoot.'

'How would you do it?' Jackman leaned forward, eager to hear Cramer's reply.

Cramer shrugged. 'The chest. It's the biggest area, you're less likely to miss. Rip through the heart or a lung, the liver even, and it's all over.'

'Faster than a shot to the head?'

'A head's easier to miss.'

'And you think it's significant?'

'You don't?'

'I just think it's his way of letting the client know that he did the job.'

Cramer put a hand up to his mouth and tapped his lips thoughtfully. 'Maybe,' he said.

'You don't seem convinced. But he can't very well leave a business card, can he?' Jackman smiled and there was something canine about the gesture, like a dog contemplating a bone.

Dermott Lynch was washing up when he heard a key slot into the front door lock. He picked up a large carving knife but almost immediately heard Marie call down the hallway, 'It's me.' Lynch replaced the knife in the soapy water.

Marie walked into the kitchen and put a plastic carrier bag onto the table. 'You're very domesticated,' she said.

Lynch shrugged. 'You have to be when you live alone. You soon learn that if you don't do it, it never gets done.'

'Why Dermott, you mean there's no young lady in your life to clear up after you?'

Lynch chuckled and rinsed the cutlery under the cold tap. 'There are several young ladies, Marie, but I don't think any of them are the type who'd do my housework.' He picked up a towel and dried his hands. Marie took a bulging envelope out of her handbag and opened it. 'It's in fifties and twenties,' she said. 'Will that be enough?'

'That's great,' he said, running his thumb over the notes. He slipped the envelope into the back pocket of his jeans, then impulsively stepped forward and kissed her on the cheek. To his surprise she turned her face so that her lips brushed his and for a few seconds she returned his kiss. Lynch put his hands on her hips and tried to kiss her harder but she reached up and put her hands on his shoulders and pushed him away. She looked at him, one eyebrow raised archly, a lock of her hair across one cheek. 'I don't think this is a good idea, is it, Dermott?' she said.

Lynch grinned. 'Aye, right enough,' he said.

Marie kept looking at him and he could see his own reflection in the pupils of her eyes. She smiled and put her head on one side as if reconsidering. 'Maybe later,' she said.

'Aye, maybe,' said Lynch. He knew that she didn't mean later that day. She meant afterwards, after Cramer was dead. He nodded, still looking deep into her eyes.

She held his gaze for a few seconds then twisted around and pulled three cartons out of the carrier bag. 'Hair dye,' she said, handing them to him. 'I wasn't sure what to get, so I got one black, one blonde and one red.'

Lynch juggled the boxes thoughtfully and Marie slipped away to the other side of the kitchen, where she busied herself filling the kettle. 'What do you think?' asked Lynch.

'I'd go for black,' she said. 'Red is always a risky colour. And it'll only advertise the fact that you're Irish. And I'm not sure you'll suit the bleached surfer look. But I wanted to give you the choice.'

Lynch put down two of the packs and took the carton of black dye into the bathroom. Marie appeared at the doorway with an old towel as Lynch was reading the instructions. 'Use this,' she said, 'and try not to get it everywhere.'

She was right; it was a messy business, and by the time Lynch had finished the bathroom looked as if a wet dog had shaken itself dry. He wrapped his wet hair in the towel and did his best to wipe the sink and mirror clean. When he walked back into the kitchen Marie was pouring him a cup of tea. Lynch took it and sniffed it appreciatively. She hadn't made the mistake of brewing it too long and she'd poured the milk into the cup first so that the milk hadn't scalded. He sipped it and sat down at the table. Marie reached over and unwound the towel. 'Who cut this?' she asked.

'I did it myself,' admitted Lynch. 'Not good, huh?'

'Not great,' she agreed, running her fingers through the thick locks. 'Let's see if I can improve it.'

She took a pair of scissors from a drawer and led Lynch through to her bedroom and sat him down in front of her dressing table. Lynch watched her in the mirror as she combed his hair. She had a thoughtful frown on her face, like a little girl facing a difficult decision. She used the scissors carefully as if she was frightened of making a mistake. She tidied up the front and gave him more of a parting, then concentrated on the back, tapering it so that it just brushed the collar of his shirt. When she was satisfied she stood behind him and patted him on the shoulders. 'How's that, sir?' she asked.

Lynch turned his head from side to side. She'd done a good job. 'Excellent. Really good. Who taught you to cut hair?'

She leant across him to put the scissors on the dressing table and her hair brushed his cheek. 'You're my first customer,' she said. Lynch turned towards her and his lips met hers. This time the initiative came from her, her lips pressed hard against his and her soft tongue forced its way between his teeth. She took sugar in her tea and Lynch could taste the sweetness on her tongue. She moved around him, still keeping her mouth pressed against him, sat on his lap and put her arms around his neck.

It was Lynch who broke away first, gasping for breath. 'Hey, I thought this wasn't a good idea,' he said.

'It's not,' she said. She kissed him again, harder this time. Lynch stood up and carried her over to the bed. He knelt on the quilt and lowered her gently. She lay there, her arms outstretched, a lazy smile on her face.

'Are you sure?' asked Lynch.

'Just get on with it, Dermott,' she laughed, reaching up for him.

Simon Chaillon flicked through his copy of *Euromoney*, looking for anything of interest. The magazine seemed to get bigger each year and if it continued to grow it would soon be the size of a telephone directory. There still seemed to be precious little to hold his attention, though. The brass plate on his office door gave his profession as personal banker and financial adviser, but Chaillon wasn't a typical Swiss financier.

Chaillon's secretary knocked gently on his door and walked into his office. 'Courier delivery,' she said, placing a Federal Express envelope on his desk.

'Thank you, Theresa,' said Chaillon, looking up from the magazine. If it came to a choice between reading the latest World Bank projections or watching the twenty-five-year-old blonde walk across his plush green carpet, it was no contest. Theresa walked slowly back to the door, swinging her hips as if she knew that he was watching, and swishing her mane of hair like an impatient racehorse. At fifty-eight, Chaillon was old enough to be her father, but there was nothing parental about his affections, or his intentions. She'd been with him for eighteen months – his previous secretary had died in a road accident – and he didn't quite trust her yet, which was why he left the envelope unopened on the desk until she'd closed the door. Chaillon looked out of his window, across the River Limmat and its flat-roofed river boats towards the twin-towered Grossmunster Cathedral. Maybe today would be the day he'd suggest that they go out for dinner. Chaillon had no reservations about mixing business and pleasure. If anything, a sexual relationship would bind her closer to him.

He opened the envelope. Inside were three colour photographs taken with a long lens. They were slightly grainy but the images were clear: a man, tall with deep-set eyes and a worried frown, was stepping away from a large Mercedes, a bodyguard to his right, a young Oriental girl just behind him; the same man, coming out of a doorway; and a close-up, just of the man. Chaillon wondered how long it would be before the man in the photograph was dead. Chaillon's client was the ultimate professional. He had never failed, he had never had to refund his fee. That was why he was so expensive.

Along with the photographs were three A4 typewritten sheets. Chaillon didn't read them, he preferred to know as little as possible about the targets. It wasn't that he was squeamish, it was simply a matter of self-protection. There was only one thing he needed to know. He picked up the telephone connected to his private line and called an office less than half a mile away. Chaillon gave a nine-digit identification number and asked if there had been any deposits made within the previous forty-eight hours. The answer was affirmative. Five hundred thousand dollars. Chaillon replaced the receiver. He put the photographs and typewritten sheets in another envelope and sealed it. The envelope went inside a fresh Federal Express packet.

Chaillon swivelled his chair around to face an IBM PC which was displaying a list of Japanese share prices. He manipulated the mouse to activate the computer's modem and within seconds he was connected to a bulletin board on the West Coast of the United States. There was one word on the board: London. Chaillon cut the connection. His fingers played across the keyboard of his computer. From the screen he copied an address in London onto the Federal Express airbill, and then he pressed his intercom and asked Theresa to come back into the office.

She knocked again before entering. Chaillon was always amused by her politeness. As she sashayed over to his desk he wondered if she'd be as polite in bed. He smiled at the thought. 'Send this right away, Theresa,' he said, handing her the packet. He had no qualms about her seeing the name or the address: it was an accommodation agency, one of more than a dozen that his client used around the world.

'Shall I be mother?' asked the Colonel.

Jackman frowned. 'Mother?' he repeated.

'It's an English expression,' said the Colonel, picking up the teapot. 'It means I'll pour.' He poured steaming tea into a white china mug and handed it to the profiler. Jackman helped himself to milk and two lumps of sugar. 'When are you going to South Africa?' asked the Colonel.

'I'm catching the red-eye,' said Jackman. He stirred his tea thoughtfully. 'Cramer didn't seem very impressed with my work.'

'He has a lot on his mind.'

Jackman nodded and pulled a face. 'He's got guts, that's for sure.' He tapped his spoon against the mug. 'The target, he's safely out of the way?'

'Well out of reach,' agreed the Colonel.

'Good. What have you done with him?'

'That's need to know.'

'And I don't need to know, I suppose,' said Jackman. 'What about the man who placed the contract?'

'Discenza? The FBI have him in protective custody in Miami. No one can get to him.'

Jackman stirred his tea again, staring at the brown liquid as it whirled around. 'Does Cramer realise how closely he himself fits the profile of the man we're looking for?'

The Colonel sipped his tea, then shook his head. 'If he does, he hasn't mentioned it.'

'Set a thief to catch a thief?'

'Not really. He was chosen for other reasons. The similarities hadn't occurred to me until you read his file and pointed it out.'

Jackman walked over to the trolley and put down his spoon. 'He lost his mother at a relatively young age, his father was rarely at home when he was in his teens, he wasn't exactly well liked at school, SAS-trained, never been in steady employment since he left the regiment. I suppose you can account for his whereabouts over the past two years?'

The Colonel smiled thinly. 'No, I can't. But Mike Cramer is not our killer, I can guarantee that. He's not the type.'

Jackman looked at his wristwatch. 'That's the problem, Colonel. He's exactly the type.'

Lynch lay on his back, his arm around Marie. She toyed with the hair on his chest, winding it gently around her fingers and tugging it softly. 'Still think it's not a good idea?' he asked.

'Definitely,' she giggled. 'But I wouldn't have missed it for the world. Who taught you to make love?'

'You're my first customer,' said Lynch.

Marie laughed and slapped his chest. 'I don't think so,' she said. She kissed the side of his neck and nuzzled against him. 'I want to come with you,' she whispered.

'You just did.'

'You know what I mean.'

'No.'

'I could help.'

'No,' he repeated.

'Why not?' Her hand began to move inexorably downwards.

'Because it's my fight, not yours.'

Her hand lingered between his legs, caressing and touching him. 'They killed my father and my mother, Dermott. It's as much my fight as yours.'

'I know that, Marie. But this isn't a sanctioned operation, it's personal. I want Cramer because of what he did to Maggie.'

'And I want him because of what he did to my father.'

'No.'

'You have to let me help you.'

Lynch rolled on top of her and took his weight on his elbows so that he could look down on her. 'You have helped. More than you know.' He kissed her again and she opened her legs, drawing them up and fastening them around his waist. She squeezed him, hard. 'And that's not going to make me change my mind,' he said. He rolled off her and headed for the bathroom.

Cramer sat between Allan and Martin in the dining hall watching the Harrods video again. It was the tenth time they'd studied the footage. Cramer felt that he knew every second by heart, but he realised the importance of getting a feel for the killer, for the way he moved, the way he held himself. He'd spent countless days on surveillance operations in the border country watching and waiting for IRA terrorists, and on many occasions he'd been able to identify targets by the way they walked, the tilt of a head, the shrug of a shoulder. At a long distance bodies were often more distinctive than faces. The problem with the video was the faked limp. It affected everything about the man's movement, and Cramer was starting to think that the video might actually prove counter-productive.

'What do you think, Allan?' Cramer asked. 'Do you think you'd spot him in a crowd.'

Allan shrugged. 'I'm getting a feel for his shape. The problem is that he can change that with padding.'

'Or dieting,' said Martin, who was munching his way

through a stack of ham and pickle sandwiches that Mrs Elliott had prepared earlier.

'Yeah. I think you were right when you said that all we know is that he's white and right-handed.'

'Could be ambidextrous,' said Martin, reaching for another sandwich.

'Terrific,' said Cramer.

'I'll tell you something, Mike,' said Allan, rewinding the tape to the beginning again. 'The guy actually looks a bit like you.'

'What?' exclaimed Cramer, then he saw that Allan was grinning and he faked a punch to his chin. Allan ducked and pressed the 'play' button and walked back to his seat as the screen flickered. Martin looked over his shoulder and the others turned to see what he was looking at. It was Su-ming. She was wearing blue jeans and a black pullover with the sleeves pulled up to her elbows. Cramer stood up and introduced her to Martin. She nodded a greeting but made no move to shake his hand.

'Are you Chinese?' Martin asked her.

'No,' she said, curtly, and turned away from him. 'Have you eaten?' she asked Cramer. He shook his head. 'I shall prepare you something,' she said and headed towards the kitchen.

Outside they heard the helicopter turbine start up. 'The profiler,' said Cramer as Allan threw him a questioning look.

'He didn't hang around for long.'

'There wasn't much for him to say. Long on opinions, short on facts.'

'Yeah?'

'Yeah. About as much use as one of those psychics that

271

reckon they can tell the police where the bodies are buried by using a pendulum or a crystal ball.'

Allan helped himself to one of Martin's sandwiches. 'Pity. I was hoping he might come up with a few specifics.'

'The man we're looking for was probably abused as a child,' said Cramer.

Martin grinned. 'Great. We'll be on the look-out for a bedwetter, then.' One of the guards came out of the kitchen carrying a fresh pot of coffee. Martin drained his cup. 'Just in time,' he said.

Cramer watched the killer on the screen walk up to the second bodyguard. Two shots to the chest. Cramer wondered why it was only the targets who were shot in the face. Jackman's explanation that it was his signature seemed too glib. He looked up to see the man with the coffee pot walking behind the television. Cramer had last seen him standing guard at the entrance to the school. He was in his mid-twenties, broad-shouldered and narrow-waisted, the build of a ballet dancer. Cramer felt himself tense inside. There was something about the way the man was holding the coffee pot that didn't look right, as if he was trying to keep it away from his body. It might simply have been that he was scared of spilling the hot liquid, but then he saw the man's eyes flick in his direction and he knew that he wasn't wrong. Cramer pushed Allan to the side as he leapt to his feet, his right hand reaching inside his sleeve for the stiletto.

The man dropped the coffee pot and turned towards Cramer. His mouth opened in surprise when he saw that Cramer was already pulling out the knife. As the stiletto emerged from Cramer's sleeve, he kept moving, keeping the momentum going, his left hand outstretched, his eyes focused on the man's throat. The coffee pot smashed onto the floor. The scalding liquid splashed Cramer's trousers but he felt nothing, he was totally focused on the man in front of him. The man's right hand had disappeared inside his leather jacket but Cramer was already close enough to slap his hand against the man's chest and jam the stiletto up under his chin, hard enough to indent the flesh but not hard enough to draw blood. The man glared at him, his eyes wide and fearful, his mouth open. 'Gotcha!' screamed Cramer.

'Yes!' shouted Martin, leaping to his feet and punching the air.

Allan's praise was more muted; he stood up and patted Cramer on the back. 'Well done, Mike,' he said.

Cramer stepped away and slid the stiletto into its sheath. The man in the leather jacket rubbed his chin and smiled ruefully. 'I almost got you,' he said.

'Almost is what it's all about,' said Cramer, sitting down again. His heart was racing and he took several deep breaths to calm himself down. He looked up to see Su-ming standing at the kitchen door, a large bowl in her hands, a look of horror on her face. He realised she must have seen the attack. Before he could explain what had happened, she disappeared back into the kitchen.

Allan stood looking down at Cramer. 'Now we're getting there, Mike. We're definitely getting there. One thing, though. Why did you use the knife, why didn't you go for the gun? You had time.'

Cramer grinned. 'Jesus, Allan, won't you ever be satisfied?'

Allan shook his head. 'Not until this is over.'

Cramer stood up and went into the kitchen. Su-ming

was chopping asparagus spears but she stopped when she saw Cramer. 'We were practising,' he said before she could speak. 'We don't know when or how he's going to strike, so Allan is testing me all the time.'

'You're going to kill him, aren't you?'

'The man has been paid to kill your boss,' said Cramer. 'He's an assassin. A hired killer. He's paid to kill people, we can't just pull out a warrant card and tell him he's under arrest.'

'You scared me,' she said, avoiding his eyes. 'Not just what you did, but the way you did it. You were like a machine. A killing machine. There was a blood lust in your eyes.'

'I was in control, Su-ming. That's what Allan is doing, he's training me to react instinctively. I won't have time to think, it'll be him or me.'

Su-ming put down the knife and folded her arms across her chest as if hugging herself. She looked absurdly young in the oversize pullover. 'You've killed before, haven't you?' she asked.

'Yes. Several times.'

'And that doesn't worry you?'

Cramer didn't answer for a few seconds. 'No, it doesn't worry me,' he eventually replied. 'Not any more.'

'When you kill this man, this assassin, I'll be there, won't I?'

'Probably. Yes.'

'So either I'm going to see you kill a man, or I'm going to see you killed. That's not much of a choice, is it? Either way, I'm going to have a man's death on my hands.'

'We're doing this to save your boss's life, Su-ming, and the rest of the people this maniac could end up killing. This man has never failed. If we don't stop him, there's nowhere that your boss can hide, nowhere he can go where he'll be safe. We have to take him out.' Su-ming shuddered as if she was standing in a draught. 'Are you all right?' he asked. She shrugged. 'Didn't the Colonel explain what was going to happen?'

'I was told that I was to accompany you, that we were to follow Mr Vander Mayer's itinerary.'

'You must have realised what was being planned?' He reached out to touch her shoulder, but she edged away from him.

'I suppose so. But I don't think anyone actually said the words. No one actually said that we were setting up a man to be killed.'

Cramer rubbed his stomach softly. He wasn't sure whether she meant that he, or the assassin, was the one being set up, or whether she cared either way. 'We'll make sure that you don't get hurt,' he said as soothingly as he could. 'Allan and Martin will do everything they can to keep you out of it. And it's me that he'll be after. Not you.'

'That's not the point,' she said, shaking her head.

'What do you mean?'

She narrowed her eyes and shivered again, then quickly turned her back to him and picked up the knife. She chopped the asparagus spears with slow, precise movements. Cramer watched, not sure what to say. Su-ming continued to cut the asparagus into small chunks, the knife making a soft crunching sound. Cramer stood watching her in silence, but realised that the conversation was over. She'd shut him out, like a clam closing itself up for protection.

*　　*　　*

Sandra Worthington looked at her watch for the hundredth time and pursed her lips, wondering if Philip would be at the office yet. She couldn't call him at home, the last time she'd done that he'd hit the roof and made her promise not to do it again. It had been a stupid thing to do. They were both married and both had a lot to lose if their affair was discovered, but there were times when she just had to hear his voice. A hurried 'I love you' or 'I miss you' was all she wanted. She checked her watch again.

'Any chance of a cup of tea?' asked her husband. He was sprawled across the sofa in front of the television set, watching Sky Sports and scratching himself.

'Sure,' she said and went into the kitchen. Their liver and white cocker spaniel followed her, wagging his stub of a tail good-naturedly. Her husband was nothing like Philip. Philip was tall and well-muscled, Philip was good-looking and kind, Philip made her laugh. Her husband just bored her, and had done for the past five years. If it wasn't for the children, she'd have left him long ago, but her own parents had split up when she was eight and she'd promised herself that she would never put her two children through the same emotional roller-coaster.

Philip had children too, three boys, and he'd made it clear that his wife would never give him a divorce, and that even if she did the alimony and child support would consign him to a dingy bedsit for the rest of his life. They had to settle for what they had: hurried couplings in the back of his Volvo, lunchtime walks in the park, the occasional luxury of a hotel room, stolen moments when her children were at school. It wasn't much, but it was better than nothing. Now even what little she had was under threat. Her husband had been made redundant and had spent the last three weeks lying about the house, watching television and only leaving to visit the pub or the betting shop. He was driving her crazy.

Sandra poured him a mug of tea and spooned in two sugars on autopilot. Philip didn't take sugar. He looked after his body. She glanced at her watch again. She had to hear Philip's voice, just to know that he cared, that he was thinking about her. The dog whined and put his head on one side. 'Stop trying to look cute, Robbie,' she said. The dog wagged his tail faster and made a soft growling noise. 'Ah, I get it,' Sandra whispered, and she winked conspiratorially at the dog.

She put the mug of tea down on the coffee table next to her husband. He grunted his thanks, his eyes fixed on the screen. 'I think I'll take Robbie for a walk,' she said.

'No need, I'll take him to the pub with me,' said her husband.

'It's a walk he needs, not a pint of lager,' said Sandra, picking Robbie's lead off the sideboard. Robbie rushed over, barking.

'Shush!' shouted her husband. 'Can't you do something about that damn dog?'

'I'll take him out,' said Sandra, grabbing her coat. She checked that she had change in her pocket and hurried to the door. 'See you later.' Her husband grunted again and she slipped out, clipping the lead to Robbie's collar as she walked down the stairs to the ground floor. Her heart was racing. There was a telephone box a hundred yards down the road but she decided against using it as it could be seen from their sitting room window. Robbie headed towards the park but Sandra pulled him back with a jerk. 'Let me call Philip first, then you can play to your heart's content,' she said.

As she walked along the pavement, Sandra wondered what she'd say to Philip. Until her husband got off his damned sofa and went looking for a job, it was going to be practically impossible for her to slip away for a few hours. Perhaps he could come around in his car and she could take Robbie for another walk in the evening? It wouldn't be the first time that the dog had sat on the front seat of Philip's Volvo while they made love in the back. She smiled at the thought.

Robbie began pulling to the gutter. 'Oh, Robbie, wait, can't you?' The dog pulled harder and Sandra relented. She let him step off the pavement. His nose was down and his tail was twitching. His feet scrabbled on the tarmac as he tried to pull away from her. 'Oh come on, Robbie, don't give me a hard time,' Sandra moaned. The dog headed towards a blue Ford Sierra. Sandra yanked on the lead but Robbie wasn't in the least deterred. He began to sniff the Sierra's bumper and his tail started to wag even faster. Sandra knelt down by his side and stroked the back of his head. 'Shit or get off the pot, Robbie,' she said testily. 'I've got a telephone call to make.'

She grabbed Robbie's collar and pulled him away. As she did so she noticed a red smear on the black bumper. She frowned. It wasn't glossy enough to be paint. She rubbed her finger on it and stared at the rusty stain on her skin. Robbie licked her finger then went back to sniffing the boot. That was when Sandra noticed the smell for the first time. She'd brought up two children and the smell immediately brought back memories of soiled nappies and filled potties. She hurriedly rubbed her finger on the tarmac, trying to get rid of the stain. She knew what it was now. Blood.

Lynch poured boiling hot water into the teapot and swirled it around, then tipped it into the sink. He knew how important it was to warm the pot first, though in an age of teabags it was something that fewer people seemed to insist on. He opened Marie's stainless steel caddy and spooned tea into the pot.

'Dermott?' Marie called from the sitting room.

'What?' he replied, as he poured water into the pot and stirred it quickly.

'Your car? Is it a blue one?'

Lynch dropped the spoon and rushed into the sitting room. Marie was standing at the window, looking out. He stood behind her and put his hands on her shoulders. Down below in the street a police car had stopped behind the Ford Sierra. A uniformed policewoman was talking to a dark-haired woman with a dog while her colleague was bending down and examining the boot. 'Shit,' cursed Lynch.

'Is it yours?' asked Marie. 'What's he looking for?'

Lynch didn't reply. He turned away from the window and went to the spare room. He retrieved the handgun from under the bed and pulled out the magazine. He checked the firing mechanism, then slotted the magazine back in and made sure that the safety was on. Marie walked into the room and stopped dead when she saw the gun. 'You brought a gun into my house?' she asked.

'Marie, love, I didn't have any choice.' He slid the gun down the back of his trousers, then pulled on his jacket, so that it covered the weapon.

'Is the car stolen?' she asked.

Lynch walked past her and back into the sitting room. He stood at the side of the window and looked down. The policeman was peering through the rear window of the car, the policewoman was talking into her radio as the woman with the dog stood behind her, looking at her wristwatch. He wasn't sure how much to tell Marie. She'd offered to help and she knew that he was an IRA volunteer, but he didn't know how she'd react to the news that he'd killed five men and that one of them was in the boot of the Ford Sierra. 'Yeah, it's stolen. And my prints are all over it.' He pounded the wall with the flat of his hand. 'Hell, I shouldn't have left the car there. I shouldn't have hung around here, I should have legged it.'

'Thanks, Dermott. Thanks a bunch.'

Lynch turned and went over to Marie and put his arms around her. 'Hey now, love, that's not what I meant. I'm just angry at myself, that's all.' He rested his chin on top of her head, his mind racing. The Russian gun was also in the boot of the car, next to Foley's body. How could he have been so bloody stupid? He'd left the clean gun in the car and was carrying just about the hottest weapon in the country shoved down the back of his pants. The police would match the bullet that killed Foley to the bullets that had killed the IRA hit team. Then they'd go through Foley's place and his own prints would be all over the back bedroom. 'I'm going to have to go,' he said.

'I'll come with you.' She said the words urgently, and she held him close as if afraid that he'd push her away.

'This is going to get really messy, love,' he said.

'Are you still going after Cramer?'

'Yes.'

'Let me come with you.'

Lynch closed his eyes. He could smell the apple fragrance of her shampoo and something that reminded him of a field in summer. She was so fresh, so young. She didn't realise what she was asking. 'No, love. I can't. It's too dangerous.' He unpeeled her arms from around his waist and went back to the window. The policeman was down on his knees, sniffing at the boot. Lynch wondered if he'd try to force it open or if they'd call out a locksmith. Either way, he didn't have long. 'I have to go,' he repeated. He patted down his pockets, checking that he had the two wallets and the money that Marie had given him.

'You won't stand a chance on your own,' she said. 'They'll be looking for you. But if I was with you . . .'

'They'd miss you at work.'

'I can call in sick.'

'They'll be starting a house-to-house search soon.'

'All the more reason for me not to be here. We can use my car.'

'You're crazy.'

'No, I'm not crazy, Dermott. This man Cramer destroyed my family, and I'll do anything I can to help you get him.' She stood before him, her hands defiantly on her hips, her chin up like a boxer at a weigh-in.

Lynch smiled.

'Damn you, Dermott, what are you grinning at?'

'I was just thinking how like your mother you are.'

'Don't try to sweet talk me.'

Lynch held up his hands as if trying to ward her off. 'I'm not.'

'We can use my car. I can help, Dermott. And I want to.'

Lynch narrowed his eyes as he looked at her. He genuinely didn't want to get her involved, but she did have a point: the police would be looking for a man travelling alone. And there was another advantage in having her with him, for a while at least. It wouldn't be long before details of the Maida Vale killings and the body in the car boot were made public, and it would be useful to see how Marie reacted to the news. It was one thing to offer her help, quite another for her to accept that she was tied in to five murders. 'Okay,' he said. 'But just until I'm safely out of London. Then we split up.'

Marie grinned. 'Deal,' she said. She took a battered sheepskin jacket from a closet and disappeared into her bedroom. Lynch paced up and down nervously until she reappeared with a large Harrods carrier bag.

Lynch raised an eyebrow. 'Marie, love, I said you're driving me out of London. That's all.'

'Relax, Dermott. It's cover. It's far less suspicious if I'm carrying something.' She opened the front door and ushered him out.

'Where's the car?' he asked, as they walked downstairs.

'Around the corner,' she said. She opened the front door. As they stepped onto the pavement a second police car went by and Lynch turned away so that the occupants wouldn't see his face. Marie looked over her shoulder. 'Don't look,' hissed Lynch.

She jerked her head around. 'Sorry,' she whispered.

Lynch forced himself to walk slowly, trying to make it look as if they were nothing more sinister than a married couple going shopping. 'Give me the keys,' he said. 'I'll drive.'

She did as he asked. The keys were on a keyring with a tiny teddy bear attached. 'Down here,' she said, leading him into a side road. Lynch relaxed a little as they turned the corner, out of sight of the policemen.

Marie's car was a red Golf GTI convertible. She climbed in and sat next to Lynch. 'Where are we going?' she asked as Lynch started the engine.

'Wales,' he said. He looked over his shoulder and drove away from the kerb.

Cramer, Allan and Martin stood behind a long table as they checked their weapons: Cramer his Walther PPK, Allan his Glock 18 and Martin his Heckler & Koch VP70. 'Okay?' Allan asked and the two other men nodded. They turned as one, raised their guns and fired at the line of cardboard targets, emptying their clips as quickly as possible. Cramer finished first because the much smaller PPK only held seven cartridges. Martin was the last to stop firing as his weapon held eighteen.

Cramer's ears were ringing as they walked forward to check their accuracy. Allan had refused ear plugs or protectors so that they would get used to being under fire. It was hell on his eardrums, but Cramer knew that Allan was right; unless he was used to the sound of gunfire, his first reaction would be to flinch and to close his eyes and, with the assassin moving towards him, the slightest delay would be fatal. All of Cramer's shots were dead centre.

Allan slapped him on the back. 'Good shooting, Mike.' He looked across at Martin's target and pulled a face. 'Fuck me, Martin, is your blood sugar low or something?'

Martin sniffed. 'It's not so bad,' he said.

'Bad? It's crap.'

'Yeah, well I'm not going to be firing at paper terrorists, am I? I was never that hot on the range.'

'You can say that again.' Allan began to stick small black paper circles over the holes made by the bullets.

'Yeah, but I was shit hot in the Killing House, wasn't I?'

'You did okay,' said Allan begrudgingly. He gave a handful of the paper circles to Cramer. 'Martin came over to Hereford with a group from the Ranger Wing of the Irish Army to brush up on his counter-terrorist tactics,' he explained.

'Great crack,' said Martin.

'Was this in the old days, live targets and all?' asked Cramer.

'Nah. Shit, I forgot, you did the single room system, didn't you?' asked Martin. 'That must have been something.'

'Yeah. It was. The good old days.' During Cramer's time with the SAS, the close-quarter battle building had a single room where the troopers perfected their hostage-release technique, with dummies as terrorists and the SAS men taking it in turn to play hostages. Live ammunition was used and the room was often in near or total darkness, to make the exercise as real as possible. Eventually it became too real and in 1986 a sergeant playing the role of hostage was shot and killed. The fatal accident put an end to the single room system, and the Killing House was replaced with two rooms connected by a highly sophisticated camera and screen system. The terrorists and hostages were in one room, the SAS stormed another, shooting at life-size wrap-around screens. It wasn't one hundred per cent realistic but it meant that there were no further accidents. As Martin said, it had been something in the old days.

The three men finished covering the holes and went back to the table. 'What do you make of Su-ming?' asked Martin.

Cramer shrugged. 'Inscrutable,' he said.

'Yeah. That's it exactly. Inscrutable. What's her story?'

Cramer began slotting fresh cartridges into the PPK's clip. 'She's the target's assistant,' he said.

Martin grinned lecherously. 'Assistant my arse. He's giving her one. Bound to be.'

'What makes you say that?'

Martin raised his eyebrows. 'Wouldn't you?'

Cramer shook his head, smiling to himself. 'You're an animal, Martin.'

'She keeps herself to herself,' said Allan. 'I wanted her to go through a few rehearsals with me, just so she'd get a feel for what's going on. She wouldn't.'

'She's unhappy about the whole business,' said Cramer. 'She might even be a Buddhist or something.'

'I thought Buddhists shaved their heads?' asked Martin.

'Only the monks,' said Allan.

'Yeah? Well, just so long as she shaves her armpits. That's one thing I can't stand, you know? Hairy armpits.'

'That's a relief to us all, Martin,' said Cramer.

'Anyway, what's being a Buddhist got to do with it?' Martin asked.

'She's against killing,' said Cramer.

'Fucking terrific,' laughed Martin. 'Some nutter's going to blow the head off her boss, and she's worried about the sanctity of life.'

Allan put his loaded Glock on the table. 'This guy's no nutter, Martin. Don't forget that. He's not crazy, he's as highly trained as you are. He knows exactly what he's doing.'

Martin raised his hands in mock surrender. 'Okay. Okay. No more crazy jokes.'

Cramer clicked the magazine into his PPK and checked that the safety was on. 'She'll be okay, won't she?'

'So long as she doesn't get in the way,' Allan replied. 'Why, are you worried?'

'I'd be happier if she took part in the rehearsals. Like you said, it'd be better if she knew what to expect.'

Allan shrugged. 'The killer doesn't shoot innocent bystanders, or at least he hasn't so far.'

'There was the doorman at the Harrods delivery entrance,' Cramer pointed out.

'He was wearing a uniform. And he was part of the security staff.'

'Yeah, but he wasn't armed.'

Allan rubbed his nose with the back of his hand. 'We'll make sure she stays in the background whenever you're vulnerable. I wouldn't worry, Mike. This guy doesn't care about witnesses. He's totally focused on the target and any bodyguards. That's you, me and Martin. I'd be more concerned about yourself than her.' Allan turned to face the targets.

Cramer followed his example and flicked the safety off. 'Yeah, I know you're right, but I just worry about her.'

'He's got the hots for her, that's all,' said Martin.

'Fuck you,' said Cramer.

'Whatever turns you on,' said Martin, grinning.

'When you're ready, ladies,' said Allan. The three men began firing and the air was soon full of bitter cordite fumes as streams of empty cartridges rattled onto the floor. Cramer fought to concentrate on the paper targets, but he couldn't block Su-ming out of his mind. Martin was wrong, Cramer wasn't in the least bit sexually attracted to Vander Mayer's assistant. And even if he was, there was nothing he could do about it; setting aside his medical condition, he was embarking on a mission which was more than likely to end in his own death. Romance was the last thing on his mind. His clip emptied a fraction of a second after Allan finished shooting and he stared at the cardboard cutout as Martin continued to fire with his machine pistol. Three of Cramer's shots had gone wide.

Dermott Lynch drove down the M4, keeping the GTI below 70mph. He was keen to get as far as possible from London but he knew it would be reckless to exceed the speed limit, especially as he still had a loaded gun tucked into the back of his trousers. They stopped at a petrol station near Windsor and while Lynch topped up the tank, Marie telephoned her office and told them that she had flu and wouldn't be in for a few days.

'Where in Wales are we going?' Marie asked as she settled back in her seat.

'Near Swansea,' said Lynch. 'Cramer flew by helicopter

from a place called Howth, just north of Dublin, and I know where it landed. I've got the map reference.'

'How did you manage that?'

'Best you don't know,' said Lynch.

'You can trust me, Dermott.' She patted his leg, then squeezed him just above the knee.

'It's not a matter of trust. It's for your own good. The less you know, the safer you'll be.' Marie took her hand away from his leg. She looked out of the passenger window and made a soft tutting noise. Lynch smiled. 'Come on, love. Don't sulk.'

'I'm not sulking,' she said, but she still wouldn't look at him.

Lynch tapped the steering wheel. A red Audi screamed past in the outside lane. It must have been doing more than a hundred and ten miles an hour. Lynch shook his head. The guy was just asking to be picked up. He looked across as Marie. She pouted and shrugged her shoulders. Lynch chuckled. 'Marie, love, this is serious.'

'I know that.'

'You're a civilian. You're not involved. You're not a player.'

Her eyes blazed. 'I'm here, aren't I?'

'Against my better judgement.'

She turned away again. Her breath fogged up the window and she rubbed it with her sleeve.

Lynch drove in silence for a while as tight-lipped young men in shirt sleeves whizzed by in company cars. 'You were never a volunteer, were you?' he asked eventually.

'Don't you know?'

'Why would I know?' She shrugged, but still didn't look at him. 'Marie, the IRA isn't a series of levels like a regular army. It used to be, but the organisation was too vulnerable to infiltration. Now it's made up of small cells, usually just four people. Of those four, only one will have contact with another cell. The other three only know the members of their own cell. It's much safer that way. If one of them is caught, it restricts the numbers they can inform on.'

'Why would they talk?'

Lynch snorted softly. 'Marie, love, sooner or later virtually everyone talks. Anyway, that's not my point.'

'I'm not a child, Dermott.'

'I know you're not a child. I'm just trying to explain why I don't want to tell you how I know where Cramer went. If I tell you who told me, he becomes twice as vulnerable. When he gave me the information, he put himself at risk and I have to respect that. If I tell you, that risk is doubled. It doesn't matter how much I trust you, it doesn't matter how reliable you are, it's just a matter of minimising risk.'

Marie nodded thoughtfully. She turned to look at him. 'I'm sorry,' she said. 'You're right.' She put her hand back on his leg. They drove in silence for a while. Occasionally Marie absent-mindedly scratched Lynch's leg with a fingernail. 'This cell system, is that still in operation?' she asked.

'One hundred per cent,' said Lynch. 'Same as it ever was.'

'But I thought that after the ceasefire the IRA was winding down.'

Lynch snorted dismissively. 'The ceasefire is temporary, never forget that,' he said. 'It lasts only for as long as Sinn Fein makes progress towards its political aims. The organisation is as well-organised and well-armed as it ever was. Don't let the rhetoric fool you, love. The hard men on the Army Council would love to pick up their guns again.'

'Do you think that will happen?'

Lynch nodded grimly. 'Yeah, love. I'm afraid I do. I'm in a minority, but I believe that it's only a matter of time before the violence starts again.'

Cramer was in his room, sitting on the bed and rereading Jackman's report, when there was a timid knock on the door. 'Come in,' he said, placing the thick plastic-bound file on the pillow.

It was Su-ming, carrying a tea tray. 'Mrs Elliott said you didn't eat lunch,' she said.

'Yeah, I wasn't hungry.'

She put the tray down on the bed next to him. It contained a small bowl of white rice, and another bowl with thin strips of white flesh and bean sprouts. 'It's fish,' she said. 'Sea bass.'

'Thanks.' He picked up the chopsticks and held them as best he could. One of them spun out of his hand and she retrieved it from the floor. Cramer pulled a face. 'It's not as easy as it looks,' he said.

'It takes practice,' she agreed. 'But you're getting better.'

Cramer smiled as he recalled Allan saying pretty much the same thing to him, albeit under different circumstances. He tried again, with more success this time. 'So you can speak Russian, huh?'

'Yes.'

'What other languages can you speak?'

'Mandarin Chinese. Cantonese. Thai. Vietnamese. French. German.' She didn't appear to take pride in the number of languages she spoke, as if it was the most natural thing in the world.

'That's pretty impressive.'

She shrugged dismissively. 'And English, of course.'

'Of course. How did you learn so many languages?'

'Some I learned as a child. Some I studied. Mr Vander Mayer said it would be useful if I spoke Russian. I attended a course in New York.'

'And now you're fluent?'

'Almost.'

Su-ming sat down on a chair in front of the dressing table and watched him eat. 'Why did they choose you?' she asked.

Cramer swallowed a mouthful of beansprouts. They were crisp and fresh, with a hint of garlic and something he couldn't quite identify. 'Why do you ask?'

'Because you don't look anything like Mr Vander Mayer. He's older, he's not as tall as you, and his face isn't as . . .' She groped for the right word. 'Sharp,' she said eventually.

'Sharp?' said Cramer, grinning.

She nodded. 'Sharp. Like a hawk.'

'It's the nose,' said Cramer, trying unsuccessfully to pick up some rice.

'You're never serious, are you? About anything?'

Cramer shrugged. 'Sometimes it's better not to take things too seriously.'

'No, it's an act with you. You pretend not to care . . .'

'But you can see through me, is that it?' Cramer finished for her. 'Don't try to read too much into me, Su-ming. I'm a soldier, that's all. I obey orders.'

'So you were ordered to do this? You were ordered to take Mr Vander Mayer's place?'

Cramer's mouth felt suddenly dry. There was a cup of green tea on the tray and he sipped it. 'No,' he said. 'It wasn't an order.'

'Because you aren't in the army any more. You're not a soldier now, are you?'

'That's true,' agreed Cramer. She'd obviously been asking about him. He wasn't sure whether to be flattered or worried.

'So why, Mike Cramer? Why are you doing this?' Her dark brown eyes bored into his. Cramer met her gaze levelly. For several seconds they stared into each other's eyes. Cramer looked away first.

'A man's got to do what a man's got to do,' he said lamely.

Su-ming stood up. 'Why are you like this?' she asked quietly. 'Why won't you ever be serious? Life is not a joke. What you're doing isn't funny.' Cramer didn't say anything. 'You're empty,' she said. 'You're a hollow man. Something inside you died a long time ago.'

Cramer looked up at her. 'Yeah? Is that a professional opinion?'

She walked out of the bedroom, her arms swinging backwards and forwards, like a small child being sent to bed. Cramer put down his chopsticks. He wasn't hungry any more.

Lynch left the M4 at Bristol. Marie had fallen asleep and she was snoring softly, her chin against her chest. Lynch smiled as he looked across at her. She was a pretty girl and under other circumstances Lynch would have enjoyed spending time with her. The digital clock on the dashboard said it was just before two o'clock. 'Marie?' he said softly. There was no reaction so he switched on the radio and twisted the tuning dial until he found a news station. He kept the volume down low and he strained to hear the headlines. The Maida Vale shooting was the second item: four men, as yet unidentified, shot, three of them dead, a man reported running away from the scene. Lynch frowned as he wondered which of the IRA men had survived. He'd have put money on the fact that he'd killed all of them. Not that it mattered, it wasn't as if the man would be helping the police with their enquiries. There was no description of the man the police were looking for, but Lynch knew that it wasn't the police he'd have to worry about. The IRA wouldn't need a description.

There was no mention of Foley, though Lynch was certain that the police would have opened the boot and discovered the body by now. Lynch cursed his own stupidity for the thousandth time. He should never have left the car parked on the street, he should have wiped the car clean of prints, he should have taken the second gun with him. He wondered how he could have been so careless. Marie sniffed and moved in her seat, turning so that her right cheek lay against her headrest. Her lips were slightly parted and he caught a glimpse of perfect white teeth. Lynch reached over and switched off the radio.

He drove into the city and made for a centrally located car park. Marie opened her eyes as he switched off the engine. 'Are we there?' she asked sleepily.

'Bristol,' answered Lynch.

Marie sat up and rubbed her eyes with the back of her hands. 'Sorry,' she said. 'I didn't mean to fall asleep. I'll drive the next bit if you like.'

'I don't mind,' said Lynch. He'd actually enjoyed the drive, it had given him time to think.

'Why have we stopped?'

'Provisions for me,' he replied. 'And a train ticket back to London for you.'

Marie's jaw dropped. 'What?'

'Don't look so surprised, love,' said Lynch. 'The deal was that you help me get out of London. I shouldn't even have brought you this far.'

'Dermott, I want to help. I want to stay with you.'

Lynch opened the door. 'We've been through this, Marie. It's for the best.' They walked together out of the car park and along Redcliffe Way, one of the main shopping streets. Marie slipped her arm through Lynch's as if they were a courting couple. 'And don't think you can make me change my mind,' said Lynch.

Marie raised her eyebrows. 'This is just cover,' she laughed. 'There's no ulterior motive.' She squeezed his arm tightly. Lynch nodded at a sign that indicated they were walking towards Temple Meads Station but Marie pretended not to notice. 'Are you hungry?' she asked.

'I could eat,' replied Lynch, half-heartedly.

'So let's,' she said, pulling him towards a café.

'There's something I want to buy first,' said Lynch. He found a camping store in Redcliffe Way, its window filled with tents, portable stoves and climbing ropes. Inside was a rack of maps and Lynch went through them. Several were Ordnance Survey maps but others were commercial versions which utilised their own reference systems. He found several of Wales but only one which used lines of longitude and latitude. It was a large scale map of the country and he had considerable trouble unfolding it. He had memorised the reference numbers that the Irish air traffic controller had given him and he ran his finger across to where the two lines met. 'Swansea?' asked Marie, looking at where he was pointing.

'Somewhere close by,' he said. 'I need a larger scale.'

Marie nodded. 'West Glamorgan, isn't it?' She went through the rack as Lynch refolded the map, laughing at his unwieldy attempts to put it back into its original form. Minutes later, Marie handed him a large scale map of West Glamorgan and took the map of Wales from him. She folded it with a few deft movements and slid it back into the rack.

Lynch opened the map of West Glamorgan and checked whether it too had lines of longitude and latitude. It did. 'Perfect,' he said. He went over to a display case. An elderly man in brown overalls came across and Lynch asked to see a pair of high powered binoculars. He bought them, the map, and a compass and then left the shop with Marie.

They went back to the café and after ordering himself a cheeseburger and coffee, and Marie a salad and Diet Coke, Lynch spread the map out over the table. Marie switched seats so that she was sitting next to him. 'There's Swansea,' she said. 'And there's the airport to the west.'

Lynch shook his head as he ran his finger down the map. 'They didn't land at the airport,' he said. He tapped the map. 'Here. This is where they went down.'

Marie peered at the name Lynch was indicating, a small village close to the tip of a peninsula which stuck out fifteen miles into the Bristol Channel, separating Carmarthen Bay and Swansea Bay. 'Llanrhidian,' she read.

'About half a mile to the north-east of it.'

Marie sat back and brushed the hair from her eyes. 'What makes you think he's still there?'

Lynch refolded the map. This time he managed to do it first time and he smiled to himself. 'I don't, but it's the only clue I've got,' he said. 'If he was going on somewhere else, I think they'd have taken him straight to the airport.' He stood up. 'I'm going to the toilet,' he said.

In the bathroom, Lynch splashed cold water onto his face and stood for a while appraising his reflection in the mirror above the sink. The new hairstyle suited him, and the colour looked natural enough. He dried his face on the roller towel then went back into the café.

Marie's head was bent over a newspaper. Lynch frowned. She hadn't had time to go and buy a paper. Then he saw copies of the *Daily Mirror* and the *Daily Telegraph* by the cash register and realised that the café owners supplied them free for customers. Marie turned the front page and ran a hand through her hair as she read. Lynch had a pretty good idea what had grabbed her attention. He slid into the seat opposite her. She looked up sharply. 'Why didn't you tell me?' she snapped. Lynch was taken aback. Anger wasn't the reaction he'd expected – he'd assumed she'd feel scared. He smiled, trying to put her at ease. 'Don't fucking grin at me like a chimpanzee with a hard on,' she hissed angrily.

'What?' he said, stunned.

'Don't give me what, you know exactly what I'm talking about.' She closed the paper and tossed it at him. It was that morning's *Daily Mail*. The story splashed across the front page had been written by the paper's chief reporter and he clearly had better sources than the radio reporter Lynch had listened to in the car. The *Mail* story identified the four shooting victims as an IRA team and named the man who had survived as Declan McGee of Belfast. Lynch didn't recognise the name, but that meant nothing. According to the *Mail*, the police were treating the incident as an internal IRA dispute. Yeah, thought Lynch, they were dead right there. The UFF and the UVF had issued separate statements saying that they weren't involved in the killings and that they remained committed to the peace process.

'So?' said Marie, jarring his concentration. Lynch held his hand up to her lips as he continued to read, but she pushed it away. She sat back in her seat and folded her arms defensively across her chest.

The reporter quoted an unnamed Security Service source as saying that the Maida Vale shootings were thought to be connected to the death of Pat O'Riordan in the Republic, which was now being treated as murder and not suicide. Lynch's eyes widened. Pat O'Riordan, dead? The news hit him like a punch to the solar plexus. Any doubts that the IRA had signed his death warrant evaporated. He was a marked man.

The reporter suggested that the killings were the result of a struggle for power in the top echelons of the IRA, with the hardliners being unhappy at the lack of progress on the political front. Lynch wondered who had fed the reporter that particular line. It could have been someone within the organisation, trying to steer the flak away from McCormack, or a Protestant source trying to discredit the IRA. Either way, Lynch knew that the deaths were nothing to do with any power struggle: the IRA was trying to distance itself from the deaths of the Americans, and

O'Riordan and Lynch had been tagged as the fall guys. The story continued inside the paper but it was mostly background material on previous IRA activities on the mainland, along with a piece written by an Oxford don speculating on the effect the killings might have on the Irish political situation and the peace process. The piece came to no conclusion, which was hardly a surprise to Lynch. Most of what was written in the media about the organisation was speculation; uninformed at best, misinformation spread by the Security Services at worst. He closed the paper and rested his arms on it. Marie was waiting for him to speak. 'I should have told you,' he said. 'I'm sorry.'

'That's not good enough, Dermott.'

A waitress carried over a tray and put Lynch's cheeseburger down in front of him. Lynch nodded his thanks and poured milk into his coffee as the waitress passed Marie her salad. He waited until the waitress was out of hearing range before speaking. 'I wasn't sure that I could trust you,' he said.

'Well I'm damn sure I can't trust you,' she replied. She picked up a fork and prodded a slice of tomato. 'How can they call this a salad? A tomato, three lettuce leaves that any self-respecting rabbit wouldn't look at twice and half a dozen slices of week-old cucumber.'

'I'm sorry,' said Lynch.

'Who do you think I am? Some tout who'd go running to the police at the first sign of trouble?'

Lynch shrugged. He looked down at his cheeseburger but he'd lost his appetite. Pat O'Riordan, dead. He remembered how the big man had clasped him to his chest on the day they'd said goodbye. 'Take care of yourself,' O'Riordan had said. Lynch intended to do just that. He took a mouthful of coffee and swallowed it as he considered what to say to her. 'I was going to tell you,' he said.

'When?'

'Eventually.'

'That's no answer.' She put down her fork and leaned across the table. 'I'm in this with you and I'll do whatever it takes to help. I don't expect you to compromise the organisation or to name names, but I don't expect to be treated like I was the enemy or something.' She nodded at the newspaper. 'Four volunteers shot in Maida Vale just before you arrive on my doorstep. Coincidence? I think not. So what am I supposed to think, Dermott? Either you were with them and you managed to get away, or you killed them. You want to know what I think?' Lynch nodded slowly. 'I think if it was the UVF or the UDA or even the SAS after you then you'd have told me. In fact, you probably wouldn't even have come to me for help, you'd have called up someone in the organisation. There's plenty of safe houses in Kilburn where they'd take good care of you.'

'Not such good care,' he said, smiling.

'A winning smile isn't going to get you off the hook that easily,' she said. 'That's something else that pisses me off. You lied your way into my bed, Dermott. It'll be a long time before I forgive you for that.'

'It wasn't a lie, Marie. Okay, I admit that I didn't tell you the whole truth, but I didn't lie. I am going after Cramer, and the organisation isn't happy about it.'

'Semantics,' she said dismissively. 'You're playing with words. Anyway, like I was saying, I don't think that you were working with the men who were killed last night. Am I right?'

'You're right,' he said. 'They tried to kill me. I was defending myself.'

'And why would they want to kill you, Dermott? They can't all have been jealous husbands.'

Lynch pointed at the paper. 'You read about the farmer who died? Pat O'Riordan?' Marie nodded. 'The IRA murdered him. It might even have been the same four guys who tried to kill me.'

'That's who. I asked why.'

'Pat and I were involved in an operation in the border country. It went wrong, two tourists were killed. Americans. I'm not sure what happened then. We were told to get out, to lie low for a while, but it looks as if someone decided that a more permanent solution was called for.'

'They'd do that?'

'Of course. They don't want anyone else to take care of their dirty laundry. They want to show that they can discipline their own. Plus, if the authorities had got hold of us, we might have talked. I'm not saying we would have, I'm saying that the Army Council would worry about the possibility. So rather than take the risk, they decided to have Pat and me killed.'

Marie's mouth fell open. She shook her head, then gulped half her Diet Coke. 'This is unreal,' she said as she put down her glass.

'I wish it was,' said Lynch. He picked up his cheeseburger and bit into it.

'So they attacked you and you killed them?'

Lynch swallowed and nodded. 'I was on my way to the flat where I was staying. A van pulled up, a guy asked me if I was Dermott Lynch. They were all armed. If they hadn't been planning to kill me there and then, it would only have been a matter of time. Somewhere nice and quiet, out in the country maybe. Perhaps they were planning to make it look like a suicide or an accident, but Marie, love, there was no way I was going to hang around to find out.'

Marie began to prod her salad again, but she made no move to eat it. 'So why didn't you just make a run for it? Why didn't you just take your car and drive? And why were the police looking at your car this morning?'

Lynch put down his cheeseburger and wiped his hands on a paper napkin. He realised that there was no point in lying to her. The discovery of Foley's body would be front page news in the following day's papers, but that wasn't why he had decided to tell her everything. She was right – he owed her his honesty. 'There's a body in the boot.'

'What?' She looked around, left and right, as if she feared that somebody would overhear, but the nearby tables were all empty and their waitress was busying herself at a hissing cappuccino machine.

'There was another guy, the guy I was staying with.'

'You killed him as well?'

'It was an accident.'

Marie's eyes widened. 'An accident? Jesus, Dermott, how the hell do you accidentally kill someone?'

A thick scum was forming on the top of Lynch's coffee and he used a fingernail to drag it to the side of his mug. 'He tried to grab my gun. It went off. Honest to God, I had no intention of shooting him.'

Marie used both hands to brush her hair behind her ears as she studied Lynch. 'Do the police know it was you?'

'My fingerprints were all over the car.'

'So the police are going to be after you, as well as the IRA? And you're still going after Cramer?'

'That's about the size of it, love.'

'You don't exactly make it easy for yourself, do you?'

'Marie, if it was easy, everyone would be doing it.' He smiled, though he was watching her carefully to assess her reaction. Helping him get back at the British soldier who'd been partly responsible for the death of her parents was one thing; helping a murderer on the run was quite another.

The door to the café opened and Lynch looked over to see who was coming in. It was an elderly couple, both overweight and wrapped up in wool coats and matching tartan scarves. They fussed over each other as they sat down at a table by the window, then they both put on glasses so that they could read the menu.

Marie pushed her plate away. 'I can't eat this,' she said.

Lynch looked down at his burger. Grease was congealing on the plate. 'Yeah, I've had enough, too,' he said.

'We can get something else in Wales,' said Marie. She looked at him as if daring him to argue.

Lynch sipped his coffee. It was lukewarm. He watched her over the top of his mug. Any thoughts about arguing with Marie disappeared when he saw the intensity in her eyes. He knew that nothing he could say would dissuade her. Besides, now that she knew the trouble he was in and where he was heading, it made more sense to keep her close to him. 'Are you sure?' he asked.

Marie nodded, her eyes fixed on his. 'Oh yes, Dermott, I'm quite sure. I wouldn't miss this for the world.'

*   *   *

Cramer sat in the rear seat of the Mercedes and stared at the back of Martin's head. 'You okay, Mike?' Martin asked.

Cramer realised that Martin was watching him in the rear-view mirror. He forced a smile. 'Yeah. Just fine.' Actually he felt far from fine. He felt as if a metal clamp was biting into his intestines. The previous night the pain had been worse than anything he'd ever felt before in his life, worse even than on the two occasions when he'd been brutally tortured. At least then he'd had someone to blame for his pain, someone he could curse and hate. Having a focus for his anger had helped take his mind off the damage that was being done to his body, but with the cancer there was nothing to fight against. The pain was the result of his own body working against itself; he had no one to hate but himself.

Allan was walking around the rear of the Mercedes, his head swivelling from side to side. As his hand gripped the handle of the door next to Cramer, Martin nodded. 'Here we go,' said Martin, opening his own door. Cramer grunted as he stepped out of the car. Martin moved to stand directly in front of him as Allan closed the door, then the three men moved together towards the steps that led up to the front door of the school. Cramer's stomach churned and he tasted something bitter and acidic at the back of his mouth. He forced himself to swallow whatever it was that he'd thrown up and then took several deep breaths.

One of the guards came along the gravel path from the croquet lawn and Martin stepped to the side to provide cover. The man was too far away to be a threat but Martin kept a wary eye on them as Allan stepped up to the front door and checked that the hallway was clear. Cramer looked up and saw Su-ming at one of the upstairs windows. 'Focus,

Mike,' Allan whispered. Cramer had stopped at the foot of the steps and both the bodyguards had been forced to stop too, so that they wouldn't get too far ahead of him. His protection depended on them never being more than a step or two from his side. The further away they were, the more he was at risk. 'In the car you're safe,' said Allan, coming back down the stone steps. 'We'll always be using vehicles with bullet-proof glass. Besides, our man has never taken a shot through a window. It's always face to face. Entering and leaving vehicles and buildings is where you're in the most danger, so you must be aware of everything that's going on around you.'

A ripple of nausea washed across Cramer's stomach and he felt his legs go weak. Allan put a hand on Cramer's shoulder. 'You tired?' he asked.

'A bit. I didn't sleep much last night.'

Allan looked at his watch, a rugged Russian model that looked as if it had come straight off a Soviet tank commander's wrist. 'We could take an hour off. We've been pushing it hard today.'

'I wouldn't mind,' said Cramer gratefully. He hated having to show weakness, but this wasn't a question of fatigue, he was really sick and if he didn't rest up he knew he'd collapse. He wasn't sure how much Allan and Martin knew about his medical condition, but one thing he was sure of, he didn't want their sympathy and he didn't want them to treat him like an invalid. That was the main reason he'd rejected the offers of treatment made by the doctors in Madrid. Radiation therapy, chemotherapy, operations; they had a host of suggested remedies none of which had more than an outside chance of extending his life by more than a few months. The doctors had admitted as much, and they had made no attempt to dissuade him when he refused treatment. There was no way that Cramer was prepared to die in a hospital bed, no way that he was prepared to see the pity in the eyes of the doctors and nurses as they waited for the cancer to run its course. He wanted to die on his feet with the blood coursing through his veins, and if everything went according to plan he'd be getting his wish within the next few days.

Allan patted him on the back. 'Let's take a break, then. Grab some scran, if you like.'

'Cheers,' said Cramer, though food was the last thing on his mind.

Martin headed towards the kitchen and Allan followed him. Cramer took off his overcoat and draped it over his arm. 'I'll be in my room,' Cramer called after Allan. He walked slowly up the stairs, taking deep breaths, willing the pain to dissipate.

He took the stairs one at a time, shuffling like an old man, one hand on the banister for balance, the other clutching the coat. When he reached the top, he leant against the wall and closed his eyes. Gradually the waves of pain subsided, though a dull ache remained, like a small block of ice lodged among his intestines. The Spanish doctors had warned him that the pain would get worse as the disease progressed, and that eventually it would become more than he could bear. Cramer opened his eyes. His jaw was aching and he realised he must have been grinding his teeth.

On the way to his room, he walked past the bedroom which had been allocated to Su-ming. Her door was open and as he went by he saw her sitting on her bed. He stopped and knocked quietly. 'Hello, Mike Cramer,' she said, without looking up. Cramer wondered if she was trying to impress him, to demonstrate that she could recognise his footfall.

'Hi. You busy?'

'Yes,' she said.

'Ah. Right.' He turned to go but she looked up and smiled at him.

'Come in,' she said.

Cramer walked into her room and dropped his overcoat over the back of a leather armchair. The room was similar in size and layout to his own, with a small bathroom leading off to the left. He looked out of the window and watched as Martin drove the Mercedes away from the front of the building, presumably to park it around the corner with the rest of the vehicles.

'More rehearsals?' she asked.

'Yeah. Allan sets high standards.'

'He cares about you. He doesn't want you to get hurt.'

Cramer turned to look at her. She was sitting cross-legged on the single bed with a leather-bound book and a notepad in front of her. She was holding something. 'He's just doing his job,' said Cramer, trying to see what she had in her hand.

Su-ming shook her head without looking up. 'You're mistaken. There's more to it than that.' She unclenched her fist and tossed three coins up into the air. They spun slowly and then fell onto the bedcover. She looked at them and then wrote in her notepad.

'What are you doing?' he asked.

Su-ming picked up the three coins and held them tightly in her left hand. 'Seeking guidance,' she said. She tossed the coins and made another note.

Cramer sat down in the armchair and leaned forward to

watch her, intrigued. She threw the coins in again. Cramer peered at the notepad. She had drawn a series of lines, one above the other, several of them broken in the centre. 'May I?' he asked, pointing at the leather-bound volume.

'Help yourself,' she said, tossing the coins again.

Cramer picked up the book. The leather was old and the pages yellowing, but it had obviously been well cared for. He opened it. It was Chinese. He flicked through the well-thumbed pages. There were several illustrations, black and white drawings of Chinese figures, birds, animals and landscapes. The book appeared to be divided into chapters, each one headed by a diagram similar to the one Su-ming had drawn on her notepad. Six lines, one above the other, some broken in the middle, others unbroken. Cramer put the book down and looked at the diagram on Su-ming's notepad. She saw him frowning. 'It's a hexagram,' she said.

'A hexagram?'

'It tells you where to look in the *I Ching*.'

Cramer smiled. 'Are you being deliberately inscrutable?' he asked.

Su-ming handed him the three coins. They were covered with Chinese characters and had small holes in the middle. Like the book, they were clearly very old, the impressions almost worn away. 'The *I Ching* is the *Book of Life Changing*. Or the *Book of Changes*. The Chinese title can be translated several ways. The idea behind it is more than five thousand years old. The copy I have is more than three hundred years old.'

Cramer raised his eyebrows. 'Three hundred years?' he repeated.

'The coins are even older.'

'How old?'

'At least eight hundred years.'

Cramer stared at the coins in the palm of his hand. He wondered how many thousands of hands the coins had passed through over the years. He couldn't even begin to imagine how the world had changed as the coins had passed down through the generations, the metal growing smoother and darker as the humans who made them turned to dust. 'I don't think I've ever touched anything so old,' he said.

'It puts things into perspective, doesn't it?' said Su-ming.

'This *I Ching*, it works?'

'It's not a television set, Mike Cramer. It's not something you plug in and watch. The *I Ching* helps you to interpret what's happening to you. It's an oracle, and the skill is in the interpretation of the book.'

'Like Tarot cards?'

'It's more detailed than the Tarot. But a similar idea, yes.'

'Fortune-telling?'

'No, Mike Cramer, it is not fortune-telling.' She held out her hands for the coins and he gave them to her.

'Do you do readings for your boss?'

Su-ming rubbed the coins between her hands as if trying to warm them. 'Every day,' she said.

'He must believe in it, then?'

Su-ming sighed as if deeply disappointed. 'It's not a question of belief. You don't have to believe in an aeroplane for it to carry you through the skies. Yes, Mr Vander Mayer believes in the integrity of the *I Ching* and in my interpretation of it, but that is irrelevant so far as its veracity is concerned.'

'So it does work?'

Su-ming's eyes flashed, then she smiled as she realised he was teasing her. 'Yes, Mike Cramer, it works. Are you happy now?'

'Will you do me?' He held her gaze for several seconds.

She stopped smiling. 'Is this a test, is that it? You want to test me?'

Cramer shrugged. 'I thought it might be interesting, that's all. If you don't want to . . .'

'It's not that I don't want to, but I'm not some sort of guinea pig. I don't need to have my abilities tested. I consult the *I Ching* for myself and for Mr Vander Mayer. I don't do party tricks.' She held out the coins and Cramer took them.

'You have to ask a specific question,' she said. 'Not a question which can be answered with a yes or a no, and it must be a question which is significant to you. The *I Ching* is not to be used for fun, do you understand?'

'Yes,' said Cramer meekly.

Su-ming nodded. 'When you have the question fixed in your mind, you toss the coins six times. Depending how they fall, each toss will be either *yin* or *yang*. If it's *yang*, I draw an unbroken line, if it's *yin*, I draw a broken line. The six throws produce a hexagram. Do you understand?'

Cramer shrugged. 'I guess so.'

'It doesn't matter. All you have to do is to frame the question and throw the coins. I will use the hexagram and the coin combinations to interpret the answer from the book.'

'Do I have to tell you the question?'

Su-ming shook her head. 'No.'

Cramer wondered what he should ask. He toyed with something frivolous but he knew that Su-ming wouldn't be amused. She clearly took it very seriously. 'Okay. I'm ready.'

He threw the coins and Su-ming drew a short line on the notepad. He tossed the metal discs another five times and when he had finished Su-ming held up the six lines she'd drawn on the pad. The top, third and fifth lines were broken, the second, fourth and bottom lines were unbroken. '*Chi Chi*,' she said. 'Completion and what happens afterwards.'

Cramer frowned. 'What's that? What do you mean?'

'The hexagram is called *Chi Chi*. The top three lines represent *k'an*, water. The bottom three lines represent *li*, fire. Together they form *Chi Chi*. It's a good omen, so long as you remain alert. It's like a kettle burning over a fire. If it's controlled, then everything is fine. But if you are careless, the kettle will boil over and the water will evaporate. You will have lost that which you hoped to achieve. You must not become complacent, that's the message of the *I Ching*.' Su-ming looked down at her notepad again. 'The hexagram is only the start,' she said. 'It provides an overall guideline, a framework. According to the way the coins are thrown, some of the lines are called changing lines. Any combination of the six could be changing lines.' She looked at the notepad. 'In your case it's the fourth line. It was *yang*, but a changing *yang*. So I consult the *I Ching* to see what it says about the fourth line. Then we change the fourth line from *yang* to *yin*, from a broken line to a complete line, and that produces a second hexagram. The oracle's advice is a combination of the first hexagram, the second hexagram, and the changing lines. There are thousands of possibilities. That's why the book is so thick.'

She opened the leather-bound volume and slowly went through it. 'Here we are. *Chi Chi*. The fourth line.' She read it silently, then looked at him. 'You must be on your guard. You must be careful. Things can very easily go wrong.'

'Tell me about it,' laughed Cramer. Her face fell as he laughed and he immediately composed himself. 'I'm sorry, I wasn't laughing at you. It's just that under the circumstances . . . you know. Obviously I'm going to be on guard.'

She looked at him seriously. 'The *I Ching* is referring to your question, remember? It is with regard to the question you asked that it is offering advice. This is not fortune-telling, Mike Cramer. The *I Ching* only answers specific questions asked of it.'

'I understand, Su-ming.'

She picked up the notepad again and drew a second hexagram, changing the fourth line from broken to unbroken. 'This is now *ko*. Revolution. A combination of *tui*, lake, over *li*, fire. The image is of a lake over a volcano, when the lava bursts through the water is vaporised. Great change. It's not a bad sign, the opposite in fact. It suggests that the present situation is about to give way to a more beneficial one. An end to sadness. But you yourself must make the change possible. It must first come from within.'

Cramer nodded. 'An end to sadness,' he repeated. 'That can't be bad, can it?'

Su-ming closed the book carefully as if she was afraid of damaging the pages. 'I suppose not,' she said. 'Was the advice helpful?'

'Of course. I must be careful, but if I try hard there'll be a happy ending.'

Su-ming looked at him with narrowed eyes. 'You sound as if you don't believe what you've been told.'

Cramer shrugged. 'It's the sort of advice I'd get in a fortune cookie. Or in the horoscope of any tabloid newspaper.'

'Your mind is closed,' she said brusquely. 'If you refuse to listen to what the *I Ching* has to say, how can you hope to be helped by it?'

'I'm just not sure how throwing coins can give me the answer to a problem that I have.'

'Because everything in the universe is connected,' said Su-ming.

'Well, I'm not convinced,' he said. 'It's like when you read my palm. I don't believe that the lines on my hand are an indication of what has happened to me in my life, much less a guide to what lies ahead of me.'

Su-ming picked up a small leather bag with a leather drawstring and dropped the coins in one by one. She put the bag on her bedside table and held out her hand. At first Cramer didn't realise what she wanted, then he slowly held out his own right hand, palm upwards. She bent forward, her face only inches away from the palm as she traced the lines with her index finger. Occasionally her fingernail scraped his skin and he felt a tingle run down his spine like a mild electric shock. He shivered, but Su-ming didn't appear to notice. She stared at his palm for several minutes, then released his hand.

'So?' said Cramer, his curiosity piqued.

Su-ming raised her eyebrows. 'So what?' she asked.

'So what did you see?'

Su-ming shrugged. 'I was just checking.'

'Checking? Checking what?'

She tilted up her chin. 'There's no point in telling you if you don't believe, is there?'

Cramer nodded slowly as he realised that she was toying with him. 'Right,' he said. He stood up. 'Thanks,' he said.

Su-ming picked up her coins again and smoothed them between her hands. She avoided Cramer's gaze. 'Are you frightened?' she asked.

'Frightened?' he repeated, genuinely confused by her question. 'Frightened of what?'

'Of what lies ahead,' she said.

Cramer rubbed his chin. 'Allan's trained me well. I stand a pretty good chance of getting through it.'

Su-ming looked up sharply. 'That's not what I meant, Mike Cramer,' she said.

Cramer swallowed. His mouth had suddenly gone dry. She continued to look at him, waiting for him to reply. 'Yes,' he said eventually. 'Yes, I'm frightened.'

She nodded. 'An end to sadness,' she said. 'Remember that, Mike Cramer.' She threw the coins and they fell silently onto the bed. Cramer walked out of the room as Su-ming drew a line on her notepad.

Lynch left the M4 and followed the A483 over the River Tawe and into Swansea. The sky was beginning to darken and he wanted to reach Llanrhidian before nightfall. Marie gave clear instructions that took them through the city centre and onto the A4118, the main road that cut through the fifteen-mile long limestone peninsula. She had the map on her lap, neatly folded with the area they were driving through uppermost. Lynch didn't know whether or not she'd been joking about being a Girl Guide but her navigation had been faultless.

'Are you sure you don't want me to drive, Dermott?' Marie asked, massaging the back of his neck with her right hand.

'I'll be okay. I prefer driving to being driven.'

'Most men do.'

Lynch threw her a quick glance. 'What's that supposed to mean?'

'Nothing.'

'You're saying that driving is a male ego thing, is that it?'

Marie held up her hands. 'Hey, if the cap fits . . .' She laughed and squeezed his neck harder. 'Don't be so sensitive. Besides, you're a very good driver.'

Lynch grinned, then just as quickly, frowned. 'You wouldn't be trying to massage my ego, Marie, love, would you?'

Marie laughed. 'Just your neck, Dermott. Just your neck. We take the B4271 after Upper Killay. The A road goes to the airport and then to the south. We keep heading west.'

'How far?'

'To Llanrhidian? About eight miles. What's the plan?'

The question set Lynch thinking. He'd been so busy getting out of London and worrying about the mess he'd left behind that he'd scarcely thought about what he would do when he got to the point on the map where Cramer's helicopter had landed. For all he knew, Cramer could have been whisked into a car and driven anywhere in Wales or beyond. 'We'll take a look around, see if we can work out where he went,' he said.

'That's the plan?' she said.

'It's not really a plan,' said Lynch.

'I'll say.'

Lynch cleared his throat. 'Do you have any suggestions?'

'No suggestions. I just want to get him. We'll find out where he is and we'll get him.'

Lynch shook his head. 'No, Marie, love. I'll do it.'

Marie nodded slowly. 'Whatever you say.'

'I mean it. I don't want you anywhere near him. He's a trained killer. He's one of the most dangerous men you'll ever meet.'

Marie raised an eyebrow innocently. 'What, more dangerous than you, Dermott?'

Lynch grinned despite himself. The road to Llanrhidian was narrow and winding and he drove carefully, aware of how easily he could lose control of the spirited Golf GTI.

The village was tiny and looked down upon a long stretch of salt marsh which ran into the Loughor estuary to the north. To the west were the gaunt ruins of a castle. 'What's that?' Lynch asked, nodding at the ruins.

'Weobley Castle,' Marie answered, looking at the map. 'The place we're looking for is to the east, just the other side of the B4295.'

They drove by the village pub. Lynch resisted the urge to stop. While he would have enjoyed a pint and a rest from driving, the pub was in such an isolated spot that the arrival of two strangers would be bound to attract attention. Marie stared at the map, rechecking the coordinates that Lynch had given her. They followed the B4295 past a sprawling caravan park, then Marie pointed to the right. 'There,' she said.

Lynch peered through the windscreen at what appeared to be nothing but farmland, most of it freshly ploughed. 'Are you sure?' he asked. Marie nodded. Lynch braked. The road curved around to the right, and as he guided the Golf into the curve, a high stone wall came into view. 'Could this be it?' he asked.

She nodded. 'According to the map, the coordinates are about half a mile inside the wall.' Lynch slowed the car to little more than a walking pace. Marie twisted around in her seat and tried to look past Lynch. 'What is this place?' she asked.

'I can't see.'

'There's a gate up ahead.'

Lynch accelerated smoothly. They passed a faded wooden sign affixed to the wall. 'Did you see that?' Lynch asked, looking over his shoulder.

'Sorry. I missed it.'

Lynch stopped and reversed the Golf down the road. The lettering on the board had once been dark brown but it was now streaked with greenish mould. LLANRHIDIAN GIRLS' PREPARATORY SCHOOL, the sign said, but a white strip with red lettering had been plastered across the board announcing that the building had been sold, along with the name and telephone number of a local estate agent. Marie took a pen from her handbag and copied the name and telephone number into the back of her diary. Lynch put the car into first gear and drove down the road towards the entrance to the school. They were about twenty yards away when he saw the two men standing just inside the wrought-iron gates. They were both in their late twenties and wearing leather jackets and jeans, not standing to attention but not lounging aimlessly, either. They were both looking at the Golf.

'Kiss me,' said Lynch.

Marie moved quickly. She leaned over and planted a kiss on his cheek and hugged her arms around his neck. Lynch accelerated and they passed the gate. He checked his rear-view mirror but the men didn't look through the gate after the Golf.

'What was that about?' Marie asked, releasing her grip on his neck.

'Didn't you see them?' Lynch asked. 'Two men, Sass by the look of them.'

'Are you sure?'

Lynch gave her a withering look and she slid down into her seat. 'Now what do we do?' she asked.

'We wait until it gets dark,' he said. 'If they're guarding the place, he's probably still there.' Lynch felt a growing excitement as he drove alongside the stone wall and he fought to control it. 'Find us somewhere where we can look down on the school so that we can get an overview, okay?'

'Sure. There's a hill to the north. We should be able to see it from there.'

Lynch turned to look at her and he saw that she was smiling. 'What?' he said.

'What do you mean, what?'

'I mean what are you so happy about?'

Marie ran a finger along his leg, scratching the material of his jeans. 'You said "we" for the first time.'

Lynch snorted softly and looked back at the road. She was right, he realised. He'd started thinking of her as part of the team. Whether or not that was a good thing remained to be seen.

* * *

Bernard Jackman looked up at the blonde stewardess and took the small glass of orange juice that she was offering. He gave her a broad smile but she was already moving on to the next passenger. Even in first class the service was perfunctory and the smiles plastic, but Jackman didn't care. He flew more than fifty thousand miles a year on scheduled airlines and regarded travelling as nothing more than a means to an end. All he cared about was that the plane arrived on time and that it didn't crash into the sea along the way.

He watched the stewardess walk down the aisle, dispensing drinks and more artificial smiles. Jackman was used to false smiles. During his time as an FBI profiler he'd interviewed hundreds of murderers, and rarely did they seem out of the ordinary. There was little to separate the serial killer from the man in the street, on the surface at least. Jackman had met serial killers who looked like kindly grandfathers, others who were as charming, handsome and charismatic as chat show hosts, and even one who was every bit as voluptuous as the stewardess. Jackman knew that it was only when you began to delve inside their heads that you discovered what separated the killers from their prey, the sheep from the wolves. He'd spent thousands of hours interviewing convicted killers, winning their confidence, peering into their minds, becoming their friend, so that he could discover what made them different. One of his bosses had said that a good profiler was like a chameleon, that when a profiler and a killer were together in a cell it should be impossible to tell them apart. Their mannerisms, their body language, the way they talked, should be virtually identical. The same man had also warned of the dangers of spending too much time in the company of serial killers. They had the same fascination as a flame to a moth: the profilers had to be careful how close they got, lest they got burned.

Jackman opened the file on Mike Cramer. Most of it consisted of reports from Cramer's time in the army and later in the Special Air Service, the British Special Forces regiment which was revered throughout the world. There was nothing to explain where the man had been over the previous three years. A colour photograph was clipped to the inside of the file cover: three pictures in a strip, left and right profiles and one full on. There was an intensity in Cramer's eyes that burned out of the photograph. The effect was almost hypnotic and Jackman spent several minutes staring at the picture. He was disturbed by the stewardess asking if she could take his empty glass. He handed it to her, still looking at the photograph.

Cramer's eyes were deep-set and his nose was slightly hooked, giving him a predatory appearance. According to the file, Cramer was thirty-seven years old but the eyes wouldn't have been out of place in an octogenarian. There was no sadness in the man's gaze, no bitterness, just a cold level stare that seemed to look right through Jackman. Jackman wondered what Cramer had seen and done to get such hard eyes. The file provided a few clues. Cramer had served in the Falklands and had worked undercover in Northern Ireland. After three tours of duty in the province he had been captured by the IRA and brutally tortured. He'd been rescued and rushed by helicopter to a hospital in Belfast where surgeons had saved his life, but shortly afterwards he'd left the SAS for medical reasons. There were no details of what Cramer had been doing since leaving the regiment, but Jackman had gained the impression that the Colonel had been holding something back. Jackman was sure that the Colonel had used Cramer on at least one operation, something so sensitive that he couldn't involve one of his own men.

The Colonel had been cagey about Cramer's motivation for taking Vander Mayer's place. On reading the file, Jackman's first thought was that Cramer felt he had something to prove, because he'd been forced to leave the army early. Unfinished business. On meeting the man face to face, Jackman had realised that there was something else driving him. Jackman would have liked to have spent more time with Mike Cramer, to have sat down with him and talked in detail, to have done what Jackman did best – probing and ferreting out what made a man tick.

Jackman smiled as he recalled how the Colonel's jaw had tightened when he'd pointed out how closely Cramer fitted the profile of the man they were looking for. Cramer's family background – losing his mother and the lack of a father-figure during his teenage years – was almost certainly what had led him to join the armed forces. But Jackman knew that it was also the sort of environment that could lead to psychological problems which, coupled with the intensive training Cramer had received, could be the perfect recipe for producing a psychotic killer. Jackman's own mother had died when he was young, and he knew all too well the void that left behind, a void that could never be filled. In Cramer's case, no one had even tried and he'd sought sanctuary in the army.

THE DOUBLE TAP

According to Cramer's service record, he hadn't shone as a regular soldier, and on several occasions had been up on insubordination charges. It wasn't until he passed the rigorous SAS selection tests that Cramer finally found his vocation. Trained to a peak of fitness that most men could only imagine and schooled in weapons, explosives and parachuting, Cramer became a government-trained killing machine. But life in the regiment gave him back something that had been missing in the past – a family. His fellow soldiers became his brothers, the regiment supplied all his needs and wants and, Jackman theorised, the Colonel probably became the father-figure that Cramer sought. Jackman knew that being forced to leave the regiment Cramer loved must have been every bit as emotionally damaging as the death of his mother, and the move back into civilian life would have echoed his original loss. The end of his army career could have opened the floodgates and allowed the release of all the emotions Cramer had been holding back over the years.

Jackman wondered what Cramer had been up to in civilian life. Men with Cramer's background tended to end up as mercenaries, or in prison, or dead. Jackman leaned back in his seat, smiling to himself. He looked forward to meeting Cramer again: there was so much he wanted to ask him. Jackman wanted to know how many lives Cramer had taken, and how he felt about it, whether he enjoyed the killing or regarded it as just another branch of soldiering. He wanted to find out what the first kill had been like, and whether the feelings had changed with the second, third and fourth. And Jackman wanted to know something else – whether Cramer missed it.

*　　*　　*

Cramer stood at his bedroom window looking down at the car park. White halogen lights illuminated the area and glinted off the cars. A ginger and white cat walked diagonally across the tarmac square with its ears pricked up and its tail erect as if it was on patrol. Cramer smiled at the thought – an SAS cat, trained to kill without emotion, a cat that could out-march, out-fight and out-drink all other cats. The cat stopped in the centre of the square as if it had seen something. A figure stepped into the light and, as it walked towards the cat, Cramer realised it was Allan.

Cramer watched as Allan walked over to the cat and knelt down beside it. The cat arched its back and rubbed itself against Allan's outstretched hand and Cramer could imagine it purring with pleasure. Allan looked up towards where Cramer was standing. Cramer wasn't sure if the bright lights reflected on the glass would allow Allan to see in, but any doubts disappeared when Allan straightened up and waved at him. Cramer unlatched the window and opened it. 'Hang on, I'll come down!' he called.

Allan gave him a thumbs up. The building was in darkness but Cramer didn't switch on any lights. He went quietly downstairs and slipped out of the back door where Allan was waiting with the cat in his arms. 'Everything all right?' Cramer asked.

'Fine. Have you met Ginge?'

Cramer stroked the cat. 'She came with the school?'

'I guess so. She seems tame enough. For a cat.' Allan bent down and let the cat go. She looked at him for a few seconds and then disappeared silently into the darkness.

'Are you okay?' Allan asked.

Cramer nodded. 'Sure. I just fancied some air, that's all.'

They walked together around the rear of the main school building and across the lawn. High overhead they saw the lights of an airliner cutting across the star-strewn sky. The man who'd attacked Cramer in the dining room was standing at the gate and he nodded to them both. Allan waved in salute.

'How did you get into this, Allan?' Cramer asked.

'The Colonel wanted somebody with bodyguarding experience, and I guess I fitted the bill.'

'How come?'

'They tend not to broadcast the fact, but the regiment supplies bodyguards for the Royal Family and politicians when they go abroad and we help train bodyguards who work for foreign heads of state. I did a six-month stint with the Sultan of Brunei before I joined the Training Wing.'

'And Martin?'

'I suggested that we use him. He left the Ranger Wing a few years back to start up his own bodyguarding business in the South of France. He's doing well, too. The Colonel had to do a fair bit of sweet-talking to convince him to join the operation, but he's the best in the business.' He paused. 'What about you, Mike?'

'What do you mean?' They turned away from the gate and headed towards the tennis courts. Cramer's eyes were constantly moving, checking out the shadows, looking for any sign that one of Allan's men was about to spring another surprise attack.

'You know what I mean. In a standard bodyguarding operation, the prime objective is to protect the client. We keep close, we make sure the environment is safe, and if the shit hits the fan we get between the client and the trouble and we get the client the hell out. His safety is paramount.' Cramer nodded. Off in the distance an owl hooted. 'Martin and I aren't bodyguarding you, Mike. You know that. Our instructions are to slot the killer. Your survival is secondary.'

Cramer cleared his throat. 'Secondary? I figured it was lower than that.'

Allan smiled thinly. 'So why did they choose you for the job?'

'For bait, you mean? Just lucky, I guess.' Allan nodded and didn't press Cramer further. They walked in silence for a while. The floodlights around the tennis court were on. Discarded cartridges glittered on the hard clay surface, the detritus of the day's rehearsals. 'Where were you before Sass?' Cramer asked. 'The Paras?'

Allan grinned. 'Not me, Mike. I was a freelance.'

'A freelance?'

'I was sitting in a pub in London and saw an advertisement in the *Daily Express* for security guards in South Africa. I figured it was for store detectives, something like that. Two weeks later I was in the Angolan bush with a bloody Kalashnikov in my hands. I was nineteen.'

'Are you serious?'

'Sure. They just wanted bodies, they couldn't care less about how much experience we had.' He shrugged his massive shoulders. 'Though, truth be told, I did exaggerate a bit. I stayed a couple of years but when things started to get a bit hot I went back to Dublin, set up my own security company, ran a nightclub, even did a bit of acting. But I missed it, you know?'

'Yeah,' agreed Cramer, 'I know.' Cramer knew exactly what Allan meant. He'd never felt so alive as when he was in the SAS. It wasn't just the adrenalin rush, it was the companionship, the fact that he was working as part of a team with men who were trained to a degree of professionalism that few could match. Cramer missed the SAS and he'd never found anything that could fill the gap it left in his life.

A small insect buzzed by Allan's ear and he waved it away. 'So I moved to London and applied to join 21 SAS. I was twenty-three and figured I was too old to join the regular army, but reckoned that the Territorials might have me. Failed the first time, but they told me to work on my fitness and try again. The following year I made it. Did the Fan Dance in eighteen hours in the shittiest weather you've ever seen. The Colonel was on the course as an observer and he approached me afterwards, asked if I'd thought about serving full time. He put in a word for me and I joined 22 SAS.'

Cramer was impressed. It was rare for a member of the Territorial SAS to be offered a place in the regiment proper. 'And you like Training Wing?' he asked.

'It's better than standing outside a Leeson Street nightclub with the rain pissing down and dealing with spotty teenagers trying to bullshit their way in.' He grinned. 'Mind you, you get laid more often in Dublin, that's for sure.'

They skirted the tennis courts and walked across the croquet lawn. Allan was laughing but Cramer remained on his guard, fearful that at any moment an attacker would come rushing out of the darkness. The PPK was in his underarm holster but unless the attack came slower than usual, he'd prefer to go for the stiletto. Under Allan's guidance he was now winning more of the confrontations than he was losing. There had been times early on in the training when Cramer had wondered about the point of rehearsing the moves over and over again, because at the end of the day he wasn't even sure that he wanted to survive the encounter with the assassin. The pain in his bowels was getting worse by the day, and he was finding it increasingly difficult to eat: his appetite had all but disappeared and when he did force himself to eat he paid for it a few hours later. He knew the discomfort was but a fraction of what lay ahead, and that the day would come when a bullet in the face would be a welcome relief, but under Allan's constant cajoling and pushing his professionalism had kicked in and he'd worked hard at perfecting the technique. Now he relished the opportunity of going up against the assassin, to prove to himself, and to Allan, just how good he was.

Cramer stepped to the side to avoid a hoop set into the lawn but kept his eyes flicking from side to side. 'You can relax, Mike,' said Allan. 'Your training's over.'

Cramer looked across, his eyes narrowed. 'What do you mean, training's over?'

'The Colonel asked me to tell you that we're leaving for London tomorrow. From now on, it's for real.'

Cramer swallowed. There was a tightness in the pit of his stomach, a mixture of fear and excitement, a feeling that he hadn't experienced in a long time. It almost made him forget about the cancer that was growing there. Almost. But not quite.

*　　*　　*

Lynch held his breath as he focused the binoculars. The croquet pitch was well lit and he had no trouble recognising the face of Mike Cramer, the Sass-man. Cramer looked in better shape than the last time Lynch had seen him – he was now well groomed and wearing what were clearly expensive clothes. Cramer and the man he was with were deep in conversation. Lynch would have given his right arm to know what they were talking about. Somewhere up above Lynch an owl hooted. Lynch had climbed a tree close to the perimeter wall which ran all around the school buildings and grounds. He'd spotted five guards, two at the main entrance and another three patrolling the grounds. There were several security cameras fixed to the buildings and they moved at irregular intervals, which suggested that they were being manipulated from some sort of control centre. The sky was obscured with thick cloud and the tree Lynch had chosen was in almost total darkness so he was certain he couldn't be seen.

Lynch licked his lips. His mouth was dry with anticipation. He could scale the wall within seconds; it had been built merely to mark the perimeter of the school grounds rather than to keep out intruders. He could cover the distance between the wall and the main school building in less than a minute and would reach the two men on the croquet lawn in half that time. The problem was, what then? The security cameras would spot him as soon as he was out in the open, and even if Cramer and his companion weren't armed, the patrolling guards definitely were. Maybe he'd be able to kill Cramer there and then, but it would be a suicide mission and Lynch was in no mood to throw his life away, no matter how strong the urge for revenge. No, there had to be a better way. He watched as the two men made their way to the front of the school and disappeared inside. Lynch hung the binoculars around his neck and climbed carefully to the ground.

The Golf was parked almost a mile away in a copse close to the road and he jogged, more to keep warm than because he was in a hurry. He figured that the men had gone to bed so there was nothing he could do until morning. He needed a way into the school, some ruse that would allow him to breach their defences. The headlights of an approaching car pierced through the night and he dropped into a ditch until it had gone by. There was brackish water in the bottom of the ditch but he managed to stay dry from the knees up. His wet feet slapped on the tarmac as he ran towards the copse. Luckily there were no other cars and he reached the Golf in just over six minutes. Marie was asleep – she'd reclined the front passenger seat and wrapped herself in a tartan blanket. Lynch smiled as he looked at her through the window.

She'd wisely locked the doors so he knocked gently on the window to wake her. She smiled sleepily at him and unlocked the driver's door. 'How did it go?' she asked.

'He's there.'

Marie's eyes widened. 'He's there? Now what?'

'Now I have to think.' He leaned down and took off his wet boots and socks.

'What happened?' she asked.

'I had to hide in a ditch.'

328

Marie gave him the blanket and Lynch wrapped it around his legs. It was cold in the car but they couldn't risk running the engine to use the heater. 'What do you think he's doing in Wales?' Marie asked.

'Marie, love, it's a bloody mystery, right enough. He's being guarded by some very heavy characters. There are security cameras all over the place, and he's dressed like he just stepped out of a Savile Row tailor's. God, I'm starving.'

Marie reached into the back of the car and picked up her green and gold Harrods carrier bag. From the bag she took out a pack of Marks and Spencer sandwiches and a can of Coke and handed them to Lynch. He pulled the tab and drank.

'Have you thought it might be a set-up?' she asked. 'Some sort of trap?'

Lynch shook his head emphatically. 'Why in Wales? Why hide here, miles from anywhere? And why is the security so obvious? When he was in Howth, now that looked like a trap. No, I think something else is going down here, but I'm fucked if I know what it is.'

The water that gushed out of the showerhead was cold and even though Cramer let it run for several minutes it didn't get any warmer. He stepped under the freezing spray and gasped, washed quickly and then jumped out. He rubbed himself with a fresh towel and dressed, choosing one of the suits he hadn't worn before.

Allan and Martin were walking out of the dining hall just

as Cramer arrived. 'Briefing in the headmistress's study,' said Allan. 'You hadn't forgotten, had you?'

Cramer shook his head. No, he hadn't forgotten. Today was the day he became the Judas Goat. Mrs Elliott followed Allan and Martin into the hallway. She beamed as she saw Cramer. 'Ah, Mr Cramer. Can I fetch you something?'

'No, thanks, Mrs Elliott. I'm not hungry.'

Mrs Elliott glared at Cramer as severely as Allan had done whenever training hadn't gone well. 'The Colonel said I was to be sure that you ate something,' she said. 'It was an order.'

'An order?' repeated Cramer, amused.

'Better do as she says, Mike,' said Martin. 'We don't want you up on a charge.'

'How about some sandwiches for later?' Mrs Elliott asked. 'Cheese and pickle?'

'Cheese and pickle will be just fine,' agreed Cramer, knowing that further resistance was futile.

'And tea?' she pressed. 'I could make a flask of tea, no bother.'

'And tea. Thanks, Mrs Elliott.' Cramer headed down the corridor towards the headmistress's office before Mrs Elliott could add to the menu.

'How are you feeling today, Mike?' asked Allan.

'Better,' lied Cramer. He'd lain awake most of the night, bathed in sweat. The pain seemed to be worse at night, even when he was lying in bed. Cramer wondered if it was because his adrenalin levels were higher during the day, stimulating the body's natural painkillers. Or maybe it was because he was always kept busy by Allan so that he didn't have time to dwell on his illness; at night he had nothing else to do but worry about the cancer that was eating him up. If the pain got much worse he'd have to ask the doctor for something else. Nothing strong enough to slow down his reflexes, just enough to take the edge off the pain. 'When are we setting off?'

Allan looked at his Russian wristwatch. 'Thirty minutes.'

'Where did you get the watch from?' Cramer asked.

'Off a dead Cuban in Angola,' Allan replied.

'Come on, if he was dead, how did you know he was a Cuban?'

Allan grinned and mimed shooting a gun with his right hand. He blew away imaginary smoke, knocked on the door to the study and opened it, allowing Cramer and Martin in first. The Colonel was sitting behind the desk, reading a file. Cramer was surprised to see Su-ming in the room, standing by the fireplace. She was dressed formally in a dark blue skirt and jacket with what looked like a Chanel handbag on a golden chain over her right shoulder. She smiled at him, but there was little warmth in her eyes.

Three straight-backed wooden chairs had been lined up facing the desk and Cramer, Allan and Martin sat down. Martin looked across at Cramer and Cramer realised that they'd had the same thought – they were like schoolboys being summoned for a caning. Both men grinned. The Colonel looked up from his paperwork as if he'd just noticed that they'd walked in. 'Everything ready?' the Colonel asked Allan.

'All set, boss,' said Allan. 'The plane has already arrived at Swansea and we've a flight plan filed for ten-fifteen.'

'Flight plan?' queried Cramer. 'I thought London was our first stop. Aren't we driving?'

'Vander Mayer always flies into London on one of his

private jets,' said the Colonel. 'He has three at his disposal, one based in the UK, one in the States and a third presently in the Philippines. According to the details we sent to Zurich, Vander Mayer left Miami in the early hours of the morning and is now on his way to Heathrow.' The Colonel leaned across the desk as if trying to narrow the distance between himself and Cramer. 'You have to think like Vander Mayer from now on, Joker. You don't open doors for yourself, you don't carry anything, you don't acknowledge strangers, you're above all that. That's what Su-ming and your bodyguards are for. The killer is going to be watching you and if he sees anything out of the ordinary, he'll run like the wind.'

'No problem,' said Cramer, rubbing his hands together.

'Once you're on the jet, you're in play. You have to live the part, you have to be Vander Mayer, and you have to be ready for the killer to strike at any moment. You've read the files, you know how he's got close before. In a wheelchair, dressed as a waiter, as a pilot, as a delivery man, the only thing he hasn't done is dress up as a woman. You have to regard every stranger as a threat, but you mustn't overreact. If our man sees you pull out a gun he'll know it's a trap. You must be sure, one hundred per cent sure.'

'You mean I don't shoot until I see the whites of his eyes,' Cramer said.

The Colonel pursed his lips. 'No. You don't shoot until you see a gun in his hand. He has to make an attempt to kill you, or we've wasted our time. I want to be quite clear on this, Joker. There are no short-cuts. We only have one chance and I don't want us blowing it. Instinct isn't going to count for anything if we get the wrong man.'

'I understand, Colonel.'

The Colonel stood up and walked over to the window. 'On the communications front, Allan and Martin will be utilising transceivers, but they will only be in communication with each other,' he said. 'That's standard procedure for bodyguards. There's no way Vander Mayer would be carrying a transceiver, so you won't be in radio contact with them. I will be monitoring their transmissions, but on no account are you to acknowledge that we're listening in. Our man is a professional and will almost certainly also be monitoring you. We will be able to transmit on your frequency, but I can't envisage any circumstances under which we'd do that. We won't be able to give you any warning, because if we did, he might hear us.'

The three men sitting in front of the desk nodded in unison. 'We're on our own,' said Cramer.

'I'll have men close by, but yes, in effect you will be on your own. You must not depend on them to protect you because that's not what they're there for.'

'Is there any way I can contact you?' Cramer asked.

'Absolutely not,' said the Colonel tersely. 'Phones just aren't secure, cellular or otherwise. Under no circumstances are you to attempt to get in touch with me.' He nodded at Allan. 'That goes for you and Martin.' The Colonel leaned back against the windowsill. 'Don't forget that we will be following you every step of the way. Even if you don't see us, we'll still be there.'

Cramer rubbed his chin thoughtfully. 'I'd be happier if there was some way we could reach you.'

'You don't need me to hold your hand,' said the Colonel. 'Any other questions?'

The three men shook their heads. 'I have a question,' said Su-ming from behind them.

The Colonel raised an eyebrow. 'Yes, Su-ming?'

'How long do we wait?'

'As long as it takes.'

'But the itinerary only runs for two weeks.'

'That was all that was asked for, which leads us to believe that the attempt will be made within the next fourteen days.'

Cramer twisted around in his seat to look at Su-ming. She looked worried but there was no trace of nervousness in her voice. 'What about Mr Vander Mayer?' she said. 'I have to be in regular contact with him.'

The Colonel shook his head. 'Impossible. What would happen if the killer were to hear you talking to him?'

'So I am not to call him?'

'Not until it's over.'

'What if he tries to contact me?'

'He won't. He understands the position. Mr Vander Mayer does have a number where he can reach me. In the event that he has to get hold of you, I will get a message to you.'

Su-ming shrugged. Cramer wondered why she was so worried about not being in contact with her boss. He turned back to face the Colonel. 'About Vander Mayer,' he said. 'What's he doing?'

'He's on his yacht,' the Colonel answered. 'It's equipped with state of the art communications equipment so he's able to carry on business as usual. He has a copy of your itinerary and will simply tell anyone he speaks to that he is at your location. Any faxes, telexes or computer transmissions he sends will also appear to be sent from your location. But he's agreed to keep his activities to the absolute minimum until we have our man.' When the Colonel saw that there were no further questions, he pointed at the door with his walking stick. 'All that remains is for me to wish you luck,' he said. 'As of now we go our separate ways.'

'How are you getting to London?' Cramer asked as he stood up.

'We'll be using the helicopter. We'll get to Heathrow after you but there are already men there waiting for you. You won't see them, not if they're doing their job right.'

Su-ming opened the door and went out into the corridor. The Colonel shook the three men by the hand as they left the room. Cramer was the last to leave. After they'd shaken, the Colonel held onto Cramer's hand. 'Good luck,' he said.

'Luck doesn't come into it, Colonel. Besides, we both know what the end result of this is going to be, don't we?'

The Colonel didn't reply. He let Cramer's hand slip from his own and then patted him on the shoulder, like a priest comforting the recently bereaved. 'I wish there was . . .' he began.

'Hey, don't worry,' interrupted Cramer. 'I'm a big boy, I know exactly what I'm getting into and it's my choice.' He held the Colonel's look for several seconds, then turned and left the room.

'Your stuff's in the car,' said Allan, handing Cramer his overcoat. 'You're carrying?'

Cramer patted the gun in his underarm holster. 'I wouldn't leave home without it.'

Mrs Elliott came out of the kitchen and handed Cramer a Tupperware box and a stainless steel Thermos flask. 'For the journey,' she said. 'And mind you look after yourself.' She hugged him and then rushed back into the kitchen.

Cramer followed Allan and Martin to the Mercedes

and climbed into the back seat. Su-ming was already there.

'All set?' asked Martin.

'Let's do it,' said Cramer.

Martin looked over his shoulder at the flask and sandwiches which Cramer had in his lap. 'Mike . . .' he began.

'Sure,' said Cramer before Martin could finish. He passed over the sandwiches and Martin practically snatched them from his hand.

Dermott Lynch watched the Mercedes nose slowly out of the school entrance and on to the road. He took his binoculars away from his eyes. 'It's him,' he said. 'He's in the back with a girl.'

'What do we do?' asked Marie.

Lynch scratched his chin and frowned. They were parked at the side of the road almost a quarter of a mile away from the entrance, the opposite direction to that in which the Mercedes was heading. He had only two choices: follow Cramer or try to find out what was going on inside the school. Marie sat watching him. She knew that it was his decision. Lynch stared after the Mercedes. It was Cramer he was after. He reached forward and started the engine. 'Get the map out,' he said as he eased the car into gear.

Marie opened the glove compartment and unfolded the map as Lynch drove past the entrance to the school. The guards had gone as if the fact that Cramer had left meant that there was no further need for security. Lynch had a feeling that Cramer wouldn't be coming back, that whatever the Sass-man was up to was now moving into its next phase.

'What are their options?' Lynch asked, fixing his eyes on the Mercedes. He tried to keep as far away from it as possible, but the road twisted and turned and he didn't want to risk losing it. He found he was accelerating and braking constantly, racing towards each bend and then braking hard once he had the Mercedes in sight. He couldn't afford to be too far away when they reached the intersection with the B4295 or else he wouldn't know whether the Mercedes had gone north or south.

'Assuming they're not just heading for a day at the beach, I'd say the airport, or Swansea and then maybe on to London. Unless they're heading for a boat, the peninsula is dotted with small ports.'

Lynch ducked involuntarily as something roared over-head. It was a huge helicopter, the red, white and blue Sea King that he'd last seen picking up Cramer from the sea wall at Howth. The Sea King was flying low towards the school. 'They're pulling out,' he said to Marie. He braked sharply as a tractor pulled out of a field ahead of the Golf. 'Jesus Christ!' he hissed as the wheels skidded on mud that was being thrown up by the tractor's massive tyres. He managed to get the car under control, then followed the tractor impatiently, trying to see if the road was clear.

'I think you're okay,' said Marie uncertainly as she peered out of the passenger window.

Lynch craned his neck to the side but all he could see were hedgerows. He stamped on the accelerator and overtook the tractor. It was only when he drew level with it and saw that the road ahead was empty that he realised he'd been holding his breath. He let it out in a mournful sigh and accelerated.

When he reached the B4295, the Mercedes was nowhere to be seen. 'What do you think? North or south?'

'They'll only go north if they're staying in Wales,' said Marie, this time with more conviction in her voice.

'Yeah, I think you're right,' agreed Lynch and turned left. After three minutes of hard driving they saw the Mercedes in the distance, just arriving at Llanrhidian village. 'Got them,' said Lynch with satisfaction.

The Mercedes turned onto the B4271, heading east. 'They're going to the airport,' said Marie, looking up from the map. 'Or Swansea.'

There was very little traffic about and Lynch realised that it wouldn't be long before the occupants of the Mercedes realised that they were being pursued. 'Hold the map up, play the tourist,' said Lynch.

Marie did as she was told and Lynch accelerated. He pulled up behind the Mercedes, indicated that he was about to overtake, and passed it on a long, straight stretch of road. Marie put down the map. 'So now they're behind us, now what?'

'Now they won't think we're tailing them,' said Lynch. 'We're pretty sure they'll stay on this road until the junction with the A4118, so we'll go on ahead.'

Marie nodded. 'What was the helicopter doing?'

'I think it's picking up the rest of the men at the school.'

'Why didn't they pick up Cramer, too?'

Lynch pulled a face. 'I'm not a mind-reader.'

'It's not a normal helicopter, is it? The army ones are usually green, right?'

'It belongs to the Ministry of Defence. It's the one that brought Cramer to Wales.'

Lynch checked his driving mirror. The Mercedes was out of sight. He slowed a fraction and within a minute or so it came into view. Confident that he wasn't going to lose his quarry, he accelerated once more.

Marie's hand stroked his knee. 'When, Dermott?'

'I don't know, Marie, love. You saw the two heavies in the front of the car?' She nodded. 'They're tough-looking guys, right enough. I saw one of them talking to Cramer last night and he's big. Looks like he can handle himself. Both of them are almost certainly Sass. They're not the sort of odds I want to go up against. One on one, fine. But one against three, no chance.'

'Two,' said Marie, her voice almost a whisper.

'What?' said Lynch, checking his mirror again.

'There are two of us. Don't forget that. I'm in this as much as you now.'

Lynch was about to argue but he decided to say nothing.

Simon Chaillon wrapped his wool scarf tighter around his neck and hunched his shoulders against the cold breeze that was blowing off the River Limmat. He pulled back the end of his lambskin glove and took a quick look at his slim gold wristwatch. He was early, a clear sign of nervousness. Like most Swiss, Chaillon was punctual to the point of paranoia, and for him to be early was every bit as irritating as arriving late. He pushed his gloved hands deep into his overcoat pockets and went in search of a café. He found one in a side road and slid into an empty table.

A waitress took his order and within two minutes a cup of hot chocolate was on the table in front of him.

He stirred the drink slowly, a slight frown the only sign of how troubled he was. The coded fax had been lying in his in-tray when he'd arrived, and once he'd deciphered its contents he'd been able to think of nothing else. Even the sight of Theresa in a white silk shirt and the flimsiest of bras hadn't relieved his anxiety. She'd asked him if anything was wrong but he'd just shrugged and said that his ulcer was troubling him. She'd made sympathetic noises and leaned over his desk so that he could get a closer look at her breasts, but even that hadn't cheered him up. He'd been unable to concentrate and had told Theresa to hold all his calls. Most of the time he'd sat staring out of his office window at the twin towers of Grossmunster Cathedral, wondering what was so urgent that the meeting had to be in Zurich and at such short notice.

He put his spoon down and looked at his wristwatch again. Five minutes. Chaillon hated to be unpunctual, hated it with a vengeance. Every minute in his life was accounted for as precisely as the funds in a company's accounts, and five wasted minutes was time lost for ever. He picked up his cup of hot chocolate and raised it to his lips, but then put it back on its saucer, untouched. Normally there was nothing he enjoyed more than a cup of milky hot chocolate on a cold day, but today was special. Today was the day he'd been summoned to a meeting by a man he'd met only once before. A man who, to date, had paid Chaillon more than two million dollars in commissions for nothing more arduous than sending sheets of paper and photographs to accommodation addresses around the world. The fact that the people featured in the photographs were always murdered within days of the envelopes being sent was something which Simon Chaillon hadn't dwelt on over the past two years. Since the arrival of the mysterious fax, he'd thought of little else.

The waitress came back and asked him if there was something wrong with the hot chocolate. Chaillon smiled and shook his head. No, he said, everything was fine. Just fine. He picked up his spoon and stirred it again. There had been no clue in the fax as to why the meeting was necessary. Apart from the first meeting more than two years earlier, the two men had communicated only by fax, computer bulletin boards, messages left on answering machines and couriered envelopes. Chaillon's client hadn't needed to spell out the importance of the two men never being seen together, which made the fax all the more worrying. Something must have gone wrong. He looked at his wristwatch again. It was time.

He pushed back his chair, dropped a handful of change onto the table, and left the café. The fax had given detailed instructions of where Chaillon was to go, but he was at least a hundred yards from the meeting point when he heard his name being spoken. Chaillon flinched as if he'd been struck across the face. He forced a smile and turned to face the man he knew only as Monsieur Rolfe.

'A cold day, isn't it?' said Monsieur Rolfe. He spoke perfect French but Chaillon doubted that he had been born in France. Monsieur Rolfe was wearing horn-rimmed spectacles and a dark overcoat and looked like a mid-ranking bank official on his way to his office. There was something different about his hair, Chaillon realised. It was darker than he remembered from their first meeting, and curlier.

'For the time of year, yes,' said Chaillon. He swallowed.

His throat was dry and he wished that he'd drunk the hot chocolate. 'Is there something wrong?' he asked.

'Wrong?' Monsieur Rolfe frowned. 'Why do you think something is wrong?'

'This isn't where you said you wanted to meet. You said . . .'

'I changed my mind,' interrupted Monsieur Rolfe. 'Come. Walk with me.'

They walked away from the river, with Monsieur Rolfe leading the way confidently as if he was no stranger to the city. 'I received your fax,' said Chaillon. He regretted the words immediately they left his mouth and he cursed himself for his stupidity. Of course he'd received the facsimile. Why else would he be there?

'Good,' said Monsieur Rolfe as if unaware of Chaillon's *faux pas*.

'You received the details I sent you? The Vander Mayer contract?' Chaillon wondered if there had been a problem with the last envelope he had couriered to London.

'Yes. Yes, I did,' said Monsieur. Rolfe. There was something almost absent-minded about his conversation, as if his thoughts were elsewhere.

'Business has been good, hasn't it? It has been a very profitable arrangement. For both parties.'

'Yes, it has,' Monsieur Rolfe agreed. 'Very profitable.'

Monsieur Rolfe turned into a side street. Chaillon noticed that from time to time his companion looked over his shoulder as if he feared that they were being followed. 'Something is wrong?' Chaillon asked.

'No. Nothing is wrong.'

Chaillon swallowed nervously. Something was wrong. Something was most definitely wrong. Chaillon's mind whirled. He pulled a handkerchief from his trouser pocket and blew his nose.

'You have a cold?' asked Monsieur Rolfe.

Chaillon wiped his nose and put the handkerchief back in his pocket. 'Maybe. I'm not sure. I don't feel well.'

'You must take care of yourself,' said Monsieur Rolfe.

'I will. I will.' Chaillon no longer recognised the streets they were walking through and it had been some time since he had seen anyone else on the pavement. Monsieur Rolfe took another look over his shoulder. 'We are not being followed,' said Chaillon.

'No. We are not being followed.'

'Good. So now we can talk?'

'Soon.'

A narrow alleyway led off the street and Monsieur Rolfe stepped to the side to allow Chaillon to walk in first. Chaillon nodded his thanks and stepped into the darkness. There was a stack of cardboard boxes to the left and an abandoned bicycle with one wheel missing. Chaillon noticed a damp, cloying smell about the place, as if something had died there and been left to rot. 'Surely this can't be . . . ?' said Chaillon, but before he could finish Monsieur Rolfe's arms came down either side of his head and something tightened around Chaillon's neck. It was a wire, Chaillon realised, and the only thing that was stopping it biting into his flesh was his wool scarf. He tried to speak but the wire was pulled tighter and he couldn't even gasp for breath. His fingers grasped at the wire but it was too tight. He felt a nail break and a sharp pain and then his chest began to heave. He fell forward, his face slamming into the cold concrete floor and then a knee pressed into the small of his back and the wire was pulled even tighter.

Chaillon's lungs began to burn and his eyes bulged and then it all went black. The last thought in his mind was what a pity it was that he would never get the chance to make love to Theresa.

The boy stood by the sink and rinsed the plate clean before putting it on the draining board. He winced as he heard his mother moan upstairs. The boy had asked his father why the doctor didn't take her into hospital, and his father had said that it was because there wasn't anything more that could be done. The boy had spent hours on his knees, praying to God, praying for Him to end his mother's torment, but it hadn't done any good. The boy didn't believe in God any more. He didn't believe in God and he didn't believe in doctors.

His mother's medicine was wrapped in a dish cloth at the back of the larder. The boy had seen his father put the bottle of tablets there after taking out his mother's night-time dose. The boy had asked his father why he didn't give her more of the tablets so that she wouldn't cry so much, and he had explained that it was because too many would be bad for her.

The boy wiped his hands on a tea-towel, poured milk into a tall glass and put it on a tray. Upstairs his mother groaned, a deep, throaty sound that made the boy shiver. He opened the larder door and took out the bottle of tablets. He weighed the bottle in the palm of his hand as he read the label. It warned that no more than twelve tablets should be taken each day. He tried counting how many there were but he kept losing track. There were at least sixty. He put the bottle on the tray next to the glass of milk and carefully carried it upstairs.

THE DOUBLE TAP

His mother looked towards the door as he walked into the bedroom. She had her knees drawn up to her chest again and was hugging a hot water bottle to her stomach. The boy took the tray to the bedside table. His mother stared at the bottle of tablets as if she didn't believe what she was seeing. She slowly pushed herself up into a sitting position, grunting with each movement. The boy watched silently. She didn't look like his mother any more. There were dark bags under her eyes, her hair was damp and sticking to her face and her lips were crusted with brown stuff. And she was thin, thinner than the boy thought a person could be without being a skeleton. He handed her the glass of milk and she took it with her left hand. Her eyes stayed on the bottle of tablets as he unscrewed the cap and poured a dozen or so into the palm of his hand. She reached over and put a claw-like hand on his arm. The nails were yellow and brittle and the skin was so pale he could almost see through it. He held out one of the tablets and she took it from him. He watched as she put it to her lips. The tablet disappeared into her mouth and she swallowed. He gave her another tablet. And another. After the fifth she took a sip from the glass of milk. She smiled and he gave her another tablet. 'How many do you want?' he asked. It was the first time he'd spoken since entering the room.

His mother shrugged. 'I don't know,' she said. He held out another one and she took it. She swallowed six more before taking another drink of milk.

'Do you feel better?' he asked as he shook more tablets into his hand.

She nodded and took another tablet. The boy watched her eat the tablets as if they were sweets and wondered why he didn't feel sad any more. The bottle was half empty. His mother sighed and leaned back on the pillows. 'You're a

good boy,' she said. 'You're a good boy for helping me.'
There were deep lines around her mouth that made her look
like the old women whom he saw sitting in the park feeding
breadcrumbs to pigeons.

'Dad's going to be mad,' he said, his voice little more than
a whisper.

'He won't be mad,' she said. Her eyelids seemed heavy,
as if she was having trouble keeping them open. 'Will
you do something for me?' she asked, holding out the
glass.

'Of course,' he said, taking it and putting it on the
tray.

'Tell your dad that I love him,' she said. Her voice sounded
suddenly stronger, more like the mother he remembered, more
like the way she was before she got sick.

'I will,' the boy promised. 'Cross my heart and hope to
die.' He crossed himself solemnly.

'You're not going to die,' she said, and swallowed another
tablet. 'Not for a long, long time. Just tell your dad what I
said, okay?' The boy nodded and held out more tablets. His
mother took them and touched them one at a time as if she
was counting them. 'Why don't you go downstairs and watch
television?' she said.

'But . . .'

'I'll be okay now,' she said.

The boy leaned over and kissed her on the cheek. She
smelled of sick and something else, something he couldn't
identify. It wasn't his mother's normal smell.

'It's time for you to go now,' she said. She slurred
her words and she was having to fight to keep her eyes
open. He slid off the bed and left the room without
looking back.

THE DOUBLE TAP

*   *   *

Martin guided the large Mercedes to a stop at the intersection with the main road and waited for a gap in the traffic. A red Golf was parked by the side of the road and the couple inside were bent over a map and arguing. Cramer smiled to himself as he remembered what a struggle map-reading and navigation had been for him. Compared with negotiating his way across the Falklands in total darkness, a drive through the Welsh countryside was an absolute breeze. A truck full of sheep rattled by and Martin turned right and followed it.

Cramer had a sudden thought. 'Allan, where exactly are we?' he asked.

'A couple of miles from Swansea Airport,' Allan replied.

'So the Brecon Beacons are where?'

Allan shrugged his massive shoulders. 'Thirty miles or so to the north-east.' He turned around and grinned. 'Do you want to go back and relive old times?'

Cramer snorted softly. 'I don't think I could finish the Long Drag these days, never mind do it on time. I was just wondering. I guess I'd lost track of where I was, that's all.' Cramer sat back in his seat and closed his eyes. It seemed like a lifetime ago. Hell, it was a lifetime ago. The Brecon Beacons was where the SAS tested its men almost to destruction. Deaths weren't unknown on the barren, windswept mountains, and the most demanding of the tests was a sixty-kilometre solo march which had to be completed in under twenty hours. The Long Drag, they called it, or the Fan Dance, after the highest peak,

Pen-y-fan. It wasn't just endurance that was tested, but navigation skills and something deeper. Without an inner drive, without a burning desire to succeed, the Long Drag was an insurmountable barrier. Cramer had completed his solo march in a little over eighteen hours, despite getting lost twice. So much had changed since he'd arrived at the final checkpoint and been slapped on the shoulders and told that he'd earned his winged dagger badge. They'd poured hot coffee down his throat and helped him into the back of a truck and he'd never been happier, never been prouder of what he'd achieved. So much had changed since then. He'd seen men die, he'd been tortured, and he'd killed. The young man who'd fought back the tears of joy at being allowed into the regiment hadn't cried for more than ten years. It was hard for Cramer to determine exactly what emotions he did feel these days. Anger sometimes. Certainly not happiness. Fear? No, he wasn't afraid. He'd been through too much to be afraid. He wasn't scared of death, he was sure of that. He'd faced death before and he'd been responsible for the deaths of others, and he knew he was being honest when he said that the thought of no longer being alive didn't worry him. What scared him was dying. He didn't want to die a shrivelled husk of the super-fit human being he'd once been, a lifetime ago. He would always be grateful to the Colonel for offering him that, the chance to die like a warrior.

'Here we are, Mr Vander Mayer.' Allan's voice jarred Cramer out of his reverie.

'Huh?' Cramer grunted, rubbing his eyes.

'I said we've arrived, Mr Vander Mayer.'

Cramer realised that Allan was using Vander Mayer's name deliberately, so that Cramer would get used to answering to it. 'Great,' Cramer replied. He smiled at Su-ming. She hadn't expressed surprise at hearing her boss's name, so Cramer guessed that she'd already been briefed by the Colonel.

Martin showed his paperwork to a bored security guard and they were waved through to the apron. Cramer whistled when he saw the plane. It was a gleaming Lear jet, the stairway down and two uniformed pilots standing to attention at the bottom. 'They've been briefed,' said Allan before Cramer could speak. 'And don't worry – they've been checked out.'

'They have been with Mr Vander Mayer for more than five years,' said Su-ming.

The Mercedes came to a halt by the side of the jet. Cramer stayed in his seat until Martin climbed out and opened the door for him. Allan went up the stairs first, disappeared into the plane and after a few seconds reappeared and waved to Martin. Cramer went up, followed by Su-ming and with Martin bringing up the rear, carrying the pack of sandwiches and the Thermos flask. The pilots nodded a greeting to Cramer, but he could see that they were weighing him up, trying to work out what sort of man was taking the place of their boss.

Cramer ducked inside the fuselage and stared at the interior. It was more luxurious than any first-class cabin he'd ever been in. The windows were as large as those in a train, there were half a dozen seats each as big as an armchair, and at the rear was a matching leather sofa facing a walnut cabinet which held a large television and video recorder. Thick grey carpet covered the floor and Cramer's shoes sank into it as he walked into the centre of the plane. 'There is a bathroom and shower beyond the galley,' said Su-ming. 'The sofa converts into a double bed if needed.'

'How the other half lives,' said Martin.

'Sure beats a Hercules,' agreed Allan.

One of the pilots closed the hatch as the other disappeared into the cockpit. 'At this point I'm supposed to give you a full briefing, but I reckon we've all been through this before so I'll just tell you to keep your belts on during takeoff and landing and wish you a pleasant flight.' He followed his colleague into the cockpit.

Cramer sat down in one of the huge leather chairs and buckled his seatbelt. Su-ming dropped into the seat next to him.

'Hey, Su-ming, what time does the in-flight movie start?' asked Martin.

'No movies,' said Su-ming, taking him seriously.

The two jet engines whined and then roared into life, and a minute or so later the plane began to roll across the tarmac. Cramer took several deep breaths. He could feel the adrenalin surging through his body, so much so that he felt almost lightheaded. It was all starting to come together.

'Now what?' asked Marie as Lynch watched the Lear jet power down the runway. The jet soared into the air, climbed steeply, and then banked to the right. Within seconds it had disappeared into the clouds.

'Give me the pen, quick,' said Lynch. He repeated the jet's registration number to himself, then quickly scribbled it down on the corner of the map when Marie handed him the pen. 'I can find out where they're going,' he explained.

'The same guy who told you they were in Wales?' Lynch nodded. 'Then what?'

Lynch smiled at her eagerness. 'That depends where he's gone, love.'

'I'd put my money on London,' said Marie.

'Yeah? Why?'

'It's a British-registered jet, and it was heading east. Could be Europe, though, I suppose.'

'How do you know it's British?'

'The first letter of the registration was G, right? All British registered planes start with a G.'

'How do you know that?'

She patted him on the thigh. 'I went out with a pilot for a while,' she said. 'Let's go use the phone. I want to call the office and say that I'll be off for another couple of days.'

'You're staying, then?' asked Lynch, tearing off the piece of map on which he'd written the number.

'Oh yes, Dermott. I'm sticking to you like shit to a cow's tail.'

'Nice analogy,' said Lynch. He put the car in gear and drove to the short-stay car park. After they'd parked, Lynch tucked his gun under the front seat.

They found a bank of call booths in the departures terminal. Lynch went through his pockets and pulled out a handful of change. He dialled McDonough's work number. A woman answered and at first she was reluctant to get McDonough, but Lynch told her that his car had been involved in an accident. He pushed two pound coins into the slot as he waited. When McDonough came to the phone, he was clearly worried. 'Who is this?' he asked.

'Easy, Luke,' said Lynch. 'It's me. Dermott.'

McDonough's voice dropped to a whisper. 'What the fuck are you doing calling me here?' he said.

'I need a favour,' said Lynch.

'You said it was a one-off,' said McDonough.

'It was,' said Lynch. 'And I wouldn't have called you if this wasn't important. Jets file flight plans, right?'

'Look, maybe I'm not making myself clear. You said . . .'

'Shut the fuck up!' Lynch hissed. 'I need one favour, that's all. Now get a pen and write this down.'

McDonough went quiet and Lynch could practically hear the man thinking. McDonough knew who Lynch was, and what he was capable of. 'Okay,' McDonough said eventually. 'Okay, but just this once.'

'Thanks,' said Lynch. 'I appreciate it, I really do.' There was no point in rubbing the man's nose in it. Lynch read out the number from the torn map corner.

'It's a jet, you say?'

'Yeah. Some sort of executive jet. I need to know who it belongs to as well. Can you do that?'

McDonough went silent for a few seconds. 'Yeah. I can do that.' His voice was cold and flat, almost robotic.

'Luke, I'm sorry I snapped at you,' said Lynch as kindly as possible. Lynch needed the air traffic controller to do what he wanted, and if that meant smoothing his feathers then Lynch was prepared to do it. If he'd been in the same room as McDonough and he'd had a gun in his hand, then his approach might well have been different. 'Do this for me and I won't ask anything else of you, I promise. I swear on my mother's life.' Lynch's mother had died of a massive stroke five years earlier and was buried next to his father in a cemetery outside Castlewellan, but he felt no shame at invoking her name.

'I'll do it,' said McDonough, less bitterly this time.

'How long do you think it'll take?'

'A couple of telephone calls,' said McDonough. 'Give me your number and I'll call you back.'

'I'll call you,' said Lynch. 'Half an hour, okay'

'Okay.' The line went dead and Lynch replaced the receiver. Marie was still talking on her phone. She waved animatedly at Lynch and he went to stand behind her.

Marie replaced the receiver. 'Curiouser and curiouser,' she said.

'What's curiouser and curiouser?'

'I rang the estate agents, the one whose name was on the school sign. Told them that my boss was interested in the property. The girl there said it had been bought by a Bristol company who are planning to turn it into a conference centre. They're taking over in two months.'

'So who's in now?'

'She wouldn't tell me. I even played the overworked secretary, told her my boss was giving me a hard time, but she still said she couldn't say. Said it was confidential. To be honest, I don't think she knows.'

'There's something strange going on, that's for sure.'

'What about your guy?'

'Half an hour. I'll get back to him.'

They went to the cafeteria. Lynch ordered two coffees and they chose a quiet table. 'What are you going to do, Dermott?' asked Marie as she stirred her coffee.

'In what way?'

'The police are after you, the organisation seems to want you dead, you've no visible means of support.'

'Sure, but it's not all going my way.' He grinned but could see that she was serious. 'What do you want me to say, Marie?'

'I was just wondering what your plan is?'

Lynch put his head in his hands and watched her with amused eyes. 'I'm in deep shit, I know I'm in deep shit, but dwelling on it isn't going to make it go away. I could run, but the world's smaller than it used to be. There aren't many places I could do a Lord Lucan, and, as you say, I'm not exactly flush with funds. So in terms of planning ahead, I'm not. In the words of Doris Day, *que sera, sera*. If you're asking me what my short-term aim is, it's to see Cramer dead and buried, and maybe dance on his grave.'

Marie nodded sympathetically. 'You're sure?'

'What do you mean?'

She shrugged and put her spoon down on her saucer. 'Getting Cramer isn't going to be easy. I just want to be sure that you're going to go through with it.'

Lynch exhaled slowly as he stared at Marie. There was an enthusiasm about her that was almost child-like. It reminded him of Davie Quinn. Poor, dead, Davie Quinn. 'You've never been engaged have you?' he asked.

'No.'

'You've never met anyone you felt you wanted to marry? Someone you wanted to spend the rest of your life with?'

Marie shook her head. 'No.'

'Sometimes you meet someone and you just know they're right for you. Twin souls. It's as if your whole life had been leading up to the point where you meet that person. It was like that when I met Maggie.'

'Love at first sight,' said Marie.

'I know, it's a cliché. But when she walked into my life

it was like everything clicked into place. Like we belonged together. She was twenty-two when we met, she'd just left Queen's with a degree in electrical engineering and she was going to change the world. She had hair that gleamed like copper and eyes like a cat, green like emeralds.' He stopped when he realised that Marie was grinning at him. 'I know, I know, I'm talking in clichés.'

'No, Dermott, you're talking like a man in love.'

'Aye, I was that. Head over heels. Nothing I've felt since has ever compared with how I felt then. Like I could live forever. Like I wanted to live forever.' He picked up his coffee and sniffed it, holding the cup in both hands. 'You know what was crazy? I knew she sympathised with the IRA, but she never told me she was a volunteer. She was in an active service unit and she didn't say a word. Mind you, she was Scottish, so I guess it didn't occur to me that she'd have been recruited.'

'Did you tell her that you were part of it?' Lynch shook his head and sipped his coffee. 'So why are you surprised that she could keep a secret? Didn't you tell me that only one member of each cell knows anyone else in another cell?'

'Aye, of course. But she was so close to me, so close you wouldn't believe.'

'She was being professional.'

'I know.' He put down his cup. 'Do you want something to eat?' Marie shook her head. 'I think she was recruited before she went to university,' Lynch continued. 'It might even have been the organisation that suggested she study what she did.'

'Electrical engineering?'

'Yeah. She got a first. She was sharp, all right. Sharp

as a knife. You couldn't pull the wool over Maggie's eyes, she'd let you get away with nothing.'

'Why electrical engineering?'

Lynch looked at her levelly. 'She was a bomb-maker. She made bombs.' Marie stiffened and Lynch gave her time to digest what he'd told her. 'We were at war,' he said eventually.

'You don't have to explain anything,' said Marie.

'I know, it's just that . . .'

'It's just that you thought I might get nervous, that I might chicken out. No chance, Dermott. If the IRA hadn't done what it did, the British would never have talked to Sinn Fein in the first place. So you don't have to explain anything, okay?'

Lynch nodded. 'Okay,' he said. 'We got engaged the year after she graduated. She was working for a company outside Belfast, making video recorders. I was on the dole but by then I was already a volunteer. I never told her, but I think she guessed. I had to go away at weekends for training, and she never asked where I went.'

'It seems a strange relationship. Both of you keeping secrets from each other.'

Lynch sighed. 'It had to be done. I couldn't say anything to her, it would have been against standing orders. Her controller was a member of the Army Council, even the rest of the council didn't know what she was doing. She was sent to London, told me she was going to see her folks in Glasgow. I was sent south for advanced weapons training, I don't know if it was a coincidence or if it was planned. The next thing I knew was all the bombs going off in London. Real spectaculars. Huge bombs.'

'I remember,' said Marie quietly.

'The SAS discovered that the active service unit was based in a flat in Wapping. They stormed it, all the volunteers were killed. Maggie was shot in the back, Marie. She was shot in the back while she was lying on the floor. That came out at the inquest. Cramer gave evidence, hidden behind a screen. Soldier B, they called him, but it was Cramer. He said that Maggie was reaching for a gun.' Lynch sneered. 'Heckler & Kochs they had, and she was lying face down. Why the fuck would she be reaching for a gun? They executed her, Marie. Cramer shot her in the back because they didn't want a trial. They killed them all. That's what the SAS are. Government assassins.' Lynch's hands had clenched into fists and he banged them on the table. Marie reached across and held his hands. 'She was pregnant, Marie. She was two months pregnant. That's what they found when they cut her open. Maybe she didn't even know. Cramer killed her, and he killed my baby. So you don't have to ask me if I'm going to go through with it. I swore on Maggie's grave that I'd revenge her. Her and our baby. Oh yes, Marie love, if it's the death of me, I'll kill Cramer.' Lynch suddenly realised that he was glaring at her, so intense were his feelings. He forced himself to relax.

Marie looked at him earnestly. 'I'll help,' she said softly. 'I want him dead as much as you do.'

They sat in silence for a while. Lynch looked at his watch. 'I'm going to call him again,' he said. 'You wait here.'

Lynch went back to the line of telephones and dialled McDonough's number. The air traffic controller answered himself this time. 'It's a privately-owned jet, not a charter firm. The owner is registered as Vander Mayer. Andrew Vander Mayer. Do you want the address?'

'Definitely.' Lynch copied it down. It was an office in

Kensington. McDonough even had the postcode and a telephone number. 'Where was the plane going?' Lynch asked.

'They filed for Heathrow. They should be landing just about now.'

'What then? Are they going on somewhere else?'

'They haven't filed another flight plan, if that's what you mean. Look, I've got work to do, okay?'

'Thanks, Luke.'

'Yeah. Right.' McDonough cut the connection. Lynch stared at the name and address he'd written down. Andrew Vander Mayer. Who the hell was Andrew Vander Mayer? And why was the Sass-man flying around in his corporate jet?

Lynch turned around to find Marie standing behind him. He raised an eyebrow. 'Not worried that I'd do a runner, were you?'

Marie held up the keys to the Golf and jangled them. 'Not really,' she said. She tossed the keys to him. 'So, what did he say?'

Lynch gave her the name and address. 'Unusual name,' she said. 'What do we do now?'

'Back to London.'

'Isn't that dangerous? Bearing in mind what's back there.'

Lynch weighed the keys in the palm of his hand. 'We could leave the Golf here and rent another car. So long as we keep away from your house, we should be okay.'

'But they'll be looking for you, right?'

'Let's check the papers and find out.' They went over to the newsagent's in the departures terminal and bought *The Times*, the *Daily Telegraph* and the *Independent*, and most of the tabloids. Only the broadsheets carried the story of Foley's body being discovered in the boot of the Sierra, and none had connected it with the deaths of the IRA men in Maida Vale. Lynch frowned as he read the story in the *Telegraph*. The police were sure to have dusted the car for prints, and unless the technicians had been totally incompetent, they wouldn't have had too much trouble getting a match.

'No mention of you,' said Marie.

'Aye, but it could be a trap. It could be they want me to think it's safe.' He made a clicking sound with his tongue, then quickly came to a decision. 'What the hell, I'm no worse off in London. And the longer we leave it, the more likely it is that Cramer'll disappear again. Come on, let's go.'

'Why don't we fly back?'

'Because Special Branch cover all the airports as a matter of course. You don't always see them, but they're there, checking all arrivals. Besides, we'd never be able to get the gun through the metal detectors. No, we're better off driving.'

'Do you want me to do it in my name?' she asked.

'No, love. I've got a licence in another name, and a credit card.' Lynch thought it better not to mention that the licence and credit card had belonged to Sean O'Ryan, one of the men he'd killed in Maida Vale.

The Lear jet touched down gently, its tyres kissing the tarmac so softly that Cramer couldn't even discern the point at which they made contact with the ground. 'Smooth,' said

Allan appreciatively. 'These guys know what they're doing.' He unclipped his seatbelt as the jet taxied to its parking space, guided by a man in blue overalls. A large Mercedes pulled up in the distance. It appeared to be a twin of the one they'd left behind in Swansea. The man in overalls guided the Lear to a halt fifty yards from the Mercedes.

'Okay?' Allan asked Cramer.

'Sure,' said Cramer.

'From this point on, you don't relax, you don't let your guard down for one second, you don't trust anyone.' He loomed over Cramer and put his hands on Cramer's shoulders, staring straight into his eyes like a hypnotist attempting to induce a trance. 'You can do it, Mike. You can take anything that this guy throws at you. You're better than he is. Okay?'

'Okay,' Cramer repeated.

'Don't let me down. If you let this guy beat you, I'll be mightily pissed off at you. Right?' Allan straightened up. 'Okay, Martin, check out the vehicle and then we'll be off.'

The pilot who'd given them the abbreviated safety briefing stepped out of the cockpit and opened the door. A mobile ladder was pushed up against the fuselage and the pilot signalled that Martin could go down. Cramer asked Su-ming for a look at the itinerary and she handed it to him. According to the typewritten schedule, they were heading for Vander Mayer's flat in Chelsea Harbour, and the afternoon was to be spent in his Kensington office. Cramer looked out of the window. Martin had opened the bonnet and was giving the engine compartment the once over. 'Just to remind you, the Merc's windows are bullet-proof and the side panels are reinforced,' said Allan.

'In the car you're completely safe, but you're vulnerable getting in and out.'

Cramer stood up and stretched. He took several deep breaths. 'I'm ready,' he said.

Martin reappeared. He'd produced a peaked chauffeur's cap from somewhere and was wearing it sergeant-major style with the peak halfway down his nose. He gave Allan a thumbs-up. They headed down the steps. Martin held the rear door open for Cramer and Su-ming and closed it behind them. Once again Cramer felt as if he'd been wrapped in a luxurious cocoon. He wondered what it must be like to spend one's life insulated from the dirt and discomfort of the real world. The car alone would have taken Cramer several years' salary when he was a sergeant in the SAS, and he could only imagine how many millions of pounds the jet had cost.

'Okay if I put the radio on?' Martin asked.

'Sure,' said Cramer.

Martin flicked through the channels and found an all-news station. They listened as they drove into central London, but there was little to hold Cramer's attention: the Prime Minister had announced a minor reshuffle of his Cabinet, the police were still searching for a man who had killed three and injured one in a Maida Vale shooting, England were losing at cricket. Cramer had long since given up reading newspapers, watching television or listening to the radio. There was nothing happening in the world that he was the least bit interested in any more. He sat back in the leather seat and closed his eyes. He was dog tired. The previous night he'd slept fitfully and when he did sleep he'd had a succession of nightmares. In most of them he was being chased by a shadowy figure with a gun and it didn't take a psychiatrist to tell him what was troubling him. At first light he'd climbed out of bed, wrapped a bath towel around himself and sat by the window, going over the assassination files for a final time. One shot to the face, one to the chest. Bang bang. Was that going to be his own fate? Did the victims hear the second shot, or were they already dead by the time the bullet blasted into their chests? Cramer's interest was more than academic; he knew there was an even chance that he would end up as the subject of another file, and that the Colonel would pass it on to the next man selected to go up against the assassin. Cramer could imagine the conversation. 'The last killing was one of ours. Name of Cramer. Former SAS, but he'd let himself go. He'd lost his edge. Hopefully you'll do better.' Cramer shuddered.

'Are you cold?' asked Su-ming.

Cramer opened his eyes. She was looking at him, clearly concerned. 'Someone just walked over my grave, that's all.'

'You didn't eat today, did you?'

'I wasn't hungry.'

'I will cook for you when we get to the apartment.'

Cramer rubbed his face and yawned. 'Where do you call home?'

'What do you mean?'

'I've never heard you refer to anywhere as home.'

'We have homes all over the world.'

'Houses. Apartments. Not homes.'

She studied him as she considered what he'd said. 'You're right,' she said eventually. 'I suppose I don't really have a home. What about you?'

Cramer interlinked his fingers and cracked his knuckles.

It had been a long time since Cramer had ever thought of anywhere as home. The regiment, maybe. That had been a home, even though he was constantly on the move. Home to Cramer wasn't somewhere to hang his clothes, it was a sense of belonging. And since he'd been forced to leave the SAS, he had never felt that he belonged anywhere. 'I guess I'm the same,' he said. 'Home is where the heart is, so they say.'

'They?' she asked. 'Who's they?'

Cramer began to wish he'd never asked her about her home. 'I don't know. It's a saying.' He looked out of the window. They were driving through Fulham, though driving was hardly an accurate description of the snail's pace at which they were crawling through the traffic-choked streets.

'Not far now,' said Allan, twisting around in the front passenger seat.

'You've been here before?' Cramer asked.

'I did a preliminary look-around before I went to the school. The flat is close to the top of the tower, each floor is a separate apartment with one elevator which has a security code, and two fire escape stairways. The door to that can only be opened from the inside, so it's an easy place to secure. Same old problem, though. You're vulnerable entering and leaving, but we'll be doing that through the underground car park.'

'Doorman?'

'Several. They've all been checked out and Martin and I have photographs of them all. If there's a new face on the door, we'll know right away. The foyer leading onto the underground car park is the most important, so we'll have our own man there, but on no account must you acknowledge him. Treat him like one of the staff.'

Cramer nodded. 'What do you think, Allan? Do you think he'll try it here? In London?'

Allan pulled a face as if he had a bad taste in his mouth. 'We've got to assume he will. But hand on heart, I think it's more likely he'll wait until you're in the States; that's where most of the killings have taken place. Now, that's probably because almost half of the targets have been Americans, but I get the impression that that's where he's most comfortable. He's got your itinerary so he knows you're going to be in New York in three days.' He pointed his forefinger at Cramer. 'Not that you can let your guard down, though. As far as you're concerned, you're at risk no matter where you are, no matter who you're with.'

They turned off the main road and Martin took the Mercedes through the back streets with the confidence of a licensed taxi driver. They drove along King's Road and its trendy antique shops and then they turned onto the road that led to the Chelsea Harbour complex, a mixture of modern offices and apartment blocks. One apartment block towered above the rest – a grey steel and glass finger that pointed skywards, topped by a cream pagoda-like pyramid. 'That's where we're heading,' said Allan, nodding at the tower. 'Each apartment costs about a million quid. It's a different world, isn't it? Who the hell can afford a million quid for a place to live?'

'Me,' said Cramer, grinning. They drove by a huge white hotel, the Conrad, and then Martin guided the Mercedes into an underground car park. He made two sharp left turns and brought the Mercedes to a smooth halt in front of the entrance to the tower block. He left the engine running as he got out and walked around to open Cramer's door. Allan was already in place as Cramer slid out of the back seat and the three men walked together to the entrance, exactly as they'd rehearsed time and time again, with Su-ming bringing up the rear. The double glass doors hissed open electronically and a doorman in a charcoal grey uniform looked up as they entered. Cramer recognised him as one of the men who'd been on guard duty at the school in Wales. His name was Matt but Cramer followed Allan's instructions and ignored him, playing the part of Andrew Vander Mayer, a man far too rich to bother with the hired help.

They rode up to the ground floor, where there was another doorman on duty wearing an identical charcoal grey uniform as the first. He was in his early sixties with the lined face and wiry grey hair of a former merchant seaman. He smiled a greeting at Su-ming and handed her a small stack of mail. If he realised that Cramer wasn't the usual resident of Vander Mayer's apartment, he showed no sign of it.

They had to walk across the foyer to a second elevator which led up to the higher floors. The lift arrived within seconds of Allan pressing the button and they stepped inside. Su-ming keyed in an access code on a small keypad above the buttons panel and the doors quietly slid shut. There was merely a vague sensation of movement, the sort of ride that only very expensive Japanese technology could produce. The doors hissed open again. Cramer was just about to step out into the lobby when Allan's giant hand fell on his shoulder. 'Me first,' he said. 'You never exit or enter an elevator until Martin or I have checked it out.'

Cramer flushed. The first day and he'd already forgotten

one of the rules that Allan had drummed into him from the start. He waited until Allan had stepped into the lobby before following. Su-ming took a keycard out of her bag and ran it through a reader at the side of the front door. The door clicked open and she stood aside to allow Allan and Martin to go in first. 'They are very thorough,' she said.

'Doesn't your boss have bodyguards?' Cramer asked.

'Yes, two Americans, former Secret Service agents. They're always with him.'

'How do they compare with Allan and Martin?'

She put the keycard back in her handbag. 'I always felt that Mr Vander Mayer's bodyguards worked only for the money. For them it was just a job. Your friends care about you. It's more than a job to them.'

Before Cramer could say anything else, Allan returned. 'All clear,' he said, holding the door open wide.

The apartment was huge, with panoramic views of the Thames and south London from the floor-to-ceiling windows. The sitting room ran the full length of the block and its size was emphasised by the minimalist furniture: stark black sofas, steel and black leather armchairs, glass and marble coffee tables and low level black ash sideboards. The floors were pristine bare oak boards, the walls painted white with just a hint of blue, the light fittings were stainless steel. Everything about the apartment was hard, it was full of sharp edges and gleaming surfaces. It had style, it was clearly very, very expensive, but it belonged in the pages of an architectural magazine. There were no personal touches, no indications that anyone actually lived there. 'Who cleans it?' Cramer asked.

Su-ming smiled. 'That's a funny thing to ask,' she said.

'It's just that it looks so perfect. How often do you come here?'

'A few days each month. It depends.'

'On what?'

'On whether we have business here. The cleaning is done by an outside firm.'

Cramer rubbed a finger along the edge of one of the glass coffee tables and inspected it. 'They do a good job. It's as clean as an army barracks,' he said.

'Mr Vander Mayer sets very high standards,' said Suming. 'In everything.'

'The bedrooms are through there,' said Allan, indicating a door to the right of the sitting room. 'You should take the master bedroom, Su-ming has her usual room, Martin and I'll take turns to sleep in the first bedroom, closest to the door. One of us will be in the bedroom, the other will be out here.'

'I'm going down to park the Merc and bring up the cases,' said Martin, doffing his peaked cap.

As Martin went back out into the lobby, Su-ming dropped her handbag on a sofa and opened another door that led off the sitting room. She motioned for Cramer to follow her. It was a huge kitchen, some twenty feet long and almost as wide, lined with oak units and spotless German equipment. Su-ming stood by a massive refrigerator. 'Are you hungry?' she asked.

'Not really.'

She pulled open the refrigerator door. It was packed with food. Cramer frowned. 'The same company that cleans the apartment keeps the fridge and larder stocked,' she explained. She took out a carton of low-fat milk and a plastic wrapped polystyrene tray containing two fresh chicken breasts. 'There's rice in the cupboard behind you,' she said as she knelt down and began pulling polythene bags of vegetables from the bottom of the refrigerator.

'Does your boss like your cooking?' Cramer asked as he took out a plastic container and shook it. It sounded as if it was filled with rice.

'That's it,' she said without looking around. She straightened up and closed the refrigerator door. 'Yes. He likes most Oriental food. Wash a handful of the rice and put it in a saucepan.' Cramer did as he was told. Su-ming watched him as she used a large cleaver to slice the chicken breasts into small pieces. He put the pan of rice onto the cooker. 'You'll need water,' she said, smiling. 'Two cupfuls.'

Cramer took the pan over to the sink and poured in cold water. 'What's the deal with you and Vander Mayer?' he asked.

Su-ming froze. The cleaver glinted under the overhead fluorescent lights. 'What do you mean?' she asked.

Cramer shrugged as he put the pan back on his stove. 'I just meant that you're quite young to be doing such a job. He's obviously a very important man, it must be very demanding to be his assistant.'

'Turn the heat on. Medium,' she said. She paused. 'I've been trained to look after his interests,' she said. She began chopping the meat again with small, precise movements.

'What, like secretarial college?'

'No. Mr Vander Mayer trained me.'

'Trained you? How?'

'He taught me about his business. He introduced me to all his contacts. He showed me how to deal with people.' She finished cutting up the meat and scraped it off the chopping board and into a small, white bowl. She wiped her hands on a kitchen towel. 'But he didn't teach me cooking.' She took a steel wok down from its hook on the wall and put it on the stove.

'What about the fortune-telling?'

She looked at him sharply, then she saw from the amused look in his eyes that he was deliberately teasing her. She waggled a finger at him. 'You're trying to upset me, Mike Cramer.' There was a blue and white striped apron hanging on the back of the door and she put it on and tied her hair back. 'My grandmother taught me how to use the *I Ching*. My mother showed me how to read palms when I was a child. Most of it can't be taught. It's an ability. An inherited ability.'

'A talent?'

'A gift.'

'Is that why Vander Mayer chose you, because of your gift?'

Su-ming folded her arms across her chest. Her chin was thrust defiantly up as if she was preparing to pick a fight with him. 'Why? Why do you keep asking about him?'

Cramer leaned back against the sink. 'It just seems strange, that's all.'

'Strange? What's strange?'

'He's American, you're . . . hell, I don't even know where you're from.'

'I'm half Thai, a quarter Chinese, a quarter Vietnamese. My father was Thai, my mother half Chinese, half Vietnamese. What difference does that make?'

'Because it feels like there's more to your relationship than just work. It's like . . .'

'Like what?' she said coldly. Her eyes had gone hard.

Cramer held up his hands in surrender. 'Hey, I didn't want

to offend you. It's obviously something that you don't want to talk about.'

'No, you brought it up, you tell me what you think is wrong with my relationship with Mr Vander Mayer.'

Cramer took a deep breath. He wished that he'd just kept his mouth shut. 'The way you talk about him, the way you're so defensive, it's like he's your father or something.'

Su-ming licked her lips. Her tongue was small and pointed. Cramer said nothing for a while. Su-ming waited for him to speak. 'Back in Wales, you said you'd been with him for fifteen years?'

'That's right.'

'You couldn't have been more than a teenager.'

'I was eleven.'

'So Vander Mayer adopted you, is that it?'

'Sort of.'

'And your parents are dead?'

'No. They're not dead.'

'So they gave you up for adoption?'

'Sort of.'

'Vander Mayer's not married, is he? Isn't that sort of unusual?'

'I suppose it is. Mr Vander Mayer is a very unusual man.'

The rice began to bubble over on the stove and Su-ming turned down the heat. 'My parents were very poor,' she said, keeping her back to him. 'All they had were children. I had five brothers. We lived in northern Thailand on a small farm, near the Cambodian border. It was a very hard life, Mike Cramer. You have no idea how hard it was. It was dangerous too, when I was a child. There were mines everywhere, left by the Khmer Rouge. My father had to clear the fields by hand because the mines were so small.' She used the cleaver to slice vegetables, her head bent low over the chopping board. 'Mr Vander Mayer came to our village on the way to the border. This was a long time ago, his business wasn't as big then as it is now. He had this big car and a driver and a translator. There was a place in our village, a noodle shop. They sold Thai food and soft drinks. Mr Vander Mayer stopped there. He saw me and tried talking to me but of course I couldn't speak English and he knew no Thai or Chinese. My mother asked him if he'd like me to read his palm. He thought that was so funny. He was quite a young man then, handsome and always smiling. He gave my mother five baht and sat down on a stool so that I could see his hand.'

Su-ming put the wok on the stove and turned on the burner under it. 'He knew something about palmistry because he asked my mother how I'd learned. It's not something Orientals do, you see. The Chinese read faces, but palm reading originated in France. My grandmother was Vietnamese and she learned it from an old French woman in Hanoi. My mother told him about my gift. Palm reading isn't just a matter of interpreting the lines, anyone can do that. A machine could do it. It's what you pick up from the person that makes the difference. I don't think he believed her. He was laughing, I think he expected me to tell him that he would have a long and happy life and have three children and that seven would be his lucky number.' She laughed bitterly, a harsh exclamation that sounded more like a cry of pain. 'At first his translator wouldn't tell Mr Vander Mayer what I was saying. He kept arguing that he'd be annoyed, that I should only tell him good things. My mother scolded him and eventually he translated exactly what I said. I told him things that had happened to him in the past. Things he thought no one else knew about, things no one else could possibly know about. Secrets. He stopped laughing then. I can't even remember what I told him, not all of it. After a few minutes I stopped looking at the lines on his palm. I was still holding his hand but I was looking through it. He started asking questions of the interpreter, and he translated them for me, but I couldn't answer them, I could only tell him what I saw.' She splashed a little oil into the hot wok and swirled it around. 'Then I saw something in his future. I told him to be careful of an older man, a man who wouldn't look him in the eye and who was always smiling. I warned him not to turn his back on the man, that he planned to harm him, that he wasn't to be trusted. He asked me when, but I didn't know, that's not how it works. He wanted to know more, but I was tired and my mother told me to stop. You can't force it, it either happens or it doesn't.'

Cramer nodded, even though she wasn't looking at him. He could picture the little girl, the man's hand appearing enormous in hers, her eyes wide as she stared at his palm. 'And it came true?'

'He got back into the big car with his interpreter and they drove up north, to the border. I never thought I'd see him again. My mother took the money and used it to buy kerosene for the lamps and some material to make me a dress. She was sewing it that evening when the big car drove up to our farm.'

She dropped the chicken pieces into the hot wok and used a pair of chopsticks to keep the sizzling meat turning. 'It was Mr Vander Mayer. He was on his own. The back window of the car had been shattered and there were bullet holes all along one side. He'd used his shirt to make a sling and there was blood all over the inside of the car. He'd come back to thank me. He said that I'd saved his life and he gave me ten thousand baht. It was more money than my father had earned in his whole life. Then he went, back to Bangkok, I suppose.' Su-ming scraped the vegetables into the wok and a cloud of steam billowed around her. She used a wooden spatula to stir the frying chicken and vegetables.

'Your prediction came true?'

'That's what he said. He never told me the details. Later that year we had floods and we lost our crops and our animals. All the money was spent. Then Mr Vander Mayer came back. He told my father he wanted to help. He had a deal. He's always been good at doing deals. He'd pay for my education, he'd take care of me, and he'd give my father one hundred thousand baht a year. In return, I would live with him, like a daughter.'

Cramer's jaw dropped in surprise. 'He bought you?'

'Not bought, no.'

'He paid for you, Su-ming. That's like slavery.'

She shook her head as she stirred the contents of the wok. 'You don't understand what it's like in Thailand. You can't even imagine how poor we were. I had brothers who needed an education, medicine, food even. My parents had given me everything and they were about to lose the farm. It was a small sacrifice, Mike Cramer. And look what he was offering me. A chance to travel, to see the world. To learn things I couldn't even dream about. And in return, all I had to do was to help him. Help him run his business and tell him things, tell him what I sensed about people.'

'And what about your family? Do you still see them?'

She took the wok off the stove and poured the steaming chicken and vegetables onto a plate. 'Of course I do. I see them whenever I want to. They're very rich now, the richest people in the village. One of my brothers is a doctor, the other is at university in Bangkok. Mr Vander Mayer has been very good to me, and to my family. Get the rice, please.'

Cramer drained the rice as Su-ming took small bowls and ivory chopsticks from a cupboard. She stopped as she saw Cramer looking at her. 'Don't,' she said.

'Don't what?'

'Don't pity me, Mike Cramer. I chose the life I have. Nobody forced me.'

'Are you happy?'

She shrugged as if her own happiness was a matter of absolutely no importance. 'Eat,' she said.

Lynch could see Marie's hands tense on the steering wheel as the police car roared past, siren wailing and lights flashing. 'Easy, Marie, love,' he said. The police car flashed its headlights and a white Toyota pulled over to the roadside.

'Sorry,' said Marie. They were on the outskirts of West London and had made good time in the hired Rover. Marie had offered to drive once they'd reached Bristol and Lynch had readily agreed. Marie drove well, albeit a little aggressively. A couple of times he'd had to remind her to keep within the speed limit and she'd smiled shamefacedly and slowed down.

'We're going to need a street map,' Lynch said.

'I'll stop at a newsagent's. They're bound to have an *A to Z*. What's the plan? To go to this Vander Mayer's office?'

'I suppose so,' replied Lynch. 'I wish I knew more about him.'

'It's an unusual name.' Her brow furrowed as if she was deep in thought.

Lynch patted her thigh. 'Don't worry, I'll think of something. You're right, we can start with his office.'

'I've an idea. I've a friend who works for *The Times*. He could get me into their cuttings library.'

'Wouldn't he want to know why?'

'He's never asked why before. I'll tell him it's for work. Researching a possible client.'

'Are you sure he won't be suspicious?'

'Positive.'

Lynch thought about it as Marie drove. 'This friend. Boyfriend, was he?'

'With the accent on friend, Dermott. We went out a few times, I jumped his bones twice. Okay, three times maybe. Now he's just a mate. It's worth trying, they'll have any story ever written about this Vander Mayer. They might even have his picture. Look, I tell you what, I'll call him first, test the water. If he seems okay about it, we can drive to their offices in Wapping.'

Lynch looked at his wristwatch. He wanted to get to Vander Mayer's office before rush hour, but they had plenty of time. 'Okay, give it a go.'

Marie found a newsagent's in Hammersmith. She left Lynch in the car and returned a few minutes later with an *A to Z* of London which she dropped through the window. 'There's a call box over there, I'll give him a ring,' she said.

Lynch watched as she went over to the phone. She played with her hair as she spoke to her friend and she winked at Lynch, letting him know it was okay. He caught sight of himself in the rear-view mirror and realised that he'd have to shower and shave before too long. A scruffy appearance always attracted attention, that was one of the things that had been drummed into him when he'd first enlisted as a volunteer. Marie looked good, considering they'd spent more than twenty-four hours on the road, but even she'd need to freshen up. Lynch decided that he might as well drive the rest of the way into the city so he moved across to sit in the driver's seat. Marie came back to the car and got in the passenger side. 'He said I can come around whenever I want. I'm to call him from the gate.'

'Okay, let's go,' said Lynch. 'We'll get a ticket if we sit here any longer.'

Martin drew the Mercedes up in front of the office block. 'Here we are,' he said.

Cramer looked out of the side window. It was a nondescript building, grey stone with square metal-framed windows and double glass doors. A security camera was mounted above the door to provide video coverage of the entrance. A young man sat huddled in a duffel coat next to a black and white mongrel. On the ground in front of him was a piece of brown cardboard on which had been written 'Please Help The Homeless'.

'I see him,' said Allan, as if reading Cramer's mind. Martin was already out of the car and opening the passenger door. Allan moved quickly, striding around the back of the Mercedes and putting himself between Cramer and the beggar.

Cramer got out of the car. The suit and overcoat felt more confining than ever. The gun was snug in its holster and Cramer could feel it pressing against his flesh through the handmade shirt. He shrugged his shoulders against the restrictive clothes, tugged nervously at the sleeves of the overcoat, and then followed Martin towards the double doors. Allan looked from side to side but his eyes kept returning to the beggar.

A man in a dark suit carrying a furled umbrella walked quickly down the street towards them and Cramer tensed. The man was the right size, the right age, the right build, but then so was half the male population of London. The man walked by at speed. He had the bearing and stride of a military man and Cramer marked him down as a former soldier who'd taken a job in the City.

Martin opened the double doors and quickly checked the foyer before nodding to Cramer to let him know that it was secure. Allan kept himself between Cramer and the beggar as Cramer followed Martin inside. A uniformed concierge looked up from his newspaper. He frowned at the men but smiled benignly when he saw Su-ming.

They headed over to the lift. It arrived empty and Allan stepped in first, followed by Cramer and Su-ming. The lift doors closed and Cramer took several deep breaths. 'You okay, Mike?' Allan asked.

'Yeah,' said Cramer. 'I just wish he'd get it over with.'

'Take it easy, we don't know how long it's going to be. You'll wear yourself out if you stay this tense.'

Cramer put his finger inside his shirt collar and tried to loosen it. He could feel rivulets of sweat trickle down his back though his mouth was still as dry as sandpaper. 'I'll be okay,' he said.

'Remember, you've got to be alert, but not tense. If you're tense you'll slow down.'

Cramer nodded. Su-ming was watching him anxiously and he smiled to reassure her, though he didn't feel like smiling. He felt trapped within the made-to-measure clothes and he had a hollow feeling deep inside his stomach, a cold dread that, despite all the training, when he came face to face with the killer he wouldn't be able to react in time.

The lift doors opened and Cramer followed Martin and Allan down a grey-carpeted corridor with Su-ming bringing up the rear. As they walked by an office door it opened and Cramer's hand reacted instinctively, jerking upwards towards his hidden gun. It was a middle-aged woman in a tweed suit. Cramer let his hand fall to his side, cursing himself under his breath. If he carried on like this, he'd be a nervous wreck by the end of the week.

Vander Mayer's office was at the far end of the corridor. Cramer waited outside with Allan while Martin and Su-ming went in. Through the open door Cramer could see a brunette, her hair tied back in a ponytail, sitting behind a teak desk. Su-ming was talking to her while Martin prowled around the office. Martin turned and nodded to Allan and he ushered Cramer inside. Cramer saw a second desk as he walked into the office. It was unoccupied.

A door led through to Vander Mayer's private office and Su-ming motioned for him to go through. The inner office was much bigger, and furnished in much the same way as the flat in Chelsea Harbour – oak floorboards, polished to a deep shine, a simple black oak desk and steel and leather furniture. The desk was bare except for a personal computer, but one wall was lined with television monitors which showed share prices and news wires from around the world, and below them was a bank of fax and telex machines.

'We're going to wait outside,' said Allan. He looked at his watch. 'The Russian won't be here for a couple of hours. We'll search him before we let him in to see you, but be prepared, okay?'

Cramer gave Allan a Boy Scout salute. 'Dib, dib, dib,' he said.

'I'll give you dib, dib, dib if he pulls out a gun and shoots you,' said Allan. He made a gun with his fingers and pretended to shoot Cramer in the face. 'Be on your feet when he comes into your office. It's much harder to draw your weapon when you're sitting.'

Allan and Martin closed the door behind them, leaving Cramer and Su-ming alone. Cramer stood behind the chair and rested his elbows on it. He nodded at the monitors. 'What exactly does he do, your boss?'

'I thought the Colonel had told you.'

'An arms dealer, he said. 'So what's all the financial stuff for?'

Su-ming leaned against the desk and studied the monitors. 'Mr Vander Mayer has many investments and he prefers to handle them himself.'

'He doesn't trust anyone else to touch his money, is that it?'

Su-ming looked at him over her shoulder and flashed

him a thin smile. 'It's not a question of trust. No one can do it better than him.'

'So how much is he worth?'

Su-ming shrugged noncommittally and turned away from him again. 'He is a very rich man.'

'Rich? Or rich rich?'

'Very rich.'

'Millions or billions?'

'That depends on which currency you're using.' She pushed herself away from the desk and went over to the telex machine. She toyed with the keys. 'Is money that important to you, Mike Cramer?'

Cramer sat down in the chair and tried to open the drawers. They were locked. Cramer wondered whether they were always locked or if they'd been locked because he was using the office. 'No. Money's never really mattered to me. Is that what drives him?'

Su-ming stopped playing with the telex keys. 'I suppose so.'

'So tell me, what does he do? He has these offices, he has three jets, but I can't get a feel for what it is exactly that he does.'

'He puts deals together. Say you're running a country in Africa and you want to buy armoured vehicles. And suppose you can't buy direct from the manufacturers. Then you'd have to go through a middle-man. Someone like Mr Vander Mayer.'

'Why couldn't I buy from the manufacturer?'

'It could be that the country of origin preferred not to trade with you.'

'Because I'm a dictator?'

'Whether someone is a dictator or a leader is often a

matter of semantics. When Saddam Hussein was in favour, governments all around the world were more than happy to trade with him.'

'Then he invaded Kuwait.'

'And suddenly he became *persona non grata*. That didn't mean that the West stopped trading with him, it just meant that businessmen like Mr Vander Mayer started to make a lot of money.'

'Vander Mayer's still dealing with Iraq?'

Su-ming nodded. 'Of course.'

'You don't see anything wrong with that?'

'He's a businessman. More than that, he's a realist.'

Cramer ran his finger along the edge of the desk. Like the furniture in Vander Mayer's flat, it was spotless. 'What sort of arms does he sell?'

Su-ming turned to face him. 'Anything.'

'Anything?'

'You sound surprised. Arms are a commodity, like anything else. There are sellers and there are buyers.'

'Jets?'

'Yes.'

'Missiles?'

'Yes.'

'Is he doing much business with Russia?'

'Quite a bit.'

'Is that why he wanted you to learn Russian?'

'It gives him an advantage during negotiations. They don't expect an Oriental to speak their language.'

Cramer swivelled his chair around so that he could look out of the window. 'I suppose there's a lot of Russian equipment going cheap following the break-up of the Soviet bloc.'

'They're desperate for foreign currency. And that's one thing that Mr Vander Mayer has a lot of.'

'Do you know what this Russian is trying to sell?' He swivelled around and could see from the look on her face that she did.

'Mr Vander Mayer said I wasn't to say.'

'But it's a weapon?'

'In a way. It depends how you use it. In the right hands, a pencil can be a weapon, or it can be used to write a poem.'

Cramer laughed. 'Give me a break, Su-ming. You don't believe that fortune cookie philosophy. A bomb's a bomb. A gun's a gun. You've heard that other great saying, "It isn't guns that kill people, it's people that kill people." Well that's crap, kid. Guns kill people. Guns and bombs and missiles and grenades. And I don't like the way I'm being used. I don't like it one bit.'

Su-ming studied him silently as if embarrassed by his outburst. 'I'm sorry,' he said. 'I know you're just doing as you're told.'

She nodded. 'Like you, I'm following orders.'

Cramer slumped back in the chair and looked up at the ceiling. 'Where did I go wrong? I spend my life training with weapons and I end up with nothing. He sells the stuff and makes millions.'

'You choose your own life,' said Su-ming.

Cramer sighed. 'Yeah, I guess you're right.' He put his hands behind his neck and interlinked his fingers. 'So, what do I do?'

Su-ming took the itinerary from her handbag and looked at it. 'We wait here until five o'clock.'

'Can't I do a deal or two while I'm here? Maybe I could sell a few F-16s, what do you think?'

Su-ming studied him with amusement. 'I think, Mike Cramer, that I shall miss your sense of humour when this is all over. That's what I think.'

Dermott Lynch dropped Marie off at the front entrance to the huge News International complex. A line of sixty-foot delivery trucks were queuing up to enter the site, in preparation for the evening's print run. The throbbing diesel engines vibrated up through his seat. He drove alongside the high brick wall which surrounded the newspaper offices and printworks and parked next to an old warehouse which had been converted into upmarket apartments. All the old ironware which had once been used to haul sacks and crates up to the storage areas on the upper floors had been painted a bright red, and wire baskets of brightly coloured flowers were hanging by the windows.

He switched on the radio and listened to a phone-in programme where listeners were calling up to give their views on the death penalty. Lynch half-listened as he watched the trucks file into the printworks. *The Times*, the *Sun*, the *Sunday Times*, the *News of The World*, most of the country's large circulation newspapers were printed there. The IRA had drawn up plans to bomb the plant several times and at one stage they had actually stored over a ton of fertiliser explosive and several kilos of Semtex in a lock-up garage on the Isle of Dogs, in preparation for the go-ahead from the Army Council. Lynch had helped put the explosive in place and another active service unit was instructed to commandeer one of the delivery trucks, fill it with the explosive and drive it into the plant. The 1994 ceasefire had put an end to the planned spectacular, and the explosive cache was now buried somewhere under the New Forest in plastic dustbins. A pity, thought Lynch. It would have made one hell of an explosion. And he'd never liked the *Sun*, anyway.

Most of the callers to the radio station seemed to be in favour of bringing back the death penalty, and several offered to do the deed themselves. Lynch smiled to himself. He had long thought that there was a vicious side to the British character, a nasty undercurrent that was never far from the surface, and radio talk shows seemed to bring out the worst in the population. String 'em up and hang 'em high appeared to be the consensus, and even the presenter agreed with the majority. It was as if the British public had never heard of the Guildford Four or countless other miscarriages of justice, where if there had been a death penalty, there would have been no chance of an appeal, no chance to prove that evidence was faked or juries misled.

The programme was coming to an end when Marie walked out through the security gates and down the street towards the Rover. There was a spring in her step and her hips swung from side to side as she walked. It was a sexy walk, a youngster's walk, the walk of a girl who was used to being watched. It was also a walk that men would remember, and that could be dangerous. It wasn't a good thing to be remembered, Lynch knew. Better by far to blend, to remain anonymous, so that you could come and go without anyone knowing you'd ever been there. All the volunteers had that quality, an ability to remain unnoticed in a crowd. The idea that members of the IRA were big, threatening figures was a figment of the media's imagination. They weren't the monsters that papers like the *Sun* painted them, most of them looked no more threatening than an assistant bank manager. It wasn't physical size or strength that counted in a war, it was a mental attitude, mental toughness. Character. Lynch wondered if Marie had what it took. She had the enthusiasm, and the motivation, but there was a world of difference between wanting to see another person dead and helping to pull the trigger.

Marie opened the passenger door and slid into the car. 'Your man Vander Mayer's a secretive soul,' she said.

'Secretive?'

'He's been mentioned twice in the last ten years.'

'In *The Times*?'

'In any British or American publication. They've got this on-line computer database which lets you put in key words and call up any article that ever used the words. It goes back ten years with most publications, even further with some. And Andrew Vander Mayer has had two honourable mentions, one in a feature on arms dealers in *Newsweek* three years ago, and another in the *Asian Wall Street Journal* five years ago.

'What was that about?'

'The Chinese planning to sell tactical nuclear weapons. They were said to have approached several international arms dealers and he was one.'

'Jesus Christ, nuclear weapons?'

Marie handed him a computer printout. 'Read it for yourself. The story is pretty thin on facts, but it names him as an American arms dealer who has contacts all over the world.'

Lynch sniffed and took the cuttings. He scanned them quickly. As she said, the mentions were brief; one sentence in the *Newsweek* piece, two paragraphs in the *Journal*.

'I think you can pretty much discount the nuclear weapons stuff,' said Marie. 'It was three years ago and it never happened. It reads to me like one of those "what if" stories.'

'Yeah, but he's obviously pretty high-powered. It makes you wonder what he's doing with Cramer.' He stuffed the printout in the glove compartment. 'What about photographs?'

Marie pulled down the sunvisor and checked her make-up in the mirror. Lynch realised she must have kissed the journalist she'd met. 'No photographs. There were no photographs of Vander Mayer used with the two articles, and none in *The Times'* files. My friend called up Reuter and AP and the news agencies don't have any either. Andrew Vander Mayer has never been photographed.' She folded the sunvisor back up. 'What now?'

'Vander Mayer's office. It could be that Cramer's there. If he isn't, maybe we can get hold of Vander Mayer. We'll play it by ear.'

The man Simon Chaillon had known as Monsieur Rolfe popped the tab on a can of Diet Coke and put his feet up on the coffee table. The television was tuned to CNN, a financial news programme. A blonde with blow-torched hair and a middle-aged man with matinée-idol looks were discussing the strength of the dollar against the yen with the measured seriousness of people who weren't quite sure of what they were talking about and were frightened of being caught out.

The man had no interest in the world's financial situation. He had more than enough money, more than he could reasonably be expected to spend, tucked away in safety deposit boxes around the world. Interest rates and currency fluctuations didn't concern him one way or the other. He picked up the remote control unit and channel-surfed for a while as he drank from the can but he found nothing to hold his attention. He settled for a channel which was playing country music videos. A manila envelope lay on the table next to a stack of new magazines. He put down his soft drink and picked up the envelope. Inside were three colour photographs, but he tossed them to the side. It was the three A4 typewritten sheets he was interested in. The top sheet was a biography of the target, Andrew Vander Mayer, and details of his entourage. He leaned over and picked up the photograph of the target walking away from a Mercedes. A young Oriental girl, pretty but with a frown creasing her forehead, was just behind him. Su-ming, her name was. There was no mention of a surname. The man studied the picture, tracing his finger along her face and down her body. She had a boyish figure, trim and tight, just the way the man liked them. He'd have enjoyed meeting Su-ming under other circumstances, but he doubted whether they'd get to spend much time together. The man kissed his forefinger and then pressed it onto the photograph. 'Don't worry, Su-ming, it's not you I'm after,' he whispered.

He dropped the photograph back on the table and read through the Vander Mayer itinerary. London. Then New York. Then back to London and on to Hong Kong. Vander

Mayer's residence in London was in Chelsea Harbour, a place the man had visited several times. It boasted an excellent restaurant, the Canteen, part-owned by the movie star Michael Caine, and a five-star hotel. It was generally a quiet area, especially in the evenings – a perfect place for a hit.

The man put the sheets of paper back into the envelope. The Vander Mayer assassination could wait. He had more urgent business to take care of first. He took a long drink from his can of Diet Coke and turned up the sound on the television.

Dermott Lynch parked the Rover in a side street overlooking the building which housed Vander Mayer's office. Marie got out and fed the meter, then leant into the car through the window. 'There's a call box over there,' she said. 'I won't be long.'

'Just be careful,' he said, handing her a ballpoint pen and the piece of paper on which he'd written down the details of the owner of the jet. 'Be relaxed, low-key, don't give them any reason to remember you.'

'Yeah, yeah, yeah,' she said.

Lynch grabbed her wrist, hard enough to hurt. 'Marie, this isn't a game,' he hissed.

Marie suddenly became serious. 'I know.'

Lynch let go of her arm. 'Be careful,' he repeated.

She rubbed her wrist. 'I will be. Don't worry. I won't let you down.' She patted the top of the car as if saying goodbye to a family pet, then walked along Kensington High Street to the call box, one of the old-fashioned red boxes that were fast disappearing from London's streets. She dropped in a coin and dialled the number on the piece of paper.

A girl answered with the jarring vowels of an Essex accent. Marie could picture her, short skirt, too-tight top, high-lighted hair and, in all probability, white high heels. 'Hello,' said Marie in her best Cheltenham Girls' School voice, 'can you tell me if Mr Vander Mayer is there today?'

'Yes, he is. Do you want me to put you through?'

'No, I'm just about to send him a brochure for our conference facilities and I wanted to make sure that I had the correct address. Can I just check it with you?' Marie read out the address and the girl confirmed it was correct. 'Does Mr Vander Mayer have offices in other countries?' Marie asked.

'Oh yes,' said the girl enthusiastically. 'He has an office in New York, one in Los Angeles, and another in Bonn. That's in West Germany.'

'West Germany, really?' said Marie. 'Do me a big favour, will you, and let me have their addresses. I'd like to send brochures there, too.'

The girl did as asked. Marie copied down the addresses, thanked her and replaced the receiver. She went back to the car and climbed in next to Lynch. 'He's there. Vander Mayer's there.' She was panting like an over-excited dog. 'Now what do we do?'

'Now we wait. If Vander Mayer's in there, maybe Cramer's there too.'

* * *

Allan looked up from his copy of *The Economist* as the secretary put down the telephone. 'Problem, Jenny?' he asked.

Jenny smiled and fiddled with her ponytail. 'Nah, it was a woman from some conference centre checking her mailing list.'

'Nothing out of the ordinary?'

'Happens all the time. Junk mail and junk phone calls are pretty much all we get to deal with, unless Mr Vander Mayer's in town. Then it's a mad rush, I can tell you.'

Martin was sitting on the unoccupied desk and staring vacantly out of the window. 'I'm hungry,' he said.

'You're always hungry,' said Allan.

'Do you want anything?'

'A Ferrari. A house in the country. A woman who loves me. The sort of stuff every man wants.'

'I meant food,' said Martin patiently.

'Yeah, I know. A cheese roll.'

Martin straightened up. 'Do you want anything, Jenny?' he asked.

'Nah, I'm on a diet. Thanks anyway.'

Allan flicked through *The Economist* as Martin left the office. He looked at Jenny over the top of the magazine. She was a pretty brunette who couldn't have been much more than nineteen years old. She was shapely and obviously intelligent – Allan had been impressed by the confident way in which she'd lied to the caller about her boss being in the office. She'd been briefed to say that Vander Mayer was in the office and if it was a business call to transfer it to Vander Mayer's yacht.

Jenny beamed at Allan. He smiled and nodded and started reading again. Under other circumstances he'd have been tempted to chat her up a little, but he was too much of a professional to mix business with pleasure. That and the fact that her accent was as annoying as fingernails being scraped across a blackboard.

'So, Allan,' she said, fluttering her long eyelashes, 'how long have you been a bodyguard then?'

Jim Smolev locked the door to his Dodge and walked slowly to the hotel. It was a hot morning, the Florida sky a brilliant blue, devoid of clouds, and the sun was beating down relentlessly. He ran his hand absent-mindedly across the bald spot at the back of his head. He'd discovered the thinning patch only a month ago, but it had become a regular ritual to check it in the bathroom mirror first thing each morning. It was only the size of a quarter, but Smolev's father had been as bald as a bowling ball by the time he was forty-five. Smolev was in his mid-thirties and had resigned himself to the fact that he was heading the same way as his father. Smolev's wife had made all the right noises, telling him that his hair didn't matter, that she'd love him just as much if he didn't have a single hair on his body, that it didn't look so bad anyway. It was, Smolev knew, all Grade A bullshit. She'd never look at him the same way again. Smolev had started reading all the adverts for hair-weaves and had even thought about asking his doctor for details of Rogaine. He was determined not to lose his hair without a fight.

He walked through reception. One of the agents from the Miami field office was sitting on a sofa facing the main entrance and he nodded discreetly at Smolev. Smolev nodded back and headed for the elevator. The rear of the elevator was mirrored and after the door closed Smolev twisted his neck and took a quick look at the bald spot, using his hand to smooth a lock of hair over it. He turned his head left and right as he checked the coverage. It would do. He sighed deeply. His whole body seemed to be in revolt. He'd gone to the dentist to have his aching back tooth checked out only to be told that he needed root canal work. His glasses didn't seem to correct his vision as well as they used to, and his wife kept telling him to go and get his prescription checked. And his knees kept clicking when he climbed out of bed. He was thirty-five years old and he felt like an old man.

The elevator doors hissed open and he walked down the corridor towards Frank Discenza's suite. A single agent stood guard outside the door. 'Hiya, Jim. What's up?' asked the man. His name was Ted Verity, a recent addition to the Bureau's Miami office. He was wearing what looked like a made-to-measure suit and a pair of Armani spectacles, and he had, Smolev noticed with a twinge of envy, a head of thick, black hair.

'My blood pressure, for a start,' said Smolev. 'Is he still giving you trouble?'

'Just moaning. You heard what he's asking for?'

'That's why I'm here.'

'Yeah? Better you than me, Jim.' Verity grinned and ran a hand through his hair as if emphasising how thick it was. 'Pimp's an ugly word, isn't it?'

'My instructions are to persuade him to accept a blow job from you instead,' said Smolev. He smiled as Verity's face fell. 'Only joking, Ted. Just kidding.'

Smolev patted Verity on the arm, opened the door and stepped inside. Discenza was sprawled along a sofa, a stack of magazines and newspapers at his side. A football game was showing on the large-screen television, the sound turned down to barely a whisper. Discenza swung his legs onto the floor and sat up. 'Well?' he said, his eyes gleaming eagerly.

'They're not happy about it, Frank,' said Smolev.

'I don't give a shit whether they're happy about it or not,' said Discenza. 'They're not the ones sitting locked up with only *Playboy* for company. I tell you, Jimmy, I've been seeing too much of my right hand recently and the other one's starting to get jealous. I want a woman, and I want one now.'

'It'll all be over in a few days, Frank. The photographs have already arrived in Zurich. Just a few days more. Can't you wait?'

'Are you married, Jimmy?'

Smolev sighed patiently. 'Yes.'

'How long?'

'Eight years.'

Discenza beat a rapid tattoo on his knees with the palms of his hands. 'Well, unlike you, I still enjoy sex, Jimmy. Lots of it. I like sex, I enjoy being with a woman. Twice a day, sometimes three times. I like pussy, the hotter and tighter the better. Keeping me locked up here is totally unnatural. It's driving me crazy, it's like I'm gonna explode.' He leaned forward conspiratorially. 'I gotta tell you, Jimmy, even you're starting to look pretty tasty. Now, what did they say?'

Smolev fought to control his disgust. 'They said okay. If there's no other way to shut you up, it's okay.'

'Trust me, Jimmy. There's no other way to shut me up.'

There was a knock at the door and both men looked towards it as Verity stepped inside. 'Room service,' explained Verity.

'Great,' said Discenza. He leered at Smolev. 'You hungry? I'm having steak, I could get you something. After all, Uncle Sam's paying, right?'

Smolev watched a white-jacketed waiter push a laden trolley across the carpet. There was a plastic hotel identification badge clipped to the waiter's pocket and the small colour photograph seemed to match. The man looked vaguely Mexican, with a darkish complexion and a thick moustache that curled down either side of his lips. Smolev looked across at Verity and Verity nodded, confirming that he'd checked out the waiter.

'No, thanks, Frank. I've already eaten.'

The waiter reached for the silver cover with a cotton-gloved hand and Smolev felt his stomach tense but when the cover was removed there was just a large rump steak with onions, a fried egg and French fries. Discenza nodded his approval and waved his hand at Verity. 'Sign the check, Ted, will ya? And give the guy a ten dollar tip, yeah?'

'Whatever you say, Mr Discenza,' said Verity, barely able to conceal his disdain. There were two bottles of Budweiser on the trolley, beaded with condensation, and the waiter deftly whipped off the metal tops before handing the check to Verity. As Verity signed for the food, Discenza picked up one of the bottles of Budweiser and drank deeply. He drained half the bottle in one go. 'You sure?' he pressed Smolev. 'The food's great here.'

'Considering what it's costing us, I'm sure it is. You go ahead.'

Discenza carried the plate and Budweiser over to the sofa. 'Get me the ketchup, will ya?' he said.

Smolev stared at Discenza's back and imagined plunging a large butcher's knife into it again and again. 'Sure, Frank. I'll get the ketchup.'

He put the dish of tomato sauce down on the coffee table and Discenza jabbed a French fry into it. He smacked his lips and began cutting his steak up into small pieces like a mother preparing food for a toddler. 'So, when do I get the girls?' he asked.

'Girls?' repeated Smolev. 'We're talking about one girl. One visit. And I'm not even happy about that.'

Discenza shook his head. 'How I get my rocks off is my own business,' he said. He popped a piece of steak into his mouth and chewed noisily. 'Sure you don't want something?' he asked, his mouth full of food.

'I'm not an escort agency, Frank. You asked for a woman, I'll arrange it. But that's it.'

'I asked for company. Female company. I never said how many I wanted.' He dunked a handful of French fries into the ketchup and thrust them into his mouth, smearing his lips with sauce. He looked as if he'd cut his lip.

'Don't jerk me around,' Smolev warned.

'That's an option,' retorted Discenza, 'but between you and me I'd prefer a couple of eighteen-year-olds.'

The waiter left the room, followed by Verity. Smolev went over to the window and looked out at the car park.

'Is it hot in here, or is it me?' Discenza asked.

Smolev turned around to face him. 'Feels okay to me. You want me to turn the air-conditioning up?'

Discenza nodded and took another swig from the bottle of Budweiser. He burped as he put the bottle down on the table. Smolev looked around for a thermostat but couldn't find one. Discenza took a card from his jacket pocket and held it out to Smolev. 'Call this number,' he said, 'tell them I want Terry and Amanda.'

Smolev took the card. 'How stupid are you, Frank?' he said.

Discenza's jaw dropped. The man's mouth was full of half-chewed food and Smolev averted his eyes. It was a disgusting sight. 'Now what's wrong?' Discenza asked.

'What's wrong is that you're in protective custody, and you expect me to call your regular hookers and invite them over. Don't you get it? The man we're after is a stone-cold killer. And if he finds out that you've betrayed him, how long do you think it'll be before he comes after you?'

Discenza swallowed. 'You said I'd be in the clear, you said you and the Brits would get him, that was the deal, right?' He loosened his collar. A trickle of sweat ran down the side of his cheek.

'If you let us take care of you, sure. But if you contact dial-a-hooker, it's just asking for trouble.' He paused. 'Terry is a girl, right?' he asked.

Discenza scowled. 'Of course Terry's a fucking girl. What do you think I am?'

Smolev fought the urge to sneer at the man. He knew exactly what sort of man Discenza was. A liar, a fraud, a cheat, a man who was prepared to pay to have another man killed, a man who'd do anything to save his own skin. A man without honour. 'Just checking,' he said, and forced a smile. 'I'll arrange the girl.'

'Girls,' said Discenza.

'Girl,' repeated Smolev.

The two men stared at each other for several seconds. Eventually Discenza smiled. 'A blonde,' he said. 'With tits out to here.' He held out his cupped hands in front of him.

'I'll see what I can do,' said Smolev.

Discenza nodded and drained his Budweiser. He put it down and then drank from the second bottle. His forehead was damp with sweat. He stabbed a chunk of steak with his fork. 'Does the Bureau use a regular agency?' he asked.

'Oh sure, we have an account with Tits 'R Us,' said Smolev. 'What do you think, Frank? You think we call up and say the FBI's got a hard on and would they send someone over?' Smolev went back to the window. A large white delivery truck with the name of a laundry service drew up in the car park.

'Jesus, it's hot in here,' complained Discenza.

'It's not that bad,' said Smolev.

'Yeah, well you're not cooped up here all day,' said Discenza.

'It won't be for much longer,' said Smolev, turning around. 'Like I said, the pictures have been delivered. Vander Mayer's out of the way, our man's in place. A few days, max.'

Discenza squinted over at the FBI agent. 'How the hell did you find someone dumb enough to take Vander Mayer's place?'

Smolev's tooth began to ache and he rubbed his jaw. 'I don't know. The Brits got him.'

'Yeah? Does he know what he's letting himself in for?'

Smolev shrugged. 'That's not my business. All I've got to do is keep you safe until we've got the killer.'

Discenza thrust another handful of ketchup-covered French fries into his mouth and washed them down with Budweiser.

Smolev spotted a thermostat on the wall by the bathroom door. It was set at sixty-five degrees and Smolev felt comfortable, but he lowered it anyway. 'Tell me, Frank. Why did you take out the contract on Vander Mayer?'

Discenza sneered. 'That's between me and my lawyer, Jimmy.'

Smolev sat down opposite Discenza. 'Come on, Frank, you can tell me.'

Discenza loosened his tie and undid the top button of his shirt. 'It wouldn't be smart for me to tell you, now would it?' He pushed the plate away.

'Something wrong with the food?'

'I'm not hungry any more. Maybe the steak's gone bad.'

Smolev picked up the plate and held it under his nose. 'Smells all right to me. The food's supposed to be first class here.'

'Yeah? Well maybe the chef's having a bad day.' He took another swig of beer then slumped back on the sofa. 'So you wanna know why I wanted Vander Mayer taken out, right? I guess it can't hurt to tell you, what with the deal my lawyer's worked out. The conspiracy charge has been dropped, right?'

'That's the deal, Frank.'

'How much did they tell you?'

'Me? They're treating me like a mushroom.'

'A mushroom?' frowned Discenza.

'You know, they keep me in the dark and feed me bullshit.'

At first Discenza didn't get it, then he broke out laughing. 'Good one, Jimmy. A mushroom. Good one.' He picked up a white napkin and used it to wipe his forehead. 'He killed my brother.'

'Yeah?'

'Killed him or paid to have him killed. Comes down to the same thing: one dead brother.'

'How come?'

Discenza undid another button on his shirt. 'We were putting together a deal in the Keys, a hotel development. Vander Mayer was putting up most of the money, I was doing the legal work and bringing in extra investors and a management team. My brother Rick was helping me. Keeping everyone sweet, you know? He was just a kid. Twenty-five years old. Just out of Harvard.' Discenza rubbed his throat. 'God, I'm thirsty,' he said. 'Get me some water, will ya?'

Smolev was going to protest but he could see that Discenza was in considerable discomfort. He went to the bathroom and filled a glass tumbler with water. 'Why did Vander Mayer kill your brother?' he called through the open doorway.

'He's got this assistant, this Oriental girl. Chinese or something. She's always with him, he never goes anywhere without her. She's some sort of adviser to him, and God knows what else. She took an instant dislike to Rick. Wouldn't have anything to do with him. You got that water?'

'Coming,' said Smolev. He carried the glass of water out to Discenza, taking care not to spill any.

'Seems she told Vander Mayer that Rick wasn't to be trusted,' said Discenza, taking the glass from Smolev and drinking greedily. He drained the glass and put it down on the coffee table. 'Funny thing was, she was right. Even I didn't know. He was planning to put Mafia money in the investment through a company in the Bahamas. He'd lost a bundle gambling and some pretty heavy guys were putting the screws on him.'

Smolev went over to the window and stood looking out. The laundry truck was driving out of the car park. 'So Vander Mayer had him killed?' Smolev asked.

'Not right away. Rick went around to talk to the girl. Things got out of hand.'

'Out of hand? How exactly did they get out of hand?'

'Depends who you believe. Rick said she led him on, she says he tried to rape her. Two days later Rick disappeared and the deal was off.'

Smolev saw a man walk out of the front entrance of the hotel. Smolev vaguely recognised him but couldn't place the face.

'I knew it was Vander Mayer, but I could hardly go to the cops, could I? A friend in Dallas gave me a number, told me that a Swiss banker could get the job done for me for half a million dollars. Jimmy, I don't feel so good. Maybe I need a doctor.'

Smolev tapped his fingers on the windowsill as he stared at the man walking away from the hotel. He frowned. Suddenly he realised that the man was the waiter who'd delivered Discenza's food. But his appearance had changed: his hair was shorter now, and he was missing his moustache. Smolev turned around. Discenza was lying back on the sofa, his mouth open, his chest heaving. Frothy white saliva dribbled from between Discenza's lips and his eyes were wide and staring. 'Oh shit,' Smolev gasped. He rushed over to Discenza. 'Ted!' he yelled. 'Get in here.'

Discenza's legs began to thrash about and Smolev pushed the man's shoulders down onto the sofa. 'Try to lie still, Frank. The more you move, the faster it'll spread.'

The door opened. 'Did you want . . . ?' Verity began, but he stopped when he saw what was happening. 'What the . . . ?'

'The waiter!' Smolev interrupted. 'He's lost the hair and the moustache and he's wearing a black leather jacket and jeans. He was on foot but he must have a car nearby. Go!'

Smolev stood up and went over to the telephone as Verity rushed out and ran down the corridor. He told a girl on reception to call for an ambulance and to see if there was a doctor staying at the hotel. He slammed the receiver down and went back to Discenza. Discenza's back was arched and the tendons in his neck were as taut as steel wires. Discenza grunted and his right hand fastened on Smolev's shoulder, gripping like a vice. Discenza began muttering, but Smolev couldn't make out what he was saying. 'It's going to be okay, Frank,' Smolev said. 'Lie still.'

Discenza kicked out and one of the Budweiser bottles skidded across the carpet. The poison must have been in the beer, Smolev realised. He cursed himself and he cursed the waiter and his white cotton gloves. No fingerprints, and a description that was worse than useless. His only hope was that Verity would apprehend the man, but Smolev knew that was no hope at all. The killer was a pro. Suddenly Discenza went rigid, and then he flopped back onto the sofa. Smolev searched for a pulse in the man's neck, but he knew he was wasting his time. Discenza was dead.

And so, thought Smolev bitterly, was his career with the Bureau.

The intercom on the desk buzzed. Cramer looked at Su-ming expectantly and she walked over and pressed a button on the device. 'Yes, Jenny?' she said.

'It's Mr Tarlanov,' said the secretary.

Cramer got to his feet and adjusted the cuffs of his shirt as Su-ming opened the office door. He heard Allan arguing with the visitor and went over to see what the problem was. A tall man in a fawn raincoat was standing by Jenny's desk clutching an aluminium case to his chest, a look of alarm on his face. He was in his late thirties with thick eyebrows that almost met above a thin nose. He had several days' stubble on his cheeks and chin and his face was drawn and tired.

Allan was standing in front of the man, his arms out to the sides, blocking his way. Tarlanov was saying something rapidly in Russian and shaking his head. Then in heavily accented English he said, 'No. No. Leave me.'

'Stay where you are, Mr Vander Mayer,' Allan said as he continued to obstruct Tarlanov.

Martin moved over to stand next to Cramer, putting his body between Cramer and the Russian.

'What's the problem?' Cramer asked Su-ming.

She spoke to Tarlanov and he answered, clearly relieved to find someone who could speak his own language. 'He won't open the case,' she said.

'Why not?'

The Russian must have understood because he spoke to

Su-ming again. She nodded and looked at Cramer. 'He says he'll only open it in front of you.'

'We have to search him, Su-ming,' said Allan. 'Tell him that.'

Su-ming began to translate but Tarlanov was already shaking his head. Cramer could see that the man understood at least some English.

'Go back into the office and close the door, Mr Vander Mayer,' said Allan.

'It's okay, Allan,' said Cramer. 'Su-ming, tell him that we're just going to pat him down, nothing more. He can open the case in my office, we just want to make sure he doesn't have a weapon.'

Su-ming moved past Martin and she spoke softly to the Russian, as if she was trying to calm a spooked horse. He nodded, still nervous, and then put the aluminium case on the floor and held up his hands. He watched Cramer as Allan searched him.

'Hello, hello, what's this?' Allan said, reaching behind Tarlanov's back. His hand reappeared with a small automatic and he held it up for Cramer to see. Martin pushed Cramer back into the inner office and took out his own gun.

Tarlanov spoke quickly in Russian as Allan continued to search him.

'He says it's for his own protection,' Su-ming explained. 'He says London is a dangerous city.'

Allan took a small aerosol from the Russian's pocket. He examined it and then sniffed it warily. He wrinkled his nose. 'Mace,' he said.

The Russian nodded eagerly. 'For protection,' he said.

'You speak English?' Cramer asked.

Tarlanov smiled ingratiatingly. 'A little,' he said.

'That's all,' said Allan, stepping back. He wiped his eyes which had started watering from the mace. He looked at the gun in the palm of his hand. It was a small automatic, not much bigger than the one Cramer had in his underarm holster.

'May I?' Cramer asked, holding out his hand. Allan gave him the weapon. Cramer didn't recognise the make, though there was Russian writing along the barrel.

'For protection,' the Russian repeated. Cramer ejected the clip, slipped it into his pocket and gave the empty gun back to the Russian.

'I'd feel happier searching the case,' Allan said to Cramer.

'No. Only Mr Vander Mayer,' Tarlanov insisted, in his heavy accent.

'Watch him, Martin,' said Allan. Martin grunted. He still had his VP70 machine pistol in his hand. Allan nodded at Cramer to back into the inner office and he followed him inside, closing the door behind them. 'He's the right build, give or take, I'm not sure about his accent and he had a gun. It could be him, Mike.'

Cramer pulled a face. 'I don't think he's faking it. And our man wouldn't just walk in here like that, he'd have shot you and Martin and then blown me away. He's never given anyone time to search him before, he just starts shooting.'

Allan sighed deeply. 'I don't want him alone with you.'

'Where's he going to go, Allan? You and Martin will be on the other side of the door. It'd be suicide, and we know the killer doesn't have a death-wish.'

Allan thought about it for several seconds. 'Okay,' he

said. 'But keep close to him, watch him when he opens the case and if he makes any threatening moves . . .'

'Get my defence in first. Yeah, I know.'

Allan held Cramer's look, then turned and open the door. 'Let him through,' Allan said to Martin.

Martin held his machine pistol down at his side as he stepped away from Tarlanov. The Russian picked up the metal case and carried it through to the inner office. Su-ming closed the door and stood with her back to it. Tarlanov nodded and smiled at Cramer as he put the case onto the desk.

'I didn't expect you to be able to speak English,' Cramer said.

Tarlanov frowned and looked at Su-ming. She translated and he shrugged. 'A little,' he said.

'Where in Russia are you from?'

Again Tarlanov immediately looked at Su-ming and Cramer realised that the Russian spoke hardly any English at all.

Su-ming looked at Cramer. 'I don't think we should be asking him questions,' she said, speaking quickly so that the Russian would be even less likely to understand.

Cramer raised an eyebrow. 'Ask him where he's from, please,' he said. Su-ming's eyes hardened. 'Let's not have a scene,' added Cramer, smiling pleasantly.

Su-ming looked for a moment as if she might argue, then she spoke to Tarlanov. 'St Petersburg,' she said.

Cramer nodded. 'Okay, let's see what's in the case.' He pointed at the metal case and mimed opening it. The Russian nodded. He reached into his raincoat pocket and Cramer tensed, even though he knew that Allan's search had been thorough. Tarlanov's hand reappeared with a set of keys. He sorted through them and used one to open the locks.

Cramer moved towards the desk so that he was standing just behind the Russian. He peered over the man's shoulder as he lifted the lid. Cramer held his breath, his right hand straying towards his hidden gun.

The lid opened and Cramer saw a sheaf of papers. Tarlanov picked them up and handed them to Cramer. He spoke in Russian and Su-ming translated. 'This is the documentation about the process and details of the consignments available,' she said.

Cramer flicked through the sheets. They were all in Russian, and scattered through the text were chemical symbols and equations. He gave them to Su-ming. 'Can you make sense of these?' he asked.

As she read through the paperwork, Tarlanov stood to the side and waved his hand over the open case. The bulk of the case was filled with grey foam rubber, but in the centre, nestled into a snug cut-out hollow, was a metal canister shaped like an artillery shell, grey at the top, red for most of its length and with a brass fitting at the bottom. The object was about nine inches long with Russian writing on the red section, mainly numbers.

Cramer bent over the case and stared at it, scratching his chin thoughtfully. It wasn't a shell, he was sure of that. In fact, it didn't look like any weapon he'd ever seen. 'Ask him if it's okay to touch it,' he told Su-ming.

'I don't think that's a good idea,' she said.

'Just do it,' said Cramer, keeping his voice as pleasant as possible. He didn't want Tarlanov to guess from his tone that there was anything wrong.

Su-ming spoke to Tarlanov in Russian, listened to his

answer, and then replied. 'It's not dangerous.' Cramer picked it up gingerly. It weighed several pounds. 'But he says be careful not to drop it,' Su-ming added.

Cramer turned the object around in his hands. It was smooth with no rivets or screws, and the brass fitting appeared to be screwed into the red metal part. It reminded him of a Christmas tree light only much, much bigger. 'Where does it come from?' Cramer asked. It wasn't a shell, he realised. It was a flask. A metal flask.

When Su-ming didn't translate, Cramer turned and looked at her. She was glaring at him, her arms folded across her chest. 'That's not what we're supposed to do,' she said.

'Keep smiling, kid,' said Cramer. 'And do as you're told.'

The Russian looked at Su-ming expectantly. She forced a smile and spoke to him in Russian. His reply was a single word. 'Ekaterinburg,' said Su-ming. 'It's a city in the Urals, about 600 kilometres to the east of Moscow.'

Cramer nodded. Tarlanov spoke again and Su-ming listened intently. 'But it was manufactured in Krasnoyarsk-26, that's a military city in Zhelenogorsk,' she translated.

Cramer could get no information from the writing on the flask so he put it back in its cut-out in the case. He really wanted to ask the Russian what was inside the flask, but that was out of the question: Vander Mayer would obviously know what the Russian was bringing him. 'How much does it cost?' he asked.

Su-ming translated and the Russian replied with a careless shrug. 'It depends on how much you want,' she said. 'The base price is four hundred thousand dollars for a kilogram.'

The Russian closed the case. 'Ask him how much he can get hold of,' Cramer asked.

Su-ming spoke to Tarlanov in Russian. He nodded, then turned and headed towards the door. Cramer realised that Su-ming had told him the meeting was over. She dashed ahead of the Russian and opened the door, ushering him out before Cramer could protest.

As soon as the Russian stepped out of the inner office, Su-ming closed the door and stood with her back to it, her eyes flashing. 'You weren't supposed to ask him anything,' she said. 'Mr Vander Mayer said you were only to take delivery of the consignment. You didn't do as you were told.'

'He's your boss, not mine.'

'You could have ruined everything.'

Cramer shrugged dismissively. 'That's not my problem.' He pointed at the case. 'Now, what the hell is that? What's so important that it's made in a Russian military city and it costs four hundred thousand dollars a kilogram?'

'It doesn't concern you.'

'You're wrong, Su-ming. You're dead wrong. I'm looking after whatever it is that's in that case, it's my responsibility, and if it's some sort of germ warfare weapon then I have a right to know.'

'It's not germ warfare,' she said, pouting like a little girl who wasn't getting her own way.

'So you say. What if I drop it, what if the car gets involved in an accident? Suppose whatever it is in the flask escapes? We could all die.'

Su-ming shook her head. 'It's safe.'

'How do you know?'

She waved the typed sheets in front of his face. 'Because

it says so, here, that's how I know. Until it's activated, it's virtually inert.'

'Activated? What the hell do you mean, activated? What is it, Su-ming?'

She tapped the papers against the palm of her hand as she looked at him. 'Red mercury,' she said. 'It's only a sample for Mr Vander Mayer to test.'

'Red mercury?' Cramer repeated. 'What is it, some sort of explosive?'

'I shouldn't even have told you that much,' she said.

Cramer walked over to her. She looked so small when he stood next to her. She barely came up to his shoulder and she had to tilt her head back to keep looking into his eyes. 'What's it used for?' he pressed.

She frowned. 'Fuses, mainly.'

'For bombs?'

She nodded. 'It's got civil applications, too, though. Mining companies can use it to help extract gold from ore.'

Cramer kept looking at her. He was sure she wasn't telling him everything.

Marie looked at her wristwatch. 'Do you think I should put more money in the meter?' she asked.

Lynch stretched his arms out in front of him and opened and closed his hands. He sighed. 'Aye, I suppose so.' He tapped his fingers on the steering wheel as he stared across the crowded street at the block containing Vander Mayer's office. 'Come out, come out, wherever you are,' he whispered.

Marie got out, fed the meter, and climbed back into the Rover. 'Of course, Cramer might not be in there,' she said.

'He's in there,' said Lynch. 'I know he's in there.'

'What about something to eat? A sandwich or something?'

Lynch shook his head. He rubbed the back of his neck. His whole body seemed to be aching. It felt as if he'd been sitting in the car for months. 'Maybe a coffee,' he said.

'Tired?'

'Knackered.'

'It's just after five, the offices should start emptying soon. I'll get you a coffee before the rush starts.'

She was reaching for the door handle when Lynch sat bolt upright. 'Wait,' he said.

Marie's hand jerked away from the handle as if she'd received an electric shock. 'What?'

'Look.' Lynch nodded at the office block. A Mercedes had pulled up and the driver, a large man in a dark blue suit and a peaked cap, was getting out.

'That's the same car they had in Wales,' said Marie.

'Same type. Different registration number. But that's the driver all right.' He started the engine. 'Keep the map out. Rush hour isn't the best time to be tailing someone in London.'

Lynch pulled away from the kerb and indicated that he wanted to turn right. He had to make sure he didn't get stuck in the side road when the Mercedes drove off. A middle-aged woman in a battered MGB flashed her headlights and Lynch nudged the Rover into the traffic. The only place he could find to park was on a double yellow line but he didn't think he'd have to wait long so he pulled in and watched the

Mercedes in his driving mirror. Marie twisted around in her seat to watch the building itself.

'Oh shit,' said Lynch under his breath. A black traffic warden was walking towards them, notebook in hand. He was about fifty feet away.

'The driver's gone inside,' said Marie.

Lynch drummed his fingers on the steering wheel. The traffic warden was heading purposefully towards the Rover. Marie opened the door. 'What are you doing?'

'I'll talk to him,' she said. She got out of the car and walked towards the traffic warden, smiling and waving the street directory. She said something to the man and showed him the map. Smart girl, thought Lynch, but he doubted whether the ruse would buy them more than a minute or two. The traffic warden took the map from Marie and began talking to her and pointing down the road.

Lynch turned to look through the back window of the Rover. The door to the block opened but it was a young woman who came out. 'Come on, come on,' Lynch muttered. He felt exposed and vulnerable, sitting on the double yellow lines with a traffic warden only yards away. There were no other parking spaces nearby and if they had to drive off they'd have to double back, and that could take ages in the heavy traffic. The door to the office block opened again and the driver came out. He stood at the entrance, looking left and right, and then held it open. Another big man came out wearing a dark grey suit, and Lynch recognised him immediately: it was the man he'd seen walking with Cramer in the grounds of the school in Wales.

Marie was still talking to the traffic warden. Lynch didn't want to risk sounding his horn, even though the street

411

was bustling with vehicles and pedestrians. He flashed his headlights a couple of times and she waved at him before spotting the two men. Marie took the map from the traffic warden, said something to him and then walked quickly back to the Rover. Lynch kept his eyes glued to the driving mirror. A third man came out. Lynch's eyes narrowed. It was Cramer. He was carrying an aluminium briefcase.

Marie got into the Rover and closed the door. The traffic warden was still walking towards them. Marie wound down her window and gave him a wide smile. 'Thanks for your help,' she called, waving the map at him. He walked by, but looked over his shoulder. 'You're going to have to go,' Marie whispered. 'He's watching us.'

'Pretend to give me directions,' Lynch said. Marie leaned over and made a show of holding the map in front of him as he kept an eye on the rear-view mirror. The three men were getting into the Mercedes. The two large men moved efficiently, and as he watched Lynch realised how cleverly they were shielding Cramer. The young Oriental girl came out of the office block and opened the rear door of the Mercedes herself. Marie continued to point at the map and nod her head. Lynch nodded as if agreeing with her. In the mirror he saw the traffic warden walking away. 'Okay, he's going,' said Lynch.

The Mercedes drove away from the kerb. As it drew level with the Rover, Lynch turned his head away. He let a couple of cars go by and then edged the Rover into the traffic. Marie had the map open on her lap and she kept looking at it as Lynch followed the Mercedes. The traffic was moving slowly and while Lynch wasn't worried about the Mercedes getting away, he wanted to stay fairly close in case he got held up by traffic lights.

A taxi forced itself in front of Lynch and he cursed. 'He's turning left,' said Marie.

Lynch indicated and followed the Mercedes down the side road. The Mercedes made another two turns in quick succession. For a brief moment Lynch wondered if the driver had spotted them, but then the Mercedes drove straight on for almost half a mile. Lynch allowed two vehicles to overtake but kept reasonably close.

'Fulham,' said Marie. 'They're heading for Fulham. They could be crossing the river.'

'If they're driving back to Wales I'll be really pissed off,' said Lynch through clenched teeth.

'No, they're going north-east. If they were going to Wales they'd be heading west to the M4.'

They drove by antique shops full of gilded furniture and extravagant light fittings, then past a football stadium. 'Chelsea,' said Marie. 'It's where Chelsea play.'

The traffic had thinned out and Lynch hung back, giving the Mercedes plenty of space. There was little chance of losing it; the driver was sticking religiously to the speed limit.

'I think we've got a tail,' said Martin, glancing in his rear-view mirror.

Su-ming began to turn around but Cramer reached over and took her hand. 'Don't look around,' he said. 'Are you sure?' he asked Martin.

'I noticed it about five minutes ago, but this is the best

way to Chelsea Harbour so it might be coincidence. Two people, one's a woman, I think.'

'Our man usually works alone,' said Allan.

'Yeah, but not always,' said Cramer. 'Remember the Kypriano killing? Someone else was in the boat that picked him up. And there've been other cases where he's had someone driving a getaway car.'

Allan turned his head and surreptitiously moved the wing mirror so that he could see directly behind the Mercedes. 'The metallic grey Rover?'

'That's the one,' said Martin. 'It's not one of ours, is it?'

'No, it's bloody well not. And if it was, I'd have their balls on toast. Can you make out the registration number?'

'Too far away,' Martin replied. 'Shall I lose them?'

Allan looked at him scornfully. 'If we lose them, they'll know we're onto them. That's not what we're trying to achieve here, right?'

'I was joking, Allan,' said Martin.

'Slow down, see if we can get the number.'

'I guess I should do that without braking, right?' Martin flashed a grin at Allan and took his foot off the accelerator.

Allan watched the Rover in the mirror. 'He's slowing too.'

The driver of the black taxi behind them beeped his horn impatiently. Martin accelerated again.

'Drive to the apartment,' said Allan. 'They can't do anything while we're in the car. Let's see what happens when we get to Chelsea Harbour.'

Cramer smiled at Su-ming. 'It'll be okay,' he said. She nodded, unconvinced. Cramer realised that he was still holding her hand. He released his grip and folded his arms. 'It might not be him,' he said.

'They're still there,' said Martin.

Cramer squeezed his arms. He could feel the gun in its holster pressing against his ribs but wasn't reassured by its presence.

Martin turned onto the road that led to Chelsea Harbour, his eyes flicking between the rear-view mirror and the way ahead. 'He's indicating,' he said. 'Yeah, here he comes. Still too far away to get the registration.'

They drove by the Conrad Hotel towards the towering apartment block with its blue-framed balconies and pyramid roof. Martin turned left to follow the road around to the car park. 'False alarm,' said Allan. 'They're pulling up in front of the hotel.'

Cramer tried to relax. He uncrossed his arms, rested his head on the back of the seat and sighed. His heart was racing and his palms were sweating.

'Okay?' asked Allan as they drove down into the underground car park and stopped in front of the entrance to the apartment block.

Cramer nodded but didn't reply. Martin and Allan got out of the Mercedes and walked around to Cramer's door. The area outside the entrance was clear but the two men still formed a protective barrier as they escorted Cramer inside. The doorman nodded at them.

They took the elevator up to the ground level and walked across the marble-floored foyer. The doorman on duty wasn't the man who'd been there when they'd left that morning. He was younger, with a thin face and pale blue eyes. Cramer transferred the metal case to his left hand. The doorman waved a greeting to Allan, then reached under the counter. Cramer tensed and flexed the fingers of his right hand. 'Easy,' said Allan out of the corner of his mouth, 'he's one of ours.'

The doorman brought an envelope out from under the counter and held it out for Su-ming as Allan and Martin walked either side of Cramer to the elevator.

Marie opened the door of the Rover and climbed in, her face flushed with excitement. 'They went into an apartment block, the tall one,' she said. 'The two big guys kept really close to him as they went in.'

'They're bodyguards all right,' said Lynch.

'Why would Cramer need a bodyguard?' asked Marie. 'Do you think they know we're after him?'

'I can't see how,' said Lynch. 'Besides, it doesn't make sense. If they were trying to protect him, they'd make him disappear. The Brits could give him a new identity, a new passport and a ticket to anywhere in the world. They wouldn't put him on full view like this. Maybe Vander Mayer's in the apartment. What did they do with the car?'

'The chauffeur came out after a few minutes and parked it.'

'So it looks like they're staying for a while, doesn't it? And who's that girl hanging around with them?'

Marie shrugged. 'I don't know. But the bodyguards definitely aren't for her. She was following them.'

Lynch made a clicking sound with his tongue. It was a nervous habit, and he didn't realise he was doing it until

Marie started to copy him. 'Sorry,' he said. 'I've always done that when I think, ever since I was a kid. Used to annoy the hell out of my teachers during exams.'

'I bet. What are you thinking about?'

'I'm working out what to do.'

'What are our options?'

Lynch put his head on one side as he looked at her. 'We can keep following him, we can try to find out what Cramer's up to. Or we can pull back, see if the bodyguards are a permanent feature. Or we can go for the hit now.'

Marie put her hand on Lynch's shoulder. 'You know what my choice would be?'

Lynch stared into her eyes. 'Yes,' he said. 'Yes, I know what you want.' He sighed and rubbed his hands over his face. 'I'm knackered,' he said. 'Whatever we do, we should rest for a while.'

Marie nodded at the hotel. 'Well, we're in the right place for that,' she said.

As soon as they entered the flat, Su-ming disappeared down the corridor towards the bedrooms with the metal briefcase. Cramer heard a door shut and he figured she was probably putting the case into Vander Mayer's safe.

Martin went off into the kitchen and Cramer and Allan followed him. 'I'm starving,' said Martin. He pulled open the door to the refrigerator and peered inside. 'Jesus H. Christ, there's enough food in here to feed a regiment,' he said. He took off his jacket and hung it on the back of a chair, unclipped his underarm holster, then stripped off his shirt to reveal the dark blue bullet-proof vest he was wearing. He ripped away the Velcro straps, slid the vest off and dropped it onto the table. The table shuddered.

'Should be enough to keep you going until tomorrow, then,' said Allan as he switched on the electric kettle.

Martin put his shirt back on, then took a carton of eggs, a plastic-wrapped pack of Danish bacon, a pack of Walls sausages and half a pound of butter from the fridge. 'You can't see any bread, can you?' he asked.

Cramer pointed at a large stainless steel bin with 'BREAD' etched into its side. 'Shot in the dark, but that could be it,' he said.

Martin piled the foodstuffs onto the work surface by the stove and opened the bin. 'Perfect,' he said, taking out a loaf of Hovis. 'I love a bit of fried bread.' A large frying pan was hanging from a hook on the wall and Martin took it down. 'One egg or six?' he asked Allan.

'Two. Fried. Black on the bottom, runny on the top, same as you always do them.'

'Mike?'

Cramer shook his head.

'Not worried about your cholesterol level, are you?' asked Martin. 'That Su-ming's got you on some sort of health kick, hasn't she?'

'Yeah, she's taking a real interest in you,' added Allan.

'Leave it out,' said Cramer. 'She's just doing her job.'

Martin ripped open the pack of bacon with his teeth and laid the slices down on the pan. They started to sizzle and Martin prodded them with a plastic spatula.

'Either of you guys heard of red mercury?' Cramer asked, leaning against the kitchen door.

'It's a con,' said Allan. He opened one of the kitchen cupboards, looked inside, and closed it again.

'What do you mean, a con?'

'A hoax. There's no such thing.' Allan opened another cupboard and took out a jar of coffee. He took off the lid. The paper seal inside was untouched. 'There've been rumours for years, but as far as the Ministry of Defence is concerned, it doesn't exist.'

Cramer ran a hand through his hair. 'What's it supposed to be?'

'Something to do with nuclear weapons. It's supposed to make them more effective or something. It's supposed to be a sort of Russian secret weapon, there were rumours that they came up with it just before the end of the Cold War.'

'So why do you say it's a hoax?'

'Because no one has ever been able to deliver the stuff.' He spooned coffee into three mugs. 'Every now and again some middleman will claim to have a supply of the stuff but it always turns out to be something else. The Russian Mafia have been making a fortune duping Arab buyers.'

'Yeah, ragheads will buy anything,' agreed Martin, dropping sausages into the frying pan. 'Except sand, maybe.'

'So if it's a hoax, why do they keep buying it?'

'Because,' said Allan, 'there's always a chance that it does exist and that the powers-that-be are lying.'

'Why would they lie?' asked Cramer.

'Habit,' said Martin, but Allan and Cramer ignored him.

Allan poured hot water in the mugs and stirred the coffee. 'The way I heard it, if the stuff does what the Russians claim, they can use it to produce a nuclear bomb the size of grapefruit.'

'So they'd try to suppress it?'

'If it exists,' said Allan. 'And that's a huge bloody if. The Russian Government says there's no such thing.'

'Yeah, well they would, wouldn't they?' said Martin. He used a fork to juggle the sausages and bacon onto two plates and then began cracking eggs one-handed into the hot fat.

'Yeah, but if there was such a thing and the Russians had it, they'd sell it to the Yanks, or the Yanks would pay to get it off the market,' said Allan.

'Yeah. I guess.'

Cramer didn't sound convinced and Allan looked up from the coffee mugs. 'Hey, wait a minute. Are you saying that's what's in the case? Vander Mayer's buying red mercury?'

'That's what he said.'

'Well he's wasting his time,' said Allan, handing one of the mugs to Cramer.

'There's documentation with it,' said Cramer.

'In Russian, I suppose,' said Allan. Cramer nodded. 'So it could be anything?'

'Yeah, you're right.' Cramer put his coffee mug down on the work surface. 'But Vander Mayer doesn't strike me as the sort of guy who'd go on a wild goose chase.'

Martin used the spatula to lift the fried eggs out of the pan, and he replaced them with two slices of brown bread. 'It's not our problem though, is it?' he said.

'I guess,' said Cramer. 'How do you know so much about it, Allan?'

'Only what I've read in the papers. And I think *Newsweek* did a piece on it a while back. Hey, Martin, I want mine fried, not cremated.' Allan went to stand behind Martin and looked over his shoulder at the frying pan and its sizzling contents.

'Bit of charcoal never hurt anyone,' said Martin, flipping the fried bread over.

'The thing is, Vander Mayer offered me money to make sure no one asked questions about the case.'

'How much money?' asked Martin.

'A lot.'

'So take it,' said Allan. He reached into the frying pan and took out one of the pieces of fried bread with his fingers and dropped it onto his plate. He scowled at Martin.

'He wouldn't do that unless he was pretty sure that it was the genuine article, right?'

'Hell, I don't know, Mike. Maybe he's got more money than sense.' Allan carried his plate back into the sitting room. Cramer followed him. Allan sat down in one of the steel and leather armchairs and ate off his lap. 'If I were you, I'd take his money, hand over the case, and not worry about it,' he said.

Lynch went over to the window and looked across at the apartment block. 'Perfect,' he said. Down below he could see the entrance to the tower, though the angle was too steep to look inside the foyer.

'It's a nice room all right,' said Marie, dropping her Harrods bag onto the large bed. 'Should be, too, for what it's costing.'

'I meant the view,' said Lynch.

Marie walked over to stand next to him. She rested her

head on his shoulder as she gazed at the tower block opposite. 'He's in there,' she whispered. 'The bastard who killed my parents is in there.' She shuddered as if she'd been caught in a draught.

Lynch wondered which floor Cramer was on. He couldn't see into any of the apartments, either the windows were slightly tinted or the evening sun was reflecting off the glass. Either way, the tower block windows gazed blankly back at Lynch, like the eyes of a dead man. He turned away from the window. 'I need a shower,' he said.

The bathroom was luxurious, gold fittings and flawless marble. Lynch stripped off his clothes and turned on the shower. He studied himself in the mirror behind the twin washbasins. He looked tired, the whites of his eyes were flecked with red and his hair was greasy and unkempt. They'd been worried that his dishevelled appearance might cause comment at reception, so Marie had done the talking and had used her credit card to pay for the room. All he needed was to get clean, followed by a few hours' sleep. Then he'd work out what to do next.

He stepped into the shower and let the steaming hot water play over his face and neck. He lathered up a bar of soap, keeping his eyes closed as the water cascaded over his aching muscles.

He didn't hear Marie get into the shower, and he jumped when he felt her hands slip around his waist. 'Easy, boy,' she whispered, pressing herself against his back. Her hands slid between his legs and she took hold of him. He gasped and the soap dropped from his fingers. Lynch started to turn around but Marie tightened her hold on him and told him to stay put. He raised his arms and placed his hands on the tiles, as Marie continued to caress him.

She kissed him between his shoulder-blades, her soft breasts pressed tight against his back, her hands making him hard and erect. 'Tell me what you're going to do, Dermott.' Her hands tightened and he moaned. She loosened her grip and then rubbed him, agonisingly slowly, teasing him until he was almost crazy with desire. 'Tell me, Dermott. Tell me what you're going to do.'

Lynch tried to turn again but she pressed him against the wall of the shower cubicle, keeping her grip on him. 'I'm going to kill him,' he gasped. 'I'm going to shoot him like a mad dog.'

Marie let him go and he twisted around. He grabbed her and picked her up. She pushed herself away from him, her eyes hard. 'You promise?' she urged. 'You swear you'll do it?'

'Yes,' he gasped. Marie raised her legs as he pushed her against the wall and he entered her, so hard that she almost screamed.

Cramer walked along the corridor to his bedroom. A strip of light shone from under the door to Vander Mayer's study. He stopped and listened but couldn't hear anything so he knocked gently. Su-ming asked who it was.

'It's me.'

'What do you want?'

Cramer thought about that for a few seconds. He wasn't sure exactly what he did want, or why he'd knocked on the door.

'Come in,' she said eventually. Cramer pushed open

the door. She was sitting on a black leather sofa at the far end of the room, her legs curled up under her. By her side was a small stack of paper and she was holding a sheet in her hands. Cramer saw to his surprise that she was wearing glasses, a pair of oval lenses in a thin wire frame. She took them off as she looked at him. 'What's wrong, Mike Cramer? Can't you sleep?'

Cramer walked over to the window. The study was as big as the master bedroom with views to the north, towards the hotel with its curved balconies and white stone walls and the brick-built office complexes of Chelsea Harbour. Between the tower block and the hotel was a small marina with a channel leading to the Thames. The boats moored in the marina were big, expensive models, vessels to be seen on, not to sail. To the left and right of the marina were smaller apartment blocks, their walls as white and gleaming as the boats in the water. 'I'm sorry about earlier on,' said Cramer. He paced the length of the room. The far end was covered with mirrored tiles, giving the illusion that the office was twice its true size. He watched her in the mirrored wall. She looked like a teenager studying for an important exam.

'Earlier?'

'That business with the Russian. I was out of order.'

She didn't reply and he turned to face her. She was watching him with an amused smile on her face. 'You were like a child who'd been told he couldn't open his Christmas present yet,' she said.

Cramer grinned sheepishly. 'Yeah. I behaved like a kid, didn't I?'

'You're not a man who likes secrets. But you're right,

424

you did behave badly. You could have jeopardised our position. Mr Vander Mayer has spent a lot of time and money trying to get in touch with Mr Tarlanov.'

Cramer pointed at the papers she was reading. 'Those are the papers he left?'

Su-ming nodded. 'They're very technical. I'm having trouble with some of the terms.'

'I'm amazed that you can even speak Russian.'

She pulled a face. 'Languages aren't that difficult. Grammar and vocabulary, that's all. Once you've studied two or three you start to see the patterns, then it's just a matter of memorisation.'

Cramer walked over to the large desk that dominated the far end of the study, facing away from the mirrored wall. Apart from a computer and VDU and two telephones, it was bare. On the wall behind the desk was a large map of the world. Cramer stared at it. England looked so small, so insignificant, compared with the total land mass of the world. There was something egocentric about the way it was placed dead centre, as if everything else revolved around it. That might have been the case in the days when most of the map was coloured pink and the British had an empire, but now it was little more than a small island on the edge of Europe.

'Are you trying to find yourself, Mike Cramer?'

Cramer smiled. Nothing could have been further from the truth. He knew exactly where he was and where he was heading. He turned away from the map. 'Do you go to New York a lot?' he asked.

'Fairly often. In the last year we've been out in the Far East most of the time. That's where the fastest growing markets are.'

'What about the red mercury? Do you think your boss plans to sell that out there?'

Su-ming put the paper she was holding onto the stack. 'It's a possibility,' she said. 'Why?'

'It's for making bombs, you said?'

She put her hands together, like a child about to say its prayers. 'That's one of its uses, yes. It can be used for lots of other things, too.'

'What you didn't tell me was that it's used in nuclear bombs.'

If Su-ming was surprised at Cramer's newly acquired knowledge, she didn't show it. 'Red mercury isn't a bomb. It's a chemical. And it's a chemical with many uses.'

'Is it used in nuclear weapons, yes or no?'

'The honest answer is that we don't know. Nobody knows. Nobody has yet detonated a nuclear weapon containing red mercury.'

'Yet?'

'I mean ever. It's never happened, maybe it never will.'

'And what about those documents? What do they say?'

She waved her hand over the papers. 'According to the section I've just been reading, it can be used to start up civilian nuclear reactors, nothing more sinister than that. And there's a section describing a coating based on the substance which appears to make whatever you paint with it become virtually invisible to radar.'

Cramer went over to her. The coffee table was carved from a solid block of black and grey marble, more than capable of bearing his weight, so he sat down on it, facing her. He linked his fingers together and leaned towards her. 'So Mr Vander Mayer just wants to kick-start nuclear reactors and help keep the friendly skies safe, is that it?'

'Mr Vander Mayer is a businessman. He does what business he can.'

'Tell me about the other uses for this stuff.'

Su-ming pulled a face as if she had a bad taste in her mouth. 'I told you about the fuses. It can be used to detonate bombs. All sorts of bombs, not just nuclear. I don't quite understand how, but it also makes nuclear bombs more effective.' She patted the pile of papers beside her. 'The chemistry is way beyond me, but it's some sort of catalyst.'

'And your boss will sell it to the highest bidder?'

'Of course.'

'Even if it's to terrorists?'

'Terrorists? No. Mr Vander Mayer wouldn't deal with terrorists.'

'Are you sure?'

She frowned as if she was considering his question, then nodded. 'Yes. I'm sure.'

Cramer shook his head in amazement. He could scarcely comprehend what sort of life Vander Mayer must live, travelling the world selling instruments of death to anyone with the money to pay for them. 'The sample that Tarlanov gave us. How is it made?' he asked.

'Why do you want to know?'

Cramer shrugged. 'Just curious, I guess.'

Su-ming studied him for a while, then picked up the papers and riffled through them. She put her spectacles back on and looked at Cramer over the top of them. 'It starts off as mercury antimony oxide.' She studied the sheet of paper for a few seconds, her mouth working soundlessly. 'Okay, it's a ternary oxide with a cubic pyrochlore structure.' She smiled up at him. 'I've no idea what that means.'

Cramer returned her smile. 'Me neither.'

'They take the oxide and dissolve it in mercury and irradiate it for three weeks.'

'So the stuff in the case is radioactive?'

'Slightly. Don't worry, it's shielded.'

'Yeah? So was Chernobyl.'

'I'm being serious, Mike Cramer. If the red mercury is going to be used in nuclear weapons, plutonium has to be added and it's irradiated again. Then it is radioactive, but it can only be stored for thirty days. The sample we have is inert.'

'So what is it that your boss is hoping to buy? The inert stuff or the radioactive stuff?'

'I don't know,' she replied. Cramer narrowed his eyes. 'Really,' she insisted. 'I don't know.'

Cramer nodded at the stack of papers. 'What else does it say there?'

'Most of it's very technical.' She scanned the sheet of paper. 'It explains how the red mercury works – it's something to do with the way it changes the mass value of isotopes which makes the nuclear material more effective. Do you understand what I'm saying?'

Cramer shook his head. 'You lost me at the cubic structure part.'

Su-ming smiled. 'I don't follow it either. I can translate it, but that doesn't mean I understand it. Mr Vander Mayer has experts who will be able to tell him what it means.' She took off her glasses again. 'It's not something you should be worried about. You should be more concerned about the man who's trying to kill you.'

Cramer shrugged. 'There's nothing I can do but wait.'

Su-ming stared at him for several seconds, then suddenly

428

she leaned forward and kissed him gently on the cheek, close to his lips. It was a fleeting touch, little more than a peck, but it electrified Cramer. He sat with his mouth open as she moved away and put her glasses back on. 'What was that for?' he asked.

Su-ming didn't look at him. She began to read again. 'Just curious,' she said.

Cramer watched her, stunned by the sudden kiss, and the longer he sat there, his fingers still interlinked, the more it seemed that he'd imagined it. Su-ming brushed a lock of hair behind her ear, as she studied the typewritten sheet, her brow furrowed as she tried to make sense of the technical information. Cramer wanted to press her, to get her to tell him why she'd kissed him, but somehow the question seemed inappropriate. He stood up and rubbed the spot where her lips had brushed against his skin. 'I guess I'll go to bed,' he said.

'Good night,' she said, not looking up.

Cramer left her sitting on the sofa. He closed the door behind him and walked slowly to his room. By the time he was lying on his bed and staring at the ceiling, he couldn't even remember what the kiss had felt like.

The Colonel was studying his chess computer, his brow creased in concentration. He had the machine set to its highest level which meant it took almost fifteen minutes between moves, and after two hours of play it had the Colonel in an almost impossible situation. Computers were taking almost all the fun out of chess, thought the Colonel.

Now that they could regularly beat human grandmasters, what was the point? He sat back in his chair and pulled a face. It would be mate in four moves, maybe five, unless he was missing something. One of the three telephones on his desk rang, jarring his concentration. He stared at the black and white plastic pieces as he picked up the receiver. It was an overseas call.

'Colonel?' The accent was American.

'Yes.'

'It's Dan.'

Dan Greenberg, the Colonel's liaison in the FBI headquarters in Washington. 'What's the problem, Dan?' There was no mistaking the tension in Greenberg's voice.

'Discenza's dead.'

'I suppose it's too much to hope that it was natural causes.'

'It was a hit. Poison.'

The Colonel slumped back in his chair. 'That's the last thing I want to hear right now, Dan.'

'Tell me about it. Heads are rolling as we speak.'

The Colonel closed his eyes and rubbed the bridge of his nose. If Greenberg had been one of his own men, the Colonel would have ripped into him. There was no excuse for losing a man in protective custody. None. And Discenza had been Greenberg's responsibility: if anyone's head was going to roll, it should have been his. 'Do we know who it was?'

'White male, early thirties, about six feet tall, brown eyes. Got in as a waiter. Had the right ID, Discenza had just ordered room service . . .'

'And the real waiter turned up dead?' The Colonel opened his eyes again. He looked out of the window at the Conrad

Hotel to his right. The Colonel was sitting in a disused apartment which had been requisitioned because of its proximity to the tower block which housed the Vander Mayer apartment. In an adjoining room sat two SAS troopers in leather jackets and jeans, drinking coffee and watching television with the sound turned down. Another trooper was sitting at the stern of a large motor yacht moored in the marina below. The trooper had dressed for the part in a white turtleneck sweater and blue jeans and was drinking from a can.

'In a storeroom. Garrotted.'

'How many of your men saw the killer?'

'Two.'

'And that's the only description you have?'

'He was wearing a false moustache and a wig,' said Greenberg defensively. 'We're not even sure about the eye colour. One of our guys thought he might be Mexican but that was probably the moustache. Do you think it was our man?'

'How close did he get to Discenza?'

'He stood right next to him. Why?'

'Because if he was that close and it was our killer, he'd have used a gun. A shot to the face, a shot to the heart. Business as usual. Did anyone else get hurt?'

'Nah. He pushed in the trolley, opened a couple of beers, and left. Two minutes later Discenza was dead. We'll have the poison identified by tomorrow.'

'It doesn't sound like the man we're looking for,' said the Colonel. 'As far as we know, he's never used poison.'

'You know what it means if it was,' said Greenberg.

'Yes, Dan. I know what it means.' If the assassin had discovered that Discenza had betrayed him, then the operation was blown. 'Has Discenza got any other enemies?'

'Like a dog's got fleas. He's crossed a lot of heavy guys in Miami.'

'The sort of people who'd be prepared to kill a man in protective custody?'

'It's possible.'

'Possible or probable?'

There was a long silence, then Greenberg exhaled. 'I'm not sure what it is you want me to say,' he said. 'We fucked up. I don't know who knocked off Discenza. It could have been the killer, it could have been someone hired by people in Miami, hell, it could even be someone from out of town. And the way things are going I don't think we're going to be any the wiser, not with the description we've got. It's got to be your call. If you want to cancel the operation, we'll understand.'

The Colonel tapped the receiver against his ear. 'No, we go ahead,' he said. 'As things stand, we put Discenza's death down to bad timing. If our killer doesn't attempt to carry out the Vander Mayer contract within two weeks, we'll know then that he's onto us.'

'Agreed,' said Greenberg.

'Can you keep a lid on the situation there, at least for two weeks?'

'No problem,' said Greenberg. 'We're doing the autopsy in-house and no one else knows that Discenza's dead.'

'Good,' said the Colonel. 'I don't want to be accused of trying to teach my grandmother to suck eggs, but you might want to look into how the killer discovered Discenza's location.'

'It's been taken care of,' said Greenberg. 'If I get anything, you'll be the first to know. Oh yeah, by the way, I got our guys to cross-check with previous killings, to see if the same method had been used before the current rash of killings. The guys at Quantico had already done it, but I did a check internally, just to be one hundred per cent sure.'

'And?'

'And it's just like I said, there's no match. Not recently, anyway. There was one guy about ten years back, he used to kill his victims with a shot to the head and one to the heart, but he's in a maximum security prison. And he's a psycho, he used to torture his victims with a wire coat hanger. There's no way he's our man. He's been well-documented by the profiling boys.'

'Any chance of you sending me the file?'

'Sure, I'll have his details faxed to you, but you'll be wasting your time. You could ask Jackman, I think he was with the Bureau at the time they were interviewing him. How's Jackman getting on?'

'He said he was off to South Africa to investigate the assassination there. He gave us a briefing before he went.'

'Was he much help?'

'Frankly, not really. What he gave us was academically interesting, but what we need is a description rather than a psychological profile.'

'Yeah, I know what you mean. But I bet you a month's pay, when we get the guy, we'll find that he matches Jackman's profile exactly. He's one of the best. The boys at Quantico really like him. We're lucky to have him on the case.'

'Well I'm sure that his bill will reflect his ability,' said the Colonel dryly.

'It's not the money,' said Greenberg. 'Jackman approached

us offering to help, we didn't go after him. He's working on a book about serial killers and I think he reckons the publicity will get him onto the bestseller list. Then there's his professional pride. He wants to be the best, or at least to be acknowledged as the best. You know the type. It's like he's got something to prove.'

'Yes, I know the type.' The SAS was full of such men, men who were driven to prove that they were the best. Mike Cramer had been such a man, willing to push himself beyond the limits of normal human endurance for no other reason than to demonstrate that he could. It wasn't only Cramer's terminal condition which had led him to accept the mission that the Colonel had offered. Cramer's willingness to go up against the killer was also a result of his desire to demonstrate that he was as good as ever, a bid to recapture his glory days. Yes, Cramer and Jackman had much in common, though Cramer's quest was likely to result in his own death while Jackman was only risking his professional reputation.

The Colonel stared at his chess computer as he replaced the receiver. The cursed machine had forced him into a corner, and there was nothing that the Colonel hated more than to have his options decided for him. He stared balefully at the pieces and stroked the side of his often-broken nose. He was no longer enjoying the game. It had stopped being fun, it was no longer even an intellectual challenge. Now it was war.

The boy stared at the television with unseeing eyes. It was some detective show set in San Francisco but he wasn't really watching. He kept on looking up at the ceiling, expecting to hear the thud of the walking stick on the bedroom floor at any minute. He stood up and paced around the room, his mind in turmoil. On the television, the two cops arrested a black guy, threw him against the car and put handcuffs on him.

He went into the hall and listened, but all he could hear was his own breathing. He went back into the living room and looked at the brass clock on the mantelpiece. It was half past four. His father wouldn't be home for another two hours. The boy swallowed. He looked up at the ceiling again, then back at the clock. He stood stock still for a full five minutes, then tiptoed upstairs and knocked timidly on the door to his mother's bedroom. There was no reply. He pressed his ear against the door and listened, his brow creased into a frown. He could hear his mother moaning. Slowly, as if afraid it would bite, he reached for the doorknob and turned it.

His mother was lying diagonally across the bed, one arm draped across the pillows, the other across her stomach. Her mouth was wide open and frothy, white fluid was trickling between her lips and dribbling onto the sheets. As the boy watched, horrified, she coughed and turned her head to the side. Her chest was heaving and she arched her back as if she was being electrocuted. Her hands were clenching and unclenching seemingly with a life of their own. The medicine bottle lay next to her. It was empty.

The boy walked over to the side of the bed and stood looking down on his mother. She began to mumble and he bent down to listen but the sounds that were coming from her mouth didn't make any sense. She'd knocked one of her pillows onto the floor and the boy picked it up. It was stained with sick and

435

saliva and spotted with blood. The boy clutched the pillow to his chest and closed his eyes, promising God that he'd do anything if only He'd spare his mother. He opened his eyes. The white stuff was coming from her nose. It was the milk, the boy realised. The milk he'd given her. He climbed up onto the bed and knelt over her, tears running down his cheeks. He kissed her on the forehead, lightly, then put the pillow over her face and pressed down with all his might.

Martin was finishing a bacon sandwich when Allan walked into the kitchen. 'Ready for the off?' Allan asked, putting his shirt on over the top of his bullet-proof vest.

Martin nodded and washed the sandwich down with several gulps of coffee. 'I'll get the Merc,' he said, wiping his mouth with the back of his hand. 'How's he doing?'

Allan shrugged his massive shoulders. 'He's quiet, but he's got a lot on his mind.'

'It takes balls to be a sitting duck, all right.' He picked up the car keys. 'I'll be outside.'

Martin took the elevator down to the ground floor and walked across the lobby. He couldn't be bothered with the lift down to the car park and took the stairs instead. The doorman on duty in the lower foyer nodded at Martin. 'Looks like rain,' said the doorman. Martin recognised him as Matt Richards, another of the SAS troopers who'd been at the school.

'Yeah, forecast said it was going to piss down.' Martin opened the door that led to the car park stairs. His footsteps echoed off the bare concrete walls as he headed downstairs.

The Mercedes was parked at the far end of the car park in the middle of three bays that had been allocated to the Vander Mayer apartment. Before he opened the door, Martin used a small mirror to check underneath the vehicle and peered through the side windows to make sure that nothing was amiss inside. When he was satisfied that the car hadn't been touched overnight, he opened the door electronically and slid in. His chauffeur's hat was on the passenger seat and he put it on, then looked at himself in the same mirror he'd used to inspect the underside of the car. He stuck out his tongue at his reflection and then dropped the mirror into his pocket. 'Hi ho, Silver, away,' he muttered to himself and started the car. All he could hear through the costly German sound-proofing was a faint purr, and there was barely any vibration. It was a beautiful car, but it wouldn't have been Martin's choice, if he'd had the money. The Mercedes was a soft man's car, built to insulate the occupants from the outside world. And it was a car designed not for driving, but to be driven in. He preferred something more aggressive, something with power, something that roared rather than purred. A Porsche, maybe, or an XJS.

He put the Mercedes in gear and slowly reversed. He didn't see the grey car until the last minute and he hit it side on, the bumper of the Mercedes crunching into the car's rear door. 'Where the hell did you come from?' he cursed, glaring at the car in his rear-view mirror. He doubted if he'd done much damage to the Mercedes, it was a much heavier car than the one he'd hit. He twisted around in his seat. The driver of the other car climbed out of the far side. Martin smiled when he saw it was a woman, and a pretty one at that.

'Women drivers,' sighed Martin, putting the Mercedes into neutral and applying the handbrake. He got a side view of the woman as she walked around to the passenger side of her car. She was a brunette, attractive, with an aerobics figure. Mid to late twenties, and almost certainly out of Martin's class. She put her hands on her hips and glared at the damage, then kicked the front wheel, hard. Martin smiled at her display of petulance, completely out of character with the designer clothes and *Vogue* make-up. He opened the door and climbed out. 'Not too bad, is it?' he asked.

The girl turned to face him, smiling pleasantly. 'Just perfect,' she said.

It was only when Martin felt the gun press into the small of his back that he remembered it was the same car that had been behind the Mercedes when they drove into Chelsea Harbour the previous evening.

Cramer was staring out of the window when Su-ming walked into the sitting room. She was wearing a cream silk suit, the trousers loose and the jacket with a mandarin collar, and she was carrying a black leather handbag. 'Good morning,' she said.

'Hi,' said Cramer. 'Did you finish your homework?' She frowned, not understanding. 'The paperwork,' he explained. 'Did you read it all?'

'Ah. Yes. Eventually. Are we ready?' She sounded curt

and business-like, and Cramer wondered again if he'd imagined the stolen kiss.

Allan came in from the kitchen. 'The car should be downstairs,' he said. 'Let's go.'

They walked together to the elevator. Su-ming stayed two paces behind Cramer as if trying to distance herself from him. Allan pressed the elevator button and smiled at Cramer. 'Sleep well?'

Cramer made a so-so gesture with his hand. He'd hardly slept at all.

Marie Hennessy wiped her hands on her skirt. They were damp with sweat and she couldn't afford to have them slipping on the steering wheel. She smiled to herself as she realised how strange it was that her hands were so wet and yet her mouth was bone dry. She swallowed but the muscles in her throat didn't seem to be working properly. Her hands began to tremble and she gripped the steering wheel tightly to stop the shaking. She was actually going to do it. She was going to go through with it. In a minute or two she was going to help kill the man who'd been responsible for the death of her parents. The anticipation was almost sexual. She'd waited so long for vengeance, and now Dermott Lynch was going to help her get it.

She pressed down on the accelerator, gunning the engine to make sure that the Rover didn't stall. The engine roared, echoing off the concrete walls of the subterranean car park, and she flinched as she realised that she risked drawing attention to herself. Soon, she thought. Soon it would all be over. All she had to do was to keep her nerve and to do exactly as Dermott had told her. She stared at the entrance to the apartment block, her heart racing. A figure appeared, walking through the double doors. It was the bodyguard, the one with the square jaw and the wide shoulders. Marie put the car in gear. It was time.

The Colonel looked at his wristwatch. It was nine o'clock and according to the schedule they should just be leaving the apartment. On the windowsill stood a transceiver. It was switched on, but only static crackled from the loudspeaker. The Colonel had insisted on radio silence until the moment that the assassin made his move. One of the Colonel's troopers came up behind him. 'Coffee, boss?' he said.

'Thanks, Blackie,' said the Colonel, taking the mug of black coffee. 'Everything ready for New York?'

'Kit's all packed.'

The Colonel tapped his stick on the bare floor. 'Tell the lads to be nice to the Yanks when we get there. No cracks about friendly fire, you know how sensitive they can be.'

The trooper grinned. 'Sure, boss.'

The Colonel turned back to the window and sipped his steaming coffee.

It was a cold morning but Cramer was sweating in the cashmere overcoat. Su-ming was still following in his footsteps. He stopped and waited for her to catch up. 'Are you okay?' he asked.

She jumped as if startled. 'What?'

'I asked if you were okay.'

She shivered. 'I'm fine.'

'You looked miles away.'

'I'm fine,' she replied. This time there was a hard edge to her voice as if she resented his intrusion into her thoughts. 'Where's the car?'

Cramer looked around. She was right. The Mercedes wasn't outside. Allan was standing on the pavement, looking around and stamping his feet impatiently. 'Stay where you are, Mr Vander Mayer,' he said. Cramer backed into the foyer with Su-ming. The doorman looked up, then visibly relaxed as he saw who it was. 'Okay,' Allan called. 'Here he comes.'

Lynch edged the Mercedes out of its parking space. Ahead of him he saw Marie in the Rover, a slight dent in the rear door on the passenger side. White smoke plumed from its exhaust. She looked apprehensive, staring straight ahead, her hands tight on the wheel. He wanted to nod or wave, to let her know that everything was all right, but he'd told her not to look at him, because any sort of acknowledgement would tip off the bodyguard.

'It's going to be okay, Marie, love,' Lynch whispered to himself. He had the peak of the chauffeur's cap pulled low over his nose and he was wearing the chauffeur's jacket. On the passenger seat lay the gun the chauffeur had been carrying in an underarm holster, but Lynch was planning to use the Czech 9mm he'd brought with him. The ten bullets in the clip would be more than enough, so long as Marie kept her nerve. Lynch turned the Mercedes to the right and headed towards the apartment entrance. On the pavement the bodyguard was waving to Cramer and the girl, urging them out of the foyer.

Allan swivelled around, checking the surroundings for possible threats. Most of the parking spaces were occupied by expensive cars, including several Rolls-Royces and a Ferrari. A young woman was sitting at the wheel of a Rover and was preparing to drive out of the car park. She seemed to be alone in the car. Cramer and Su-ming joined Allan on the pavement.

The Mercedes was about fifty feet away and Allan moved to the edge of the pavement, preparing to open the door for Cramer and the girl. The Rover accelerated. Allan frowned. She wasn't heading for the exit, she was heading directly for the apartment entrance. Something was wrong.

Allan stepped between the car and Cramer, holding his left arm out to the side, ready to push Cramer back. He kept his eyes on the Rover. He half expected to see a man with a gun appear from the back seat but the young woman was definitely alone in the car. 'Stay back,' Allan said to Cramer. The Mercedes was still heading towards them and Allan beckoned it with his hand. If Martin put his foot down he'd get in front of the Rover and the threat would be neutralised. The Mercedes continued to crawl towards them.

'Back in the foyer,' said Allan, but as he spoke the Rover's tyres squealed and the car leapt forward. Su-ming screamed. Allan reached for his gun with his right hand and pushed Cramer with his left. His fingers touched the butt of the gun, but before he could pull it out the Rover was upon him. He threw himself to the right but the wing clipped him and he heard his leg snap above the knee. The pain followed a second later as if his whole leg was on fire and he bit down on his lip to stifle a scream.

The Rover veered to the left and sped away. Allan rolled across the pavement in agony, the gun falling from his fingers. The Mercedes accelerated towards them, its engine roaring in the confines of the car park.

The Colonel blew across his coffee mug. The steam condensed on the window pane and he rubbed it away with his hand. Down on the luxury motor yacht, the trooper was washing down the decks with a bucket and sponge.

A grey-haired man in a blazer and white slacks was helping two blonde teenage girls onto a fifty-foot motor launch. The Thames was at its lowest level of the day and the channel connecting the marina to the river was empty, so the man obviously wasn't planning to take the boat out, not for a few hours at least. The taller of the two blondes stumbled as she stepped from the dock onto the boat and the man put a hand on her backside to steady her. The Colonel supposed the man might just be the girls' father, but there was no mistaking the predatory gleam in his eyes. They disappeared inside the boat. It was, thought the Colonel, entirely possible that the man was showing them the engine room. 'And pigs might fly,' he mused.

The Colonel looked over at the tower block. Vander Mayer's apartment was almost at the top of the tower. The sun was reflected off the windows so the Colonel couldn't see inside. He shaded his eyes with his right hand but it didn't make any difference.

Behind him, his fax machine rang, three times, and then it hummed as a fax began to come through. Down in the marina, the motor yacht began to rock gently. The Colonel shook his head in amazement, then he realised that it made sense. Eyebrows might be raised if an elderly man booked into a hotel with two young girls, so a luxury boat moored close to the city centre made a perfect venue for illicit assignations, providing you had the money. The Colonel wondered how much the boat had cost. A hundred thousand pounds? Maybe more.

The first sheet fell out of the machine. It was a memo from Dan Greenberg saying that he was faxing the notes on the killer they'd spoken about. His name was Anton Madeley, and he'd been held in Marrion Prison for the past nine years, mostly in solitary confinement. The Colonel stood by the machine as the second sheet began to spew out.

It was halfway out of the machine when the transceiver crackled. It was Richards, the young trooper who was sitting in the foyer by the car park. 'Allan's been hit,' said Richards. 'Allan's been hit in the car park.'

The Colonel dropped his mug as he turned and grabbed the transceiver. He pressed the transmit button. 'Move in!' he yelled. 'Everybody move in now!'

*   *   *

Cramer and Su-ming dashed over to Allan. He was lying on the pavement like a broken marionette, his right leg sticking out at an awkward angle, blood pouring from the knee. 'Get back!' Allan shouted. 'Get the fuck out of here!'

'It's okay, she's gone,' said Cramer. As Su-ming examined the damage to Allan's leg, the Mercedes pulled up in front of them. Cramer looked up, expecting to see Martin at the wheel. He did a double-take as he realised that the man in the chauffeur's cap wasn't Martin.

Allan reached along the pavement for his gun. The man in the Mercedes threw open the car door and fired twice at Allan. The first shot screamed off the pavement inches from his hand, the second hit him in the right shoulder, close to the neck. Cramer got to his feet, pushing Su-ming behind him. Allan lay on the floor, gasping for breath as blood gushed around his shoulders.

The man in the chauffeur's cap pointed his gun at Cramer's face. 'No!' screamed Su-ming from behind Cramer.

Matt Richards didn't hear the Rover accelerate but he heard the thud as it hit Allan. He yelled into his transceiver as he pulled his Heckler & Koch MP5 submachine gun from under his seat, then leapt over the counter. He almost slipped on the marble foyer but quickly regained his balance as he brought his weapon up into the firing position. He ran towards the double doors, slipping his finger onto the trigger. On the pavement outside he saw Cramer and the girl standing in front of Martin, while Allan lay on the ground, blood pooling around his neck. The car that had hit Allan was screeching away, towards the exit. For a second Richards was confused; he couldn't understand why Cramer and Martin weren't firing after the car. Then realisation hit him like a shower of freezing water – it wasn't Martin wearing the chauffeur's cap, and whoever it was he was holding a gun on Cramer.

The double doors hissed open as Richards got within three paces of the electronic sensor. He saw the man with the gun look over Cramer's shoulder. The man's eyes opened wide with surprise as he spotted Richards. Richards stepped to the side, trying to get a clear shot but Cramer and the girl were in the way. 'Down! Down! Down!' Richards screamed, the staccato commands piercing the air like bullets.

Lynch had no idea who the doorman was or why he had a high-powered automatic weapon in his hands, but he knew that he was in big trouble. What had started as a straightforward hit was escalating into a full-scale war. He aimed the gun at Cramer's face and tightened his finger on the trigger, but as he did so the doorman began to scream for Cramer to get down and Lynch knew that if he didn't react immediately he was going to die there and then on the pavement.

Lynch swung his pistol to the left and fired at the doorman. The bullet whizzed past Cramer's face, missing him by inches. The first shot hit the doorman square in the chest and it knocked him back, but Lynch could see that there was no blood. The man's face was contorted with pain but he kept hold of his weapon. Lynch realised he must be wearing a bullet-proof vest under his charcoal grey uniform.

Cramer dived to the side, pushing the girl out of the way. Lynch ignored them. He fired two shots at the doorman in quick succession. The first hit the upper part of the man's chest and from the dull thud it made Lynch could tell that it had hit the reinforced vest. There was no mistaking where the third bullet went. It hit the doorman in the throat, snapping the man's head back. Blood poured down the man's chest and his weapon clattered to the floor. Cramer and the girl were down on the pavement. Cramer was on top of her, shielding her with his body as he reached inside his coat. Lynch grinned and brought his aim to bear on Cramer's face. He grinned. He had five shots left. More than enough.

Marie Hennessy hit the brakes. She looked over her shoulder, wondering why Lynch was still standing in front of the apartment entrance. His instructions had been crystal clear. She was to take out the bodyguard with the car, Lynch was to pull up in the Mercedes, shoot Cramer, and then run to the Rover. They'd used the street map to work out the quickest way to Fulham Broadway Station, where they would abandon the car and disappear into the Underground system.

Marie had done her bit, she'd hit the guy hard, though it appeared that she hadn't hit him hard enough because she'd kept one eye on the rear-view mirror and had seen Lynch shoot him twice as he lay on the ground. There had been three more shots, but when she turned around she could see Lynch still standing there with his gun aimed at Cramer. Cramer didn't appear to be dead, he was lying on top of the Oriental girl and staring up at Lynch. Cramer's hand was inside his coat but it seemed to be frozen there. 'Come on, Dermott,' Marie hissed. 'Come on.'

Cramer glared up at the man with the gun, his teeth bared like a cornered dog. His fingers were touching the butt of his Walther PPK but he knew it would be futile to pull out the weapon. He slowly withdrew his hand, his eyes fixed on his attacker. Why hadn't the man fired? It didn't make any sense. All he had to do was pull the trigger and it would all be over. He felt Su-ming struggle and he rolled off her. The barrel of the gun followed him like an accusing finger. In the distance he heard the Rover's horn blare. The man ignored it. There was hatred in the man's eyes, a burning contempt that suggested he was going to enjoy killing Cramer. A small part of Cramer was surprised by the man's emotional intensity, because everything he'd read about the assassin suggested that he was a stone cold killer, a consummate professional.

Su-ming crawled away until her back was against the wall, her eyes wide with fear. 'Don't,' she whispered, her hands covering her face. 'Please don't.' Cramer wondered if she was pleading for her own life or for his, he had no way of telling which. Whatever, Cramer himself had no intention of begging for mercy.

'Do it,' Cramer growled.

'No!' shouted Su-ming.

Cramer rolled over, putting more distance between himself and Su-ming. He looked into the barrel of the gun. He imagined he could see the bullet there, the bullet that would shortly smash through his skull and blow his brains across the concrete. The cold, clinical part of his mind hoped that the blood wouldn't spray across Su-ming's silk suit. He forced himself to look away from the gun and into the eyes of the man who was about to end his life.

'Do it!' Cramer hissed. He pushed himself up off the ground and sat back on his heels. He glared at the man with the gun.

The man smiled cruelly. Cramer imagined he could see the knuckle of his trigger finger whiten as he increased the pressure. Cramer had an unexpected feeling of well-being, and he realised that he really wasn't scared of death, that there were worse things than a shot to the head, and that the man with the gun was actually doing him a favour. Cramer smiled.

The man with the gun seemed confused, as if a smile was the last thing he expected to see on the face of his victim. Then the confusion vanished, leaving only hatred in his eyes. 'This is for . . .' the man began, and then his face exploded outward in a mass of pink brain tissue and splinters of white bone. The bloody fragments splattered across Cramer, blinding him. He didn't see the second shot or the third, but when he wiped the blood from his eyes he saw the man with the gun pitch forward and slam into the ground.

Allan had levered himself up on one elbow. His gun was in his left hand, shaking from the effort of shooting the man. The Glock tumbled from Allan's hand as he fell back onto the pavement.

Marie Hennessy screamed as she saw Lynch pitch forward, blood streaming from his face. She threw the Rover into gear and stamped on the accelerator. She had no doubt that Lynch was dead; there had been hardly anything left of his face.

The barrier at the exit to the car park was down but Marie didn't hesitate. The Rover crashed through the pole, which collapsed in a shriek of tearing metal. The steering wheel bucked and twisted as if it had a life of its own and Marie fought to control it. She wrenched it to the right and the rear wheels skidded on the tarmac. A black taxi with its hire light on was heading down the road towards her and she narrowly missed colliding with it. The Rover banged against the kerb and a hubcap was ripped off in a shower of sparks but Marie regained control and sped off down the road.

The white walls of an apartment block went by in a blur. She risked a quick look in her driving mirror and smiled grimly as she saw that there was no one following her. As her eyes flicked back to the road ahead of her, she noticed a man in a white turtleneck sweater and jeans standing by the roadside, a large automatic held in both hands. She saw the gun kick up and instantly her side window shattered. A piece of glass sliced through her cheek but she scarcely felt the pain. As she passed the man he fired again, and she heard a dull metallic thud as the bullet buried itself in the rear wing of the Rover.

Marie was hit by a wave of elation as she realised that she'd got away. The road ahead was deserted, if she could just make it to the tube station she'd be free and clear. She pressed the accelerator to the floor, but suddenly she heard another shot and then the car juddered and veered to the left. The steering wheel twisted out of her hands and the car hit the kerb. Marie realised with clinical detachment that the man in the sweater had hit one of her tyres. The Rover slammed into a street lamp and then began to skid sideways. The car tipped up and Marie's head banged against the back of her seat, hard enough to stun her. She closed her eyes and almost passed out. Her stomach heaved as the car rolled and the top of her head slammed against the roof. The windows exploded and she was showered with broken glass and then she was thrown forward against the steering wheel, so hard that the breath was forced from her body. The car came to a halt, upside down, rocking from side to side. Marie could taste blood in her mouth and she realised she'd bitten her tongue. She coughed and spat to clear her throat, then gingerly moved her arms and legs. She was all right. She wasn't even really hurt. She felt light-headed and giggled despite herself. She'd been shot at, she'd survived a car crash, it was as if the fates had decreed that she should emerge from the debacle relatively unscathed. She reached for the door handle and tried to open the door. It was jammed, the frame had been distorted by the crash. Marie wriggled around and managed to get hold of one of her shoes. She used it to smash away the remaining pieces of glass. All she had to do was to crawl out then she'd be able to run to the tube. She was going to be okay. That was when she smelled the petrol seeping out of the ruptured tank. There was a loud whooshing sound as the petrol ignited and Marie Hennessy began to scream as she realised just what a cruel sense of humour the fates truly had.

Cramer crawled over to Allan. Blood was oozing from the wound in his shoulder but it didn't look fatal. He took off his overcoat, rolled it up and stuck it under Allan's head. 'Thanks, Mum,' said Allan, his eyes still closed. For a wild moment Cramer thought Allan was delirious but then he opened his eyes and grinned up at him. 'I got him, huh?' asked Allan.

'And some,' said Cramer. 'It's his blood I'm wearing all over my face.'

'Su-ming?'

'She's okay. Now lie still and shut up.'

'Okay, but tell me one thing first.'

'What?'

'What happened to all our fucking training, Mike? You stood there like a rabbit caught in headlights.'

Cramer felt his cheeks redden. 'I'm sorry.'

'You froze.'

'Yeah. I froze. I'm sorry.'

Su-ming came up behind Cramer. She took off her shirt and gave it to him. 'Use this,' she said.

Cramer used the silk shirt to stem the bleeding from Allan's shoulder. It looked as if the bullet had gone straight through. 'Can you move your fingers?' Cramer asked. He watched Allan wiggle the fingers of his right hand. At least the nerves weren't damaged.

'Do you think I'll be able to play the piano again?' Allan asked. Cramer couldn't help smiling.

'Will he be all right?' Su-ming asked.

'He'll be fine.'

'Now it's over?'

Cramer looked at the body of the killer, sprawled on the ground, the head surrounded by a halo of congealing blood. 'Yes,' he said. 'It's over.' As he said the words he was aware of a nagging doubt at the back of his mind.

Cramer took off his tie and threw it onto a chair. He stared out through the picture window at the sprawling city. Six million people, give or take. He wondered how many would ever be aware of what had happened in the underground car park. Half a dozen, maybe. It wasn't the sort of operation that would be trumpeted to the press. The bodies would be taken away; the trooper buried in Hereford with the minimum of fuss, his name added to the plaque on the regimental chapel wall where the SAS remembered those who had died on active service; the assassin probably cremated with no memorial to mark his passing. There would be no inquest, no investigation, no publicity. It would be as if it had never happened.

The Walther was still in its holster but Cramer was reluctant to take it out. Removing the gun would signify that the operation was over, and that was something that Cramer wasn't yet prepared to deal with. It had all happened so quickly that he hadn't had time to think about the future. His future.

He rubbed his stomach. The pain was pretty much constant, though occasionally it felt as if a knife was being twisted deep inside, a reminder that he shouldn't be complacent, that there was worse to come. While he was being trained, and while he was waiting for the assassin to make his move, Cramer had managed to blot the pain out of his mind, but now it was over it had returned with a vengeance.

He realised that Su-ming wasn't in the room with him. He went in search of her and found her in Vander Mayer's study, standing by the desk. She looked up as he walked towards her. 'Cramer . . .' she said, her voice trembling.

She was shaking as if she had a fever and there were tears in her eyes. Cramer stepped forward and held her tightly, pressing her against himself as if his life depended on it. Her small hands slipped around his waist as she buried her face in his chest. Cramer stroked her black, silky hair with his right hand as she sobbed. 'Hey, it's all right,' he soothed.

He caught sight of his reflection in the mirrored wall. Su-ming looked like a child next to him and he suddenly felt big and clumsy. Cramer saw that he still had the killer's blood on his face. He looked like he'd just walked away from a traffic accident; there were black circles under his eyes, his hair was in disarray and there was an unhealthy pallor to his skin. He hadn't realised until then how sick he looked. She squeezed him but there was hardly any strength in the movement and she continued to cry softly. Cramer wondered if it was the first time she'd seen anyone killed. Flying first-class around the world with an international arms-dealer was one thing, seeing the effects of the tools of the trade close-up was a different matter all together.

The doorbell rang. He tried to untangle her arms from around his waist but she tightened her grip and wouldn't let him go. The doorbell rang again. 'I have to get it,' said Cramer. Su-ming reluctantly released him and Cramer went back to the sitting room to answer the door.

It was the Colonel. 'Are you okay?' he asked.

Cramer nodded. 'How's Allan?'

'The paramedics said he'll be okay. Allan keeps insisting that it's just a flesh wound, but he'd say that if his arm had been blown off. You know what he's like.'

'Yeah. He saved my life.'

'He did his job. You both did, Joker. You should be proud of yourself.'

'I fucked up,' said Cramer. 'I fucked up big time.'

'We got the guy, and that's what counts.'

'I froze. I pushed Su-ming out of the way, then I froze. I did everything wrong.'

The Colonel tapped his walking stick on the wooden floor. 'Stop playing the martyr, will you? We took out a professional killer, the best in the business. And we did it with the minimum of casualties. No one's blaming you, Joker. No one. How is Su-ming?'

'She's in shock,' Cramer answered.

'The doctor's on his way. He'll give her something.'

Cramer nodded, but he wasn't convinced that it was tablets that Su-ming needed. 'What about Martin?' he asked.

The Colonel grinned. 'Just a bump on the head. He was in the boot of the Mercedes, bound and gagged. He's embarrassed more than anything.'

'He's lucky they didn't kill him.'

'There was no need. Vander Mayer was the target, and Martin wasn't a threat. Allan was.'

Cramer rubbed his forehead with the palm of his hand. He was sweating. 'That's what I can't figure out,' he said. 'Why did he hesitate?'

'What do you mean?' asked the Colonel.

'He had the drop on me, Colonel. He had me bang to rights. But he waited.'

'It was bedlam, Joker. He was in the middle of a firefight. Richards was there, Allan had his gun out, it wasn't going the way he'd planned.'

'Yeah, but he's always been such a pro in the past. Nothing's fazed him before.'

'No one had set him up before.' The Colonel put a reassuring hand on Cramer's shoulder. 'You're worrying too much.'

'Post-traumatic stress syndrome?' said Cramer, sarcastically. 'I don't think so. Been there, done that. This is different. Something's not right. He was trying to say something. Before he pulled the trigger, he wanted to tell me something.'

The Colonel squeezed Cramer's shoulder. 'Forget it. You're worrying about nothing. You did a good job, Joker. A hell of a job.'

'Thanks, Colonel.' Cramer shook his head as if trying to clear his thoughts. 'What happens now?'

'I'm winding down the operation here. We'll run the killer's prints through the Fingerprint Bureau and we should have an ID by tonight.'

'I meant, what happens to me?'

There was an uncomfortable silence as the Colonel

considered Cramer's question. 'What do you want to do?' asked the Colonel eventually.

'I don't know. I really don't know.'

'Why don't you sleep on it. We'll talk about it tomorrow.'

'It's not as if I have many options, is it?'

'We'll talk about it tomorrow,' the Colonel repeated firmly. 'Okay?'

Cramer nodded. He showed the Colonel out and then went back to the study. Su-ming didn't appear to have moved. He put his arms around her. She'd stopped trembling, now she was as stiff as a tailor's dummy. They stood together in silence, looking out of the window.

It was Su-ming who broke away first. 'I have to call Mr Vander Mayer,' she said.

'Sure. He'll be glad to hear that he's in the clear.'

Su-ming picked up the phone and looked at Cramer. The message in her eyes was obvious. She wanted to make the call in private.

Cramer shrugged and walked disconsolately back to the sitting room. He stared out of the window, deep in thought. A few minutes later she reappeared carrying a mobile telephone. 'He wants to speak with you,' she said, holding it out.

There was static on the line and a short satellite delay. 'Mike? Congratulations. First class.'

'Thanks,' said Cramer. He didn't think that two men in hospital and a dead SAS trooper was something to be congratulated on. And he was still embarrassed about his own performance, or lack of it.

'Mike, listen. Remember the conversation we had before? About the Russian consignment?'

'Yes. I remember.'

'Well I want you to stay with it until I get there.'

'It's in your safe,' said Cramer. 'It's not going anywhere.'

'I'd feel a lot happier if you'd keep an eye on it,' said Vander Mayer. 'The fee we spoke of, it's still available. A quarter of a million dollars.'

Cramer looked at Su-ming. She was pacing up and down in front of the window. 'Where are you now?' he asked.

'I can be there in eight hours. Nine, max.'

Cramer nodded slowly. 'Okay. I'll be here.'

'Great, Mike. Great. Now put Su-ming back on will you?'

Cramer handed the phone back to Su-ming. She pressed it to her ear and walked back along the corridor to the study, her shoes making no sound on the polished wooden floor. As she left the sitting room she whispered into the receiver but Cramer couldn't hear what she was saying.

The Colonel picked up the phone and tapped out Dan Greenberg's private number. The FBI agent answered on the second ring. The Colonel gave him a quick rundown on the situation but Greenberg interrupted him before he could finish. 'Hot damn, good job,' said Greenberg. The Colonel heard him shout over to his co-workers that the Brits had got their man. 'You guys deserve a medal,' said Greenberg. 'And you saved us the cost of a trial, huh?'

'That wasn't intentional, Dan,' said the Colonel archly. 'He was about to kill our man.'

'Same MO as the previous killings?'

'He was close in and going for a head-shot,' said the Colonel. 'He wasn't working alone, though. He had a woman with him. She's dead, too.'

'It won't be the first time he's had help,' said Greenberg. 'Any idea who she is?'

'No, and it's unlikely we'll ever know. Her car went up in flames. We'll run a check on her dental work, but we don't even know where she's from. We'll have more luck with the killer. His face was shot up but we're running his prints through our records now. I'm sending copies to you.'

'If he's on file, we'll match them,' said Greenberg. 'And thanks, Colonel, I owe you one.'

The Colonel replaced the receiver. 'Yes, Dan,' he said to himself. 'You certainly do.'

The doorbell rang. Su-ming was still in Vander Mayer's study so Cramer lifted himself off the sofa, grunting with pain as his stomach muscles tightened. He opened the door to find the doctor whom he'd last seen at the school in Wales. Dr Greene looked at Cramer over the top of his gold-framed bifocal spectacles. 'Sergeant Cramer, you can't believe how pleased I am to see you in one piece,' he said.

Cramer stepped aside to let the doctor in. He was wearing the same brown cardigan with leather elbow patches that he'd had on in Wales. Cramer wondered if it was some sort of uniform the man wore to put his patients at ease.

The doctor put his black leather medical bag down on

one of the marble coffee tables then turned to face Cramer. 'How have you been?' Dr Greene asked.

Cramer was going to say something sarcastic, but he restrained himself. He knew that the doctor was sincere and only trying to help. 'Worse,' said Cramer. 'Much worse.'

The doctor nodded sympathetically. 'What about your motions?'

Cramer smiled grimly. 'Motions?' he repeated.

'You know what I mean,' Dr Greene said. 'How are you in the toilet department?'

'It's painful,' said Cramer. 'And bloody.'

'Constant pain?'

'Constant dull pain, like a toothache. Then bolts of pain that come and go.'

'Getting worse?'

Cramer paused. He hated showing weakness but he realised there was no point in papering over the cracks. He was sick, and he needed help. He nodded. 'Much worse.'

The doctor bent over his bag. He clicked it open and took out a bottle of capsules. He held them out to Cramer. 'Take as many of these as you need to kill the pain,' he said. 'But no more than eight in one day. They're stronger than the others I gave you.'

Cramer took the bottle. There was no label. He wondered whether the doctor's instructions were a subtle way of telling him how many he'd need to take if he decided to end it all. 'Thanks,' he said.

Dr Greene looked at him gravely. 'They'll only do the job temporarily,' he said. 'A week, maybe a little longer. Then I'll have to give you something stronger, something in liquid form. I'll come and see you next week and we'll see how you're getting on.'

Cramer put the tablets in his jacket pocket. He wanted to swallow a couple there and then, but that would have been too much of an admission of what a bad state he was in. He forced a smile. 'Hopefully it won't be necessary,' he said.

The doctor looked at Cramer. He nodded as if he understood. 'I wish there was something else I could do,' he said.

'You and me both, Doc, but I'm not complaining.'

Dr Greene clicked his bag shut and picked it up. 'I'm told that the girl might need my attention. What's her name, Sue something or other?'

'Su-ming,' said Cramer. 'I think she's okay now.'

The doctor raised an eyebrow. 'I think I should be the judge of that,' he said.

Cramer nodded wearily. 'She's in the study. Down the corridor, on the right.' He waited until the doctor had left the sitting room before taking the bottle out of his pocket. He swallowed two of the capsules dry, almost choking on the second one. He sat down on the sofa facing the balcony and poured the capsules out of the bottle and into the palm of his hand. There were thirty-six. More than enough, said a small voice in the back of his mind. He tipped the capsules into the bottle and screwed the cap back on.

Dr Greene came back into the room. 'She seems to have calmed down,' he told Cramer.

'Have you prescribed her anything?'

The doctor shook his head. 'The best thing for her is a cup of hot, sweet tea. And someone to talk to.'

'I'll take care of her,' said Cramer. He stood up and showed the doctor to the door.

On the threshold the doctor turned to face him. He put

a hand on Cramer's shoulder. 'I hope I see you again,' he said.

Cramer looked at him levelly. 'Don't count on it, Doc,' he said quietly.

The doctor held Cramer's look for several seconds. It seemed to Cramer that he was struggling to find the right words to say but before he could speak Cramer shut the door. He went back to the sofa and sat down. The bottle of tablets was on the coffee table and he picked it up and shook it. Eight, the doctor had said. Cramer figured sixteen would be better, to make absolutely sure. He began to unscrew the cap from the bottle, but suddenly stopped. He felt ashamed of what he was doing. There was no honour in swallowing tablets, it was a coward's way out. Embezzling accountants or wronged wives took tablets. Soldiers didn't. Soldiers fought like men and died like men.

He took the Walther PPK out of his shoulder holster, ejected the clip and checked that it was fully loaded – an unnecessary precaution because he hadn't used it since he'd left Wales. He smiled to himself as he remembered a joke he'd heard while on a surveillance mission in the Falklands, lying in a trench overlooking Goose Green for three days, drinking rainwater and shitting into a plastic bag. The joke involved the Argentinians playing Russian roulette with an automatic, and at the time Cramer had thought it was the funniest thing he'd ever heard. Now, with a loaded automatic in his hand, it didn't seem so amusing. He slotted the clip back into the weapon and flicked off the safety. His throat was dry, but it was going to be easier to swallow the barrel of the gun than it would have been to swallow the capsules.

Cramer took a deep breath. The dull ache in his stomach

had begun to ease. He wondered if it was the medicine starting to weaken it or if the fear of what he was about to do was stimulating his body's own natural painkillers. Whatever, in a few seconds he wouldn't be feeling any pain. He took several deep breaths, then slowly brought the gun up so that the barrel was touching the tip of his nose. He could smell the lubricating oil that he'd used the last time he'd cleaned it. He licked his lips. They were as dry as his throat. He closed his eyes as if in prayer, but Mike Cramer had long since stopped believing in God or any higher power. It wasn't heaven he was planning to visit, just a dark empty place where there would be no pain and no regrets. All it would take was to put the barrel in his mouth and pull the trigger. He'd fired the gun a thousand times on the range in the school, with Allan shouting encouragement. He could pull the trigger one last time. He pictured Allan standing behind him. Point. Aim. Take a breath. Let half of it out. Squeeze, don't jerk. He imagined Allan's voice, calm and confident. Cramer slipped the barrel between his lips. He almost gagged on the metal cylinder as his thumb tightened on the trigger. He took a deep breath. Slowly he began to exhale.

'Cramer?' Su-ming's voice pierced his thoughts like a lance. He opened his eyes. Before he could react she had put her hands over his and pulled the gun away from his face. 'What the hell are you doing?'

'What does it look like?'

'How dare you?' she said angrily. She twisted the gun out of his grasp. He was much stronger than she was but she took him by surprise. 'How dare you do this?' She stood in front of him, her eyes flashing.

Cramer was genuinely confused. 'What do you mean?'

She held the gun in front of his face. 'You'd do this, with me here? How do you think I'd feel? You'd kill yourself with me in the next room? Just what was I expected to do, Mike Cramer? Wait for the ambulance to come? Have you die in my arms?'

'Hey . . .'

She shook her head. 'Don't hey me, don't you dare hey me.' She slammed the Walther down on the coffee table.

'Jesus, Su-ming, be careful,' said Cramer. 'It could go off.'

She glared at him and Cramer couldn't help but smile. 'Don't laugh at me,' she said. 'This isn't funny.'

He held up his hands in surrender. 'I'm not laughing at you,' he said. 'It's just ironic, that's all. There was I going to . . . you know . . . and now I'm worried that it might go off accidentally.'

'English humour?' she said dismissively. 'Well, I don't think there's anything funny about trying to kill yourself.'

Cramer sat back in the sofa and looked away. She picked up the bottle of capsules. 'What are these?' she asked.

'Painkillers,' he said.

She frowned and sat down on the sofa next to him. She put a hand on his leg, her touch as soft as a child's kiss. 'How sick are you?' she asked.

'Very,' he said. He finally turned to look at her. 'Why else do you think I'd . . . ?' He left the sentence unfinished.

'I didn't know,' she said. 'I didn't realise.'

'I thought you were psychic,' said Cramer, unable to keep the bitterness out of his voice.

'I have feelings, that's all. But I always found it difficult to read you, Cramer.'

'Yeah? Why's that?'

Su-ming lowered her eyes. 'I was confused,' she said.

'Well, now you know,' he said. He looked across at her. Her hair had fallen across her face like a black veil. 'What do you mean, confused?'

'Nothing,' she said.

Cramer snorted softly. 'Not that it matters now.'

'What do you mean?'

'I'm dying, Su-ming. I'm not going to get better, there's nothing anyone can do. I'm going to die and I'm going to die in a great deal of pain.'

'Isn't there . . . ?'

'There's nothing,' he interrupted sharply. 'There's no miracle cure, no operation, no nothing.'

Su-ming held up the bottle of capsules. 'Don't these help?'

'A bit. But they're not a cure, they just dull the pain. They're only temporary. Su-ming, I really don't want to talk about this. Just go. Leave me alone.'

'So you can kill yourself?'

Cramer shrugged half-heartedly. 'Don't make this harder than it is.' She pushed her hair behind her ears. There were tears in her eyes but she blinked them away as if she didn't want him to see her cry. 'Remember when you gave me the *I Ching* reading?' he asked.

'Of course.'

'I had to ask a question, remember?' Su-ming nodded. 'And you remember the answer?'

'An end to sadness,' she said softly.

'That's right. An end to sadness. And I had to bring about that end myself. That's what the *I Ching* said. The change must come from within. That was the answer to my question.'

'And what was the question, Cramer?'

Cramer rubbed his hands together as if trying to keep warm. 'I wanted to know how I'd die,' he said, his voice a hoarse whisper.

Su-ming said nothing for a few seconds, then she impulsively put her arms around him and held him close. He felt something soft brush against his cheek and he realised that she'd kissed him.

The Colonel sat down at his desk as two troopers carried large cardboard boxes out of the apartment. The telephones and fax machines were still in place. The Colonel had hoped to receive confirmation of the assassin's identity before leaving for Hereford, but it appeared that it wasn't going to happen. He thought about calling Dan Greenberg to see if the Bureau had managed to obtain a match through their files, but decided against it. He was sure that Greenberg would notify him if he'd come up with an identification.

A sheaf of fax paper lay in the tray connected to the fax machine. It was the information that Greenberg had been sending through when the assassin had struck. The Colonel hadn't had time to look through the faxes. He picked them up and was about to run them through a shredding machine when he had second thoughts. He flicked through the sheets. There were more than twenty sheets of close-typed reports, most of them from FBI files. The Colonel settled back in his high-backed chair and started to read. Anton Madeley was a nasty piece of work, and if he hadn't been locked up in Marion Prison he could well have been a suspect in the recent killings. Marion Prison was a super-maximum security facility built by the US Federal Bureau of Prisons to replace Alcatraz, surrounded by a thirty-foot-high fence and bullet-proof watchtowers. Only the worst of the worst ended up there, and all of them were kept in virtually permanent solitary confinement. According to the psychiatric reports compiled before Madeley was sentenced, he had psychopathic tendencies but was well aware of what he had been doing. He'd tortured more than a dozen men and women, then killed them. There was no sexual motive, the psychiatrists reported, it appeared that Madeley was more interested in causing pain. And once he'd had his fill of torturing his victims, his method of killing them was always the same: two shots with a handgun, one shot to the face, one to the heart.

The Colonel scratched his chin. According to the psychiatric reports, Madeley believed that shooting his victims in the head trapped their soul, extending their misery into eternity. The man was obviously demented, but the psychiatrists insisted he was sane and should be sentenced as such. The Colonel wondered if Madeley had a relative who had decided to carry on his legacy. He flicked through the sheets and came to a sheet of biographical data. Madeley was fifty-two years old, had never married and had no known children. He was an only child, his mother had died when he was twelve and his father had abused him, physically and mentally. Madeley was taken into care and spent four years with foster parents, parents who Madeley claimed abused him as much as his father ever did. There appeared to be no one who was close to Madeley, so the Colonel discounted his theory that it was a family member whom Allan had killed in the car park. Madeley had left the foster home when he was sixteen and spent the rest of his life in and out of prisons, initially for stealing cars and graduating swiftly to mail order fraud. He had no known friends or associates, he was a true loner.

The file included summarised reports by FBI profilers from Quantico who had visited Madeley in Marion Prison, though he appeared to be unhelpful and uncommunicative. The last two sheets detailed all the visitors Madeley had received during his time in imprisonment. The Colonel ran his finger down the list. There were no family members, no friends; every name was a law enforcement officer, legal representative or psychiatrist. Bernard Jackman's name appeared on the second sheet, initially visiting Madeley once a month, but then with increasing frequency, until at one point he met with the serial killer each day for a week. Jackman's name was absent from the final section of the list, his place appeared to have been taken by another profiler. The Colonel realised it was because at that stage Jackman had left the Bureau to set up on his own.

One of the troopers came back into the apartment. 'We're all clear, boss,' he said.

'Okay, Blackie. You can pack up the communications equipment.' He fed the sheets of fax paper through the shredder by the side of the desk. 'The shredder can go, too,' he added.

The doorbell jarred Cramer awake. He was disorientated for a few seconds until he realised he was lying on a sofa, his face buried in the soft black leather. He rolled over.

The sky had darkened outside and several stars twinkled among the clouds. He couldn't remember falling asleep. As he sat up he felt nauseous and he wondered if it was a side-effect of the painkillers. The doorbell rang again. Su-ming walked along the corridor and into the sitting room. 'I'll get it,' she said.

'Yeah, I'm sorry,' he said. 'I fell asleep.' Cramer realised that there was a blanket over his legs.

'I know,' she said, smiling. She'd changed into blue jeans and a white silk shirt and she looked fresh and clean as if she'd just had a shower.

Cramer could taste something bitter at the back of his throat. He swallowed and grimaced. As he looked around he realised that the bottle of capsules and the Walther PPK were no longer on the coffee table. Su-ming must have moved them while he was asleep. He rubbed his face with his hands. When he took his hands away, Su-ming had the door open. A man walked into the room carrying a slim leather briefcase. He was in his mid to late forties, a dapper little man who couldn't have been much more then five feet eight tall. His hair was slicked back and he had the sleek, well-fed look of a man who lived off expense accounts. 'This is Mr Vander Mayer,' said Su-ming as she closed the door.

Vander Mayer strode across the floor, his arm out-stretched like a used-car salesman greeting a prospective customer. 'Mike, good to see you at last,' said Vander Mayer.

Cramer got to his feet unsteadily, still disorientated. Vander Mayer seized his hand and pumped it enthusiastically. Cramer recognised the man's voice, but his appearance was a surprise. Vander Mayer was immaculately dressed in what was clearly an expensive made-to-measure suit and a gold Rolex glinted from under the sleeve of a starched white shirt cuff as he shook hands, but Cramer had expected a much bigger man. While Vander Mayer's voice was deep and authoritative, the man himself was unimposing. If anything he appeared to be slightly shifty with sharpish features that made Cramer think of a small bird.

'I would have been here earlier but the traffic was a bitch,' said Vander Mayer. 'I've been pushing them to get a helicopter pad installed, but the neighbours won't have it.'

'Shame,' said Cramer.

Vander Mayer released his grip on Cramer's hand and put his briefcase on a low sideboard. Cramer's gun was there, along with the painkillers. Vander Mayer raised an eyebrow at the weapon. 'Walther PPK,' he said. 'I thought the SAS used Glocks?'

'I'm ex-SAS,' said Cramer.

Vander Mayer nodded. 'Even so, it's not one of my favourite guns. May I?' He gestured at the pistol.

'Sure,' said Cramer.

Vander Mayer picked up the Walther, ejected the clip and quickly and efficiently stripped the gun, then reassembled it just as quickly. Cramer had the feeling that he was only doing it to show off his familiarity with the weapon. Vander Mayer gave the gun to Cramer and without thinking Cramer slipped it back into the shoulder holster under his jacket. He saw Su-ming look at him anxiously, but before she could say anything Vander Mayer went over to her and put his arm around her shoulders. 'How are you, baby?' he asked.

'Great,' she said. She turned up her head and kissed

him, close to the lips. Cramer felt a sudden pull inside and realised with a jolt that he was jealous. He turned away, unwilling to watch any more, suspecting that Vander Mayer's demonstrations of affection were as contrived as his manoeuvre with the Walther.

'Miss me?' Vander Mayer asked.

'Yes,' Su-ming said quietly.

Vander Mayer nodded as if satisfied. He turned back to Cramer. 'So, Mike, have you got the consignment?'

'It's in the safe,' said Su-ming before Cramer could answer. 'I'll get it.'

As Su-ming left the room, Vander Mayer went over to the picture window and looked out. 'I never tire of this view,' he said.

'Yeah,' said Cramer unenthusiastically.

'Best view in London.'

Cramer didn't say anything.

'Where are you from, Mike?'

'Glasgow.'

'Yeah? Scotch, huh?'

'Scottish,' corrected Cramer. 'Scotch is the drink.'

'You don't sound Scottish,' said Vander Mayer. He clasped his hands behind his back and squared his shoulders.

'Yeah, well I left when I was young.'

'To join the army?'

'Pretty much, yeah.' Cramer didn't enjoy talking to the man. He wasn't sure if it was because he hated answering questions about his background, or if it was a reaction to the way Vander Mayer had treated Su-ming. There had been something proprietorial in his attitude, as if she was merely an adjunct to the car, the flat, the jets.

'Well, you won't have to work again, not after the money I'm giving you.'

Cramer smiled bitterly. 'Yeah. Early retirement.'

Su-ming came back into the sitting room with the metal case. She handed it to Vander Mayer, who acknowledged her with a smile.

'What are you going to do with it?' Cramer asked.

Vander Mayer sat down in one of the leather and chrome easy chairs and swung the case up onto his knees. 'That depends,' he said, clicking open the locks.

'On what?'

'First I get my people to test it. And if it's what I'm told it is, I'll be buying as much of it as I can get my hands on.'

'And then?'

Vander Mayer took out the metal flask. He handled it reverently, as if it were a holy icon. 'Then?' Vander Mayer repeated, his eyes fixed on the flask.

'Who do you sell it to then?'

Vander Mayer grinned. 'To the highest bidder, Mike. To the highest bidder.'

'No matter who?'

Vander Mayer put the flask back in the case. He closed the lid and then took a handkerchief from his pocket and carefully wiped his hands. 'This is business, Mike. It's a commodity like any other.'

'It's used in nuclear weapons,' said Cramer.

Vander Mayer looked sharply across at Su-ming. She visibly flinched as if he'd struck her. Vander Mayer smiled and looked back at Cramer. 'So is steel, Mike. Are you suggesting that we stop selling steel?' He put the case on the floor beside his chair and crossed his legs.

'There's a big difference.'

Vander Mayer shrugged dismissively and put the handkerchief back in his top pocket, taking care to arrange it
neatly. 'Eye of the beholder, Mike. Eye of the beholder.
Besides, there are lots of potential uses for it.'

'Are you saying that it won't be used in a bomb?'

Vander Mayer leaned forward, his elbows on his knees.
'No, I'm not saying that. But that's not really any of your
business, is it?' He raised his eyebrows and nodded, as if
trying to get Cramer to agree. Cramer just looked at him,
unable to conceal his disdain. Vander Mayer stood up and
went over to a steel and glass drinks cabinet. He picked
up a bottle of twenty-year-old malt whisky and unscrewed
the cap. He poured himself a large measure. 'Do you want
a Scotch?' he asked Cramer. He smiled thinly. 'Or is it
Scottish?'

Cramer shook his head. He'd lost the taste for whisky.
He'd pretty much lost the taste for everything. The telephone
rang and Su-ming picked up the receiver. She listened and
frowned, then put her hand over the mouthpiece. She
looked at Vander Mayer. 'You have a visitor downstairs.
A Mr Jackman.'

'Jackman?' said Cramer. 'Bernard Jackman?'

Su-ming nodded.

'You know him?' asked Vander Mayer.

'He's the FBI profiler,' said Cramer. 'Well, former FBI
profiler, actually. He's the guy who profiled the assassin
who was after you. I wonder what he wants?'

'There's one way to find out,' said Vander Mayer. He
gestured at Su-ming. 'Tell him to come up. I'd like to meet
the guy.'

Su-ming relayed the message to the doorman and put
the phone down. 'He's on his way up,' she said.

'What's he like?' Vander Mayer asked Cramer.

Cramer shrugged uncertainly. 'He's clever, but to be honest he wasn't much help. It's not as if knowing the killer's characteristics helped us nail the bastard. It was Allan and his Glock that did that.'

'Don't knock it,' said Vander Mayer. 'One of Su-ming's most valuable skills is her ability to judge people. To decide whether they can be trusted or not.' He picked up the metal case and relocked it. 'I'd better put this back in the safe,' he said. 'Once an FBI agent . . .' He left the sentence hanging as he went through the hall to his study.

Su-ming walked over to Cramer. She looked as if she was about to say something, but before she could speak the doorbell rang. She jumped as if startled by the noise, and her eyes remained locked on Cramer. The doorbell rang again. Su-ming took a step backwards, then turned on her heels and went to the front door. She opened it and stood to the side. It was Jackman. He was wearing a dark green jacket and grey slacks and as he walked into the room Cramer realised that the man's ponytail was missing. Jackman's hair looked lighter, too, as if he'd been out in the sun.

Jackman ignored Su-ming and strode across the sitting room. He shook hands with Cramer. 'I wasn't expecting you,' Cramer said.

'I came as soon as I heard, I wanted to get the details from you while they were still fresh.'

'Details?'

'Of the assassination attempt. I need to know everything that happened. For the files. What about Vander Mayer? Is he here?'

'He got here just before you did,' said Cramer. 'Did the Colonel call you?'

'Hell of an apartment, isn't it?' said Jackman, looking around.

Cramer wondered if Jackman hadn't heard him or if he'd deliberately ignored the question.

'It's a different world, isn't it?' said Jackman as he turned around, smiling broadly. Cramer wondered what had happened to the ponytail. The man's accent seemed slightly different, too. There was less of a Texan drawl and a harder edge to it. More East Coast than mid-West. 'So, do I get to meet the guy whose life you saved?' Jackman asked.

'He's in the study,' said Su-ming.

Before Cramer could stop him, Jackman strode off down the corridor. Cramer and Su-ming followed him into the study where Vander Mayer was scrutinising a list of share prices on one of his many monitors. He looked up at the sound of their footsteps, then smiled. It was the same sort of smile that Jackman himself used, an emotionless baring of the teeth, a pale copy of the real thing. It wasn't a pleasant smile. 'You're the profiler?' said Vander Mayer.

Jackman nodded. 'And you're the target?' he said, his fake smile broadening.

'Not any more,' laughed Vander Mayer. He held out his hand.

Jackman laughed, too. His hand slipped inside his jacket and emerged holding a snub-nosed revolver. He walked towards Vander Mayer, his arm outstretched, and shot him point blank in the face. Before Vander Mayer's legs gave way Jackman fired again, this time at Vander Mayer's chest.

Su-ming screamed as Vander Mayer fell backwards, his face and chest a bloody mess. Cramer reached for his Walther but before he could pull out his gun, Jackman had whirled around and aimed his own weapon at Cramer's face.

'Too slow, Mike,' said Jackman. Cramer froze. Su-ming stared down at Vander Mayer. The body twitched on the floor, then went still. Jackman ignored her. 'Take out your gun, slowly,' Jackman said. 'Use the thumb and index finger of your left hand.'

Cramer did as he was told.

'Drop it on the floor, then kick it over here.'

Cramer obeyed. The gun came to rest by Jackman's left foot. Jackman crouched down, keeping his own gun aimed at Cramer. He picked up the Walther, then straightened up. Su-ming had her hands up to her face, her eyes wide with shock. Jackman motioned with his gun for her to stand next to Cramer.

'Well,' said Jackman to Cramer. 'You don't know how much I've been looking forward to having a chat with you, Mike.'

The Colonel looked around the apartment. The equipment that had been installed prior to the operation had been removed. All that was left was the furniture that had come with the flat. The Colonel was sitting on a winged easy chair by an empty bookcase. He leaned forward and clasped his hands together and bent his head as if in prayer. Something didn't feel right, but he wasn't sure what it was. By rights he should have been over the moon; he'd achieved his objective with relatively few casualties. But there was a nagging doubt at the back of his mind, a feeling of unfinished business

Blackie popped his head around the door. 'All packed, boss,' he said. 'Are you coming with us?'

'No, I'll hang on here for a while,' said the Colonel. 'I've got my own transport.'

One of the telephones on the desk rang. The trooper looked at the Colonel expectantly, but the Colonel shook his head. 'I'll get it,' he said. It was a chief inspector in Special Branch, one of the few non-military personnel in Britain who had been appraised of the operation.

'Good news, bad news, I'm afraid,' said the chief inspector.

The Colonel's heart sank. 'You couldn't get a match?'

'Oh yes, we got a match all right. The problem is, he can't be your killer.'

'I don't follow you.'

'The man you killed is Dermott Lynch. From Belfast. He's . . .'

'I know who he is,' the Colonel interrupted. He wanted to ask if there was any possibility of a mistake, but he knew that the chief inspector was too thorough to have called with inaccurate information.

'The problem is, we had Lynch under surveillance for quite some time last year,' the Special Branch officer continued. 'In Belfast and elsewhere in Northern Ireland. We know exactly where he was during three of the killings. And it would be virtually impossible for him to travel to the United States without us being aware of it. He's on the FBI's watch list.'

The Colonel said nothing, but deep creases furrowed his brow. If the man that Allan had killed was Dermott Lynch, then the assassin was still on the loose. And the Vander Mayer contract was still open.

'Are you there?' the chief inspector asked.

'Yes. Sorry. I was just thinking.'

'There's no possibility that we have our lines crossed and that the killings have all been the work of the IRA?' asked the chief inspector. 'Perhaps the IRA is moving into new territory. Selling their expertise to the highest bidder.'

'Unlikely in the extreme,' said the Colonel.

'Ah,' said the chief inspector. 'So, did Lynch have a personal reason for going after your man?'

'I'm afraid so, yes.'

'So it's an unfortunate coincidence, that's all?'

The Colonel sighed. 'Yes. Just bad luck. The worst sort of luck. Anyway, thanks for letting me know so promptly. We were in the process of standing down. Obviously, in view of what you've told me, the operation is still live. I'll inform my opposite number in the States.'

The Colonel thanked the chief inspector and cut the connection. He wasn't looking forward to telling Dan Greenberg. He was about to tap out the FBI agent's number when he realised that Mike Cramer was still unaware of the latest development. And with Allan and Martin in hospital, the Colonel would have to provide alternative protection. He punched out the number of Vander Mayer's apartment.

Su-ming jumped as the telephone rang. 'Leave it,' said Jackman. He kept his gun pointed at Cramer's head. 'Let it ring.'

'Why are you doing this?' Su-ming asked.

'You wouldn't understand,' said Jackman.

'It's all right, Su-ming,' said Cramer. 'It's not you he wants.'

'Really?' sneered Jackman. 'So tell me, Mike, what exactly is it that I want?'

Cramer stared at Jackman. Jackman stared back. 'I don't know,' Cramer admitted. 'It's not money, is it?'

'I've all I need,' said Jackman. 'More than I need. It was never about the money.' The telephone continued to ring.

'So it's what? The challenge?'

Jackman shook his head. 'There's no challenge, not really. Not for someone like me. It's all in the planning. You know that. You're a soldier.'

'Was,' said Cramer. 'I was a soldier. Not any more.'

'Sit down!' Jackman shouted at Su-ming. She had been edging towards the door but she stopped dead.

'I, I . . .' she began but Jackman waved the gun at her.

'Sit down,' he repeated. Jackman covered them both with his gun until she'd dropped into a leather and chrome armchair, then he levelled it at Cramer. 'How many people have you killed, Mike?'

'I don't know,' Cramer answered.

'Like fuck you don't know.' The telephone stopped ringing. 'How many?'

'Nine.'

Jackman smiled broadly. 'Yeah? Nine? I've killed fifteen.'

'It's not a competition, Bernie,' said Cramer. There had only been twelve in the files. He wondered if Jackman was lying about the number of kills.

'It's Bernard,' said Jackman, with the emphasis on the second syllable. 'Bernard. Not Bernie.'

Cramer shrugged as if it made no difference to him. 'Fifteen? All for money?'

'Mostly. Like I said, it's not about the money. It's power. The power of taking a life. Isn't it the most unbelievable feeling, Mike? To take another human being's life?'

Cramer rubbed the back of his neck, trying to massage away the tension that was building there. 'No. I never felt that way. I never did it for kicks. It was my job.'

'Killing isn't a job,' said Jackman. 'It's a vocation.'

'You're sick.'

Jackman smiled tightly. 'No, I'm not sick. I've interviewed psychos, Mike. I've spent time with them. I've rooted around inside their heads, I know what makes them tick. I'm not crazy.'

Cramer held his hands out, palms uppermost. 'Hey, okay. You're not crazy.'

Jackman's eyes narrowed. 'Don't humour me, Mike. You're not smart enough to play mind games with me.'

Cramer didn't reply. The telephone started to ring again. 'How do you feel when you kill someone?'

Cramer thought about the question for a few seconds. 'At the time, nothing. It's what I was trained to do.'

Jackman frowned as if he didn't understand. 'You don't get excited? You don't get a rush from it?'

Cramer couldn't believe what he was hearing. He'd never enjoyed killing. Ever. And he'd never met anyone in the SAS who did. There was nothing thrilling about taking another person's life, even in the heat of battle. He'd been in fire-fights in the Falklands and in Northern Ireland and he'd killed men to save his own life, but there had been no feelings of elation, no adrenalin kick. 'No,' he said, 'I never enjoyed it.'

'I don't believe you,' said Jackman. 'It's the best feeling in the world. It's the ultimate power. And to do it close up, to stand in front of someone and watch them as they die, that's the absolute best. It's better than drugs, better than sex, better than anything.' Jackman shook his head animatedly. 'Don't tell me you don't get a kick out of it, Mike.'

Cramer folded his arms across his chest. He felt something hard press against his right hand. The stiletto. He'd forgotten that he still had the blade strapped to his left forearm. 'I don't know anyone in the SAS who does enjoy the killing. They might enjoy being in combat, but that's because it's what they're trained to do. But the act of killing, no. No one enjoys that. Only sadists and madmen kill by choice.'

Jackman grinned. 'Yeah? And which am I, Mike?'

Cramer let his hands fall to his sides. The telephone stopped ringing again. Jackman was standing fifteen feet away, his back to the window. Out of reach of the stiletto. 'You wrote the profile,' said Cramer.

'Yeah, I did, didn't I? That was half the fun, you know? Being close to the investigation, watching the idiots chase their tails, knowing that they'd never come close to catching me.'

'Unless you wanted to get caught.'

Jackman shook his head. 'No, that's not what this is about. It's not a case of me wanting to be stopped. I don't want to be caught and punished to satisfy some inner need for retribution. I fully intend to spend the rest of my life as a free man. I've enough money tucked away to live wherever I want. South America. Africa. There are plenty of places for a rich man to hide. And I'm a very, very rich man, Mike.' He smiled at Vander Mayer's body, sprawled on the polished wooden floorboards. 'Not as rich as him, but then he's dead, isn't he? And you can't take it with you, right?'

Jackman was waving his gun around like a conductor with a baton. Cramer took a step forward, but Jackman immediately levelled the gun at his face. 'Don't even think about it,' Jackman warned. 'I can put a bullet in your skull before you get anywhere near me.'

Cramer said nothing. He could reach Jackman with three steps but that would be more than enough time for Jackman to shoot. Cramer needed a distraction, something to give him the time to pull out the knife and get in close. He looked across at Su-ming. She was staring at Jackman, fear etched into her face. He willed her to look across at him, but her eyes remained fixed on Jackman and the gun.

'What was it like for you, the first time?' Jackman asked.

Cramer was concentrating on Su-ming so intently that he almost didn't hear the question. 'What?' he said.

'The first time. What was it like?'

Cramer shrugged and didn't answer. 'Why did you kill Vander Mayer?' he asked. 'Why did you kill him when you knew that you'd be caught?'

'I haven't been caught, Mike. I'm in control here, not you.'

'But it's over now. Your cover's blown. We know who you are.'

Jackman pursed his lips. 'It was always going to happen,' he said. 'It was just a matter of time.' He licked his lips and they glistened wetly. 'Anyway, I've nothing to lose now, have I?'

Cramer took a step forward, trying to look as non-threatening as possible. 'Let the girl go.'

'Maybe I will. What was it like for you? Your first kill?' Cramer felt his teeth clench involuntarily. Jackman looked at Su-ming and gestured with the gun. 'I'm waiting,' Jackman pressed.

'The first person I killed was my mother,' said Cramer.

Jackman's jaw dropped. Then his expression changed, from amazement to admiration. He whistled softly.

The Colonel went over to the window and looked across at the tower block opposite. Most of the floors were in darkness, but the lights were on in Vander Mayer's apartment. He could make out a figure standing by the study window but it wasn't possible to see whether the figure was looking in or out. The Colonel couldn't even tell who it was. He looked around for his binoculars but they'd been packed away, along with his transceiver and the rest of the equipment he'd been using. The Colonel tapped his lips with the flat of his hand as he considered his options. The figure in the window hadn't moved.

The Colonel picked up the telephone and tapped out the number of the doorman in the main lobby.

Jackman put his head on the side as he looked at Cramer. 'Your mother? You killed your own mother? Why, did you want to go to the orphans' Christmas party or something?'

Su-ming turned to stare at Cramer. Cramer looked at her, wishing there was some way to communicate with her, some way to tell her to cause a diversion so that he could get the stiletto out, because if they didn't do something Jackman was going to kill them both. Jackman needed time to get away, and the only way to buy it would be to leave two more bodies on the floor next to Vander Mayer. 'She was dying,' said Cramer flatly.

'Cancer?' said Jackman.

'Brain tumour. Inoperable.'

Jackman nodded and there was something almost sympathetic about the gesture. 'Tough.'

'Yeah. If it had happened today they'd probably have saved her. Back then, there was nothing they could do. They sent her home to die.'

Cramer looked at Su-ming. All he needed was for her to distract Jackman for a moment. As soon as Jackman pointed the gun at Su-ming and not at him, Cramer could make his move. One step. Pull out the stiletto. Another step. Drive the knife forward. The last step. Up into Jackman's throat. It would take one second, two at most. Su-ming was staring at him, aghast, her hands up to her face, covering her mouth.

'She was in pain every day. Every minute of every day. Pain like you wouldn't believe. I used to hate getting home from school. I used to stay out of the house as much as I could.' Cramer knew he had to keep talking, to play for time.

'How old were you?' Jackman asked. His interest seemed to be academic, as if he were a psychiatrist analysing Cramer's case.

'Eleven,' Cramer answered. 'I was eleven.'

'How? How did you do it?'

'The doctor had prescribed her strong painkillers. Really strong. My father kept them hidden from her because of what she might do. She kept begging me to get the medicine for her.' Cramer took a step forward. Jackman appeared not to notice. 'I got the tablets for her, and I watched as she took them. I knew she was killing herself, but I didn't try to stop her.'

'And how did you feel?'

Cramer massaged his temples with his knuckles as if he had a headache. He wanted Jackman to get used to seeing his hands moving. 'She was in a lot of pain. And she was dying anyway. All I was doing was helping the process along.'

'A mercy killing?'

'Yeah. You might call it that.'

The Colonel tapped the receiver against his ear as he waited for the doorman to answer the phone. It was at least twenty rings before the doorman came on the line. He was out of breath and apologetic, explaining that he'd been helping a resident carry his cases to the elevator. The Colonel asked him if there had been any visitors to the Vander Mayer apartment.

'Mr Vander Mayer himself arrived half an hour ago. And I just showed another visitor up.'

'Who was that?' queried the Colonel.

'Hang on while I check the book,' said the doorman and put down the phone. The Colonel looked across at the tower block. The figure was still standing by the study window.

'Here we are,' said the doorman. 'His name was Jackman. Bernard Jackman. He wasn't expected but Mr Vander Mayer said he'd see him. Is there a problem?'

'No. Everything's fine,' said the Colonel. He replaced the receiver, frowning. Vander Mayer, Cramer, Su-ming and Jackman were apparently all in the apartment, so why didn't they answer the phone? And what was Jackman doing up there?

Jackman kept the gun pointed at Cramer's head, giving Cramer no chance of making any sort of threatening move. Cramer's palms were sweating and he rubbed them on his trousers. His right hand was only inches away from the hilt of his stiletto. One movement and he'd have it in his hand, three paces forward and Jackman would be dead. All he needed was an opening. A distraction. Jackman moved away from the window, keeping his gun on Cramer. He went over to the mirrored wall and stood with his back to it. Now he was even further away from Cramer, well out of range. Cramer forced himself to relax, to conceal the signs that he was preparing to launch an attack.

'What about you, Bernie?' Cramer asked. 'Why did you decide to leave the side of the angels?' Cramer could see Su-ming reflected in the mirrored wall. She was sitting with her legs pressed together, her hands clasped in her lap.

'For the kick. For the excitement.'

'You gave up . . .'

'I gave up nothing, Mike. I was too good for the Bureau, I knew that within weeks of joining. Have you ever felt like that? Like Gulliver, surrounded by midgets? Intellectual midgets? It was like that for me at high school, and at college. I thought that when I joined the Bureau it'd be different, that I'd finally be among people like me. The G-men, the best and brightest of the country's law enforcement officials. That's what they like you to think, but it's bullshit. They're as dumb as the cops. Dumber sometimes.'

Jackman had begun waving his gun around again, but Cramer had a gut feeling that he wouldn't shoot until he'd finished saying what he had to say. It was like a confession, thought Cramer. Except the confessor wasn't planning to leave any witnesses. 'If they were smart, they wouldn't be cops,' said Cramer.

'Right,' said Jackman eagerly. 'The really bright people don't go into law enforcement, or if they do, they leave pretty damn quickly. Like me.'

'Better off working for yourself, right?'

Jackman narrowed his eyes as if he was wondering whether or not Cramer was humouring him. 'It's not about money, if that's what you're implying,' Jackman said. 'That's not why I left. If I'd wanted money I'd have gone into business. I could have made a fortune, Mike. I could have been as rich as Vander Mayer. Richer. I've met a lot of rich people in my time, and most of them aren't much brighter than cops. You don't need brains to make money, you just have to work your balls off. Look at all the Vietnamese and Chinese who move to the States. They start with nothing, but they make fortunes. Fortunes. And they're not all geniuses, I can tell you.'

Cramer nodded vaguely. Jackman was rambling. It was as if he didn't often get the opportunity to explain himself, and now that he had a captive audience it was all tumbling out. 'So why did you leave?' Cramer asked.

'I finally met a man who was my intellectual equal,' said Jackman. 'A man called Anton Madeley. He's a genius, Mike. A true genius. It was like meeting a soulmate.'

Cramer glanced at Su-ming's reflection in the mirrored wall but her attention was fixed on Jackman.

'I was sent to interview Madeley to update our VICAP report. At first he wouldn't open up to me, but even at our first meeting I knew that the guy was special. He knew stuff. He knew how people's minds work, what made them tick. He could get inside your head and find out exactly what you wanted. What you needed.'

'He was in prison?' asked Cramer.

Jackman's eyes flashed. 'I know what you're getting at,' he snarled. 'If he was so smart, how did he get caught? Right?'

Cramer shrugged uncertainly. He just wanted Jackman to keep talking.

'I'll tell you why he ended up in prison. Because he trusted someone. Someone he thought was a friend. He opened up to this person and this person betrayed him. That's why. That's the only reason he was caught. The FBI hadn't a clue who he was, he'd never left any evidence, there were never any witnesses. He made one mistake, and that mistake was to trust. I've never trusted anyone, Mike. That's why I'll never be caught.'

Cramer nodded. 'Madeley was a killer? Is that why he was in prison?'

'Yeah, he killed. Killing is the ultimate power, Mike. That's what he taught me. I hadn't realised what killing really meant, not until I met Anton. I'd interviewed dozens of murderers, from wife-batterers who went further than they intended to serial killers, and they'd all had their own reasons for doing what they did. Anton was the first one to explain the psychology of it. The thrill of it. Not right away, of course. It took a long, long time before he opened up to me. And I had to pass a lot of tests along the way. I had to prove my worth, I had to show that I was a worthy disciple. But I did it, Mike. And then he let me inside his head.'

'He seduced you, Bernie.'

'Seduced? Maybe, but I was willing. More than willing. He explained things to me, things that I'd half known, half appreciated. It was like being short-sighted and getting glasses.'

'Didn't the Bureau realise what was happening?'

Jackman shook his head. 'I told them I was building up a relationship with him with a view to expanding our profile and they took that at face value. The reports I turned in contained just enough new information to make them think I was making slow progress. They're not too bright, Mike. Intelligent, yes. But not smart. There's a difference. Anton taught me that. And stop calling me Bernie, will you. My name's Bernard.'

'Are you saying that you never thought about killing before you met Madeley?'

Jackman's upper lip curled back in a sneer. 'Don't try to analyse me, Mike. You don't have the mental capacity.' He pointed the gun at Cramer's face. His finger tightened on the trigger.

'Answer me one thing, though,' said Cramer. Jackman didn't say anything, but Cramer saw his trigger finger relax. 'Why the head-shot? Why did you shoot them in the head and then in the chest? It wasn't just a signature, was it?'

Jackman grinned. 'It was a tribute,' he said. 'That was how Anton killed his victims. It locked in their souls, he said.' He saw the look of disbelief in Cramer's eyes and his grin vanished. 'That's what he said. I'm not saying I believed him. It was just his theory, that's all.'

'So what was the real reason? You must have wondered.'

'Of course I wondered.' Jackman paced up and down, but he kept the gun aimed at Cramer.

'So tell me.'

Jackman stopped pacing. He stared at Cramer. Cramer held the look. Jackman was three paces away. Within range. Cramer put his hands together. It was a non-threatening pose but his right hand was just inches away from the stiletto again. 'He was abused by his father as a child,' Jackman continued. 'Physical abuse of a particularly vicious kind. His mother used to watch. She'd watch and she'd encourage her husband. Sometimes she'd hold Anton down so that her husband could do what he wanted. That's what he remembered most. Not the buggery, not the pain, but her eyes. Watching him.'

'So when he started killing, he shot them in the face?'

Jackman nodded. 'You got it.'

'And you decided to do it the same way . . .'

'So that he'd know,' finished Jackman. 'He'd know that I was as good as he was. Better even, because he was in prison and I was on the outside.'

Jackman stopped speaking as if realising that he'd already said too much. He stretched his arm out, the gun levelled at Cramer's face. 'Enough talking,' he said. 'Let's get this over with.'

*   *   *

The Colonel screwed up his eyes and peered up at the windows of Vander Mayer's flat. Whoever had been standing there had moved away. He turned and picked up the phone. He was about to tap out the number to Vander Mayer's flat but he changed his mind and called the doorman again instead. 'Do me a favour, will you?' he said once the man answered. 'I'm having trouble getting through to Mr Vander Mayer's apartment. Will you go up and see if there's a problem with his telephone?'

'Of course,' said the doorman. 'Though it was okay when I called up before.'

'Well, try again. If you get through, ask him to call me at this number.' The Colonel gave the doorman the number of the apartment he was using. 'If you can't get an answer, pop up and see if there's something wrong with the phone.'

The Colonel replaced the receiver and sat down in front of the desk. He tapped his walking stick on the floor, deep in thought. Something was wrong. Very wrong.

'Let the girl go,' said Cramer. 'This is between you and me.'

'It's nothing to do with you and me,' said Jackman. 'I'm taking care of business, that's all.' He started to squeeze the trigger. 'You know what I like best of all?' Jackman asked. Cramer said nothing. 'The look in their eyes when they realise they're going to die.'

Cramer stared back at Jackman. 'Just do it, Bernie,' he said quietly. 'Pull the trigger and get it over with.'

Jackman frowned. 'You're not scared, are you?'

'No.'

'If you beg me for your life, I might not kill you.'

'Yeah?'

'Yeah,' said Jackman, flatly.

'I don't think so,' said Cramer.

'Cramer, do as he says,' said Su-ming.

Cramer turned to look at her. He'd almost forgotten that she was still in the room. 'He's going to kill me anyway, Su-ming.'

Jackman looked at Su-ming and smiled cruelly. 'What about you, little lady? Why don't you beg for his life?'

'Su-ming, don't,' said Cramer. Jackman had switched his attention to Su-ming, though the gun was still pointing at Cramer's face. Cramer moved his hand a fraction and the fingers of his right hand probed inside his left sleeve and found the hilt of the stiletto.

Jackman suddenly switched his attention back to Cramer. Cramer let his hands fall to his sides. 'You think you're better than me, don't you?'

'I don't know what you mean.'

'Yes, you do. They picked you to go up against me, and you figured you were good enough to take me on. That was the plan, wasn't it?'

'Are you going to talk me to death, Bernie? Or are you going to pull the trigger?'

Jackman's eyes hardened. 'That would be too easy,

wouldn't it? I've got the drop on you, shooting you cold wouldn't prove anything, would it?'

'Just do it, Bernie.'

Jackman studied him for several seconds. 'Why?' he said eventually. 'Why are you doing this? No one wants to die.'

'He does,' said Su-ming quietly.

Cramer whirled around and glared at her. 'Shut up!' he hissed.

Su-ming wouldn't look at him. She stood up and faced Jackman. 'He's dying. He's got cancer. He wants to be killed, it's an easy way out for him.'

'Su-ming, shut the fuck up,' Cramer shouted.

'If you kill him, you'll be doing him a favour,' said Su-ming as if Cramer hadn't spoken.

Jackman began to chuckle. His shoulders shook as he laughed, but his eyes remained hard. 'Well, well, well,' he said. 'Who'd have thought it? A death-wish.'

He backed away from Cramer and took the Walther off the desk. He weighed it in his hand. 'It's a small gun, not much stopping power,' he mused.

'It does the job,' said Cramer.

There was a coffee table to Cramer's right, black marble with white veins running through it. Jackman walked over to the table and put the gun down on it, the butt facing Cramer. Jackman slowly backed away until the gun was midway between them. Cramer looked at the gun. The safety was off. It was two paces away from him, and Jackman was a further two paces away from the table.

Jackman gestured at the gun. 'Go for it,' he said.

Cramer shook his head. 'I'm through playing games,' he said.

493

Jackman stared at him menacingly. Then slowly and purposefully he pointed the gun at Su-ming. 'If you don't, I'll shoot her first. In the gut. Then I'll shoot you.'

Su-ming wrapped her arms around herself as if giving herself a hug. Cramer glared at Jackman. 'If I try for the gun, will you let her go?' he asked.

Jackman sighed wearily. 'What do you think?' he said.

'I think you'll kill her anyway.'

Jackman nodded at Cramer's gun. 'At least if you go for it, you've got a chance of saving her life and yours.'

Cramer looked at the gun. Two paces. More than enough time for Jackman to aim and fire. He wasn't being offered any sort of chance. He put his hands on his hips and stared at Jackman.

'Well?' said Jackman. 'Shall I count to three or something?'

'You've never worried about shooting an unarmed man before, have you?' said Cramer. 'You've shot women and children and old men so why this sudden urge to give me a break?'

Jackman pursed his lips as if considering how to reply. 'The kick,' he said. 'The challenge. Everything so far has almost been too easy.'

'You want to prove that you're better than me, is that it? The shoot-out at the OK Corral?'

Jackman nodded slowly. 'Maybe.'

'Go to hell,' said Cramer. He took a step away from the marble coffee table. And another. It put the gun well out of reach but Cramer was now closer to Jackman. But not close enough.

THE DOUBLE TAP

*   *   *

The doorman tapped in the code for the Vander Mayer floor on the lift keypad and the doors began to close. He heard a shout and he pressed the button to open the doors again. Mrs Carey, a fifty-something divorcee, barrelled into the lift with her Yorkshire terrier clasped to her ample bosom.

'Good evening, Eric,' she said. She nodded at the security keypad. 'Can you press my floor, please? You know the code, don't you?'

'Of course, Mrs Carey,' said Eric. He punched in the code and the doors closed again. 'And how's little Janie today?' He put out a hand to pat the dog but it snarled and Eric pulled his hand away.

'She's got a poorly tummy,' said Mrs Carey, planting a kiss on the dog's neck.

'Poor thing,' said Eric, who would quite happily have strangled the bad-tempered dog.

Mrs Carey lived on the floor below Mr Vander Mayer and was one of the richest residents in the tower. She could always be relied on for a big tip at Christmas, unlike Mr Vander Mayer who was rarely around during the festive season. Eric wondered what all the fuss was about, why it was so important that he go up and check on Vander Mayer. There'd been something strange going on for the past few days, what with the security guys changing, and the new face who'd been staying in the apartment with Vander Mayer's assistant, and two hefty bodyguards acting as if they owned the place.

'I'm sorry, what did you say?' asked Mrs Carey.

Eric realised he must have been thinking out loud. 'Nothing, Mrs Carey,' he said. The lift stopped at Mrs Carey's floor.

Cramer suddenly felt light-headed. He wasn't sure if it was the painkillers he'd swallowed earlier or the adrenalin rush kicking in. He'd have to make his move soon and his body was gearing up for action. He took a deep breath.

'It's not much of a choice, Mike, I know, but it's more than I normally give my targets.'

'Targets? Is that what you call them? That's so you can distance yourself from what you're doing, isn't it? That's why you shoot them in the face. Because then they stop being people. It dehumanises them, doesn't it? So that you can deal with it. You know you're sick, Bernie. You know it but you can't face it.'

Jackman ignored him. 'One,' he said.

Cramer flexed his fingers. He looked at the Walther on the table. Then he looked at the gun in Jackman's hand. 'This isn't fair,' Cramer said.

Jackman's lips formed a tight line. 'Two,' he said.

Su-ming stood up. She took a step towards Jackman, her hands pressed together in front of her as if in prayer. 'Don't kill him,' she said. 'Please don't kill him.'

Jackman didn't look at her. His eyes were locked on Cramer.

'We won't say anything,' Su-ming pleaded. 'You can just go. You've done what you've been paid for. You've fulfilled your contract.'

'Don't beg, Su-ming,' said Cramer.

'But . . .' Su-ming began. Before she could finish, the doorbell rang. Cramer tensed. Jackman looked towards the front door. Cramer's right hand edged towards his left. He steadied his breathing. He felt a sudden elation. This was it. His one chance.

The doorbell rang again, more insistent this time. 'Are you expecting anyone?' Jackman whispered to Su-ming.

She shook her head. Cramer slipped his fingers inside his sleeve. He touched the hilt of the knife. Now, now, now, his mind screamed, but he held himself back. Jackman's gun was still pointing at his stomach and all he had to do was tighten his trigger finger and he couldn't miss. Cramer started breathing tidally so that his chest hardly moved. Jackman's gun wavered. It was just a few degrees but it was enough. Cramer started to move.

He went up onto the balls of his feet and took a step forward as his hand grasped the stiletto. It came out of its sheath smoothly, with the barest whisper of plastic against nylon.

Jackman noticed the movement and began to turn towards Cramer. Su-ming also saw Cramer move. Her mouth opened in surprise. She was closer to Jackman and she threw herself forward, trying to grab hold of the gun.

Cramer took another step, the stiletto low, ready to drive it upwards into Jackman's throat. He was conscious of Su-ming launching herself at Jackman but he remained totally focussed on what he was doing. He held out his left hand ready to grab Jackman's jacket, knowing that he'd get more leverage if he could pull him onto the blade as he thrust it forward.

Su-ming tried to catch hold of Jackman's arm, but he

was too quick for her. He swung the gun at her face and clipped her under the chin. Her head snapped back. Instantly Jackman brought the gun back to bear on Cramer.

Cramer was still two steps away from Jackman, but he'd built up a momentum and he couldn't have stopped even if he'd wanted to. Cramer's left hand was outstretched and Jackman kept his gun low, unable to go for the head-shot. The gun looked huge in Jackman's hand but Cramer ignored it. All he cared about was the stiletto.

His left hand brushed the lapel of Jackman's jacket. Jackman's eyes had narrowed so that they were almost slits. Cramer stared into them and he knew that Jackman was about to pull the trigger. He clawed his left hand and grabbed Jackman's jacket. The gun went off and Cramer felt a sudden kick to the stomach that knocked the breath out of him. The noise was deafening. Cramer pulled Jackman towards him and drove the stiletto up with all his strength. The point of the blade sliced up through Jackman's chin and then crunched through cartilage and bone. The gun went off again and Cramer screamed, partly in pain but more out of hatred and rage.

Jackman fell backwards and Cramer kept hold of him, forcing the stiletto higher up into Jackman's skull. They hit the ground together. Jackman's gun tumbled from his lifeless fingers and rattled across the wooden floor.

Cramer heard Su-ming scream but it sounded as if she was miles away, at the end of a long, long tunnel. Cramer pushed himself up off Jackman. He almost passed out with the pain. Jackman's eyes were wide and staring but there was no life in them. Blood was pouring down the blade and over Cramer's hands and red froth bubbled up from between Jackman's lips. Cramer let go of the stiletto. It stayed buried up to the hilt in Jackman's throat. Cramer was on his knees, fighting to stay conscious. He felt Su-ming's arms around him. She'd stopped screaming and now she was wracked with sobs.

Cramer could feel blood draining from his head. It took a long time to die from stomach wounds, he knew. A long time. And even if they managed to put him together again he'd only have to face the cancer that was eating him up. He clasped his hands to his stomach. He bit down on his lower lip to stop himself from screaming, the pain was so bad. He tried to fight it, to push the agony away, but each wave was stronger than the previous one. He tasted blood in his mouth and realised he'd bitten through his lip. He felt something warm and wet trickle through his fingers. He looked down. His thighs were soaked with sticky red blood, his own blood mixing with Jackman's. Su-ming put her head against his, as if trying to share his suffering.

'Su-ming, you have to help me,' he said. Another wave of pain washed over him and he grunted. Even with the painkillers he'd taken, the pain was almost more than he could stand, and he knew it was only a taste of what lay ahead of him.

'I will,' she promised.

'It hurts,' he moaned. 'It hurts so bad.'

'I know,' she said.

Cramer watched Su-ming in the mirrored wall as she went over to Jackman's body and picked up his gun. She stood staring at the weapon as if she wasn't sure what to do with it. She looked up and for a second their eyes locked in the mirror. She was crying. Cramer looked away. 'There's no need to cry,' he said.

She nodded. A tear rolled down her left cheek and she wiped it away with the back of her hand. 'I know,' she said.

Now available from Hodder & Stoughton

Stephen Leather's new thriller:

THE SOLITARY MAN

Chris Hutchison is a man on the run. Imprisoned for a crime he didn't commit, Hutch escapes from a British maximum security prison and starts a new life in Hong Kong.

But when a face from his past catches up with him, Hutch is forced to help a former terrorist break out of a Bangkok prison. Or face life behind bars once more.

Meanwhile the Drug Enforcement Administration wants to nail the vicious drug warlord responsible for flooding the States with cheap heroin. And decides to use Hutch as a pawn in a deadly game.

London journalist Jennifer Leigh also wants something from Hutch. She's convinced that there's more to his story than meets the eye – he could be her ticket to the front page.

Hutch's bid for freedom takes him into the lawless killing fields of the Golden Triangle, where the scene is set for one final act of betrayal.

Riveting, page-turning, filled with dramatic action and the bitter-sweet corruption of the East, *The Solitary Man* is a breathlessly exciting novel confirming Stephen Leather's position in 'the top rank of thriller writers' (*Jack Higgins*).

The prisoner lay in the damp grass and watched the building. It was in complete darkness. To his left was a line of small planes, standing like soldiers on parade, their noses pointing towards the distant runway. Two of the planes were four-seater Cessnas and he memorised their numbers. A police car sped down the road that ran parallel to the airfield, its siren on and lights flashing. The prisoner flattened himself into the grass, spread-eagled like a skydiver. He closed his eyes and breathed in the fragrance of the wet grass. Dew had coated his beard and he wiped his face with his sleeve. The siren sounded closer and closer and then began to recede. The prisoner lifted his head. It wouldn't be long before they searched the airfield.

He got to his feet and ran towards the single-storey building. There was a main entrance and a fire exit, and a window that overlooked the parked planes. Two locks secured the main door: a Yale and a deadbolt. The Yale he could pick but he'd need a drill for the deadbolt. He scuttled around the side of the building and checked the emergency exit. There was no lock to pick, but the wooden door didn't look too strong. A couple of hard kicks would probably do it. The moon emerged from behind a cloud, making thick yellow stripes that ran down both sides of his blue denim uniform glow.

A truck rattled down the road. The prisoner took a step back from the door, then waited until the truck was close to the entrance to the airfield. When the truck's engine noise was at its loudest, he kicked the door hard, putting all of his weight behind the blow. The wood splintered, and it gave way on the second kick. He pushed the door open and ducked inside. The keys were in a cabinet mounted on the far wall of the office.

He dashed over to the planes. The fuel tanks of the first Cessna he tried were almost empty. He said a silent prayer and went over to the second four-seater, a blue and white Cessna 172. He fumbled for the keys, then unlocked the door on the pilot's side and switched on the electronics. Both tanks were half-full. The prisoner smiled to himself. More than enough to get him well away from the island. He untied the chains that kept the plane tethered to the metal rings embedded in the concrete parking area.

In the distance a dog barked. The prisoner stopped dead and listened intently. There was another bark, closer to the airfield. A big dog, a German Shepherd maybe, the sort of dog that the police would use. He walked quickly to the front of the plane and climbed into the pilot's seat. He let his hands play over the control wheel for a few seconds. There was so much to remember. He closed his eyes and took several deep breaths. Carburettor heat in, throttle in a quarter of an inch, just enough to get the engine turning over. He turned the key. The engine burst into life. He pushed the throttle further in and the engine roared.

The noise was deafening. He hadn't realised how loud it would be. It was the first time the prisoner had ever been in a small plane. He shook his head. He was wasting time, and the dogs were getting closer. He put his feet on the rudder pedals and released the handbrake. The plane lurched forward.

He wrenched the control wheel to the right but the plane kept going straight ahead. Only then did he remember what Ronnie had told him; on the ground, you steered with your feet. The control wheel was only effective in the air. The prisoner took a hand off the wheel and wiped his forehead. He had to stay calm; he had to remember everything that Ronnie had taught him.

He pushed his right foot forward and immediately the plane veered to the right. He overcompensated and tried to use the control wheel to get the plane back on course. 'Rudder,' he muttered to himself.

He jiggled the pedals and manoeuvred the plane to the end of the runway. The windsock down the runway was blowing towards him, so he'd be flying straight into the wind. He pushed the top of both pedals forward to operate the brakes, and held the plane steady. The gyroscopic compass was about twenty degrees adrift according to the magnetic compass so he reset it. A heading of 340, Ronnie had said. North-north-west. He pushed in the throttle as far as it would go and let his feet slide off the pedals. The plane rolled forward, accelerating quickly. He used the pedals to keep the nose heading down the middle of the runway, resisting the urge to turn the control wheel.

His eyes flicked from the windscreen to the airspeed indicator. Thirty, thirty-five, forty. The runway slid by, faster and faster until it was a grey blur. He waited until the airspeed hit sixty-five and then pulled back on the control wheel. The plane leaped into the air. His stomach lurched and he eased back on the wheel, levelling the plane off. A gust of wind made the plane veer to the left a he pulled back on the wheel again and started to climb.

Below, houses and gardens flashed by, then a road. He began to laugh. He was doing it. He was actually doing it. He was flying.

He looked at the altimeter. Five hundred feet and climbing. Wisps of cloud hit the windscreen and then were gone. Ahead of him were grey cloud, but he could see large areas of clear sky between them.

The control wheel kicked in his hands as he hit an air

pocket and he gripped it tightly. He scanned the instruments. Everything seemed to be okay. He looked down at his feet and realised he'd left the fuel selector switch in the 'off' position. He reached down and turned it to 'both', freeing up the fuel in both tanks. That had been a stupid mistake. Running out of fuel wouldn't have been smart.

He took the plane up to a thousand feet and levelled it off, pulling back on the throttle as Ronnie had told him. He looked out of the window to his right. There was a beach below, and then he was flying over the the Solent, towards the ton of Lymington. The muscles in his neck were locked tight with the tension and he rolled his neck. Taking off was the easy part, Ronnie had warned. Getting the plane back on the ground would be a lot harder.

He flew through a patch of cloud and for a moment he began to panic as everything went white, then just as quickly he was back in clear sky. Ahead of him were more clouds. They were grey and forbidding, and the prisoner was suddenly scared. He pushed the control wheel forward and took the plane down a few hundred feet but all he could see ahead of him were the slate-grey clouds. Far off to his right was a flash of lightning. The clouds seemed to rush towards him and he turned the control wheel to the left, figuring he'd try to fly around the storm, but he was too late.

Before he could react, he was inside the storm, the plane buffeted by the turbulent air. He could see nothing but impenetrable cloud. It was totally white, as if he were surrounded by a thick, cloying mist. There was no way of telling whether his wings were level or not, no sense of which was up and which was down.

The engine began to roar and he pulled back on the

throttle. It didn't make any difference. He scanned the instrument panel and saw that his airspeed was rising rapidly. He was diving. Diving towards the sea. He yanked the control wheel back and his stomach went into freefall. His compass was whirling around but nothing he did stopped the spin.

He began to panic. He'd been crazy even to think that he could fly. Crazy. The engine was screaming now, screaming like a tortured animal, and the plane was shaking and juddering like a car being driven over rough ground.

He yelled as the plane dropped out of the clouds and he saw that he as only fifty feet above the waves. His left wing had dipped so far down that he was almost inverted. He wrenched the control wheel to the right and kicked his right rudder pedal, his cries merging with the roar of the engine.

Wreckage from the small plane was found floating in the Solent two days later. After a week police divers discovered the bulk of the plane scattered over the sea bed. There was blood on the windshield where the prisoner's head had slammed into the Plexiglas. Of the body there was no sign, but one of the doors had sprung open on impact and the tides in the area were strong, and the Hampshire police knew that it wasn't true that the sea always gave up its dead. The file on prisoner E563228 was closed and his belonging sent to his ex-wife, who was listed on his files as his next of kin.

The farmer knelt down, took a handful of reddish soil, and held it up to his lips. He sniffed, inhaling its fragrance like a wine connoisseur sampling the bouquet of an expensive claret. He took a mouthful and chewed slowly, then he nodded, satisfied. He had worked the land for more than three decades, and could taste the quality of the soil, could tell from its sweetness whether it was rich enough in alkaline limestone to produce a good crop of opium poppies.

It was important to choose the right land to grow the poppies, because if the crop was bad, the farmer would be blamed, and with blame came punishment. So the farmer chewed carefully, mixing the soil with his saliva and allowing it to roll around his mouth. It was good. It was very good. He nodded.

'How long will it take to clear the land?' asked the man on the horse. He watched the farmer through impenetrable sunglasses.

The farmer ran a hand through his hair. If he over-estimated, Zhou Yuanyi would think he was being slothful. If he under-estimated, he might not be able to finish the work in time. The trees and bushes would have to be slashed down with machetes. It would be hard work, back breaking, and they'd have to toil from first light until dark, but the farmer knew he would be well rewarded for his work. Zhou Yuanyi was a hard taskmaster, brutal at times, but he paid well for the opium the farmer grew. He paid well, and he offered protection: protection from the other opium kings in the Golden Triangle, and protection from the Burmese troops who wanted to smash the poppy-growers of the region.

'How many rais?' asked Zhou Yuanyi. A rais was just over a third of an acre.

'Twenty. Maybe twenty-one.'

Zhou Yuanyi sniffed. He cleared his throat and spat at the ground. 'Not enough,' he said. 'Find me another field as well. Soon.'

STEPHEN LEATHER

THE CHINAMAN

'Will leave you breathless' – *Daily Mail*

The Chinaman understood death.

Jungle-skilled, silent and lethal, he had killed for the Viet Cong and then for the Americans. He had watched helpless when his two eldest daughters had been raped and killed by Thai pirates.

Now all that was behind him. Quiet, hardworking and unassuming, he was building up his South London take-away business.

Until the day his wife and youngest daughter were destroyed by an IRA bomb in a Knightsbridge department store.

Then, simply but persistently, he began to ask the authorities who were the men responsible, what was being done. And was turned away, fobbed off, treated as a nuisance.

Which was when the Chinaman, denied justice, decided on revenge. And went back to war.

'As real and hard and tough as today's headlines. I couldn't put it down' – *Jack Higgins*

HODDER AND STOUGHTON PAPERBACKS

STEPHEN LEATHER

The Solitary Man

Chris Hutchison is a man on the run. Imprisoned for a crime he didn't commit, Hutch escapes from a British maximum security prison and starts a new life in Hong Kong. Then a ghost from his past catches up with him, forcing him to help a former terrorist break out of a Bangkok prison. Or face life behind bars once more.

Meanwhile the Drug Enforcement Administration wants to nail the vicious drug warlord responsible for flooding the States with cheap heroin. And decides to use Hutch as a pawn in a deadly game.

Hutch's bid for freedom takes him into the lawless killing fields of the Golden Triangle, where the scene is set for one final act of betrayal . . .

coronet

CORONET BOOKS

Hodder & Stoughton

STEPHEN LEATHER

THE VETS

Hong Kong. The British administration is preparing to hand the capitalist colony back to Communist China with the minimum of fuss.

But Colonel Joel Tyler has other plans for the British colony, plans which involve four Vietnam War veterans and a spectacular mission making use of their unique skills.

Vietnam was the one thing the four men had in common before Tyler moulded them into a team capable of pulling off a sensational robbery.

But while the vets are preparing to take Hong Kong by storm, their paymaster, Anthony Chung, puts the final touches to an audacious betrayal. At stake is the future of Hong Kong . . .

'The plot blasts along faster than a speeding bullet' – *Today*

'His last thriller was praised by Jack Higgins who couldn't put it down. The same goes for this' – *Daily Mail*

HODDER AND STOUGHTON PAPERBACKS

STEPHEN LEATHER

Pay Off

Why does a wealthy Scottish financier set up a drugs deal with the IRA? Jeopardise his career, endanger his family and lover by tangling with the East End underworld and a ruthless mercenary? The motive is simple: revenge for a cold-blooded act of murder.

His adversary is a dangerous gangland boss whose connections stretch from the Highlands to London and beyond. More than a match for a newcomer, especially when his plans contain a fatal flaw which will be discovered only when it is much too late . . .

coronet

CORONET BOOKS

Hodder & Stoughton

STEPHEN LEATHER

THE LONG SHOT

The plan is so complex, the target so well protected that the three snipers have to rehearse the killing in the seclusion of the Arizona desert.

Cole Howard of the FBI knows he has only days to prevent the audacious assassination. But he doesn't know who the target is. Or where the crack marksmen will strike.

Former SAS sergeant Mike Cramer is also on the trail, infiltrating the Irish community in New York as he tracks down Mary Hennessy, the ruthless killer who tore his life apart.

Unless Cramer and Howard agree to co-operate, the world will witness the most spectacular terror coup of all time . . .

'*The Long Shot* consolidates Leather's position in the top rank of thriller writers. An ingenious plot, plenty of action and solid, believable characters – wrapped up in taut snappy prose that grabs your attention by the throat . . . A top-notch thriller which whips the reader along at breakneck speed' – *Yorkshire Post*

HODDER AND STOUGHTON PAPERBACKS

STEPHEN LEATHER

The Stretch

Who can you really trust?

When career criminal Terry Greene is sentenced to life for a murder he didn't commit, his wife has two options. To walk away from the criminal empire he'd built up, or to take it over. To become as big a gangster as her husband ever was.

So far as Samantha 'Sam' Greene is concerned, there is no choice. All the family's assets are tied up in the business, and family means more to her than anything else in the world.

But being a gang-boss doesn't come easily to Sam, not when other criminals are trying to take over what's left of her husband's empire and she's not even sure which of his friends and associates she can trust.

As Sam gets drawn deeper into a world of drug-dealing and counterfeit money, she realises for the first time the true extent of her husband's illegal activities. And she has to answer two burning questions – can she get her husband out from behind bars? And should she?

CORONET BOOKS
Hodder & Stoughton

STEPHEN LEATHER

THE BIRTHDAY GIRL

Tony Freeman rescued Mersiha when she was fighting for her life in war-torn Yugoslavia. Now she is his adopted daughter, the perfect all-American girl – and the past is another country. Or so it seems.

But Mersiha has been trained to kill. And when she discovers that Freeman's company is subject to a sinister takeover bid, she decides to help. Whatever the risks.

The consequences of her actions are lethal – for Mersiha has unearthed a conspiracy of terrifying proportions . . .

'A whirlwind of action, suspense and vivid excitement' – *Irish Times*

HODDER AND STOUGHTON PAPERBACKS

STEPHEN LEATHER

The Eyewitness

Jack Solomon is a messenger of death.

His task is to identify the victims of ethnic cleansing and tell families that their loved ones are never coming home.

Years of working in the fractured remains of Yugoslavia have desensitised Solomon to the horrors of war, but when a truck containing twenty-six bodies is pulled from a lake, he is unable to walk away from the case.

Solomon's hunt for the last witness will lead him from the brothels of Sarajevo to the high-stakes world of London's organised crime.

Where he will discover that the killers are closer to home than he thinks . . .

CORONET BOOKS
Hodder & Stoughton

STEPHEN LEATHER

HUNGRY GHOST

'Very complicated. Fun' – *Daily Telegraph*

'The sort of book that could easily take up a complete weekend – and be time really well spent' – *Bolton Evening News*

Geoff Howells, a government-trained killing machine, is brought out of retirement and sent to Hong Kong. His brief: to assassinate Chinese Mafia leader, Simon Ng. Howells devises a dangerous and complicated plan to reach his intended victim – only to find himself the next target . . .

Patrick Dugan, a Hong Kong policeman, has been held back in his career because of his connections – his sister is married to Simon Ng. But when Ng's daughter is kidnapped and Ng himself disappears, Dugan gets caught up in a series of violent events and an international spying intrigue that has run out of control . . .

Tough writing, relentless storytelling and a searingly evocative background of Hong Kong in the aftermath of Tiananmen Square make *Hungry Ghost* a compulsive read.

HODDER AND STOUGHTON PAPERBACKS

STEPHEN LEATHER

The Fireman

Young, talented, in love with life, why should Sally have thrown herself fifteen floors to her death? But as suicide is the verdict of the uncompromising Hong Kong authorities, Sally's brother, a London-based crime reporter, begins his own investigations.

As he delves into the details of Sally's unaccountably opulent lifestyle and her mysterious work as a journalist, he is forced to recognize a very different girl from the fun-loving kid sister he remembers. And he uncovers a trail that leads him through the decadent haunts of Hong Kong ex-pat society, the ruthless wheeler-dealing of international big business and the violent Chinese mafia underworld – to an ultimate, shocking act of revenge . . .

CORONET BOOKS
Hodder & Stoughton